Critical acclaim for Night

'Her metaphors are insistent
wild, weird images are strewn
Descriptions play tricks on the reader, transforming
shards into swiping knives, faces in ecstasy into opening flowers or "the open mouths of bears, rabbits, small animals as they died". Nowhere is exactly new, Jean McNeil appears to suggest, but a jubilant baroque can dress it up in strangeness' Joanna Griffiths, *Times Literary Supplement*

'Her first novel, *Hunting Down Home*, was lauded for lyricism. Now comes *Nights in a Foreign Country* . . . a superb collection of 14 zesty short stories – sensual, razor-sharp – set in Canada, Britain, France and central America. Start reading it at the airport and you will miss your flight' Michael Thompson-Noel, *Financial Times*

'She lures the reader into her sometimes cryptic tales with sharp, descriptive language and seldom provides a tidy resolution . . . Armchair travellers will rejoice at the chance to cover an amazing amount of geographical ground guided by McNeil's gift for mining the sensual and philosophical challenges of travel . . . a collection that is not unlike travel itself: exotic, exhausting, sometimes confusing and rewarding in unforeseeable ways' *Toronto Globe and Mail*

'A haunting collection of stories . . . Her description of the Canadian landscape is breathtaking, and her poignant, melancholy evocation of the wonder of nature, and the need to escape it into city life, is beautifully done, evoking at the same time both cultural gain and the loss of simplicity'
Gay Times

Jean McNeil was born in 1968 and grew up on Cape Breton island in Canada but has lived in London since 1991. Her first novel *Hunting Down Home* was published in 1996; she is also the author of the *Rough Guide to Costa Rica* and a contributor to the *Rough Guide to Central America*. She works as an editor and researcher at the Latin America Bureau in London.

By Jean McNeil

Hunting Down Home
Nights in a Foreign Country

NIGHTS IN A FOREIGN COUNTRY

JEAN McNEIL

PHŒNIX

A PHOENIX PAPERBACK

First published in Great Britain in 2000
by Phoenix House
This paperback edition published in 2001
by Phoenix,
an imprint of Orion Books Ltd,
Orion House, 5 Upper St Martin's Lane,
London WC2H 9EA

'Bethlehem' was the winner of the 1997 *Prism International*
fiction competition (Vancouver, Canada) and was originally
published in the journal of the same name in spring 1998. It
was also nominated for Canada's Journey Prize for fiction and
published in the *Journey Prize Anthology* (McClelland & Stewart, 1998)
and in *Fortune Hotel*, edited by Sarah Champion (Hamish Hamilton, 1999).

'The Wolves of Paris' was commissioned by CBC radio in Canada for the
1998 Festival of Fiction, and broadcast nationally in May and July 1998.
It was published in *Prism International* in 2000.

'The Rainy Season' was a winner in the 1995 *Prism International* fiction
competition and was published in the journal of the same name in
spring 1996.

'Monterrey Sun' was first published in *Wild Ways: Women Writing on the Road*
(Sceptre, 1998)

The lines on p. 127 from the poem 'Monterrey Sun' by Alfonso Reyes
translated by Samuel Beckett are reproduced by permission of
Editions de Minuit, Paris.

A CIP catalogue record for this book
is available from the British Library.

ISBN 0 75381 274 6

Printed and bound in Great Britain by
Clays Ltd, St Ives plc

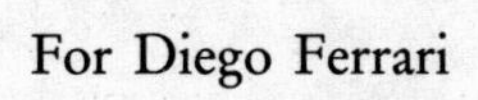

For Diego Ferrari

I would like to thank those friends who have supported and encouraged me in my writing, especially Nick Dennys. I am grateful for the support of the London Arts Board New Writers' Awards. Thanks also go to those Canadian fiction magazines that have published my work over the years, including some of the stories in this collection, and to Jane Bradish-Ellames at Curtis Brown and Maggie McKernan at Phoenix House.

CONTENTS

Bethlehem

She is running back and forth to the bathroom, getting towels to put underneath him. The boy sits on the edge of the bed.

'I'm not gay, *Senhora*.'

'That's reassuring,' she says, in English.

The boy scowls. '*Qué*?'

She switches to Portuguese. 'He's my husband.'

'Sure.' The boy shrugs. He can see she wears no ring.

She disappears into the tiny bathroom. When she emerges she is carrying a towel. She wrings her hands in it first, noticing a dark brown ring underneath her nails, next to the skin – dried blood. Suddenly her hands look alien, like mandibles, or claws; the appendages of another species.

She flicks the wall switch, turns on the fan. 'I have to dress his wound first.'

'What's wrong with him?'

The boy's copper skin has turned to onyx in the soupy light. It is the rainy season and dark has fallen at four o'clock. Outside, Peru-shaped clouds bloom – the thunder-clouds that float across the Amazon basin every afternoon.

She doesn't answer the boy. She concentrates on dressing the wound, slapping on the yellow lotion and winding the gauze around his midriff. He whispers something in her ear, but she misses the sense of it. She kisses his forehead. She does all this with the same detachment she would feel if she were watching herself on film. Everything she does seems to happen too slowly. Even the walls of the room look very far away.

'I've been shot too, *Senhora.*' He pulls up his shirt to show her a tiny puckered scar just to the right of his abdomen.

'Good for you. Here, catch.' The boy claps his hands over the small packet. He opens his hands and grins. She leans against the wall. 'Put it on.'

As the boy unbuttons his jeans she goes to sit in the chair by the window. The sheer curtain floats in the breeze and brushes her hair like an insect. She watches them closely, noting all the manoeuvres and sequences, as if she were cataloguing them. The only thing that still surprises her is how men can become aroused without really feeling any particular desire. Otherwise she is not shocked. It is really heterosexual sex she finds most disturbing; the appendages fitting each other with the puerile ease of Lego.

After a while the boy begins to moan.

'*Basta*,' she says. Enough.

She pulls him off the bed. She hates it when they moan – it sounds like the death cries of animals. She stuffs some cruzeiros into his hand. He scowls. He had been expecting dollars. He trips into his trousers, his graceless movements revealing his youth. He is all gangling adolescent limbs.

When he is in the hall she shuts the door behind him and turns to the man on the bed. He is sweating. She goes into the bathroom to get more towels to wipe him down. When she pulls on the light cord she cannot help seeing her face in the mirror. She grabs another of the too-thin towels and quickly pulls off the light.

I love to watch the rains come. It doesn't get dark so much as the sky seems to become coated with metal. Then it comes, bulleting and horizontal. Potholes open in the streets, as if they've always been there, like wounds underneath the skin of the asphalt, waiting to open.

About once a week after the rains I go to buy earrings in the market by the cathedral. I go out so often that many people know me by sight by now – there aren't too many foreigners who stay here for longer than it takes them to catch a plane or arrange some jungle adventure trip. I have even picked up the deep-throated, meowing accent of Pará. I use the *tu* and conjugate it correctly. This is an interesting regionalism; nobody but people from Pará do this, in the whole of Brazil.

The Basílica de Nossa Senhora de Nazaré is my favourite church in this city of heat-stunned churches. It is modelled upon St Paul's in Rome. Not far from our apartment building is the quarter where the rubber barons used to live. The best of these Portuguese mansions have been built, natives of Belém tell me, by Antônio Lemos and Lauro Sodré. Brazilians say their names with the gravity usually reserved for military heroes. It's one of the things I like most about this country – they hold their architects in reverence. The buildings are the colour of faded lime, oyster-hued, and peeling, as if they have been attacked by some kind of eczema. In the middle of a rainstorm the whole city looks like a torched Versailles, or the earthquake-smashed apartments of ancient Pompeii.

I could love this city, if I were here under different circumstances. I even take an interest in the riot scenes in the supermarkets, when shoppers discover rice has gone up again. Inflation is running at 46 per cent per month. To a degree I am protected by my cache of American dollars.

I don't know why he is indifferent to the city. He behaves like someone who has come here to die. He has become very interior, fixated upon himself and his reactions. As far as he is concerned, he could be in Calcutta, or Toronto. Maybe this is just his way of saying he wants to go home.

I love to watch the rains come but sometimes I wonder why I stay here. We're young: he's twenty-four, I'm twenty-one. We're almost out of money. We should go home, I should leave him. But I'm still edgy, still hungry for experience.

The nearest slum neighbourhood, *favela*, is where she goes to make her contacts for him. Without Lourdes, she could not have dreamed of entering the *favela*. Lourdes has lissom legs, trim and pretty. She can see the girl takes great care with her appearance; her hair is always neatly clipped in pink plastic butterfly-shaped hair pins, her shirts always spotlessly white. Most days she wears the same pair of blue shorts, but every day they are pressed and clean. She manages to keep up this level of hygiene and meticulousness in a one-roomed tin shack where she, her father and half-brother live.

The shacks are reached by walking through an old colonial mansion, now nearly gutted. Lourdes leads her carefully over gaping holes in the floorboards, and up and down rickety stairs. As they enter the darkened house she sees shapes shifting in the corners – people rising from the floor, or falling down; she can't tell which. They pass through the house and emerge through the back door into narrow alleyways of corrugated tin shacks. As they descend the stairs to the alleyway Lourdes walks in front of her, putting each foot delicately on the mulch-soft wooden steps.

Then she sees him, or at least she thinks it's a he, judging from his bulk. He lies on his side, his head propped up by an arm. Folds of fat droop where his bicep should be. Lying on his platform, which has the slab-aspect of a masseur's table, he looks like a beached seal. His mouth is lipsticked, his hair drawn back into a bun. He wears a purple piece of material, the exact colour of the *açaí* berries that come from the jungle, which is draped over his flounderous body in the style of a toga. His dark skin glistens as if it has been greased. His eyes, she notices, are extremely cunning.

'Is he a man or a woman?' she asks Lourdes, when they are past him.

'Who? Gorda?' The girl grins, hiding her mouth behind her hand. 'Who knows? A man. We think.'

'Then why is he called Gorda, in the feminine, as you would call a woman?'

'I don't know.'

'Is he homosexual?'

Lourdes considers this for a few seconds.

'What do you mean?'

She gives her mock-severe look. 'You know very well what that means. Don't tell me you can live twelve years in a place like this and not know. It means a man who likes men, or a woman who likes women.'

Lourdes screws up her face. 'Will you buy me an ice cream?'

'Sure,' she says, taking her by the hand. 'Let's go.'

They go to the zoo and botanical gardens, called the Emílio Goeldi museum. She has been to the zoo at least five times already. She likes to wander around its cool, ordered gardens, so different from the tangle of jungle, not much more than twenty kilometres away, that hems the city.

They enter the gardens, following a path of gravel the colour of woodchips. On either side of them are clumps of tropics vegetation. It is early morning and a weekday, so they almost have the place to themselves. She reminds herself that she should avoid the snakes, but they go up there anyway, she and Lourdes leaning over the railings, looking at the boa and the anaconda, which are kept in cages placed next to each other. The boa drapes itself over a bare, constructed tree branch like an exhausted inner tube. The anaconda lolls in the water. They can only see its eyes and its massive head.

'Which do you think is bigger?' Lourdes' vanilla ice cream drips down her fingers. She exits her tongue, small and feline, to lap it up.

'I heard the anaconda is the biggest snake in the world, so it must be bigger,' she reasons.

Lourdes licks her ice cream thoughtfully. 'I like them.'

'I hate them.'

They move on to the alligators, which lie like boats in a man-made creek. They walk over a little bridge to look at them from above. She sees the yellow glassy eye of one of them swivel in her direction.

'Come on.' She takes Lourdes' arm. 'Let's go.'

They move on to the aviary, where the macaws are making a racket. Lourdes has finished her ice cream and is looking longingly at her soggy napkin, which has mopped up most of the melted vanilla.

'There's one more thing you have to see before you go,' Lourdes says, pulling at her arm. 'The Amazon is famous for it. Do you know what it is?'

She smiles, shakes her head.

'Oh, come on.' Lourdes doubles her body up into a burlesque of impatience. 'It's *this* big.' She throws her arms out on either side of her body, her face turning pink with strain.

'*Não.*' She shakes her head, trying not to laugh. '*Não posso imaginar.*'

'The Victoria Régia lily. Do you know, this flower is like Gorda. It is both male and female. It changes overnight. That's why it's so big.' Lourdes begins to frown in concentration. 'It begins the day as a male, but then, at dusk, it traps this insect, a beetle. And it uses this beetle to pollinate' – Lourdes grins, proud of her use of the word –

'to reproduce itself. And then, by morning, it has become a female. The plant, not the beetle.'

'And does it let the beetle go in the morning?'

Lourdes frowns. 'I don't know.'

They go to the indoor exhibit, billed as The Natural History of the Amazon. '*Belém.*' Lourdes points to the sign on one of the bird displays that recounts the importance of the trade in tropical birds to the city. 'I can read that word. Do you know what it means? Bethlehem.' The girl stumbles over the consonants, unable to aspirate the 'h' and concretize the 't', so that it comes out sounding like *Betchleheem.*

'Bethlehem.'

Lourdes cracks up laughing. For the rest of the morning she coaches the girl to say it properly, in English. Lourdes insists. Still, she wonders if she has been cruel, teaching the girl to say a word she will never use again.

At noon, they part.

'You have to get back to your *namorado*,' Lourdes states, a little flatly. *Namorado* means both 'boyfriend' and 'betrothed'.

'Yes.'

'I know a good new boy for you, Esther,' Lourdes says, using the name she has given the girl but which is not her own. Lourdes doesn't normally do this. She's doing it for the same reason as a salesman would, to pretend or invite familiarity.

Suddenly she feels sullied. She wants to let Lourdes know that their friendship can be pure.

'He's not for me.'

Lourdes says nothing, just walks away from her, turning to look over her shoulder from time to time, but she keeps on walking, without turning around, heading for home.

Lone taxis scoot up and down the wide streets that lead to the docks like frightened rodents. Massive gutters are built alongside each *rua* and *avenida* to trap the daily deluge. They are so big, in any other city I'm sure they would be called canals.

Every day, all year, it rains twice a day. Once at one o'clock, once at five. The second instalment of rain is less predictable. But the sky is almost always clear in time to see the sun disappear into the river.

Our apartment is on the eleventh floor. We live in the highest high-rise in Belém, on Praça Tiradentes ('Toothpuller's Plaza'). It is American in style, furnished in chrome and mirrors, but Brazilian in intent. The kitchens all have a maid's elevator leading on to them, and a small maid's room, right next to the laundry room. For a Brazilian, an apartment like this costs a fortune. But we have dollars.

Every evening at five thirty I go out on to our balcony and watch the sunset. To the right are the docks – the oblong forms of warehouses look like greased lozenges in the setting sun. Cranes tower above them, lopsided, delicate. In the distance is the Ilha do Marajó – a wedge of green dotted with what looks like lakes. This time of year the island is a virtual floodplain, inhabited only by the horned water buffalo imported from India at the turn of the century and the four-hundred pound *pirarucú* fish, the biggest freshwater fish in the world.

To the left is the river, heading toward its intersection with the Xingú. And to the north, nothing, at least for us city dwellers. Only an untransversible forest stretching from here to the Guyanas. For most of the foreigners and the wealthy Brazilians, the only thing north of Belém of any significance is Miami. Both Varig and VASP have daily flights there. I see them taking off from the airport, which is also visible from my balcony. Planes are so different when they fly in; they seem to hover, like exhausted metal angels. When they take off they seem to be saying MIAMI OR BUST.

One or two nights a week we go out to eat. We always end up in one of the many good seafood restaurants.

'We should stop eating so much shrimp.' He makes a face, as soon as we have ordered shrimp again. 'I never thought I'd be sick of shrimp.'

I like *vatapá*, a shrimp dish in a rich sauce made from Amazonian fruit. But my favourite is *maniçoba*, meat cooked in leaves from the bitter cassava, which are toxic, at least under most circumstances. To be used in cooking, its leaves first have to be simmered for a full eight days, to drain them of their natural poison.

She opens the door to their apartment. As soon as she opens it she feels a wave of tiredness wash over her. The plants look plastic, she notes, for the hundredth time. Even though they are real. Then, that's the tropics.

He sits watching a *telenovela* to improve his Portuguese – its name translates into *As the World Turns*.

'Hi.' He grins, and turns his eyes upon her.

She has seen them hundreds of times before, but she will never tire of their magnificence. They are dark green, not large, but perfectly framed by thick ginger eyelashes. Chapped skin flakes off around his straight nose and thin, svelte eyebrows. His lips are full and crisscrossed like the stitching in a quilt. His hair is red-gold; he has a prominent but not jutting jawline, and wide-sprung cheekbones showing traces of Slavic ancestry. His face, as always, causes her to think of unlikely foreign phenomena, the loping walk of the Bushmen of the Kalahari, or the disdainful turned-down mouths of the ancient Incas. Every time she looks at him she feels a kind of exquisite shifting taking place inside her, as if she were made up not of veins and organs but sand bars.

He is not a large man, but his limbs are perfectly in proportion. He is still almost as muscled as he was when he went to the gym every day. She has never seen anyone, not even Lourdes, who has such beautiful limbs. His forearms, for instance, which are tendon-hard, and are transversed by a riverine network of veins. Sometimes she runs her forefinger along them, pointing to the places where they branch.

'That's the Tapajós,' she says, where one thick vein departs from another. 'That's the Solimoẽs.'

His skin has the delicacy of parchment. She can swing next to him in a hammock and not say anything for hours. They don't need to talk.

But she doesn't like the burnt metal taste of this supposed languor, this relatively cheap idyll. She's aware that this is not real life, even though she enjoys her friends and her life, her students. She loves the city. Even in the midst of living there, she already knows she will never forget it, and that this is not true of all experiences. But she also knows it is a place to be left behind in favour of more rigorous realities. He does not seem to realize this. Sometimes she thinks he has no aspirations in particular.

Later, they sit together in the darkness in front of the window, illuminated by the sodium light of the docks. Flecks of white dot the river – the headlamps of boats. On the inky, viscous river they seem to form a mirrored pattern of the stars.

'You are everything to me.'

Does she say this, or does she just think it?

From the moment she met him – when she had to lean against the wall for support, such was the impact of seeing someone for whom she'd been waiting – she had never expected not to know, at any point, where he was; whether he lived or died.

Sometimes she has this vision of him out in the world, without her. He is in Srinagar, maybe, the hue of his beautiful ochre skin the exact colour of deserts waiting for the rains to come. He has the grace that all people whose fingers are longer than their palms have. In his every movement is the fluidity of a lazy swimmer, heavy with supper, about to go under.

Between her fingers is his hair. It feels as soft as the tendrils of sea anemones. Noises from the docks, twenty blocks away, crackle into the apartment. Eleven storeys up, she thinks, you hear everything.

Night falls. On the equator, she has the impression that the world does not turn.

When they left behind the northern winter and came to Brazil she thought she would hear sounds of dense forests at night. She wanted to be surrounded by a breathing, whispering conspiracy of trees. But it was the sounds of the city that came to her every night – Rio de Janeiro, Salvador, São Paulo, Manaus, and finally Belém. She could only make money teaching English in the cities.

When they first came to the Amazon they flew in from Brasília. From the plane she saw Manaus rise up beneath them like a giant satellite dish. Fifty feet from the edge of the airport runway was the rainforest.

A few days later they flew to Belém. The plane took off just before dusk. From her window seat she watched the night come over the river. They flew into its mouth in increasing darkness; to her left, towards Venezuela, the sky was streaked purple. Then she lost the shape of the river beneath her in the night.

That night in their hotel in Belém, he took a wisp of her hair in his hand, twirled it between his fingers.

'It's not you I need.'

'Who is it?' she said. '*Who*?'

She thought she was shouting; her voice came out a whisper. In that way it was like a dream.

'What,' he said. His lips were dry and they smacked as he

said it, the sound of desert-bleached bones brushed by wind. 'What I need.'

That night she went out on her own, into the still-baking thoroughfares, clogged with vehicles whose axles and undercarriages were caked with red dirt from driving the Trans-Amazonian highway. Curtains of rain brushed her cheek. Beyond the phosphorous gleam of the city's lights she could feel the rainforest respiring, exchanging carbon dioxide for oxygen. Something about the city told her she would be safe there, that it would allow her a respite from her mania for knowing things.

From our balcony eleven floors above the city I can see the ferry to Macapá wandering into the river. I've never been there and from what I've heard I don't want to go. It is a heat-ragged city on the northern rim of the Amazon with a soccer field, a landing dock, and not much else.

I've seen the ferry leaving the dock, barely moving as it slogs through the liquorice viscosity of the river. It's an old rusting tub by any standard, so it won't have any navigational equipment. By some sonar instinct – like a bat – it dodges the hulks of big cargo boats, the Amazon steamers. The boat leaves Belém at midnight and takes twenty-six hours to cross the Amazon. That means it arrives at two in the morning. The transport schedules in the Amazon are unreal: buses leave at three or four in the morning and arrive at the same time. No wonder no one gets any sleep.

Caracas is a four-hour flight away. The cities which are near, at least in relative terms – Cayenne, Manaus – are still jungle backwaters. Even Lima or Bogotá is five hours' flying time away, including the inevitable stops in Letícia. Rio and São Paulo are about five hours by air, in the frigid south. Only the very rich of Belém go there with any frequency. Everyone else takes the bus to Brasília, if they really have to. That takes two and a half days. New York is an impossibility, Paris so remote as to not exist at all. Although I still hear people talk about it occasionally, in the tone usually reserved for speaking of jewels, or jaguar pelts – *París*.

Instead of the Seine and its bulb-garlanded tourist boats, the *açaí* boats land at eleven thirty each night. The berries are brought to Belém from all over the mouth of the Amazon. Some evenings I watch them come in to their docks below the Círculo Militar, the army fortress-compound. They look like migrating eels, these long, thin boats with their cyclops eyes piercing the night like fireflies. When the boats land, small, dark men scuttle to unload the heaps of fruit.

Açaí – I love the name, its medicinal, swishy sound. On their own the berries are far too sour. They can be mashed with sugar and mixed with manioc, to make a purple couscous. More often, though, they are sugared and used to make ice cream the colour of virulent bruises.

At these moments I don't feel I occupy a periphery, somewhere dreamed of only by centuries of scientists and merchants and other alarmists, but forgotten by everyone else. I feel I am at the fulcrum of the universe. Nowhere on earth is as flat and broad and significant as this part of Amazônia. All along the two-thousand-kilometre length of the river, the elevation barely rises two hundred metres. I really believe those *National Geographic* sentences, the ones that tell me I am living in the lungs of the world.

They are having breakfast. As always, he seems nervous when he eats, trembling, plucking at his napkin as if it were a chicken that needed to be defeathered.

'The newspapers in the Amazon are such crap.' He points to the corner of the table, where one of the body-count papers that dedicates itself to corpses and accidents lies in a frustrated heap.

'You knew that before we came here. Why don't you go out and buy the *Folha de São Paulo?*'

'Because my Portuguese isn't as good as yours. I can only look at blood-and-guts pictures.'

'I'll translate for you.'

'No thanks. I'm dependent on you for enough already.'

'You'd rather complain.'

'I would.' He smiles. 'Oh *God,*' he groans. 'Another story about the damage anthropologists are wreaking. This is a great joke.' He grins. 'What's a typical Kayapó family? A mother, a father, five kids and an anthropologist.'

She moans and rolls her eyes.

'Why don't we go to Salinópolis this weekend?' he says. 'I want to go to the beach.'

'I don't think we can.'

'You mean we can't even afford that? A weekend in Salinópolis, the Daytona Beach of the north-east?'

'This apartment costs a lot. You know that.'

'So,' he shrugs. 'Let's move.'

'We can't.'

'Why not?'

She pauses, looks down at her hands. 'I need the view.'

We can't afford to go to Salinópolis on the Atlantic so we go to Icoaraçi, a good river beach only half an hour by bus. For a river beach, it's okay. There are not many piranha, almost no chance of bilharzia – the water is too swift-moving. There are crocodiles, though.

The beach is crowded on the weekends with Amazonian families and their children, who glisten like lizards. The fresh water seems heavy and sticks to my skin like mercury. We drink chilled coconut milk, he meets sylph boys at beach bars. In the distance I can see the flat shape of Marajó island. I wonder where the crocodiles are.

*

'I have to go out.'

He eyes her. 'Okay.'

'Do you want me to bring anyone back?'

'No.' He shakes his head. 'Just go out and enjoy yourself.'

He hardly goes out now. On the nights when he used to accompany her ventures into the city, they would sit in the Bar do Forte, built on the battlements of the old *fortaleza*, the one that overlooks the Ver-O-Peso market. The Fortaleza once defended the entire Amazon against the English and the Dutch.

From there they used to watch ships sliding like giant glass structures over the Amazon. At night the river and sky are a seamless horizon of black, occasionally sequinned by the lights of the massive dock cranes, which warp and wink like the eyes of dinosaurs. Some nights they would go on to the Clube Lapinha, which she knew Belém natives avoided. Tourists were always fascinated by it because there are toilets for three sexes: Men, Women and Gay.

Now she has become so used to being alone in the city that she finds his presence obtrusive. Other men never look at her in the street when he is with her, and she is treated deferentially in bars and restaurants. She knows why – alone, a woman is a threat. With him she is a *Senhora*, an attached woman. Not that long ago the Amazon had been like the Wild West, she knew, a place where a woman's survival depended upon having the protection of a man. Either that or they could become prostitutes.

Most of the time now he stays in their apartment, reading classics on their eleventh-floor balcony. She comes home to find him in the chair, sometimes asleep, with Ovid and Aeschylus and Plato and Cavafy sitting at his feet like puppies.

What she misses is seeing him in action, out in the world, because his entire being is calibrated on the cusp of action-obsessiveness and languor, and she knows this is unusual. When he does things, even if it is just buying fish at the Ver-O-Peso, he does so decisively, with a need that is ragged, intense and controlled at once. He kisses her like that too, but with a languor in his lips. He lets them linger on hers until something inside her becomes insupportable. If she could X-ray him she is sure she would see something in the process of melting. That's how he feels when she touches him: frozen maple syrup or chilled chocolate warming up, returning to its natural viscosity.

When she enters the air-conditioned office that afternoon, the one that pays her meagre salary, or into a travel agency to investigate flights they cannot afford, her body breathes a sigh of relief. Her business done, she leaves the travel agent and walks on the uneven sidewalks, cracked and buckled by rain and heat, into streets full of shoestores.

The Organization of American States is in town. Heat-stunned gringos wander the broken pavements, avoiding crevasses, stepping delicately, like storks. The statesmen and their acolytes have convened in the city for six days. She tries to avoid the North Americans; their pale and fleshy faces remind her too much of what she is herself. Still, just for a moment, she wants to go home.

The nights have gotten worse, not better, since they came to Belém. Most nights now he has to uncurl her from her screwdriver sleep postures. In the middle of the night all her muscles contract, as if she were a stroke victim, and she doubles up upon herself. He prises the pillow out of her hands. He sits at her thighs. The click-click sound of the docks filters in through the window. Light from the halogen floodlights used to illuminate the nighttime loading makes its way in too, bathing them in a sick hospital yellow.

He sinks down on one elbow and swings his legs up on the bed. All this time he says nothing, but begins to stroke her hair, moving it off her forehead. Then he lays himself against her and straightens her out, limb by limb, like a store mannequin.

From time to time she would picture herself, or at least try to, with someone else – someone who returned her love at its exact pitch and frequency. But after him, she knew, everything would seem out of key: banal, like the Bahian pop songs they listened to by Djavan, full of saccharine regrets. Every time she talked to him, she felt she was going somewhere she had never been before. No one else had ever given her that sense of possibility, and she clung to it even while she understood that its promise was false in the way that a journey undertaken in a dream does not really get you anywhere, at least not when judged by the moment of waking.

Life seemed not to want her in it. No matter how hard she tried to get close to life, it repelled her. It had only allowed her to touch it as you would place a finger on a mirror. The imprint lasted for a second, seared there by body heat, then faded away. With him, the mirror disappeared; he was more real than anything she had ever encountered in her previous life of mowed lawns, country-and-western ballads played on radios, the open tailgates of pickup trucks.

But he is changing. Although he is in a way every inch the western man, his smooth limbs and chiselled face suggesting infinite progression, she can tell he is becoming increasingly dark, interior. Just talking to him is like entering an abandoned labyrinth. He often takes off his glasses to look at her, and even she would wonder if this was a calculated move of his, as if he knew the effect of the jade-threaded clarity of his eyes.

Still, she can't imagine he has any need to manipulate her. They can sit together happily for hours on the couch, facing the window of their apartment, their fingers twining and untwining. She runs her fingers through his hair, rubs the point on his neck where his hair stops and his skin begins. Her body flushes hot, just from this. If he falls asleep beside her, their thighs running alongside each other, she fingers his eyelashes, very lightly. They are extraordinarily long, like a camel's. She runs her finger through the whorls in his ear. She can do this for hours and not be aware of time passing. Then she might look up, suddenly, and see that outside the sky has turned to aluminium. Rain's coming.

The Organization of American States conference brought opportunist traders from all over the mouth of the Amazon. After she encountered a glut of Canadians, she walked down to the Ver-O-Peso. Under a massive Amazonian sky, pelicans fell like bombs into the brown waters. Or they waited opportunistically with the hunch-shouldered posture of diplomats next to the fish stalls. Some of the pelicans were as tall as the women who minded the tattered stalls. The late afternoon light was silk-washed. The sun would go down in less than an hour.

Senhora, Senhora.

She turned around to see a man, his face creased with the lines of too many false smiles. His forehead wide, his hair cut by some maniac. She could see immediately that he was a *caboclo* – of mixed indigenous and Portuguese blood. He wore a brown-stained white sleeveless shirt and blue nylon shorts. On his feet were flip-flops.

'I have something to show you,' he said, in burring English, and winked at her.

'*Qué?*' She pretended not to understand.

He switched to Portuguese.

'*Vem conmigo.*'

She did not know why, but she went with him. It was not a safe face, but she went with him anyway.

He turned his back to her, bent down, and reached into a

box, carefully, all the while whispering, *'Minha amor, minha amor.'*

From the box he pulled what looked to be an animal.

She stood back. The first thing she noticed was the smell – like rotting leaves. The animal's fur was grey and wiry and was covered with what looked to be a dark green slime.

The animal faced the man, gripping his shoulders with two short arms. Then it rotated its head, very slowly, and turned to look at her. Its eyes were the colour of black liquorice streaked with amber. Its stare was inquisitive and sad.

'Don't cry, *Senhora*. Here, she's yours.'

She approached the animal. Its nose was squashed, button-like. Over its eyes was a band of dark hair, like a racoon's mask. She realized its benevolent expression came from its upturned mouth; two thin black lips that seemed to be smiling.

'Only thirty dollars, *Dona*.'

She took it in her arms. The animal gripped her shoulders with its claws. She was made nearly delirious by the heat and damp coming from its body.

She turned to the man, smiling. 'She's beautiful.'

The sloth gripped her like a child, each leg splayed on her hip bones, its claws, snug but not biting, on her shoulders. It did everything very slowly.

She could hear the thump-thump of its heart. It was also slow. The sloth had extremely long claws. She could feel her skin being serrated, but the sloth did not puncture it.

She looked into its face but wasn't sure what it was she could see there. Its nose touched her forehead; it was hot and wet. The sloth put its nose in her ear and she flinched, then smiled.

'She's trying to tell you something,' the man grinned. Then he prised the sloth off her body.

'Thirty dollars, *Senhora.*' He put the animal back in the box.

'Wait here.' She thrust fifteen dollars into his hands. 'That's a deposit. I'll be back this afternoon.'

She wanders in and out of the afternoon rainstorms, going nowhere. She stands beneath their waterfall wetness, emerging from time to time into curtains of sunshine.

Near dusk she finds herself in Lourdes' neighbourhood. She can't remember going there. She has no appointment. He doesn't need a boy tonight.

She passes through the house and into the courtyard of neatly arranged tin shacks. As she descends the stairs she expects to see him there on his slum divan. But Gorda is not there today.

She arrives at Lourdes' shack and, as there is no door, steps into the gloom of the shed. She steps back, blinks a couple of times, re-enters. By this time the girl has lowered the gun and holds it limp, at her thigh. She blinks again. It is unmistakably Lourdes. She looks just as she has always looked – a twelve-year-old girl, long-legged and intelligent.

'What are you doing with that?'

The girl shrugs. The gun falls out of her hand, thumps to the dirt floor.

'That's loaded. You never, *ever*—' She steps forward to take Lourdes' face in her hands. 'You *never*,' she nearly squeals, her voice still constricted, 'let a loaded gun drop on the ground, do you hear me?'

Lourdes doesn't look at her.

'If you load a gun then you use it. You point it at someone and *you use it.*' She is shouting now. She is shaking the girl by her shoulders. 'Who were you going to shoot?'

The girl goes limp as a mollusc, comes to her, slides against her body. 'Oh Esther.'

She has to remember that this is not her real name, only

what she told Lourdes she was called. She feels guilty, suddenly, that this girl who trusts her thinks her name is something that it is not.

The girl puts her arms around her chest. Her flat body pinches itself against her breasts. She takes Lourdes' oblong face between her hands.

'Who were you going to shoot?'

Lourdes lowers her eyes.

'Who?' She shakes her.

'I don't know. I was just looking at it.'

She sits down on the edge of the bed and puts her face in her hands.

'Esther, what's wrong?' Lourdes waits. When she hasn't answered she says, 'Will you stay with me, just until I go to sleep?'

'Where's your father?'

Lourdes shrugs.

Later that night, they lie entwined together, listening to the fizz of rain on the tin roof. Lourdes sleeps against her, stirring occasionally, only a shard of her face visible in the moon's knife slicing through the window.

They stay like that for what seems like hours. Eventually she falls asleep. For the first time since she met him, she sleeps with her body relaxed. No one has to come in the night and prise her apart. She wakes up after the rain has stopped. She picks up the gun from where it had fallen, and leaves.

Much later that night she sits in the Tip-Top ice cream parlour, licking her favourite flavour, the bitter-lemony *cupuacú*. Families take desultory promenades around the square to the rattling sound of axle-battered cars, combatants of too many Belém potholes. The sky is clear, but it is a sideways, neon night.

In the park, women are arguing with their boyfriends.

The women always take the initiative in an argument, she observes. The men are pliant, as if drugged. They go along with everything until they start drinking.

She has only a thousand cruzeiros left. Not much. She has spent the fifteen dollars she was going to use to buy the sloth on ammunition.

In the window she sees the reflection of her face. Then she sees his reflection in their apartment window, superimposed on the river-cranes. The cranes are sawing the sky, groaning forward and back. On the bed, he is thrashing back and forth, too.

I didn't mean to hurt you.

He is barely conscious, and gasping.

We're the same, she whispers.

Then she mops up the blood, makes him a torque bandage, and takes him to the hospital. Everywhere she looks malarial men lie like exhausted bread loaves. Whenever anyone is shot in the conflicts of the *garimpo*, the nearby gold mines, they are taken to the hospital in Belém.

'To your knowledge, has your husband ever had dengue, malaria, or HIV?' they all say, when she fills out the forms. In Portuguese, HIV sounds like *Ash Ee Va* – soft, almost benevolent.

'We'd like to keep him overnight for observation and to run blood tests,' the doctor tells her. 'It's just a grazing. He was lucky. Or it was meant to be just that.'

When she tells him the story about the robbers, the doctor shrugs.

'It happens a lot. And you live in a rich neighbourhood. You should move downmarket. You can take him home in the morning.'

The doctor looks at her, sudden and sharp. 'You're not going to report this to the police, are you?'

'No.'

'Good.' He clips a piece of paper on to his board, turns away from her. 'That would get you nowhere.'

She makes sure he is asleep, then she walks out of the hospital, catches a taxi and asks the driver to take her to the ice-cream parlour.

As I work my way through the riot-coloured ice-creams – *Açaí, Cajú, Cupuacú, Castanha* – I run through the possibilities of what I have begun to call My Future.

I will go and live with Lourdes and her brother. We will save our money, the three of us, and I will take them to Miami. There they will learn English, and instead of a prostitute Lourdes will become a dark-skinned secretary in an air-conditioned office.

I will leave this city. I will swim out to the one or two ships that still make the journey up to Manaus and back again and then are spat out the mouth of the giant river, and go to Port-of-Spain, to Monrovia, to Panamá. There I will meet a Belgian businessman in a bar and we will become lovers and he will pay my passage home. Or I will go with him to Antwerp and work there for the tourist board, guiding English people around the city.

I will use all my savings to buy the sloth. I will return her to the forest. I will journey for many days in small boats, dependent upon the kindness of the people in the river settlements. They will understand what I am doing. They will help me. Even if by that point I smell of piss and green slime because the sloth will not let go, even at night, of my shoulders.

He had been out of the hospital for a week. The boy had just tripped into his trousers, closed the door. That night, like many nights before, she sat in the corner of the room, the one beside the tall faux-French window. She sat so that her hair was brushed lightly by the once-white gauzy curtains as they swung in the breeze. In front of her was the bed, which took up an obscenely large area of the room. Her legs – tanned, mosquito-bitten – were curled up beneath her, and she sank down as far as she could into the chair.

She loved to watch his face when he came close to orgasm. It twisted into an almost phantasmagoric mixture of pain and waiting. Waiting, waiting . . . and then relief. Like the slow opening of a flower, or the open mouths of bears, rabbits, small animals as they died, caught in the steel trap in the winter forests of her childhood.

She could do this too. It wasn't just the boys she brought to him. They were made for each other. His penis was thin and long, delicate. She was small. They fitted each other perfectly. Sweat even ran down their chests in synchronized rivulets.

In the morning she would change his wound. This would bind them more to each other. There was nothing about him that was foreign. Not his ruptured skin, the scar he would always carry. Every part of his anatomy seemed made to inhabit her body. And it had been even better between them, ever since he had told her she was not what he needed.

He watches her change the dressing on his wound, following the complex instructions from the doctor, which he could not understand because his Portuguese is bad. At these moments he looks at her face with an expression approaching benediction.

Later that night she lies beside him on the bed, so hot she thinks she might be breaking into a fever. She rolls over, away from him, careful not to touch his body.

In the morning she got him a glass of water, took his gold-rimmed glasses delicately in her hands and cleaned them with her silk scarf. She replaced them quietly on the bedside table.

Quietly, without looking him in the eye, she went around the room gathering her things. She stuffed them in her bag. The claustrophobia was getting worse with each second, but she tried not to appear rushed. He looked like a wounded animal, faultless and uncomprehending, lying tense and waiting for the moment to be over, the one when she would close the door behind her.

Eel Fishing

As the plane descended she pressed her face against the cabin window. The city was a nexus of light, but within it she could see individual orange dots that flickered in the night like sequins scattered across a piece of black velvet. When the plane dropped lower she saw that these wavering dots were fires. Indistinct figures rimmed them, standing in ragged circles.

After the long, snaking journey from the airport on the underground she emerged on to the sidewalk to see packs of young men swigging from brown cans and dragging straw figures dressed in baseball caps and old football shirts. She watched as the effigies, dripping straw, were bumped down the street like recalcitrant children being carted off to school.

The whizz-boom of what sounded like rockets or mortar fire rang in her ears. She looked at the sky and saw that its edges were seared by an orange burn. She knew nothing of Bonfire Night and she felt afraid, going to sleep in this new city of fire. The next morning it rained and she recognized it immediately, the smoke-bitter smell of carbonized wood cooled by rain.

A man burst in the door. He was lightly dusted with snow and his glasses were fogged.

'Sorry I'm late. I had to go back to the house to get my camera,' the man said as he struggled out of his jacket.

'Why, are you art-directing a shoot today?' said Niles, one of the account managers.

'No, it was something I saw on my way to work.' The man took off his glasses to clean them and Keir saw two peat-coloured eyes. There was something unusual about them; they were clear and pale and looked as if they were covered by a thin layer of ice.

'I started across the park and there's this funfair, all covered in snow. And this ride – what's it called – Spider or Octopus or something?' The man grinned, his peat-eyes shining. 'All its arms were frozen and covered in snow, like a dinosaur skeleton.' He threw his arms open wide and limp in an imitation of the construction. 'It was amazing. I just had to get some pictures.'

'That's so like you, Dan,' Niles said. 'Out photographing snow-covered funfairs when you should be in a meeting.' He leaned over to Keir. 'Dan's an artist.' Niles rolled his eyes, as if to say, *What can you expect?*

In the meeting she stole sideways glances at him, saw unkempt hair the colour of light honey, the black fuzzy jumper and combat trousers. Later she would not be able to remember ever saying hello to him, or even exchanging names. At the time she thought the lack of introduction was odd, but then explicably neurotic in that English way, like how an English person could pass you in the street and not say hello, even if you had been introduced, even if they knew you.

She was beginning to get used to these cultural tics. She had been in the country for a total of three months. Less than a month before she'd got the job, much to her amazement. She had no experience with charities or medicine. The organization raised money and supported research into a number of degenerative diseases for which there was no cure and which attacked the body slowly, over time, like a sadistic subversive.

An hour after that first meeting Dan came into her cubicle. He flashed a quick, hesitant smile. 'I'm wondering what to do with this page.' He indicated the rolled-up pieces of paper he carried under his arm. He unrolled them and laid them on the floor so they had to bend over.

On each of the posters were pudgy, long-eyelashed faces. Under each baby was a trial slogan: THIS IS YOUR FUTURE; FOR THE FUTURE; WHAT WILL HIS FUTURE BE?

'It's a well-known rule in charityland,' he said, answering her frown. 'Babies bully you into giving money.'

'Not me they don't.'

'Oh well, I guess you're a marketing anomaly.'

Most of their exchanges began like that: in discussions about Quark Xpress or word length, and then transformed themselves in a subtle, meandering way into treatises on films or books or music. For months they skirted the periphery of friendship, fuelled by these quiet forays into each other's interests, until there came a point when, if they ran into each other in the lift or while swishing through the grey-blue prairies of the office, they would greet each other with smiles that threatened to erupt into grins.

Still, after three or four months of working together she knew only two things about him: that he had been an artist and he was married.

*

In August it started. Trains of eels would swim downstream and out to the sea, coursing out of rivers, creeks, inlets in a living flood. On these nights her father put on her rubber boots and took her by the hand. The flashlight's beam wobbled in front of them as they swished through the wet grass.

When they arrived at the river it sounded different: slow,

sluggish, not gushing, as it usually did. The river was full of thick brown cords; it was so full it had stopped flowing, like a sauce that had been heated to thickening.

'Where are they going?'

Her father scanned the horizon and his vision seemed to snag on some feature he knew well. He pointed south-west, in the direction of the gypsum cliffs that lined the coast. 'Down there. They've got four thousand miles to cover in the open ocean. They're going back to their spawning grounds.'

The next day she stood on the edge of the sea. It was true: the land felt emptied. For months she had seen their fat brown bodies, thick from a year of gorging on river-feed, and suddenly they were gone.

Above her she saw the eagles spiralling, riding the thermals in search of fish or squirrels. Above the eagles she could see the quilt of exhaust drawn on the sky by Europe-bound airplanes. She tried to imagine the destinations of these planes but could see only a vague tapestry of light woven out of unfamiliar colours: strange transparent blues, old burnt siennas. Each day on the lonely shore she wove this tapestry tighter until it became a drawing, a photograph, a map. She could already feel it, the pull of the gulf stream.

*

There was a tap on her shoulder as she slid her name from IN to OUT. She turned around to find Dan behind her.

'Do you want to get a sandwich?'

'Sure.'

'It's warm enough to go to Bunhill Fields. Have you been? It's where all the famous dissenters are buried. Wesley's there, so's George Fox, the guy who founded the Quakers.'

'Great.' She smiled. 'I love nonconformists.'

They sat on the bench opposite William Blake's headstone. Dan said he couldn't remember if he was actually buried there, or in Westminster Abbey. In any case it was pretty ordinary, she decided, a thin tranche of stone blackened by centuries of grit.

'So,' Dan said. 'Do you get out much, I mean, beyond work?'

'It's hard when you've just moved here. It takes a long time to get to know people in London.'

Dan nodded; he seemed to understand, even though he was a Londoner and had always known people there.

'At least I don't have to be friends with the office women,' she said. The office women wore loose-fitting batik dresses bought in Bali or India, or leggings worn with long jumpers on cold days. They floated from room to room, looking preoccupied. They seemed to avoid discussing realities that did not contain the possibility of helping people. 'I'm surprised how rabid they make me,' she continued. 'They're just so smug in their batik dresses and their serial pregnancies.'

'Michaela's pregnant.'

'Who's Michaela?'

'My wife.'

'Oh. Sorry. I didn't know.'

'She didn't either, until a few weeks ago. But that's what she wants.' Dan smiled his quick smile, the one that flashed across his face like a fugitive and transformed it from ordinary to something momentarily astonishing. Dan was not beautiful, but certain elements – his eyes, his smile – would occasionally conspire to be dazzling.

'I don't know what I'm doing there either,' he said, sounding suddenly deflated. 'That's how it's been for me: I started out with installations, then photography. I won prizes. I thought I was invincible. Now I've got a job in which I have to apologize for my most creative ideas.'

'Why do you work here then?'

He shrugged. 'I try not to think about it too much. I remember I had that obsessiveness that you need to make it. The weather or love had no effect on me; I just wanted to work. But I wasn't paying attention to experience,' he continued, chewing his sandwich slowly. 'I wasn't respecting it. I was just using it as fuel in my routine of flinging myself every day at art. The good thing about working is that it's a little more real.' He gave her a look that told her he expected her to understand, and she returned it carefully to him, intact, to show that she did.

'But do you really think it's real, what we're doing? Helping people who are dying of a terminal illness, whose bodies are disintegrating around them?'

If you were one of them, you'd want to know we were there, working for you, wouldn't you?'

'I guess.'

'We'd better be getting back.' He crinkled his sandwich wrapper into a ball and tossed it into the rubbish bin in a deft arc. He threw a glance at William Blake's tombstone. 'Ciao, Bill.'

On Saturdays she goes to Camden Market and Portobello Road where she wanders past tables of silver and pewter, fingers racks of musty-smelling cashmere sweaters. On Sundays she goes to Spitalfields or Brick Lane and to the Whitechapel gallery, where she sees threatening installations made from organic substances – ice or lard or chocolate.

She wanders the streets of the East End: Peartree Street, Milk Yard, Tobacco Dock, Swedenborg Gardens – that strangely thrilling mix of philosophers and commodities – forming her own internal geography of this confusing new city of twisting streets and sudden rainstorms. She is never aware of feeling lonely, only that time has taken on a breezy, astringent taste. Everything was supposed to be so new – Dan, the fact that they said *trainers* and not *sneakers*, the bad pay, the estuary weather, names of groups: Blur, Pulp, Suede, all those four- and five-letter snappy names that were to her the sound of Englishness even more than the music they produced. Yet everything felt new in a pre-exhausted way, like when she bought food at the dusty corner shop and took it home only to discover that its sell-by date had passed.

On that March Monday, walking back from Bunhill Fields with Dan, she notices that sparrows are singing and the afternoon sun is warm. There is so much to her life now, she tells herself, as they walk together in a new, slow silence she interprets as companionable, his arm occasionally brushing hers; so much more than the concerned job, her weekend mappings of the city, her minute speaking role in the cast of city dwellers. There is him.

*

She studied it as if it were the encyclopedia, reading the strange names of the fish that surrounded her: *Tompot Blenny*; *Five-Bearded Rockling*; *John Dory*; *Gudgeon. Fish of the Atlantic* was one of only three books her father owned. It was the eels section that caught her attention.

At an early larval stage the eel looked similar to a silver leaf, with ribbed gills, then it grew longer, its chevron gill-pattern still visible. The larva lived for one or two years before turning into an eel. In adult stage the eel began the migration to the northern waters. They swam as much as eight thousand miles to reach the freshwater river where their parents had lived.

In the fresh water of those rivers they grew fat together, never straying more than a few metres from the spot they chose as their home. There they stayed until one day a switch was thrown inside their minds and they began to get ready to leave. On one of those dark and choppy nights they loved, they left the continent that had been their adult home. They charged into the salt waters of the Atlantic, swimming towards the Sargasso Sea in their multitudes.

But then something odd happened, something for which there was no explanation. When the eels reached the mid-Atlantic bight, near the Sargasso, they vanished. In the Sargasso there are no spawning eels among the mats of seaweed and flotillas of jellyfish, only young eels, drifting on the ocean currents for thousands of miles to reach their parents' home waters. Eels have never been observed mating or spawning. An adult that is ready to spawn has never been found in nature, the book said. How they perpetuate their species is a mystery.

*

'So what do you think of him?'

Keir turned around to find Alison there. Alison worked in their department. She had come into the kitchen to make a cup of tea and caught Keir staring blankly into an empty mug.

'Of who?'

'Dan. Everybody notices Dan when they start.'

'Only when they start?'

'Well, you have to admit' – Alison gave a shrug – 'attractive men aren't exactly thick on the ground in the charity sector.' She moved her coffee cup next to Keir's. 'Almost everyone has a crush on him.'

'Do you?'

'Do I what?'

'Have a crush on him.'

Alison gave her a disappointed look. 'There's no point.

Haven't you noticed that all his sentences begin with "My wife"? Dan's very happily married.' Alison rolled her eyes. Keir caught the false tone of commiseration in her voice that said, *Doesn't it make you sick?*

She didn't really know if it did or not. She had oscillating views on marriage: at times she saw it as a state of moral poise, at other times as one of almost childish fantasy, like those Dickensian stories of children who spend years in each other's company, slowly, seamlessly falling in love, expecting their love to keep them protected from a certain kind of penetrating knowledge. She already knew that Dan was one of many people who used his marriage as both a defence and a weapon against those who inhabited a less enchanted state.

'He *adores* her,' Alison went on. 'Of course, it helps that her family is fabulously wealthy. A real old Italian family with a real old castle in Tuscany.'

'Amazing.'

'But don't let his cool, creative guru posturing fool you. That's what he really wants, a family. His parents split up, you know. Really nasty. He's vowed it would never happen to him.'

The kettle boiled and Alison poured water for them both and left. Keir stayed in the kitchen, flipping the tea bag back and forth in her mug, watching the liquid turn from the colour of light pine to oak.

She felt like a character in one of those spy films, the guileless one who has just undergone a covert interrogation by a top double agent. Was it a warning, or just girl chat? It felt like high school, when girls would carefully stage conversations in bathrooms in order to stake their claim on some guy or protect a boyfriend from the attentions of some marauding cheerleader. But she was nearly thirty, Dan was thirty-two. Adults didn't do things like that.

*

In June, one of the sudden deluges the English weather was capable of brewing out of nowhere swept in, and by six o'clock it was raining too hard to leave. Keir and Dan sat together in the empty office, watching the rain run down the windows.

'You know, on days like this I think how everything seems so diluted,' she said. 'Even the light. It's so transparent. Almost yellow.' She wanted him to know how unreal she felt in this watery new country where the sunlight was the colour of pale egg yolks and the sky seemed tilted at the wrong angle.

'I know,' Dan sighed. 'I sometimes think I'm a Mediterranean myself. I can barely get through the winters here. I look forward to my summer holidays like a kid. Sometimes I even count the days. This year we're going to Sardinia. I'm so excited.'

That was the source of his interest for her, she realised. He was so fresh. He wasn't worried that enthusiasm would make him look ridiculous. She also perceived he was still very angry about something, and that he had kept this anger intact since childhood, but somewhere along the line he had taken a decision to express it in jokes, in nervousness, in self-doubt.

She reminded herself he was married. To an Italian woman. His wife would be sharp, transparent, like a good olive oil.

They looked out the window to see sun battling toward them through heaps of dispersing clouds. Dan flicked his eyes up to the clock. 'We should head home.'

Before she knew it they were outside, the traffic screaming around the corner from the Old Street roundabout. 'It was a Roman road, Old Street.' Dan pointed. 'Did you know? Even before they came, the Celts used it. It was here before London existed.'

'No,' she said. 'I didn't know.'

'You live north, don't you?'

She nodded, expecting the invitation to walk home together. They stood there for a moment, vibrating toward each other, or away. Then the moment passed, the moment in which he didn't invite her and she didn't invite him, so in the end they went their separate ways.

'Now, about Alzheimer's, how are we doing on that, Rob?' Their boss, Marcella, shifted in her seat, carefully rearranging her skirt. Keir knew Marcella wore tight-fitting black skirts to work to elevate herself above the batik-wearing hordes.

She watched as Rob gathered his face up into a wrinkled blanket of seriousness. 'I would propose that we take this new campaign forward with a maximum of tact if only because our supporters simply might find guerrilla tactics—'

'—or scaremongering—' said Marcella.

'After all, we have to show some compassion for the people actually afflicted with the disease, rather than scaring the hell out of them—'

'Exactly—'

'Exactly—'

Keir threw a renegade look at Dan, who sat next to Marcella. He was looking straight at her with an expression that was unmistakable. His eyes were liquid and his face had the softened, faintly smudged features that signal desire.

She was stunned. She readjusted the features on her face, as if pulling them more tightly to her bones, and sat up straight. At first she was afraid. Then, within a second, angry. She threw him a look that said, *I'm the one who shoulders this, not you. I'm the only one who is allowed to look at you that way, then put myself through hoops of burning flame like a trick pony.* Then a helpless, so far unknown voice spoke from inside her. *Please don't love me back or I don't know what I'll do.*

All this cacophony passed through her in two seconds, maybe three. By the time she looked back at his face the expression was gone.

*

In the long summer evenings they played dusty board games that made her sneeze when they opened the boxes after winters spent underneath the sofa: Monopoly, Clue, Snakes and Ladders and an old mauve Scrabble, its box shattered at the edges.

She was terrible at these games for the same reason he said she was never much good at fishing. No patience, her father said. Or at least, not enough. But it was card games and their tactics she loved: forty-fives, blackjack, cribbage, gin rummy, poker. They rewarded risk, strategy, betting, not just the ability to wait.

They played games to pass the time. There seemed to be a lot of time that needed to be passed. In these evenings Keir and her father began to knit the complex quilt of silence that would keep them warm for so many years.

Other nights, though, the cabin was full of voices, eight people around the table, the smell of men and women woven into a single mat of Old Spice and Cacharel. The women came carrying handbags loaded with sympathetic smiles. The men clapped her father on the back heartily and she heard the hollow, drum-like sound as the thwack of their palms echoed in her father's lungs.

She sat on the fringes of these games, making cigarettes for her father, inserting empty filters into the roll-o-matic, pushing the lever, forcing the thin tube of tobacco, taking it out and tapping it sharply on the table, one, two, three. When she did play, most of the hands she was dealt were no good. She said, *Pass, pass, pass*. She fell asleep head on her elbow, watching the moon slide across the kitchen table and settle into her mother's empty chair, the game's ninth ghost player.

*

The office picnic took place on a muggy Thursday. As the afternoon went on they drank warm wine which turned their faces red and their tongues into deserts.

By late afternoon they still hadn't spoken to each other. She knew they wouldn't, unless the silent choreography of those around them were to shift and suddenly maroon them together. Even then they would probably spiral away from each other, their eyes hunting desperately for someone to join them and make the proximity bearable.

The young Irish account manager stood up, his face flushed. 'Let's go to the top of Parliament Hill.'

Keir stood up; it would be good to get some exercise. She didn't notice that Dan had stood up too. Then, suddenly and through some amorphous group dynamic, the impulse to go for a walk deflated and everyone sat down again, one by one, until only Keir and Dan were left.

'Nobody wants to go to the top of the hill?' Dan sounded lost.

'There's Keir.' Somebody pointed to her and she swivelled around to see him there.

The sun entered her head like an axe. 'No, that's okay,' she said, woozily, and went to sit down.

'No, you two go,' said Marcella in the tone of voice she used in the office when issuing an order.

Keir stared at their boss in disbelief. They were supposed to protect him: her boss, their colleagues, the postal delivery men, the café cashier. Everyone was failing Dan and his wife by allowing them to go to the top of the hill together. What was happening to the fabric of society?

Simultaneously Keir and Dan perceived that it would be

more conspicuous for them to abandon the walk than to set off together up the hill, shoulders hunched, keeping a distance between them. A strange misery settled on her as they walked, like a blanket thrown over her head. The heavy picnic food they had just consumed stuck in her stomach, the greasy chicken nestling queasily beneath strawberries.

When they reached the top they stopped and surveyed the cityscape with their hands held over their brows, like military tacticians. The city lay beneath them in a haze, punctured only by the bright orange plinth of Canary Wharf reflecting a late afternoon sun.

Keir pointed to the blue plateaux in the distance. 'What are those?'

Dan squinted into the horizon. 'The Downs.'

'It's strange, to call something that's so obviously up the Downs.'

Dan laughed. 'You make terrible jokes.'

'But don't you think it's odd, how you never question the things that are most familiar to you? Where I come from there are all these strange place names, or everyone says they are strange. But for me they're the most normal thing.'

'Like what?'

'Tangier Bank. Mushamush. Judique. Grand Etang. Memramcook.'

'*Mushamush.*' Dan grinned. 'That's great. What do they mean?'

'They're the rivers where my father fished. He fished eels.'

'You mean, for a living?' Dan flashed her another of the looks she received from him more and more often, a look that teetered between incomprehension and admiration.

'I know, it must seem strange, but it's a good living.' She tried to laugh in the merry way that showed she accepted she was just another foreign curiosity in his landscape.

'Then there's Kougibouguac. That's my favourite name. Although that's a park, not a river.'

'It sounds French.'

'Where I grew up the names of everything are French or North American Indian, sometimes both mixed up.'

'God,' Dan sighed, still squinting into the sunset at the city. 'Why on earth did you want to come here?'

*

It was the third time that week they'd found one of their eels in the grass near the river. It had crawled out and around the weir and was heading towards open water.

'They can survive two days out of water,' her father told her. 'As long as they keep damp.'

'Why do they try so hard to go away?' she asked.

'It's instinct. Eels aren't like us. They can't think. They can just do.'

She tried to imagine being an eel: no thoughts buzzing through her mind; day turning into night, over and over, and the dreamless place in between; lonely journeys through the cold and dark to a place where she has never been but which she knows because something has implanted the memory of it inside her.

In early September her father was ready for the heavy weeks of the eel season. The first night that was cloudy and the moon dark – the conditions eels liked best for migrating – she went with him. The river looked brown and angry. She watched him open and close the weirs, then sit back on his heels.

Soon the weirs were full of hundreds of brown bodies, thrashing and whiplashing. Before her father could stop her, or even notice what she was doing, she had run to the last weir at the bottom of the river, and tugged on the rope. Like a guillotine blade rising, the little door at the bottom of the weir came up and the eels flowed through, then out towards the Atlantic.

Her father's hand landed on her shoulder with a thud.

'What in the Jesus do you think you are doing? Hey?' He shook her by the shoulder the way she had seen him shake dogs.

'I wanted to let them go.'

'You need your head examined.' She realized he was shaking, even trembling. 'You just cost me five hundred dollars.'

He didn't hit her, but she could see he wanted to.

He never trusted her after that, not really. Eventually they grew apart. Her father began to fill the holes in his memory with his confusion and disappointment in her. They were incarcerated together, she realized, in a peculiarly indifferent interdependence. The moment she understood this, she began to plan her departure. She would leave in the autumn, when brisk ribbons of light began to lay themselves across the sky in alternating gold, blue, orange. She would leave her father and the cabin, the eels and the bald eagles and their lonely sorties. She would start again somewhere untainted by memory.

*

They shuffled along the high street, walking past clumps of people standing limply at bus stops. It was the first time they had walked home together and they were nervously silent, keeping a distance between them.

A sign in wobbly handwriting caught her eye – *Live Eels Inside! Eel Pie, only* 90p! She stopped and peered in the shop window to see eels arranged on crushed ice in marble banks. The eels were dull and grey, like the colour of office equipment.

Dan caught her expression reflected in the window. 'What's wrong? You look sick.'

'I was just thinking how far they swim from the Sargasso to North America and back. Then they end up dead in Dalston. It doesn't seem fair.'

Dan nodded absently. 'Listen, I've got to get some cash.'

They went to the cashpoint. As Dan inserted his card she looked up to where thin banks of cloud had spread themselves over an estuarine sky. How intimate it was, she thought: taking money from the bank machine together, each with the little numbers that were passwords to their separate existences. She thought how you must really know someone when you knew their PIN.

The machine spat Dan's card back and bleeped angrily, releasing the card twice and drawing it back, like a lizard flicking its tongue.

'What's wrong?'

Dan peered into the screen. 'It says there's no money in my account. Here, you go ahead.'

She inserted her card and took her money – twenty pounds, two tens. She held one up to him. 'Here, I'll lend you a tenner.'

'No thanks. I'm married to a rich woman.'

Dan had said it so lazily, so effortlessly, that it took her a moment to absorb his sentence.

He looked up to the sky, smiling. 'I think it's going to rain. Wouldn't that be amazing?' He brought his head down to find that Keir had lurched off up the street. He looked after her, frowning. It wasn't like her not to say goodbye.

That night she sits at her desk in the room she has rented in someone else's house. Rachmaninov's Prelude in B minor booms out of her stereo. Long-overdue rain finally droops outside and a candle burns on the mantelpiece behind her. She puts the two tenners she has taken out of the machine on the desk in front of her. She picks one of them up, stares at it for a few minutes, scrutinizing the Bank of England's secret silver strip. It's a good trick, she thinks. She stands up and takes the tenner over to the candle on the mantelpiece. She holds it to the flame and watches it burn.

*

Of that night she remembers only dark and rain. Outside lightning split the sky in two. The cabin had lost power and they sat in the orange pool of the kerosene lamp.

Her father put his hands on the table. By then arthritis had turned his fingers into crab's legs. He couldn't fish another season with those hands. Besides, his memory was going. He seemed to have trouble remembering faces and she would come home to find the stove left on, or a fire burning in the fireplace. It was this that had first given her the idea.

'You can't do it,' he said, when she had explained it to him.

'But how are we going to pay for you? Who's going to take care of you? I've been here with you for nearly twenty years.' The way she said it, it sounded like a sentence. He gave her the watery, reproachful look he had learned from his eels.

'If we do it then the insurance money will buy you ten years in that home. You know I can't stay here any more.' She said this in the manner she had learned from characters on television shows, people who spoke only in that frequency of the obvious and the inevitable. 'We can take out everything that's valuable and put it in Rory's house. No one will know.'

Before she started she went down to the river and stood beside the weirs. One by one she tugged at the ropes attached to their floodgates. She had to use all her strength:

the river was high and the water murky. One by one they came up and their cargo of eels flooded into another holding pen until she reached the last one and, with a tug that wrenched her shoulders, they were free. She watched them spill downstream, tumbling towards the ocean.

She got them both in the rowboat and they rowed out into the water, him hauling on the oars in the middle while she watched from the stern. From that distance the burning cabin looked like a distant flare in the darkness. In the night the water and the sky were navy and there was no line between them. She watched the flames leap from the pile of wood that had been their home. She never thought anything burning could be so beautiful. She thought, this is the beginning of forever.

*

They crash into each other outside the bathroom and leap away as if they have been electrocuted.

'Sorry.'

Dan gives her a wobbly smile but his eyes are full of an indistinct hurt. She reads their encoded plea: *What do you want from me?* She sends him a mute message back: *I don't know. Please don't hurt me.*

The rest of that afternoon she spends surfing the net, logging on to sites that hold no interest for her and have nothing to do with her work. She clicks in and out of these individual phantom web universes, thinking how they talk all the time. They are two culturally literate people, so they talk about the films of Antonioni, Jose Saramago's winning of the Nobel Prize, Danish interior design, Portishead's appeal in France, Malcolm Lowry's obsession with the Cabbala. But somehow, like a deft goalkeeper, he blocks her every attempt to really connect.

She knows sex would be only the most tawdry, imprecise

way to get close to him. What she really wants to do is to be able to say to him: How did we get here? I'm sure when we were children we never thought, I want to grow up and work for a charity for people whose minds and bodies are falling apart.

But at the same time, she thinks, it can't be an accident, that they are both there. At least they have each other; at work they can talk, bizarrely cosseted by the surveillance of their colleagues, telling each other about films, set design, the genius of Truffaut, their love for cinéma verité, its insistence upon verisimilitude, the extent to which art can recreate life, can mimic reality.

'Hummous and peppers on a baguette, please.'

God, she hated hummous. She was trying to impress him by being a vegetarian. It didn't matter. She knew she would feel too sick to eat her sandwich if she had to look at him at the same time.

They left the sandwich shop, both wading through a sudden ripe silence. There was a pause stuffed full of hesitancies before Dan said, 'Do you want to come over for dinner?'

'No.' It had come out of her mouth, unwanted and unmeant. What she meant was, *I have been trying to forget you. Why do you do this to me*? She said, 'I mean, why?'

'Why?' He looked hurt. 'Because you're invited. That's why.'

'Is Michaela going to cook?'

'Michaela's in Italy.'

'Oh.'

'I thought you'd like to see my work. You always used to ask.'

'Oh yes. Your work.'

He shrugged. 'Just bring a bottle of wine, then.'

'I beg your pardon?'

'You know. Bring—' He folded his arms and made a cradling motion. 'Off-licence. Wine. Dinner. Polite.'

She laughed. Suddenly she felt safe with him. His humour would protect them.

'I'm sorry. Tired.'

'Ah.' Dan raised his eyebrows. 'Tired. No speak. Understand.'

'Yes,' she said. She was laughing helplessly. 'Yes.'

That night she has a dream. She is covering enormous distances. She can see a blueprint of the ocean floor hanging in her mind; she isn't sure but this seems to come from a microchip embedded in her nose. She has left the Sargasso and is swimming. She is a leptocephalus, a transparent creature, shaped like a willow leaf; then a glass-elver, then a cylindrical adult. She has a silver skin, a cord of solid muscle. She began yellow, then became silver, now she is turning brown. As eels get closer to their destination they get darker.

She is swimming between scattered balleen and forests of kelp. Whales and submarines pass beneath her like submerged planets.

A gulfstream night. And in the sky, the shattered hieroglyphs of stars.

They don't even make it to dinner.

She turns around to face him. He swivels his hands on her waist, as if they were dancing partners. In just one glance she sees fear, hurt, embarrassment. Although she can't really identify it, lust, which can look like so many things. To her, when she thinks she sees it – flashing, metallic – it looks like hatred.

An hour later they lie on their backs. Dan's bed is bare, with no sheets or pillows. Their legs are splayed and they are looking at the ceiling. She feels she has just been involved in some tremendous fight in which there has been no clear victor. She feels like she has arrived at an airport only to find her flight cancelled. She is – what is the word? Stranded.

*

At first she had gone to visit him often. The smell in the home was vegetable and smothering, as if she had stepped into a vat of mashed peas. Vaguely camp young men wearing soft-soled assassin shoes trotted after her father with kidney-shaped bedpans.

After a while he didn't seem to recognize her. They would sit playing silent card games, the ones they used to play in the cabin: crib, forty-fives poker. She didn't know who he thought she was. Perhaps he thought her a roving card player, sent to partner men who were perpetually lost between words and meanings. Sometimes she thought she could see the flames flickering in his eyes. The navy water, and in it, the reflection of their burning home. Sometimes he wouldn't look at her.

The cabin was wood and dry: no one had questioned it. Of that time, the time after, all she can remember is talking to investigators, to men in work suits and business suits, filling in forms, and not having to fake her tears. But her dreams of leaving had filled her head like cool water poured into an empty glass. Her father wouldn't have known how, in those childhood meanderings on the shore underneath the silent white arrows of transatlantic jets, she had been rehearsing her disappearance.

When she left on the plane she did not look beneath her to see the blue-black patches of matted forests slipping away. Her instinct was already that of an exile; she wanted a complete cut, a deliberate circumnavigation of destiny.

*

'Do you want me to stay the night?' Even as she said it she knew it was too tentative, too filled with remorse. It begged to be answered, *No.*

'I don't think so.' She knew he was trying to avoid saying, *I think you should go.*

Her eyes patrolled the unfamiliar darkness of the room, saw the streetlight falling through trees outside the window and drawing filigree patterns of Victorian wallpaper on the bare floorboards. In the distance she could hear the whee-whee sirens of emergency vehicles. It was the same sound pattern as the double-time telephones that went ring-ring, ring-ring. She wondered if this were an accident, that everything in this new country sounded like a short-short code of distress.

After a while she realized he was asleep, although his breathing was shallow and irregular, as if in his sleep he sensed he was lying next to a stranger. That was what she was, she thought: a stranger. Unknown, unplaceable. Might do anything. Might sleep with your husband. Might disappear tomorrow.

She remembered that in a week it would be her birthday. She had lost all markers of time in this wet seasonless country. Her birthday was on that cusp time of year, early September turning to autumn. At home the seasons changed overnight; there was no warning, no transition. One day the skies lost their summer haze and the next they were glassy and sharp.

Those years when she was eleven, twelve, thirteen, they would have a birthday bonfire on the beach below the cabin. All the kids she grew up with came. Her father would bring wieners, marshmallows, hot dog buns for them to roast, skewered on the ends of sharpened alder branches. The dogs would bask beside the fire, their golden fur melting to amber in its light. Even though autumn was in the air, they would all go for a midnight swim in the warm black water beyond the fire's halo. She remembered the nights were still warm enough, but in a few days it would be cold. She remembered swimming in an ocean warmer than the air.

Cachoeira

I

Cachoeira, 2/8/8—

Town the colour of oysters. Or petrol.

The old railway station is yellow and gouged by guano. I'm told it was built by a Czech who modelled the clocktower on one in Prague. The hands fell off the clock long ago; some numbers too: there's no two, and no eight. In what was once the forecourt kids totter on those bicycles made in the seventies, with banana-shaped seats and deer antler handlebars.

No one on the streets, or anywhere. Such a strange town. Like a living memory of itself.

He got in his car and drove twenty kilometres in the general direction of the sea without looking at the map. He arrived at an inlet choked with tall reeds. He got out of the car and squinted at them; they were brown and tightly rolled, like elongated cigars. They must be six feet tall, he thought.

He got back in the car. *Giardia, amoebic dysentery, leishmaniasis, leptospirosis, Chagas' disease*. He recited tropical illnesses silently as he drove. His malaria pills were in his room, their packs unruptured.

Although it was nearly forty degrees he did not sweat. He had never perspired much. Maura had once told him, 'You always smell like mint, do you chew it or something?' In hot places people could always smell him before they saw him. They wrinkled their noses, remembering forced washings when they were children, the bristle of their mother's scrub-brush hands.

He turned on the radio. A mellifluous hum of Brazilian Portuguese poured from it; he thought again how everything in Portuguese – even 'You're going in the wrong direction' – sounded like someone's last words before sleep, dreamy and sophisticated, sexual in that way of sounding just one step short of letting go.

In the two hours' drive from Salvador he saw only three or four other cars. It was on one of those IMF-built roads that looked more like airport runways, with no meridians and liquorice-black asphalt. By the roadside, tall sugarcane swayed in the breeze, undulating in waxy waves of green. He was looking at these so intently he almost missed the tiny rusted plaque: CACHOEIRA.

A turnoff appeared, then a potholed spur road. The town came upon him quickly, as if it were rushing to meet him. It swallowed him into sudden clean cobblestoned streets lined with neat houses painted colours that reminded him of the icing on supermarket cakes: watery peach, lemon yellow, chemical pink.

At the Bahiatursa office a luminous black woman named Estelle showed him to his hotel. 'It used to be the convent,' Estelle explained. 'You'll be sleeping where the nuns used to live.'

By seven o'clock it was pitch dark. There was no moon and few streetlights. The biographer sat on his narrow bed, reading the journals of his friend, the writer, who had been through Cachoeira nearly fifteen years before. He smoked and listened to the clack-clack sound of the old air-conditioner. Outside, a metallic tide of crickets rose and fell in perfect unison, like a practised cathedral choir. He allowed himself to think they were the convent's crickets, trained by the nuns. He smiled at the deliberate whimsy of his own thoughts. All this solitude was getting to him. He stubbed out his cigarette and went to sleep.

Cachoeira, 3/8/8—

Today: met Luis at Bar do Nair. Luis: thin forearms in a land of muscled men. Piano-player's fingers. He speaks English well – an inheritance from his father, who learned it from missionaries. He said his family originally came from what is now Gabon, a country of small, lissome men with soft eyes prone to religious conversion.
Said we would meet again, Thursday.

Hot night. One week to go, until the rains.

The biographer set out from the convent with an energetic step. He was wearing his Englishman-in-the-tropics uniform (serious version): beige cotton trousers the Americans called chinos, a clean, pressed green Oxford shirt. On the first day of research in a new place he always felt eager. In each country he broke open a new notebook, liberating it from the plastic wrapping he had kept it swathed in since he had bought it in W.H. Smith. He loved putting his pen to the clean, dry, empty prairies of their pages.

No sooner had he walked a block than he was approached by a rickety old black man. 'The King used to live here. Every day he came and bought a new little girl fresh from Africa! Did you know that?' The man grinned, but where there should have been teeth were only a few yellow stubs.

He ducked into the tiny grocery store to avoid the man. He decided to buy a cold drink and some chocolate that turned out to be mouldy. The two teenage girl cashiers gave him furtive looks and shy smiles.

Back on the street he passed a shop selling nothing but religious candles. He decided to ask the man and woman behind the counter, who had the weary automaton look of long-married shopkeepers. At the sound of his phrasebook Portuguese the husband-and-wife creature threw each other a symbiotic look. They shook their heads and went back to pricing candles.

He made his way to the church. He had taken the advice of the old biographers he was reading and their eighteenth- and nineteenth-century wanderings. 'Talk to the priest and the mayor,' they suggested. 'Go to the convent,' one biographer of a famous Italian Catholic novelist had advised. The biographer was pleased he had already penetrated the convent – and so effortlessly! He frowned. He was beginning to tire of his own jokes. Another hazard of excess solitude, but then he couldn't have known about that before.

He knocked on the door of the church. He waited a few minutes, knocked again, and was about to turn away when he heard shuffling footsteps inside. The door opened and a cool draught rubbed itself on his shins like a cat. A fleshy face peeked out.

'Are you Padre Paulo?'

The face nodded, causing its chins to wobble.

'I need some information. I'm told you might be able to help.'

The face opened the door. The biographer saw the round, cassocked body attached to the face and, behind, a long, dark hallway. A few minutes later he sat with the priest in a room full of paintings of mildewed monsignors.

The priest smoothed his skirt. 'So what do you think of our little town?'

'It's lovely. A bit like a museum, though.' The biographer smiled to show he meant no harm. What he meant was the town surprised him with its scrubbed look, so different from Salvador and its slatternly apartment buildings and gaping wrecks of colonial mansions, their façades faded to the dull lime of gooseberries. He hadn't liked Salvador at all – the thin, cobblestoned streets that his guidebook told him thieves used for quick getaways, the way the woman at the hotel had warned him not to wear his watch, which was plastic and cost ten pounds, in the streets. Even Africa hadn't been like that.

'Cachoeira means "dam", doesn't it?' he asked the padre. The dam was visible from the window of the priest's office: an ugly, low structure that looked oddly like a medieval catapult.

'It was one of the first dams built in Brazil. Of course, compared to the ones in Amazônia, it is a child's toy.'

The biographer cleared his throat again, his pad poised on the dusty table. 'I'm here because I'm looking for a man named Luis. Do you know anyone in town by that name?'

'Luis?' The priest frowned. 'There are many people named Luis in this town.'

'What about a Luis who lives in a blue house on the hill?'

'What else do you know about this Luis?' The biographer caught a disapproving, confessional-box tone in the priest's voice. He decided to be clear about his intentions.

'I am researching a biography. An English writer came through here ten years ago and became' – he paused very briefly, but the priest caught it, – '*friends* with a man named Luis.'

'Ah-hah,' the priest said. 'The English writer. I never met him but he wrote that book, didn't he, on the northeast? *Candomblé*?' The priest smiled a private smile. 'It was full of inaccuracies, but I admire his energy.'

The biographer looked up sharply from his notepad. 'Which mistakes are you thinking of?'

'Nothing, really. Just little things.' The priest shrugged. 'I remember a line, for example, about Cachoeira: "A town of wet colours mixed with four-hundred-year-old dried slaves' blood from Dahomey, Angola and Guinea, their midnight faces bound for the fields of Pernambuco." The slaves brought into this town stayed to work on the sugarcane plantations you drove through on your way to Salvador. Or they went to the Bahian *sertão*, the interior. They never went to Pernambuco.'

The biographer pursed his lips. 'He must have liked the sound of the word. Writers often eschew a strict interpretation of the truth for the sake of art.'

'I wouldn't know much about that. I'm sorry I can't help you with your enquiry,' The priest said, rising. 'You've considered of course that your friend might be using another name, a false one, to protect the identity of Luis.' The priest opened the heavy door and a dazzling wedge of sunshine forced its way into the darkened church.

'I knew he might have changed his name in the book, but not in his journals, he wouldn't.' The biographer scowled into the sun. 'It seems Luis has just vanished off the face of the planet.'

The priest raised his eyebrows. 'Or maybe he never existed. If what you say about writers is true.'

He left the priest and wandered around town. He passed the small triangular park that marked the spot where the slaves used to be auctioned. There was no monument, just a tree enclosed within a triangle of benches where a little boy in shorts sat eating ice cream.

2

It was an ordinary book launch, studded by red-faced journalists in misjudged suits who were there only for the booze; aloof writers; glossed publicity girls and agents with marauding smiles. Of course it was too hot, and of course I feel ill at ease in these things. Everyone is *friends*, supposedly, and puts on smiles that only make them look like cheetahs trying hard to relax.

I looked across the room and noticed a tall man standing on the periphery, holding a long-stemmed wine glass tentatively between two index fingers, the way you would hold the thorn-studded stalk of a rose. He had curly hair, shiny and dark, which fell around his face in curls the colour of squid ink. Poet, I thought.

Then suddenly we were being introduced by my publisher, who was conscious of my lack of social viability and who consequently thrust me in the path of anyone who wasn't surrounded by acolytes.

Nick gave a little smile. His mouth was not as attractive as the rest of him; it seemed too small in such a wide-boned face, like a hole that had been cut halfway and then abandoned. He was a reviewer, he said, and a journalist. He laughed sharply before adding, 'A hack.' An unhappy look fizzed into life then died just as quickly in his eyes.

We went on from there, our friendship tripping along on that peculiarly unspontaneous London rhythm of infrequent meetings that were never happenstance, luncheons and book launches. When I published my first novel he gave it a glowing but trenchant review. When he was promoted to literary editor of the daily I gave him a congratulations party in my flat.

After a year in the job, however, he was bored.

'I need *challenge*,' he told me as we met for lunch in a Covent Garden restaurant.

'Write a book, then.'

'But that will mean an even drearier existence. I'll sit in my study for a year and make things up. That's no way to experience anything.'

I was taken aback. He had just described the previous two years of my life.

'Write a travel book then,' I suggested. 'That's going to be the next big thing. Ride round Chile on horseback. Or infiltrate a Tibetan monks' school. Study the tension between old values and new in the Bushmen of the Kalahari.'

'Hmm?' He was staring out the window. His eyes snagged on something. I looked and saw a tanned, blonde-haired man.

'I have to go.' He picked up the briefcase he took everywhere with him. He always had a manuscript or a C.V. or a list of publications in it, ready to whip out and hand to whomever he was meeting. We paid our bill and left.

I started work on my troublesome second novel and did not hear from him again for some time. Then I began to receive postcards from unusual places: Senegal. Congo. The Cape Verde islands And the town where I write now, Cachoeira, northeast Brazil.

I was upset when the book appeared without a mention of our conversation. I thought at least he would have thanked me for suggesting the idea of a travel book to him. He thanked his parents and the woman who was to be his wife. They were followed by a slew of foreign names.

His book and my second novel appeared at roughly the same time. My novel was an autobiography of a fictional composer, written in a series of letters to intimate friends. It was hailed as erudite, and reviewed in the *Telegraph* and on Radio 3.

Nick's book was quickly lauded as the book of the year. It was about a month before I got around to reading it. I found he wrote in short, pungent sentences. His eye for detail – colour, the angle of light, a type of bird, the composition of tarmac on the roads – was acute.

Perhaps most surprisingly, he had an intimate, personal voice (something I have always found difficult, as a writer). He seemed to be communicating to you, personally. This surprised me, because he himself could be so remote and diffuse. I expected him to have that arched, stylish voice of the writer who is approaching experience from the intellectualized angle of someone who only wants to put his stamp on it. Instead he drew scenes and situations with a distinct, almost painfully sharp acuity. He was faithful to the reality of the moment, even when he fictionalized it. Most of all, he had this tone that made you believe everything he said. As any writer knows, that's a gift.

Cachoeira, 5/8/8—

Late afternoon. The sun embroiders the edges of everything – chairs, bridges, houses – with gold trim.

We meet in the square. Luis is silent and melancholy. I give him a cigarette. We have a beer, a tall, slender bottle of the beer they call Brahma.

'I don't feel like talking,' he says. 'There are whole days when I do not want to talk. I would rather tend my garden, feed my chickens, listen to music.'

I say, 'I can't imagine a day without talking.'

Luis shrugs again. I can see it's not going to get any better. From the beginning our meeting has the taste of a sour tryst. We get up to leave. On an unobserved corner we part with a lingering sundown of a kiss.

Thought I'd take a break today. I went to Maragojipe, a tobacco-exporting port twenty-two kilometres away.

The town turned out to be more ragged than Cachoeira, with houses painted in appleskin colours: light green, pale yellow, brick-dust red.

I pulled up at what Nick's journals tell me used to be a cigar factory. It's shut now, its white paint fading to grey. Straight away I was approached by a black man wearing the sort of suit Kenneth Kaunda used to wear: grey, open-necked shirt, grey pressed trousers. An enormous cyst stuck out of his neck like an extra limb.

'*Bom dia, bom dia,*' Kenneth Kaunda said, grinning recklessly. As he spoke, the thin skin covering his cyst moved up and down, revealing the marled cartilage of the growth. It looked as if it would burst through any second.

'Can't you do something about that?'

'*Não, não tenho dinhero*,' he said, meaning, no money. Behind his square glasses his eyes were moist. Suddenly his whole body teetered sideways while remaining rigid, like a building leaning into an earthquake. I realized he was drunk.

He bent down to the cobblestones and picked up a cigar end dropped outside the door of the old factory. 'The factory close three years ago, and this still here. You looking for the owner? The Dutchman? I show you.'

Kenneth Kaunda delivered me to a white house bigger than the other white houses. Then he turned and without a word of goodbye veered down the street, his cyst bobbing along like a toy bird kept on his shoulder.

I knocked once, twice, three times. I was about to turn away when the door was flung open by a tall, spindly man with a shock of white hair and watery blue eyes the colour of Portuguese tiles.

'Hello. I'm from London. I'm visiting town and this gentleman' – I pointed in the direction in which Kenneth Kaunda had gone – 'and someone I met suggested I speak to you. About the history.'

'Hes.' A once-substantial voice thinned by age came from somewhere deep inside the tall Dutchman. He looked about ninety, but in good health. 'Cume een.'

He led me down a dark corridor, then into an enormous ballroom where tall French windows cast rectangles of caramel light on the wooden floor. The room was empty except for two chairs. Dust fell from one of the chandeliers. He saw it and brushed it off my shoulder.

As I sat down I thought I saw a figure, something small and dark, a woman perhaps, flit by in the doorway. A second later I saw another follow her down the corridor at a quick pace.

'Who are those women? Do they work for you?'

'Women?' The Dutchman looked at me as if I had just suggested tigers were inside his house.

'I just saw two women go by the door. A cleaning lady, perhaps?'

'Hes. But she comes on Fridays. Today is—'

'Tuesday.'

'Well.'

'Well.'

'I read sometimes in English,' he said abruptly. 'The last time I speak English was with another Englishman. He came here many years ago. I can't remember. But he was writing a book.'

'Do you remember his name?'

'No. But he was tall, like me.' The Dutchman pointed to his own body. 'Very black hair. A gut-looking man.'

'Nicholas Myers?'

'Meers?'

'Yes.'

'Hes. That may be it.'

'I'm writing his biography.'

'Biograafie?'

'Biography. A book about his life. That's why I'm here in Brazil. I am following in his footsteps.'

'And then you will write this book, of your journey?'

'Not really. Not of the journey itself. This is research. I'm trying to find out everything I can about him. I have to cover everything.'

'That is a lot of travel.'

'I know. A lot of travel.' My head felt very heavy. 'He's dead now, Nicholas,' I explained. 'I feel I owe it to the memory of him to get things right.'

'But he was a young man.' The Dutchman turned his watery eyes on me. They had a peculiar cascading expression, as if understanding was washing down them like rain on a window. His mouth worked from side to side. 'You are chasing the ghast of a man who came here chasing another ghast. Are you not afraid of becoming a ghast yourself?'

'A ghost?'

'Hes.'

'What do you mean?'

But he just shook his head sharply as if to drive away a fly that had settled on his cheek.

'I am having trouble locating a person who was very important in Nick's time in Bahia,' I ventured. 'His name is Luis, but I have asked the people in the church, the town hall, the candle shop, and they haven't heard of him.'

'Luis?' The Dutchman looked at me carefully. 'What else do you know about him?'

'That he was very thin. He had worked in the sugarcane fields. He was most likely black. But very well-to-do. He had his own house. A blue house on the hill.'

'Oh, that's Zé.'

'Who?'

'Zé. He has a *pousada*. A little hotel. The house used to be blue but he painted it orange. To make it look more . . .' He searched for the word. His eyes cracked open with triumph. 'More *jolly*.'

'But his name is not Luis?'

'His second name, hes. His full name is Jose Luis. Here Jose is usually cut to Zé: Zé Luis. Everyone knows him as Zé.'

The sun slipped from his face. I looked out the enormous windows, a greased late afternoon sky. 'Well, I should be getting back.'

The Dutchman rose. As I went to cross the threshold I felt long fingers curl themselves around my shoulder. 'Could I ask? Do you have any photographies with you?'

'Of Nick?'

'Of Europe. Europe now. Current photographies.'

'No. I'm sorry.'

'Nick, when he was here, he showed me photographies.'

'Oh. I'm very sorry.'

I looked back to thank him, and caught it; a very subtle look of shock, and pleasure. Perhaps he hadn't had a visitor in ten years. Perhaps he would never have one again.

'Goodbye.'

'Goodbye.' I waved. The look came alive again in his eyes, for a second, before fizzing and dying like an extinguished match.

3

Two dusty boys helped him find the house. He paid the boys and mounted the stairs alone. There was a knocker on the door with the face of a lion. He picked it up and it made a dull, humid sound as he knocked once, twice, three times.

After what seemed a long time he heard footsteps. They stopped for a second. Then a man flung open the door. He was black, thin, with delicate limbs and the discerning eyes of an innkeeper.

'I am looking for Zé Luis.' The biographer said it first in Portuguese.

A light flickered in the dark pool of the man's eyes. 'That's me.'

'Is this not a good time?' He said it in English, hoping the man would remember some of the good English Nick said he spoke.

'A good time for what?' The English came back, fluent, hardly accented.

'I'm the friend of a man who knew you, who came here ten years ago. An Englishman.'

Luis held the door open wider and the biographer passed through into a darkened hallway. He called a name that sounded like Mariela, or Maristela. A light-skinned, much younger woman appeared.

'My wife.' Luis smiled. He turned and said something complicated involving *amigo* and *Inglaterra*. His wife looked at him and smiled.

'She has just finished putting the children to bed. We have three.'

'That's wonderful.'

Luis led him into a living room with smooth walls of some dark tropical wood. The mantelpiece and shelves were studded with antiques: a silver clock, a tiny chest of drawers, a barometer.

'It's a very beautiful house.'

'It used to belong to a very rich man.' Luis' breezy voice said he had heard this compliment many times before. 'A white planter. He left it to my father.'

Luis moved towards a large box which sat on a shelf in a dark corner. It looked like a lamp. As the biographer neared it he realized it was a massive antique phonograph, with a real old horn, enormous and trumpeting. He realized he had never seen one before. It looked like a deranged lily.

'You will excuse me if I play music. I like to play music.' Luis took out a record, flipped it over and slid out the black disc. The record began to wobble over the old player and before long the cracked grandeur of Maria Callas' voice poured itself into the room like cool water into an empty glass.

'Most divas I don't like. They are so *heavy*,' he sighed. 'But this one. There is something really true in her voice. Do you know her?'

'Yes. I know her. I know what you mean.'

Luis sat down in a rocking chair, folding his body into its frame delicately but with precision, as if he were practising origami with his own limbs. He was middle-aged, the biographer decided, about Nick's age, in fact. The overall impression Luis gave was one of an almost pained dignity.

They looked around the house in silence; there was so

much to admire, the dark wood, hard and shiny like brown marble, the stocky antiques studding every corner.

'It's a wonderful house.'

'It was my father's. But not really his.'

'What do you mean?'

'He inherited it from a white planter who had no family of his own. No wife, no children. My father was his foreman. He trusted him. The people in the town they could not believe it, of course,' Luis shrugged. 'Someone even tried to burn down the house, rather than have it go to a black man.'

'Hmm.' The biographer nodded. Then he found, to his surprise, and after searching for days for the man who now sat in front of him, that he didn't know what to say. He felt strangely reluctant to talk about Nick.

The record had finished. It hissed, snagged on the end of the album. Luis rose and turned it over.

'So you are his friend?'

The biographer flinched. He had intended to ask Luis that question: *Were you friends*? His heart beat faster. He was paid to get the information, the detail. He should be like a shark moving in for the kill.

'Yes. We were. I mean, we worked together. We were writers together.' Even as he said it, the biographer thought, no. That's not right. Writing is something you do alone. We were never together, in that way. 'In his last years I got to know him better through—' The biographer paused. 'Through his illness.'

'Illness. He is ill?'

'He is dead.'

Luis sat down abruptly in his chair. '*Morto?*'

'*Dead.*'

Luis lowered his eyes to somewhere around the tips of his knees.

The biographer looked at his watch. 'I should go. By the way, do you have any rooms?'

'I have all my rooms.'

'I mean are any free?'

'They are all free.'

'Right. Well, I'll come and stay then. Tomorrow. If that's all right with you. As a guest. A paying guest,' he added.

Luis held out his hand. He said, 'Tomorrow.'

Cachoeira, 7/8/8—

From my balcony I can see the empty squares. It is noon and everyone is inside, eating or sleeping.

I can't imagine what attracts me to these heat-exhausted towns. There's no cinema, certainly no bookshop.

A smell of aloe. Shuffling priests.

Here it is difficult to imagine the future as anything other than a slow exile.

Luis brought coffee, papaya, and juice made from green oranges. He moved like a waiter, swift and unobtrusive. His children were at school already and his wife had gone to work at the small town hospital, where she took care of 'old people with mental problems', as Luis put it.

'Come out and see the garden.' The biographer walked out the back door and into a vast tangle of vegetation. There were outsize tropical flowers with faces like leering masqueraders, other plants that were only marled ribbons of green. He could recognize oleander, hibiscus, and the zigzag of heliconias.

'Did you learn to do this all by yourself?'

'This? Oh.' Luis shrugged and smiled. 'I've known this since I was a boy. My father taught me. Everything else I have taught myself. I'll be doing some gardening tomorrow. You can give me a hand, maybe. Tell me how you would arrange things in England. Unless you're doing more research.'

'I'd love to help out.'

'Good.' Luis smiled. 'We start at seven.'

Over the following days Luis went around the house fixing things – drains, pipes, the doorbell. There seemed a lot of things that needed to be fixed. He made telephone calls to get business cards printed, mulled into the faces of flowers in his garden, went shopping for new shoes for his youngest child.

In the evenings Luis' wife Maristela came home with a preoccupied expression. It was unusual, the biographer thought, for a man in a country like Brazil to give the children their evening meal as Luis did. But the children were more used to him. They spent more time with their father. When Maristela came home they clung to his body like jellyfish.

In the evening the biographer sat in the kitchen watching Luis shell peas and strip manioc, the potatoes of the north-east.

He remembered Nick watching him peeling potatoes once, near the end, the way he was watching Luis now. He was in his London kitchen, Nick was in a wheelchair by then, a granny rug spread across his knees. His face had been hollowed out by the disease, and a single glass of red wine had already made him giddy. He saw Nick's eye rest on the thin strips of potato skin exiting from the peeler blades. He said, in a voice glazed with the same substance that had covered his eyes, 'What a miracle. I can't believe how simple it all is.'

'You mean peeling potatoes?'

'So many things have taken on this marvellous symmetry. When I look at things I feel as if I am drawing them in my own head. I feel like I'm coming up with the blueprints to everything: spoons, a wallet, the spider crawling across your floor—'

Nick was sitting in his chair, his eyes roving around the room like remote-controlled sensor beams. The biographer would remember that look: concentrated, almost burning, despite the smudge that had covered his eyes in the form of cataracts.

The biographer retreated to his room in Luis' house. He lay down and listened to the silence of the town. He thought of his flat in London, its narrow rooms dark and empty. There was no lover in his life, there hadn't been for years. He saw himself walking home from the Tube, one of many men in soft-soled shoes, a single plastic carrier bag of dinner-for-one groceries dangling from their arms.

He had to count back through his books, his career as a novelist, to remember when Maura left. It would have been after his second book was published. They had been to a party and Maura had been telling him on the way home about some 'interesting young novelist' she had met and he had almost driven the car off the road. He hated those words individually: *interesting; young; novelist*. Put together their effect was toxic.

She had left him after that, calling him bitter, competitive, volatile. She said, 'How long are you going to go on thinking you have no career, letting it poison your life? You have a career. So many people struggle to get published. You're just selfish, self-involved. A typical writer.'

He published his third novel, about a fictional Arctic explorer. After three months of gruelling research in northern Norway and six months of agonizing writing at his desk in London, trying to locate the emotional centre of his character, he finally packaged it up, not hopefully, even joyously, as he had done with his first two books, but with a sense of defeat, and sent it off to his agent.

It was published. A similar book about a similarly

fictional, this time Antarctic explorer had just won the Pulitzer Prize in the States and it got all the attention. Bad timing, said his agent. He remembered the time he got frostbite, his dark hours in the Maritime Library at Greenwich, flipping through the log books of the ships of the Arctic explorers, the long hours spent at his desk.

By then Maura had gone to live in the States. She was younger, she could do those things. He was stuck now, a tired figure on the London literary scene who merited a few minutes of interested conversation at book launches but who never got invited to the post-party dinner.

After Maura there had been no one – that was, how many years ago now? Nearly eight. No one until Nicola.

4

I found her, as usual, in the garden. Rain dripped from the shoulders of her coat, one of those ones made to protect Australian sheepshearers. She pushed her hair back behind her ear and smiled at me.

'I'm so glad you've come.'

Nicola loves her animals and her garden. When I visit she sits me down at the kitchen table and tells me about the benefits of gardening without peat and companion planting.

Pieces of Nick are still scattered around the house. A few masks bought in dark African countries, his leather briefcase he took everywhere. His pens, books, photographs of him in some sunlit place.

Nicola went to a desk and took out a pile of notebooks. Actually they were the books sold in nautical shops: ship's logs, covered in oilskin. She put them on the table in front of me, all wrapped up in string, like a birthday present.

'You must never show them to anyone,' she said. 'You

have to promise me. Anything you want to quote has to be cleared with me first.'

'And the man thing,' I said, out of the silence, temporarily stunned by the inarticulateness of how I had said it: *the man thing*. 'What do you want me to do about that?'

She looked hard out the window, although there was nothing there except rain. 'I don't know much about that side of his life. But on a certain level, I mean' – she gave me an appealing look – 'I don't want to be crass, but don't you think it would be a bit like drawing parallels between someone's bowel movements and their writing? How relevant is it, if what you are trying to do is to discuss the man, the writer? Not the writer, the man.'

'But his friends know, surely.'

'Did you?'

'No, but – I'm not, I would never be—'

'I didn't know either. Until he got ill.'

'But I can hardly write a book about him and not go into—'

'Are you interested in that – *yourself*?'

'No. I don't have any interest in that side of experience, *myself*.'

'Do you think it informs his writing, every word, the reason he wanted to write, the reason he wrote as he did?'

'No. He wrote as he did because he was Nick. Not because—'

'Exactly—'

'Exactly—'

We shook hands. We told ourselves we understood each other, that we wanted the same things for the memory of Nick. But when we said goodbye she smiled and I thought I could see in her eye an expression ever so slightly pained. But then English women are like that, with their opaque blueness, their swallowed hurts.

That night on the train back to London I remembered

what Nick's friend Rory said about his marriage. *She's from the same class, she's got the same name, or almost, she's a female version of himself, which is what Nick is looking for in a lover: himself.*

The biography would bring us together. I would discover so many things about her in the course of writing this book, and so many things about her husband, that I would replace him as the most intimate relationship in her life, both of us circling closer around the magnetic pole of her husband. I would find out what she thinks of him, how she thinks of him.

Does she see him still as she knew him first: the young, slightly slippery, very clever man, a real catch? The up-and-coming writer of the London literary scene?

Or the man she came to know, later. Still her husband, but this man was in towns in North Africa, in Malaysia, in Cachoeira, looking at quick-eyed men with nervous hand gestures, men who open their mouths wide to laugh, gulp the air, men who wear white robes, their hems embroidered by dust. His white limbs entangled with other, darker ones.

Does she wonder what it must be like, if it is a harder passion, brewed up out of the moment, the appreciative yet dispassionate eye men turn on other men? Does she wonder about the appeal of it, sex between men? Does she wonder if it might be a more extreme kind of experience, like being in a car crash with a stranger; binding you together in the sheer jolt of it, the sweat, the unfamiliarity, the blood?

That night I took the train back to London, rattling through wet villages, past red metal benches empty on station platforms, travelling towards the sulphur explosion of light that is the city.

'No light again.'

We sat at the table with a kerosene lamp at the end. It was one of many nights when there was no electricity, despite the dam and the hydroelectric project – 'They're selling it all to Paraguay,' Luis explained.

I reached into my bag and put them on the table one by one. 'Here are Nick's books. I have them all.'

'Is that the one he wrote about Brazil?'

'You've never seen it?'

'He said he would send it, but it never arrived.' He flipped it over to the back cover, where there was a photograph of Nick, taken about the time he had returned from Brazil. Luis looked at the photograph for a long time, scowling. He gave the book back in silence.

'And you write these kinds of books too?'

'No, I never wrote the kinds of books Nick did.'

'But you write books.'

'Yes. Unsuccessful ones.'

Luis laughed. He thought it was a joke.

'We did things for each other. You know. Favours. If he needed some inside information, in publishing, what was going on. That sort of thing. Writing doesn't bring you together with people much. You're more likely to be in competition. That's what it is, a lonely competition that never ends. We did have things in common, Nick and I. We were good friends. But there wasn't anything terribly *emotional*' – I noticed I said the word in the same tone I could have said the word *sexual* – 'between us. Oh. And—'

And a rough-sketched intimacy. The kind men usually have, skirting lonelinesses. Keeping our affection for each other like coffee, a stimulant that you sip but are careful not to let spill over.

'And what happened to Neek?' Luis looked away, into the darkened corners of his dining room.

What happened to Neek?

There's Nick in some African country formerly run by the French. Revolution in the streets. Snipers are firing through the windows of hotels known to be frequented by foreigners. Nick and the only other foreigner in the hotel, a Belgian, are under the bed reading each other the Air France International Timetable to keep calm and eating the only food they have, a box of Belgian chocolates the man had bought in Antwerp.

Nick at the launch of his third and most successful book. It's a party at his place and everyone is dancing. Nick grabs one of the catering staff, a young, dark-skinned man with a close-shaven face and neat glasses who turns out to be a Spanish guitarist, takes the tray of canapés out of his hands and in front of everyone (including his wife) pulls him on to the dance floor.

There's Nick dying in an NHS hospital, the nurses only blue blurs. He is going blind. It's a drizzly day in March, the sky the dull pewter of England. Outside the hospital black cabs fly down Gower Street like crows.

Nick is asleep. His wife has popped out for a coffee. His hand lies on the bed, open-fingered, as if it has just been held. Only the hand isn't Nick's. It belongs to some other creature, it is red and shrivelled, like a pigeon's foot.

It is the hand that wrote the books I am carrying around the world with me now, like a talisman, looking for the ghost of the tall, black-haired man whose eye had been indiscriminate, who had searched out things – nuns, trains, maps, seagulls, men, women – as if they were of equal interest. Which of course, I think now, they are.

The kerosene flame has dropped. Luis' face is just a dark question mark.

'You are not jealous?'

'I beg your pardon?'

Luis shrugged. 'Perhaps I mean envious. I never really understood the difference between them in your language.'

'Jealousy is when you want something someone else has.

Envy is when—' I paused. 'When you want something someone else has.'

Luis smiled.

'No, I'm not jealous of Nick. Nick was my friend.'

How could I explain? He was so much more complex than me. He could be slippery. I suppose he was the kind of person who could turn himself off and on like a tap. Many found him insincere. At times even I thought he was like an octopus, prodding into every darkened corner of the ocean and consuming what he found there.

I could have told Luis how Nick was indiscriminate but incredibly discerning. Maybe this is the true nature of discernment: to look everywhere, deny yourself nothing, in order to discover what it is you really like. I could have told Luis how Nick seemed to have his eye fixed permanently on some distant horizon. When he was deep into one book he was already thinking about the next. He had that ability, crucial to any truly successful person, of imagining himself into his own future.

People have accused him of making things up, then presenting them as fact. (As if that were a crime.) I think the truth is closer to his love for arcane details that often sounded as if they could only have been concocted, or at least embellished. He took an interest in the type of tractors used in Chile, he loved explaining the mechanism by which camels store water, or the Maya's long meditations on calendrics, or the techniques of cornet players of the twenties, the blood pageantry of voodoo traditions, the way the sun went down on the equator. He seemed to be able to find meaning anywhere.

Luis rose and picked up the kerosene lamp. 'Time to sleep.'

In the bedroom the moonlight draws silverpoint patterns at the foot of my bed. I can't sleep. I think about Nick.

The truth is, Nick and I come from what is probably the

last generation of writers who can say we really knew each other, who met from time to time or from city to city – bumping into each other while on book tours in New York, in Amsterdam – and talked about politics, or India, or our latest trip to the Himalayas. We are all well-educated men of a certain class. Perhaps we are the last such men to become novelists and travel writers in the great democratization of culture that is taking place.

We have plenty to share: scare stories of being stuck in the Holiday Inn in Luanda, being in Sarajevo on assignment for the *Independent*, hanging out with Susan Sontag, covering Los Angeles during the riots for *Granta*. We are thoughtful, well-seasoned people, used to exoticism and being shoved on and off aeroplanes.

And then there's that looming sense of posterity, too, hanging over our friendships – even while we are alive we know we will be writing each other's biographies. Perhaps we even embellish ourselves for each other, embroidering anecdotes, inflating daring escapes. Our heroes are Hemingway, Henry Miller, Graham Greene. We all want to be larger than life, writers with a capital W, who live writing and not just do it. We have given our lives over to pure expression. We go to the ends of the earth in search of an experience that might one day become a novel. Nick was the one who had really succeeded. Oh yes, and he had managed that most impressive and demanding of performances: dying young.

In the years when Nick was off discovering new idiosyncrasies in foreign countries, I was slipping into the midlist. My books were concerned with the ebb and flow of time, with memory, the destiny of the artist, ethics, the nature of inspiration. They were novels populated by the obvious shadows of Greek philosophers, lost souls, set pieces in modern-day Hades. Some of my reviewers (who, as time went on, were always younger than me) laughed openly at my work. Then I stopped getting reviewed at all.

I thought, maybe I should try travel writing. But I hated travelling; travel brings you to places like Cachoeira, places whose stunning eventlessness makes you feel you are in moral danger, as if the stasis will suck you down and soon you too will be wearing only a pair of nylon shorts and drinking beer at eight in the morning. In London the sheer effervescence of the city, the fizz, can lift you above the confines of your life. I never feel more of a Londoner than when I travel, I never feel more certain that I want to live and die in London.

But I am also a writer. I need to write. Then, just when I was losing hope, the biography came along. And here I am. Travelling.

On my last day I decide to be a proper tourist. I go to the church, the Capela de Nossa Senhora da Ajuda, but it's shut. Then to the Hansen Bahia Museum, a tiny house dedicated to a German engraver who lived in Cachoeira. But this too is closed.

I sit down under the big tree in the square. Next to me is the same little boy I saw here a few day ago, eating ice cream. We smile at each other. He offers me some of his ice cream. We sit there, eating the ice cream together, the child and I, watching the stupefied quiet of the town gather like smoke, become viscous, then swirl away in thin threads.

8/8/8—

The rain comes streaking down in wet knives. There is something falling down inside me, too, in that same glissando way.

I will have to go; if not tomorrow then the next day.

The riot sunsets, yellow rain. The sun roaring through the latticework.

'So, tomorrow you will leave Brazil. Where will you go next?'

Luis went to his phonograph and removed a record from its sleeve.

'Back to England. I need a break from researching, to write my notes.'

Luis laughed. '*England.*' The way he said the word it came out shaped like disappointment. 'I wanted to go there.'

'Why didn't you?'

'Neek – he said he would write when he got back to England, and send money for me to study English. He wrote. Once. I think, maybe a year after he left here. I used to go around saying it. Only like two words: Eng. Land.' Luis laughed. 'It did make me angry for a while. Not long. Perhaps a year. Then I forgot about it.' Luis looked away. 'Until you came.'

The voice of Callas soared through the dining room. I thought, not for the first time, now eerie it was to listen to a voice when the person who produced it is dead.

Luis turned his ear towards the phonograph. 'What I love about her is that she sings every moment as a distinct experience. It is like how you feel things when you are in love. Perhaps that's the connection between love and music. They both say, You have to try. To really *try*. To not tell lies. To not betray. Not the music or the feeling. It's about more than pleasure. To me, Callas commits herself to the moment, and that is why she is such a great singer.'

'I've always loved her too. But I never knew why.'

15/8/8—

Last night in Cachoeira. The moon scatters silver threads on the river, the town. What was that kind of drawing they used to do? Silverpoint. Eerie, luminous tracings on the parchment. That's what most lives are: stacks of skin-thin parchment. And on each sheet, half-forgotten drawings no one will ever see.

I leave at five thirty in the morning, the dawn a red smudge on the horizon. In England it is nine thirty in the morning. Nicola will be tending the special Edwardian roses whose seeds she ordered from Mottisfont Abbey in Hampshire.

I am here with one of her husband's lovers, with her husband's journals, on this jutting triangle of Brazil, reaching out to Africa. I wonder how I will write this book without mentioning who he loved. What he loved. I wonder if I am only looking for what other people will salivate over as undiscovered squalor in the life of my friend.

I wonder if I have come all this way to lie. Or just not to mention it. I wonder if that is lying.

A Biography of the Biographer: He takes a commission to write a book for reasons he doesn't quite understand. This book will make his life a piece of tracing paper thrown over a sharper drawing.

We see him crossing oceans to verify details. Corroborate stories. Apocryphal, or real?

Prising open the clenched fist of the past.

Crossing oceans to set you free.

Back in Salvador. I was wrong; it's a beautiful city, actually, with its white apartment buildings studding lush hillsides, the blue arc of the widest bay in the Americas. Flocks of schoolchildren flutter past, buses clang. Businessmen wearing sunglasses enter and exit from the dark interiors of the city's three hundred churches. I sit in the colonial district drinking a cold beer, eating a meal of fish and manioc. It's so good to be back in a city.

From the Foot of the Volcano I Write to You

NOTES FOR A NOVEL

Landscape: the shimmering, vertiginous tropics. An island with twin volcanoes, one dormant, the other active. The active one has just begun to erupt, after twenty-five years of silence. She (the character – name? just 'she') has exiled herself for unknown reasons, to a place where beauty and threat intermingle, become indistinguishable.

It took an hour on a lurching fishing boat to reach the island. Girls in white dresses sat primly on benches while agitated waves smacked the boat from all directions. The men seemed to have more delicate stomachs; they leaned over the side of the boat in a neat row, like sports spectators in the upper reaches of a stadium, vomiting.

As the boat approached the island the shadows of the volcanoes threw a cool shroud over their heads. The water had calmed and changed colour to a deep mauve, glassy and viscous.

The volcano that overlooked the town was called Concepción. Tall and perfectly conical, Evelyn had read in her guidebook that its crater was almost permanently obscured by a small oval cloud. Looking at it now, this close, she wasn't at all sure she liked it: it looked less majestic than gauche, like a giant barnacle or a serrated molar. The other volcano was about twenty kilometres to the south and was friendlier, smaller, its eroded edges coated with rainforest. Hemming the skirts of both volcanoes was a band of shimmering, almost plastic green – she had read these were cultivated fields of tobacco, bananas and papayas, dotted with pockets of rainforest.

The boat slid into the docks. Simultaneously a flock of young boys picked themselves up and flew over to the boat, each fighting to carry the passengers' bags. Evelyn peeled them off her gently until finally one boy wrested her backpack from her hand.

'Hotel? Hotel?' The boy looked at her hopefully. 'I know a little hotel.' Tired, she let him take her there, even though she knew he was on commission and it was bound to be a mistake.

They turned a corner and she saw a sign – HOTEL PIRATA. On it a winking pirate in a striped shirt leered. She paid the boy and entered into a dark lobby where a large woman sat watching a black-and-white television. She greeted Evelyn indifferently, even though by the looks of it she should have been falling over herself. The full key rack behind her head told Evelyn there were no other guests and the dust on the keys suggested there hadn't been for some time.

As she wrote her name with a defeated pen in the register she asked, 'Do they ever erupt?'

'*Las hermanas*?' The woman squinted. She noticed people in this country did a lot of squinting, usually at the sound of her accent.

'What sisters?' Evelyn asked, confused.

'We call them the sisters.'

'And they're not active?'

'Oh no,' the woman laughed. '*Está tranquilo*.'

She gave Evelyn the key to a dark, rancid-smelling room. Within a few minutes she discovered the real – possibly the only – advantage to the hotel: it was set on a spur of land next to the lake, with a well-kept garden by the water in which a few tables and even multicoloured party lights were strung. Pen and paper in hand, she sat under the weak pool of light thrown by an orange plastic bulb and tried to lose herself in the thick folds of the humid night.

THE SCENE
A woman sits by the edge of the lake, writing a letter by candlelight.

> Night fell half an hour ago. I wanted to write to you from this island, which I would have liked you to know. I write by the light of a candle I bought from the priest, it really belongs on the church altar but he sold it to me so that he can buy Venezuelan shampoo.
>
> The night here is a carnival of fireflies and burning moths hurling themselves into the candle. Did you know the island is in the middle of a freshwater lake? The lake is the only habitat left of the endangered bull shark, which changes from saltwater to fresh as it travels up the river here from the Caribbean. Behind me is the volcano. It is almost invisible, black against black. Only the moon picks up the shiny nap of its velvet pleats, corrugates it with silver.

Pleased, she put down her pen. Then she thought for a second, picked it up again and wrote:

SUMMARY OF THREATS
Threat from above (the volcano). Threat from the water (the shark). Threat from the past (the lover). Have to find a way to introduce the lover.

*

The kitchen was arranged around a courtyard, with its walls open to the air. Thick-leaved plants grew sideways along the ground; they looked exactly like those plants in horror films, she thought, the ones that turned out to be carnivorous.

She could hear the muffled roar of traffic outside the guesthouse, and the drip of rain as it tumbled from the leaves of the horror-film plants.

As she stood by the toaster waiting for her 'supper' – two pieces of toast with cream cheese and ham – to pop up, she was vaguely aware of a man at the other end of the kitchen, standing over a pot of boiling water. With a clandestine sideways look she recognized him from the supermarket, where she had seen him roaming the aisles, basket in hand. She had dismissed him then as just another American ecotourist in his waist pack, jungle shorts and surfer sandals.

'Would you like some soup?' he asked, startling her. 'I've got way too much here.'

'Thanks.' She accepted half out of surprise. She had been at the guest house for two weeks and no one had ever offered to share their dinner before.

'So,' the man ventured, still stirring his soup, 'are you just passing through?' His voice was polite and open, but with a cool, disinterested current running beneath it.

What would she say? She wanted to avoid the conversation she always ended up having with men like him, men who had probably come to study rare vipers or to build schools for poor kids. They would nod their heads appreciatively but she could see them thinking, imagine, going around the world for no better reason than to write stories.

'I'm researching.'

'Oh really?' It was in the way he said those two words that she first noticed his trick of being simultaneously cool and enthusiastic. He turned his face towards her for the first time: a square face, but with alert, direct eyes buried behind graduate-student glasses. She guessed him to be about twenty-eight, if only because there were a few lines around his eyes, and his hair was starting to recede.

'Are you a scientist?'

'A writer,' she conceded, in a voice she knew reeked of defeat.

'What kind of writing?' His voice was wary. She had heard the tone before: nobody likes a writer, she reminded herself. He had probably already begun to wonder if he would appear thinly disguised in her next book.

'Fiction, mainly. Some journalism, some travel writing.'

'Oh wow. I read fiction at night. It helps me get to sleep.'

She wasn't sure if this was an insult. 'You do?'

'Yeah. If I read anything else my mind just goes round in circles.'

Her toast finally popped. She buttered it with the local orange-coloured industrial-tasting butter. 'I wonder what they put in this?' she said, almost to herself. 'It looks like suntan lotion.'

He laughed. 'I think they add Agent Orange.'

'So what are you doing here?' she asked, trying to match her tone to his, detached, yet friendly.

'I'm an anthropologist-in-progress.'

She couldn't help smiling. 'You mean you're unfinished?'

'You're not really an anthropologist until you've done your fieldwork. I'm doing it here. I start in two weeks.'

'Where are you studying?'

'At—' He named a university she had only ever seen in American films, the ones about a group of privileged kids finding life and love together on campuses filigreed with ivy and studded with big puffy trees.

'Wow,' she couldn't help saying. 'That's top of the line.'

'It sure is,' he said grimly. 'But I did my undergraduate degree at Brown, so I'm pretty used to the hothouse atmosphere.'

'I took a couple of classes. I really enjoyed anthropology.'

This was partly a lie. She remembered her classes at university as being full of young women named Sidonie and Imogen listening to a bearded seventies refugee tell them how men in primitive societies concerned themselves with religion, transcendent drug experiences (supposedly related to religion), copulation (sometimes with each other) and wife-beating. The lecturer was young but prematurely wrinkled from too many years in Thailand or Ghana. The Imogens and Sidonies would listen to him wide-eyed, biting the tops of their pens.

'Everybody seems to agree it's pretty useless, though,' he went on. 'I mean, in terms of an actual career.'

'I don't know. I think an anthropologist's methods are very similar to a journalist's. Or a fiction writer's, for that matter,' she said.

'Really?' He gave her a wide-eyed look that suggested he was flattered by the comparison.

'Well, if you think about it, they're both interested in the same thing: depiction of reality through writing.' She said this fluidly, as if it were obvious, although the truth was she had never considered the subject before. 'Their methods are the same, after all – social observation, uncovering truths, eavesdropping, learning the importance of gossip and how to reproduce it in written form.'

They talked about this and other things for five hours seated at the kitchen table. The conversation progressed from idle and meandering to something more urgent as they exchanged ideas. By the end she had a stomach ache, she was so excited.

At the same time she wondered why he was talking to her. The other denizens of the guesthouse were Americans like him: tanned blonde girls in surfer sandals and flowing Earth Mother skirts. She had tried to start conversations with the girls but there was something stubborn and opaque about them. They would merely nod and get up to make themselves more herbal tea. More often than not they wanted to talk about endangered species of sea turtle or some monkey they had seen.

She learned his name was Mark and he was from California. She was surprised. He had a certain gravity and also a deft sense of self-deprecating humour – she hadn't associated either with California. His face was expressive; she thought she could see shafts of light and dark gather on his face, alternately, then disperse themselves, like little thunderstorms.

'I've been on the road now for a month,' he sighed. 'I travelled through Mexico with some friends. When we got to Guatemala they went home. Since then it's been just me and my backpack. I love my backpack. I can get everything I need in there. Except company.' He smiled in a way she interpreted as an admission of occasional loneliness. This made her like him even more.

'So where are you headed next?' he asked.

'Oh, an island. You've probably heard of it – Ometepe. I want to do some research for my next novel.'

'That's great,' he beamed. 'I haven't been myself, but I hear it's a really mystical place.'

'That's what I'm looking for, mysticism.' She frowned. 'I've never found it in my own life, I have to go looking for it. It's quite a potent ingredient in literature, a real crowd-pleaser. Look at that Brazilian who writes those loopy books full of alchemists and soul twins. People fall for that in droves.'

'I love the way you talk.'

She looked up sharply. The way he said it, honest, admiring, gave her a feeling like warm water washing through her.

'Thank you. I like the way you talk too.' Her own voice suddenly sounded absurdly formal and English.

Later she sat in the kitchen on her own, except for the

gardener, who was trimming the plants in the courtyard, lopping off thick limbs with his machete – *whoosh, chop, whoosh, chop*. A clear gel oozed from the white stumps where he had cut them.

It was true – Mark was a strange Californian. Not once did he say *awesome,* or *like, hello*? or *totally*. Sitting there with her back to the garden, she made a list.

Words he uses:
neophyte
hyperbole
agitated
maudlin
beatific (!)

They had talked for nearly five hours, and she had had no sensation of time passing. For once time had gone too quickly and she wanted to call it back, to rewind the reel of their conversation and go through it all again. Just talking to him made her feel she had been going for years with a reduced supply of some vital substance – oxygen, or water.

She had never seen herself falling in love before; it had always happened slowly, imperceptibly. Maybe she had never really fallen in love before. Nor had she ever watched someone falling in love with her – she was not the kind of woman who seduced, who enthralled. But for once these things seemed to be happening transparently, simultaneously. It was there for both of them to see. It was intoxicating.

*

Her first day on the island, Evelyn rented a Suzuki Samurai with a dodgy clutch and tripped around, taking the wide gravel road that encircled the larger volcano. She passed through three or four dusty towns. Schoolboys ran up to the jeep as she slowed at speed bumps and yelled things she couldn't understand. On the open road cowboys would hear her coming, pull their horses to the side of the road and laugh openly as she passed. She would look at them in her rear-view mirror, wiry men in dusty jeans, their eyes sunk in the dark pools cast across their faces by their hats.

She arrived on the other side of the island, which harboured the second-largest town of any size after the port in which she had arrived. Her map showed the road going straight through town and out the other side, but she couldn't find the way out. At one point she had to put the jeep in four-wheel drive and climb mountainous screes to get out of a dead-end street. Other times the road just ended in a couple of chickens in someone's farmyard.

'Excuse me.' She approached an old man near the church. 'Could you point me the way to the road out of town?'

He raised his thin arm and pointed the way Evelyn had entered the town. She shook her head. 'I just came from there.'

The man's eyes watered. Either he wasn't used to being contradicted or perhaps he couldn't hear her right. She saw a white flag with a red cross flying above a building. Inside, the stout woman behind the counter pointed in the same direction.

'No, no. The other way, please. The road goes all the way around the island, doesn't it?'

The woman shook her head. All her movements were excruciatingly slow. She wondered if this was the woman who would be dispatched in an emergency.

'It's been washed out,' the woman said, her voice monotonous and nasal. 'You have to go back the way you came.'

She put the jeep in gear. Just in front of the car were loose stones and one enormous boulder that marked the end of a lava flow. She leaned forward and through the windscreen looked up into the volcano's enormous, shattering verticality. Looking at it this close made her heart constrict oddly. She thought she could feel it turning the same hue as the volcano, the dead purple of bruises.

When she got back to her hotel she bought a cold beer and took it down by the lakeside. This is just where my character would sit, she thought, pleased. Her character, her nameless 'she': what is she thinking, looking over the now-calm lake, the brown peat of its water, a far-off Pacific sunset forming on the horizon? Is she thinking of her lover?

> You would have liked this island. The blue mists of morning, the purple volcano behind me, the shiny rubberized organic coffee plants. Behind my tiny house is the beginning of the rainforest, a thick wall of green gouged to make way for my house, the exposed trees forming a half-moon-shaped sylvan chorus of silence.

She took her pen away from the notebook. She thought about the structural necessities of a novel. She brought her pen back to the paper.

> NEED A REVOLUTIONARY LEADER
> Has to be charismatic, philosophical. The lovers meet him on the island where the volcano is about to explode.

'The revolution?'

The man – or boy, as the hairless face underneath the baseball cap at the gas station was about eighteen, she realized – narrowed his eyes.

'I'm just wondering what happened here.'

'*Pues, nada*,' he said, with a verbal shrug.

'Well, if anything had happened, who would know?'

The boy thought for a second. He refused to meet her

eyes and instead stared hard at some concrete oracle located between their feet. 'Don Julio, I suppose.'

She was dispatched to the other side of the island again to find Don Julio, passing through the same straggling towns in the same jeep with the same schoolboys running after her. Eventually she found him (she avoided asking the woman at the Red Cross for directions).

He was a wiry, bent figure mending a water pump in the backyard of his house. On hearing her approach he turned around and arranged himself into a standing posture. He smiled a wonderful smile. He had a full mouth of teeth, neither yellowed nor pitted. 'You have beautiful teeth,' she said, by way of a greeting.

Don Julio brightened. 'Don't smoke.' Another lazy, octogenarian smile flashed across his face.

He led her to a flower-strewn courtyard, where two rocking chairs sat like old friends nodding at each other as gasps of wind set them rocking.

She settled herself in her chair and composed her speech.

'Don Julio, I've come to see you because I am a writer, and I am going to set a novel on the island. People tell me you know everything. I'd like to know some stories about the revolution.' (She stopped short of saying she needed a Revolutionary Leader.)

The old man thought for a minute, rocking back and forth. 'How long are you going to spend here?'

'I don't know. Two weeks.'

Don Julio frowned. 'I have lived on the island all my life. I have never thought about writing a book. To write a book you must know everything. You must go to the archives in the capital. You must interview everyone. You need to stay a long time to write a book.' The old man's gaze was stern, not entirely disapproving, rather disbelieving.

'I know.' She looked down. She couldn't meet that gaze.

'It's not much time. But I was wondering about the revolution.'

'The revolution?' Don Julio said it as though this was the first time he had heard of it. 'Yes.' He gestured, throwing his arm out to the north, in the direction of the bulk of the country. 'People went to fight. Yes, many, many people died. But they needed us to stay on our farms. We were the only ones who could grow things, to feed the revolution. It was the only place in the country that remained prosperous,' Don Julio explained. 'At least we had enough to eat. We had no need to revolt.'

She had a quick vision of the years of civil war, carnage all around, and the islanders left placidly to tend their tobacco and oranges.

'No revolutionaries then?' she said. 'Not any?'

'There are many heroes of the revolution from this island, many martyrs,' Don Julio said, his voice level, perhaps conscious, she thought, of the pride seeping into it. 'But they are all dead and in the ground for ten years now.' He looked at her with alert eyes, a little crushed and ridged, like raisins. His expression, careful, evaluating, seemed to ask her: *What more do you want?*

She got up to leave. Don Julio rose with her and smiled. 'Listen, I'll give you the number of my grandson Roberto.'

'Can he tell me about the revolution?'

'A little bit, maybe.' He tore off a piece of paper from an old damp notepad. 'He's a professional guide. He'll take you hiking up the volcano.'

She took the number, thinking, thanks, but I'm not a tourist.

She drove the road slowly to the by-now-familiar chorus of kids yelling *Chela, chela*. Blondie! On her way out of town two cowboys pulled their horses over to the side of the road. In the rear-view mirror she saw them pumping their hands up and down in front of their crotches, phantom penises held between their cupped palms, grinning through the dust the jeep threw in her wake.

*

She met Mark again in a restaurant in the university district, which consisted of three or four chaotic streets of photocopying stalls and cheap diners.

She saw him first, sitting alone in the corner. He was wearing a clean, pressed khaki shirt and chinos and an elaborate pair of hiking boots. She slid into the chair opposite him. He looked up, surprised.

'Did you think I wasn't going to come?'

'No, why?'

'You look surprised.'

'My friends tell me I flinch a lot. If I'm surprised or when I'm moved.'

'And what would it take to move you?'

He didn't answer her, only gave her a look of such exceptional clarity that she felt exposed.

She turned to the menu. 'What shall we have?'

'Well, there's pizza, pizza or there's pizza.' He laughed and she understood he had let her comment pass.

They ordered their pizzas. As they talked she was almost afraid to look at him because when she did she felt something stab her in the stomach. It was his eyes, mainly: they were such a changeable brown, morphing from amber to chocolate to onyx to purple in a single moment.

She decided to say it. He would understand her intentions, she thought. He was an American: open, straightforward, honest. 'You know you have the most amazing eyes,' she said.

'I don't know. I come from brown-eyed people. There are so many of us.' His voice was very serious, as if he had just instigated a debate over an intellectual position. 'But you know, your eyes were actually the first thing I noticed about your face,' he said. 'They're amazing. I was going to say the same thing to you but I didn't have the guts.'

'Oh yes,' she said, her voice grim. 'Guts. I've got those in spades.'

'You say it like it's a bad thing. I really admire people who can take risks.'

'And you don't?'

He shook his head. 'I've never been much of a risk-taker. I don't know why.'

In the background, Mercedes Sosa droned leftist anthems. Evelyn's eye snagged on a group of Che Guevara posters in which Che was forever twenty-seven, his face rigid with valour.

She pointed. 'Speaking of risk-takers, there's the prototype. Every time I look at him I think, now why don't I want to fight for social justice?' She sighed. 'Instead I consume things, just like everyone else.'

'Hmm,' Mark said. 'Speaking of which, his must be one of the best-known faces never to have been hijacked for advertising purposes. Things Che could legitimately hawk' – Mark smiled – 'Guevara Beer, Guevara Berets, Guevara Cigars.'

'Guevara Life Insurance.'

He laughed and flinched (his friends were right). 'He has great eyes,' he said appreciatively, in the same tone he had told her he loved the way she talked. 'They're full of the future. That's where he was looking, every day of his life.'

She looked down at her hands. 'I'm still trying to learn to live in the now.'

'I think about it,' he said thoughtfully. 'I mean, the future.'

'What are you going to do?'

'When?'

'In the future. *Your* future. What is it you want to do?'

'What do I want to do?' Mark repeated. 'Now there's a question.' He got hold of a ringpull, which he turned over and over in his fingers. 'I think—' he ventured, then stopped. 'I think it has everything to do with fragmentation. With fixing the broken connections.'

'Which connections?'

'Any connections. I want to put the broken pieces back together. Before the puzzle is lost. I want—' He stopped again, seemed to gulp. As she watched him struggle to articulate his desires it struck her again, the symphony of passivity and aggression, pride and embarrassment flickering through him with the delicacy of grace notes. 'I want to change the way people think,' he finished.

'You're going to change the way people think through anthropology?'

He gave her a sharp look. His eyes had changed again. Now they were dark purple, with gleaming edges. 'Why not?'

'It's just a tall order.'

'Why do you write then? Surely you don't just want to entertain people.'

She wanted to say, *Of course not*. She thought about what she could say. Why did she write? She wanted to explain to him, but it was like catching a glimpse of something elusive, like the tail of an animal as it disappeared around a corner.

'I think I want to make the things that should have been true, and weren't, true,' she said, in the end.

'Oh really?' He sounded suspicious.

'What exactly do you want to change about people's thinking?'

He flinched. 'You know, no one's asked me that before. Not even my professors. Not even my supervisor. Well—,' he began, frowning so that the lines on his forehead formed beautiful waves, 'for starters the way they think about the earth and how we relate to it. I mean the natural world, the world un-created by man. I want to show people what is valuable, what is worth saving. Because I want us to understand that there are possibilities beyond our own inexplicable behaviour or patterns of consumption. That there is a world beyond this one. I mean, the world of Man.'

'It sounds almost mystical.'

He smiled. 'Back to mysticism. 'Hey—' He put his hand in his pocket and searched for something. 'I left the guesthouse today—'

'You *left*?' She could hear the alarm in her voice. She tried to turn it off. 'I mean, where are you staying?'

'I'm moving into this shared house. It'll be my base in the city while I'm doing fieldwork. Here, I'll give you the number. Give me a call and we'll go out for a drink. I know a good place where we can hear *peñas*, even though they're completely inauthentic in this context of total political apathy. What's so funny?' He had caught her expression.

'It's just the way you speak,' she said. 'It's not funny at all. It's like hearing me talk. You're familiar. Your thoughts—'

'Here.' He handed her the piece of paper on which he had scrawled a telephone number. 'It's a great house. You'll have to come visit.'

They left the restaurant and stood in the street waiting to hail taxis that would take them in opposite directions. She got hers first and they said goodnight with a strange awkwardness, both of them shifting from one foot to the other before making their ungainly exits, like bad actors unsure of their cues.

*

She drove to the narrow isthmus between the two volcanoes where the land was flat and sandy. Tall, reed-like grasses grew there, towering over the bony cattle that grazed on them.

She decided to take a walk along the beach. She took off her shoes, felt her toes sink into the soft, seal-grey sand. She wanted to walk along the shore at night, to get the feel of the moonlight, the water, for the passage she would write about the lovers sleeping on the beach, a campfire illuminating their faces. It was in this scene that they would look up at the sky, see the shattered hieroglyphs of stars, and be moved by their remoteness and by how they had come to this lost corner of the world together.

By the time she started back to her jeep it was five thirty and the sun was slipping behind the volcano. By six o'clock it was pitch dark. The wind had picked up suddenly with the night. The lake began to hurl surprisingly large waves at the shore. Pieces of driftwood that had looked so harmless in the day now assumed the glistening shape of lizards or snakes.

She walked on a little until she saw the silhouetted shapes of two bodies walking towards her. The shapes had rangy shoulders, long arms, slim waists and no hips: men. She began to run. She reached her jeep, jumped in and locked the door before she started the engine with her heart racing.

When she arrived back at the Hotel Pirata she had two beers in quick succession to calm her nerves. Then she sat down in one of the rickety plastic chairs by the lake and began to write.

> When we met you were still in the process of becoming, while I had already forfeited the youthful enchantments of the state of being in progress, which serves as an automatic pardon for so many crimes – innocence, for example, or other cavalier brutalities. Your vulnerability was intoxicating. Your coolness, your hesitancy and

uncertainties had a slow montane slope, declining gradually into fevered flatlands and hot microclimates where plump avocados are bred.

During those two months, months which had the same inconstancy as the unseasonably heavy rain, I began to perceive that there was something grave in you, something really careful. The frequency emanating from you was of a green mountain turning to blue, so deep was its verdancy. I wanted nothing more than to finger its tightly strung threads, from which I was sure I could pluck some dark music. I thought: I think it has a voice, this uncertainty. If I can make this speak it will say things to me neither of us has ever heard before. I was already filling vast anterooms, storing, against my will, monstrosities of tenderness.

She read over what she had written. At the bottom of the page she wrote in cramped, almost indecipherable sentences without thinking, without even understanding what she was writing,

How can I describe this? The way in which I am moved. The way I am moved by people, the anger, the helplessness, like being shut tight in a bathysphere as it is lowered into the obliterating waters of an ocean.

*

'"Martyrdom and abdication: A study in the sex appeal of revolutionaries".'

'"Surfer sandals and enclave identity among upper-middle-class university students".'

'"Emotional apathy and the myth of infinite sexual choice: Some five-minute histories".'

'"The enshacklement of freedom-seekers: The desire for non-knowledge through knowledge".'

They sat in the Bar el Tomate trading fake anthropology essay titles. After a few minutes they were laughing so hard the manager of the bar had to come over and ask them to be quiet. She watched Mark's face rise towards the broad, disapproving one of the manager. He sorted out the situation in his perfect Spanish, with an assurance that was both delicate and firm.

He turned back to her and fixed her with a tentative gaze. So many of his looks were like this, feathers brushing across her face.

'I'm happy out of the city.'

'I'm only happy in it.'

There was a silence in which Mark fiddled with things on the table. 'I guess that means compatibility is out of the question.'

Evelyn grimaced. 'I hate that yuppie language. "Compatibility". We're not computer software.'

'I've got a girlfriend.'

'Oh well.' She resisted the urge to shrug. 'I've got a boyfriend.'

It was true. But what was also true was she was having trouble recalling her boyfriend's face. Each time her mind snagged on his image it slipped away again, like a fish sliding off a hook.

They parted on the street in another taxi confusion. Mark was going to his new house, she back to the guesthouse. They hailed two taxis which waited, their drivers watching them with amused faces.

'There's a party at my house on Saturday. Although I can't imagine what a student squat party in the suburbs of a characterless Central American city could offer you.' He stood, nervous and also defiant, willing her to refuse. Then a smile hacked its way through his hesitancy and she was captivated again. 'Well,' he said. 'It's been intense.' In his voice she thought she heard the tone of something over and completed.

'You think that's intense?'

He flinched and gave her the same look he had given her in the pizza restaurant.

'Well,' he said.

'Well,' she said.

The next day she went to a telephone booth. She would call him, tell him she couldn't come. She had to leave early for the island. She was sick. She knew what would happen if she went to the party. He knew too.

She dialled his number. The phone rang and rang. She left the telephone booth and went to do some photocopying, a laborious process involving three men in shirts and ties and one slow cashier. She went back to the phone booth. Still no answer. This went on all day, then the next, and the next.

On the island she will have dreams – or nightmares – in which she is dialling his number and the phone doesn't work, or she forgets his number, or the keys won't move, or she's putting in the wrong coins. In the mornings she wakes, exhausted from her nights spent in phantom phone booths, his number ringing in her head.

*

Roberto turned up in the afternoon. He was a short man with a sweet face and the jaunty stride and nervous energy she equated with maleness. He arrived dressed in taupe cotton shorts and a shirt of the same material that had too many pockets. On his feet were Nike knock-offs.

Roberto saw her eyeing his outfit. 'I know,' he shrugged. 'My aunt sent it to me from the States. The tourists like it. They think I'm going to wrestle jaguars or something.'

He handed her a little map of the south island with the smaller volcano sketched on top, and a broken line showing their trail.

'You like it?' Roberto smiled. 'I drew it myself. Okay, I'll pick you up tomorrow morning at four, then we'll get to the foot of the volcano by four thirty. We'll have an hour walking in the dark while it's still cool.'

'The dark,' she gulped. 'Aren't there snakes and things around in the dark?'

Roberto gave her an odd look. 'Of course.'

The next morning she hauled herself out of bed to the discreet beep of her alarm, shrugged on her backpack and went out into the dark. She expected the pre-dawn streets of the little town to be like those of a big city: deserted except for a few drunks and overnight workers. But everyone was up. Farmers clattered through the streets in horsedrawn carts, women were on the move, carrying unidentifiable bundles. Children were yawning sleepily in doorways, spooning papaya into their mouths.

Roberto picked her up in his small truck and they drove, kicking dust and gravel in all directions, to the road she had taken when she explored the isthmus beach. About half an hour later, after bone-jarring juts and rattles, he parked the truck. 'Okay,' he smiled. 'Time to go meet those snakes.' He saw Evelyn's face. 'Sorry,' he said. 'Really, it'll be okay.'

They started off steadily through grassy fields, Roberto shining a torch in front of their feet. Soon they were on a steep, muddy path winding through rainforest. A dense blanket of sound wrapped itself around her – chirrings, squeakings, and a strange metallic bop like a pinball machine when the ball drops through the hole.

'Bellbirds,' Roberto called over his shoulder. 'Weird, isn't it? The squeak is from the oropendolas. They're the ones who build nests that look like lacrosse baskets. You ever play lacrosse?'

'Oh, did I.' She had a flash of big-kneed girls running around in kilts on cold English mornings.

Roberto paused and inhaled deeply. 'Sweet, isn't it?' He sighed. 'I love the dawn air.'

She looked up through the mesh of rainforest trees and found the sky paling rapidly. With each second more light leaked into its porous fabric.

'I just can't believe how fast the dawn happens here.'

'Everything happens fast here. You get old fast, you get hot fast, you die fast.'

For two more hours they hiked steadily and in silence, Evelyn keeping her eye on the back of Roberto's boots. She didn't dare look to either side of the trail for fear of what she might find there.

They stopped for a while halfway up the volcano for her to dab on suncream. Roberto took a seat on a stone while she looked around at the forest. Everything seemed to be growing on top of everything else: mosses on wood, flowers on mosses, strange plants that looked like the tops of pineapples sprouting from the Vs of tree branches. Now that daylight had arrived the forest had the empty quietude of a cathedral.

'What do you remember about the revolution?' she ventured.

'Remember? Well, that depends. I probably remember a lot. I don't think about it much, though.' Roberto paused. 'I had to leave school for a while.'

'Why?'

'To be a soldier. I was drafted.'

'But you must have been sixteen years old.'

'Fifteen. I didn't do much fighting. For a long time I was on burial duty in the mountains. One day we buried twelve children.'

'Were they killed fighting?'

'Oh no. Cholera. Malnutrition. The diseases that are here

all the time got worse with war. That was the worst day of my life. It was raining and by the twelfth little coffin the path to the cemetery was a sea of mud. We kept slipping and dropping the box.' Roberto looked up at the canopy of trees. 'Anyway, by the time the war ended I was nineteen. I went to university. Then I spent a year in Germany as a refugee.'

'You speak German?'

'Pretty well.' He smiled. 'A little English too, not much. Hey,' he grinned. 'You could teach me. I really have to learn. Most of my customers are gringos.'

'Sure.'

'So when I came back from Europe I came home to the island to help my dad. And now I'm a volcano guide.'

'How old are you now?'

'Twenty-five.' He saw her face. 'Is something wrong?'

'Just you're very young.'

'Twenty-five isn't young here.'

'Do you have a family?'

He nodded. 'I have a wife and two kids. I love it, family life. There's always someone around to talk to. In Germany I was very lonely. I never want to be lonely again.'

'You've done so much for your age.'

'The way I see it, there's a lot I want to do, and not much time.'

He rose and they started back up the volcano path. On the lip of the crater Roberto guided her to a lookout spot. In the distance she saw Concepción for the first time from a position of equal height. 'You never worry,' she said to Roberto, 'that the volcano might erupt?'

Roberto narrowed his eyes and gave her the same look his grandfather had given her when she had asked about the revolution. 'You can worry about anything if you want to.'

An hour later they reached the crater, Roberto using his machete to hack at the dense foliage. They were protected from the wind now. A hollow silence filled her ears only to be ripped open suddenly. A swarm of green bodies filled the air, rising skyward in a flurry of noise and alarm.

'Parrots,' Roberto mouthed.

'They scared the hell out of me.'

'Nothing to worry about. They live in the crater. There's no predators up here and we scared them. There's a really strange thing about these parrots, they don't mind the sulphur gases. They live in a place that's poisonous for most living things.'

The sulphur smell was strong now; metallic bordered with something rotting. 'Phew,' Roberto said, holding his nose. 'It's a bit like eggs, isn't it. Here, we can swim.' He pointed to the black mirrored waters of the lagoon.

She took a step back, then steadied herself. 'No.'

'Why not?'

She looked at the water. Mist was still rising off the lips of the lake.

'I'm scared.'

'Oh, like there's a monster at the bottom?' Roberto grinned.

'It's just so dark. It must be very deep. And then there's that – that hole at the bottom.'

'That's long dead, that hole.' Roberto's face was serious. She realized he wasn't going to make fun of her fear.

'Okay, I'm hot now,' he said. 'Let's go for a swim.'

She lagged behind to take off her shorts and her shirt, her swimsuit underneath. Roberto went in wearing a pair of boxer shorts.

She followed Roberto to the edge of the crater. The water was surprisingly cold and had a strange consistency, dense and heavy. She brushed a few pieces of driftwood in panic, thinking they were waterborne snakes. After a few minutes she relaxed and swam through the cold, dark water with confident strokes.

They hauled themselves out of the lake.

'Time to descend,' Roberto said, looking at the sky. 'It's going to rain.'

She dried herself with the towel Roberto had brought. She felt tired and happy. She felt like they had been up the volcano forever, but when she looked at her watch she saw that it was ten o'clock in the morning.

*

At the party everyone sat around on collapsing couches drinking beer out of cans. In the corner a few blonde girls bobbed to Madonna.

'I know,' Mark said, as soon as she entered the room and he saw her disbelieving look. 'It's just like the parties we used to have at my frat house.'

'Frat?' Evelyn said. It sounded unpleasant, like a house where they ate fried food and held contests to see who could spit into the rubbish bin.

'Frat house. You know, fraternities. I guess you don't have them in England. Anyway, mine was terrible. It was supposedly the most intellectual of the houses, the hardest to get into. The motto of my house was "Beer like water, dope like smokes, women like tissue paper".'

Her mind went blank for a moment. 'Women like tissue paper?'

'As in, use them like.'

'Oh.'

He gave her that quick, appraising look that reminded her of delicate-eyed animals: raccoons, otters. Then he looked down at his knees. 'I know, it's totally politically incorrect.'

They sat down on the groaning sofa and drank beer. She turned the conversation to his fieldwork.

'The one thing I know about fieldwork is that you can't

go looking for experience,' Mark said, his expression tense. 'I have to *find* it.'

She nodded. 'Otherwise you end up tailoring the experience to fit your thesis, which is like ignoring the reality in favour of hope . . .'

'. . . which is like lying . . .'

'Exactly.'

'Exactly.'

'Do you ever think you've made the wrong choice?'

'What? Anthropology?' Mark pursed his lips. He looked as if he was really searching his conscience. 'I suppose in the beginning I was interested in philosophy. But what can you do with philosophy? I didn't want to sit around and think all the time. Anthropology seemed so much more active. I could go out there' – he jabbed at the air with his finger, in the direction of the mountains – 'I could participate.'

'What interested you about philosophy?'

'Oh, you know, theories of self. The diaphanous curtain. The smudged lens. The various obfuscations of the self and its desires. How the ego gets things wrong – "all is clouded by desire". That sort of thing.'

Mark looked sheepish again and she felt her stomach lurch. She felt overwhelmed by his combination of vulnerability and academic prowess.

'You look like you're ashamed.'

'Of what?'

'Of how articulate you are. The way you speak, what you say.'

'I had to learn to tone it down for my frat brothers, I guess,' he said, in that tone of his, both detached and appreciative, as if he were always reserving his final judgement. 'It wasn't cool to be a philosopher in Sigma Chi. All my brothers are on Wall Street now, making a fortune. Or they're in the CIA.'

He leant across the table to grab them another beer. As he

sat back, she noticed he had begun to throb. He was inflating, then deflating, to the accompaniment of pounding, like a giant heartbeat she belatedly came to realize was her own.

Someone changed the record to M People. The blonde girls began to bob again.

'This is going downhill.' She rolled her eyes in the direction of the stereo.

'I know,' Mark said, although she could tell he didn't really mind the music. 'We could go upstairs,' he said carefully. 'Do you want to see my room? It's great. There are screened windows on one side opening to the garden. It's really quiet and sunny in the morning. It'll be a great place to write.'

She followed him up the stairs. Suddenly everything seemed to be happening very slowly. She watched the heels of his cowboy boots move, then stop, move, then stop. Finally, after what seemed like years, they reached the top.

He opened a double door on to a white room. In the middle was an enormous bed. Above it a mosquito net hung from the ceiling. This was the beatific net, the saint-like whiteness he had spoken of going to sleep under on so many thick tropics nights.

He closed the door behind them.

THE LOVE SCENE

Has to combine all the elements: suspension, growth, humidity, the tropics' urge towards self-regeneration.

> I can feel my pupils dilate like a baby's as you come towards me into the extended, prolonged moment. Your mouth, expectant, waits underneath me between mollusc-fold lips opening and closing, revealing your tongue curled there like a viper in its anticipation of the coming entwinement.

There is a burning somewhere; every filament, every tiny sinew, like white phosphorous or the igmibrite used for adobe houses in this country's old colonial towns. It is at once hot, dry and metallic, but unstable in its properties, so that within seconds it becomes wet, moist, earth-wooden – the cloudforest. Along with this chemical fecundity there is a sharp taste of fear in my mouth.

It is nearly dawn and I am lying there like an animal; watchful, wide-eyed, breathing shallowly into the cheesecloth puff of the mosquito net. Beside me you sleep a heavy post-ejaculatory sleep. It is amazing, the sedative effect sex has on men. As if they can sleep easy because all is right with the world now; they have done their work. Then there's your secure posture, as if your limbs have never failed you, you've never questioned your existence. Your body asleep has the unthinking, oblivious certainty of a child.

Who said it (Foucault or Freud, they seem the likely candidates) – that the lover is only a child with an erection? The lover is both a child, your child, and you; a cunning creature. One who is happening over and over again, who never ends, but rather slips over the unmapped boundary between self and other. Someone caught, like the forest, in the continual fluid dream of becoming.

Next to me, this person's sunny-climate back; tanned and freckled. Outside, in the backyard the *lapa verde*, the green parrot, sings the dawn into existence, gaggling in his suburban tropic tongue.

Her heart is still pounding. It is that post-sex time which people who smoke fill with cigarettes but nonsmokers like Evelyn and Mark fill with silence.

She is thinking how they will do their research together, she as a novelist, he as an anthropologist. They will go together to the island, which will become their personal intellectual fiefdom. They will catalogue every detail, know every inhabitant personally, chart the rites and describe the uniqueness of the islanders' complex diagrammatic interpretations of the universe.

They will share information, work on their books together. She can see them in their separate studies in the house where she lives with him, the dark-panelled American studies of Ivy League universities, the ivy itself crawling like tentacles along the windows. They will be the golden couple of anthropology/fiction. He will write for the *Nation* and she will contribute stories to the *New Yorker*. It will be as if Margaret Mead and Claude Lévi-Strauss had married (only with Margaret Mead writing fiction, which, from what she understands, is the general verdict of the anthropological community on her work anyway).

Mark turns to her. Backed by the white of the mosquito net he looks very brown – his eyes, hair, eyelashes, skin. His eyes are bloodshot. She can see the little red veins branching off into the whites of his eyes like tiny rivers.

He slurs his words.

She finds herself saying, absurdly formal, 'Pardon me?'

'I said I have to get up early in the morning,' he repeats. 'I have to go see someone at the university. I have an appointment.' He reaches out and switches off the light.

There is a loud bird in a tree in next door's garden. She recognizes it as a *sorococa*, a tropical screech owl. It has a call that sounds like an obscene laugh. *Hee hee hee*, it calls, then flies out of the tree with a crack.

*

It is four o'clock in the afternoon, that time of the day when she always feels less dense, less believable. She wants to sleep but it's too late for a siesta. She wants to have a beer but it's too early; the man who runs the little Bar el Naufragio (the unluckily named Shipwreck Bar, which she notices the locals avoid) will think her an alcoholic.

The heat is intense, seems to be building towards something. She wonders if it will rain.

*

'I've got a girlfriend. I told you. I have commitments.'

Evelyn looked around the Bar El Tomate. Che Guevara scowled back with the annoying smugness of a hero, pointing out to her, rudely, that a twenty-five-year-old – a man four years younger than her – was telling her about commitment.

Why did you do it then? she wanted to ask. But she only nodded. She wanted to be reasonable. She wanted to be emotionally independent. Maybe they could be friends. After all, he was only telling her what he felt, what he could and could not do. Like the way last night he had reached for the alarm clock and said, *Do you mind if we go to sleep now? I've got an appointment in the morning.*

But she has to wonder. What does it take for someone to fall in love with you? Their conversation is pure delight. They think the same, they speak the same. They are of about the same height and the same attractiveness. They each think the other has beautiful eyes. They had good sex, despite being unfamiliar with each other and operating in fugitive conditions. They both love the word *beatific*.

He has a girlfriend, she has a boyfriend. She tried to push the thought out of her head, but it bounced back, stubbornly, like a mischievous child on a pogo stick.

She thought of her semi-love affairs, her boyfriend with whom she had not had sex in a year, the flirtations and distractions which seemed, from her present perspective, so insubstantial. Twenty-nine was not an age for crushes and flirtations. When would the alchemists and the soul twins make themselves known in her life? Maybe she'd have to give in and join the millions who read the Brazilian mystic's novels.

What would it take? If it didn't happen now, it would never happen.

'Look,' she said, drumming her fingers on the table. She felt a vast impatience bubbling in her gut. 'We've got, what? Twenty-four hours left together. And then we never need see each other again. I'm not going to hound you from afar' – she was particularly pleased with the way she said this, it sounded both muscular and vulnerable – 'and the truth is I'd rather see you now than not see you.' She finished her speech and sat back in her seat. She threw Che a challenging look that said, *Who's the hero now?*

'Okay,' he said cagily.

Relief spread through her stomach. The truth was, she wasn't thinking beyond the next twenty-four hours. What was her life beyond the next day, her life back in London? A desk, a computer, her lonely struggle with words and meanings. Besides, she had to get on a plane, and who knows? She might not even have a beyond-the-next-twenty-four-hours. She was so pleased to finally be living in the *now*.

She sleeps with him again that night. The sex is better, less fumbling. This time they talk for a bit longer before Mark drifts off to sleep.

In the morning she runs into his housemates outside the bathroom. The handyman who has come to fix something or other takes one look at her and bursts into an idiotic grin. Mark gives her lukewarm black coffee in a chipped aluminium cup and walks her to the bus stop across from the Super Sindy, the overpriced twenty-four-hour supermarket run by entrepreneurs from Florida.

In the distance she can hear the gnash of gears as the bus rumbles towards them.

The bus screeches to a stop. She plants a ridiculous kiss on his lips and jumps on the bus. All the seats are full and she has to stand in the aisle. The man in the seat beneath her crosses himself every time he passes one of the city's many churches. She can smell the grease he wears in his hair. She looks down at his bare fingers: he wears no wedding band. He is the sort of man who still lives with his mother, she decides. Everyone in this country is married by the time they are twenty-two or twenty-three. She wonders what happened to him.

*

NEED SOME TRAGEDY
How is the lover going to die?

Roberto plunked their beers on the table. It was her last day on the island and she wanted to buy him a beer at the Shipwreck Bar.

'My grandfather tells me you're writing a book.'

She nodded. 'I'm trying.'

'So tell me about it.' Roberto sat back in his chair, a professorial expression on his face.

She told him about the main elements of the story: the island, the rainforest, the love affair, the conflict, the death, the tragedy.

Roberto pursed his lips. 'Are you sure he has to die?'

'It's the only way of preserving his perfection,' she sighed. 'To make sure his meaning doesn't die. And it's more powerful, don't you think,' she argued, 'that she's writing a letter to a dead man but the reader doesn't know he's dead. At least, not until the end.'

Roberto gave her a strange look. At first she took it for

the evaluating stare men unconsciously give women. But then she realized it wasn't sexual – he was evaluating her seriousness as a human being, just as his grandfather had done.

'How are your wife and kids?'

Roberto took a swig of beer. 'They've gone to my brother's grave for the day. It's the anniversary of his death.'

'Did he die in the revolution?'

Roberto shook his head. 'In a river.'

'How did it happen?'

She watched Roberto square something within himself before replying, as if rearranging objects on a desk. 'He went to work on a farm in the mountains. One day he went swimming. It was the end of the rainy season. He didn't know the area that well. In the highlands you have to be careful in rivers that start in the mountains. Up there it's raining sometimes, but in the lowlands the day is clear. And what happens is the rain comes, and a big wave' – Roberto spread his hands wide on either side of his body –'it sweeps down the river. Before you know it, it's on top of you. A lot of people here are killed that way.'

'By a river tidal wave?'

Roberto nodded. 'We call it a *cabeza de agua.*'

'Head of water,' she translated. 'Flash flood.'

'How do you say it again?' Roberto leaned forward, looking at her intently.

'Head of water. Flash flood.'

'Ead or wader,' he repeated. 'Flish flod.'

'Very good,' she smiled.

They sat in silence for a minute. 'How old was your brother?'

'Twenty-five. The age I am now.' Roberto took another swig of beer, draining the bottle. A confused look had settled on his face. She was afraid she had taken the conversation too far.

'Here we consider it impolite to talk too much about our misfortunes.' Roberto pursed his lips. 'Tragedy is such an everyday thing. That was always the case, even before the revolution.'

She nodded, absorbing his rebuke.

'We never got the body. He was washed away so fast. The doctor told us he probably ended up in ribbons. Sticks, stones.' Roberto stopped. 'The strange thing is—' He paused and looked over her shoulder, to the afternoon calm of the lake. 'I keep expecting something to happen to me. I'm watching my back all the time this year, as if I'm convinced God won't let me outlive my brother.'

'I'm so sorry.'

'Thanks.' Roberto shrugged. 'But it's all pretty clear to me. When someone dies we don't know how to compensate ourselves for that kind of loss.'

'Maybe there is no way,' she said.

'But if you're a writer, you can write it all down. You can change the ending. Write a different story. Give it a happy ending.'

She looked down at her hands. 'I don't think a story is much compensation. At least, not compared to the real thing.'

'Hmm.' Roberto pursed his lips again. He stood. 'I promised I'd say goodnight to my kids.'

Roberto wouldn't let her pay for their beers. He insisted and she gave in. *Que le vaya bien*, he told her. *Igualmente*, she said. They shook hands and parted.

On her last night on the island she sits under the serene shadow of the unmoving volcano. The rainy season was coming, Roberto had told her. Soon the clouds would arrive like relatives gone away for a visit and returned clutching their liquid baggage.

In the last night under clear skies she writes:

> I have seen pictures of corpses of people who have been washed away. Their faces are bruised purple where they have been bashed into rocks and logs. Their fingernails and nostrils are filled with silt.
>
> You were still beautiful, I am sure, despite the violence you suffered. I do not know if I have made that clear, your beauty. Your skin had the plasticity and resistance of a young person's skin, despite the fine lines that played around your eyes when you laughed, a result of having been brought up in a city where it hardly ever rains and where water has to be piped in from the Colorado river so that young people can grow like trees.
>
> His bruised hands, drowned face.
>
> Where is your body? Where are you?

*

She arrived back at the guesthouse to the lonely lump of her luggage and the clothes she had discarded the night she dressed for the party.

That afternoon she tried to call him but one of his housemates answered the phone. 'He's left for the mountains,' he said. That meant he had gone to do his fieldwork. She had no address for him, and no telephone number, although she could probably find him if she wanted to. She put the phone down, went to the bus station, and booked her seat to the island.

Now, on her last night, she reads through the pages she has written. She sees their contents all too clearly, as if she has only recently acquired a new pair of eyes.

First, she has broken the cardinal rule of writing. She has

told, not shown. Then there's the cloying melodrama, the thick foliage of verbosity, the style whose call is shrill and garish with emotion, like the screeching technicolour parrots that inhabit the volcano crater. But more than anything there is – its tone is unmistakable and gruesome, like a thousand tuning forks ringing flat – the hope.

Of course she had wanted to live a love story, the one in which the character accidentally meets the person she is destined for in a rainy Central American guesthouse. They speak each other's sentences. They fall precipitously in love. They sleep together and both decide, on the strength of their sudden passion and sudden understanding, to change their lives so that they can be together. It's an old story, although she herself hasn't tried writing it until now.

She looks idly away from her page and at the red canvas of her sunburnt shoulders. Melanoma, melodrama: there must be some connection. She has a brief vision of malignant pustules of hope bursting forth on the skin of her mind. But that's the task, she thinks, slapping away the last of the horde of mosquitoes that have feasted more or less undetected on her for over a week now: how to draw blood without calling attention to yourself.

*

The boat ploughs through the waves. The lake is even rougher than the day she arrived. The other passengers are vomiting uproariously. Only Evelyn and the boys who work on the boat are fine. In fact, she's starving.

From time to time she shoots a parting look at the twin volcanoes. *Las hermanas*, the devilish sisters. She sees it for the first time, their annoying smugness, their complacency. She can tell by the way people call the volcanoes sisters that these sisters are the opposite of women like her: they will always be both beautiful and dangerous and people will love them for it.

An hour later she has let all the taxis, old battered Ladas, speed off to the nearest town. Shallow waves roll in from the lake. She watches the local kids frolicking. They wear soiled T-shirts and ragged shorts instead of swimsuits. It is five o'clock and the sun has settled on the flanks of *las hermanas*, turning them violet. Evelyn sits on a rock jutting out into the water, feeding the pages of her manuscript one by one into the lake.

Monterrey Sun

OCTOBER 15, TORONTO

Yesterday Julia asked me to go to Mexico with her. She says she's sick of slinging overpriced food at overpriced people. She wants to get away from restaurants, from the city. 'Nothing will ever happen here,' she says, with that look I've seen in her eyes before: hard and prophetic. 'Come on, it'll be an experience.'

I said no. I only met her six weeks ago. All I know about her is that she's older – she must be twenty-four – and she's gay. She has a girlfriend but she can't go because of her job, that's why Julia asked me. 'What will she think of us going to Mexico together?' I asked Julia. She shrugged. 'Why would she think anything?'

I still said no. The next day I was walking to work as usual, passing the string of Vietnamese cafés on Dundas West. I saw this sign locked to a fence outside a house. Someone had painted on it in yellow free-hand capitals:

BE BLATANT
BE EMOTIONAL
RISK EVERYTHING

I was sure I had never seen it before, even though I walk those blocks every day. I just went on to work and forgot about it until the afternoon. When I got back to the place I had seen it, it was gone. I retraced my steps, then I knocked on the door of the house. A tiny old Chinese woman came to the door. I asked her where the sign was but she just shook her head and smiled beatifically. She didn't understand a word of English.

NOVEMBER 26, RALEIGH, NORTH CAROLINA

We came this way because Julia wanted to drive through the Carolinas and Georgia; she hasn't been back since she was fifteen and she wants to see them again. I didn't even know she had lived in the States until we reached the border and she flashed her American passport.

'You're *American*?'

'Relax. It's a passport, not an identity.'

I had always thought there was something American about Julia. She seems to have an innate sense of her self-worth, and I can't see her ever apologizing for anything.

We haven't actually seen much of the country so far from the interstates, just one unbroken procession of starched poplars and sycamores lined up outside the window as if for inspection. So far we've settled for interstate chain hotels. 'We don't have to sleep at all,' Julia said at some point, and patted her pocket. 'Nose candy is cheaper than a hotel.'

'You brought coke across the border?'

'Relax, honey. We'll blow it before we get to Mexico. That would be like taking coals to Newcastle, or china to Dresden, or whatever.'

Tonight was one of those Ramada Inn nights and we sat on blue chenille bedspreads, tractor trailers slipstreaming through the dark outside. We poured our beer into the evangelicized plastic cups we had bought in a grocery store.

I turned mine to the front. TODAY IS THE DAY it

announced, with a sun leaking out of a bank of clouds that had the same shape as the state of Georgia. Julia took the SHINE ON, JESUS one. It showed a skinny, sad Jesus in a yellow velour robe. In his hands was a guitar.

'I didn't know Jesus played the guitar,' Julia said. 'God, tomorrow we'll be in Georgia,' she sighed, looking out the window. 'It all looks so familiar. My father was working in Atlanta when we left the south.'

'What was he doing?' Julia still hasn't told me exactly what her father's job was. That was the reason why they had moved to Canada.

'Playing a lot of golf.'

'What did you do?'

'Played with his golf partners.'

'You were sleeping with your father's friends?'

'Their wives too.'

I didn't believe her at first. What would she want with these Dolly Parton women?

'They're not all southern belles, you know,' Julia said.

'Were you in love with them?'

'Not in love. More in lust.'

I propped myself up on my elbow and faced her. 'I can't imagine ever feeling lust for a woman.'

'Well that's all right.' She took a sip of beer. 'There are things I can't imagine either.'

'How old were you?'

'I don't know. Sixteen. Seventeen.'

'Jesus. Didn't you fall in love with any of them?'

'I thought I did, with one, anyway.'

'So what did she look like?'

'I'm surprised you're so interested.' I felt her eyes on me and turned away, embarrassed. 'She was a typical Southern woman,' Julia said, slowly. 'Very well brought up. *Bred*, as they say down here,' she laughed. 'She looked ten years younger than she actually was. She was so bored it frightened me. She used to have fantasies about running away to New York or Europe and I would say to her, "What then?" The scary thing is, I was seventeen and I think I was the most exciting thing that had ever happened to her. I mean, *seventeen*.'

She lay back down on the bed and looked at the ceiling. Suddenly the transport trucks had vanished and the only noise was the wheeze of the air-conditioner.

'What are you thinking?'

Julia didn't say anything, just spread her arms and legs out wide until they touched the sides of the bed. She swished them in and out, like when you lie on your back in the snow and make a snow angel. The bedspread bunched up between her legs and arms.

'I'm thinking that I hope she's happy, somewhere. I'm thinking she didn't deserve a string of stupid, vain young women for lovers,' Julia said, still staring at the ceiling. 'Women like me.'

NOVEMBER 30, SAVANNAH, GEORGIA

Early this morning we left the coast and headed inland through South Carolina. On our way out of town we passed Corinthian-pillared houses and then, not much further down the road, tin-roofed shacks and pools of swamp-poverty.

'When I lived down here I was oblivious to all this,' Julia said. 'I didn't even *notice* the tar-paper shacks and the trailers.' She turned to me, a helpless look on her face. 'I can't believe myself five, six years ago. I mean, as a teenager you're trapped in some interior country like Chile – thin and authoritarian. You only see what you want to see. Now I think, Jesus, it looks like the Third World. Or what I imagine the Third World to look like.' Julia blew her cigarette smoke out into the slipstream. 'We just entered our white houses like moths,' she continued. 'They were always this *searing* white. I guess it's called Suburban Gothic. In the cities it was always condominiums. We went to places like Bermuda or Jamaica on vacation. We still do.'

She shrugged and lit another cigarette, taking both hands off the steering wheel to do it and driving for a moment with her elbows.

'All I wanted to do when I was a teenager was travel,' I said. 'To be anywhere other than the place I was living.'

'And where was that?'

'Oh.' I sighed, and named a provincial town. 'The sort of place that breeds future hockey players and lawyers. When I was sixteen I was reading all these F. Scott Fitzgerald books,' I explained, waving my hands around in some kind of valedictory gesture to show her that was all over and done with. 'You know, like *Tender is the Night*. What I really wanted to do was to go to the south of France and wear striped bathing suits and develop a delicate sensibility, through psychosis, if necessary. But when I was sixteen I was wearing floral dresses and had a perm. They never would have let me into France.'

DECEMBER 4, NEW ORLEANS

I don't believe in the distances Julia says we are covering. I can't believe that *this* is travel, so flat and uncomplicated that we move from place to place simply by pressing an accelerator.

Julia does most of the driving; I sit in the passenger seat. The world has become a backdrop to her profile, passing blurrily behind her face. With every day the outlines of her face seem to be evolving, coming into and slipping out of focus against miles and miles of low cotton-dotted landscape. A serious profile, blonde hair, cut short, enormous blue eyes. I keep seeing this one expression: a small face with two dark eyebrows squinting in concentration. From the side, it really is difficult to tell whether she is male or female. Her face has the beautifully blank savagery of the animals I grew up with, the cunning, generous creatures of the Canadian winter: an otter, a wolverine, a fox.

DECEMBER 8, AUSTIN, TEXAS

When you see it on the map, Texas looks huge and unnavigable and *in the way*, as Julia says. We drive over a series of interconnecting bridges and estuarine developments, by rows of wet-roofed warehouses looking like greased lozenges. The sky has a chemical burn. In Louisiana we drive through a town called Sulphur only to find, on the other side of the border, an identical one called Orange.

When we finally arrive in Dallas we hit the make-up counter at Nieman Marcus. There isn't anything of interest to see. We hang out there for an hour or so. Julia doesn't buy anything. She dresses simply; jeans and a nice shirt, no jewellery, only a black plastic watch.

Out in the glaring empty plazas of the city, men in lightweight suits and dark glasses race past us before launching themselves into skyscrapers and their arctic air-conditioned atria. All the women we see are blonde and are dressed in yellows, greens or reds – often all together, like tropical birds.

Back on the road, heading south-west to the border, it is the cows and not the truckers who look at us most kindly, their wet, inquisitive eyes peering through the steel-slat trucks. The only other cattle we see surprised us in the night with their pinto patterns and sleek eyes. They stand motionless beside the road, more like mechanical creatures than cattle, as if they have been planted there just to signpost us along our way.

We drive through the tornado belt of the Texan south-west, hoping to see one. But it is too late in the year and all we see is a sky like broiling seaweed spitting hailstones the size of baseballs. The headwinds are so strong we go through twice as much gas and Julia has to pull into countless gas stations. I watch as she leaps out of the jeep, dusts off her thighs like a trucker or a cowboy and says, 'Hey, Bobby, fillerup. The missus in the truck'll pay,' and the Bobbys screw up their faces and I can tell they are wondering whether she is a boy or a girl.

Then she disappears into the gas station to buy *USA Today* or some bad Texan paper that dedicates itself wholly to drifter stories and murdered prostitutes.

'What do you think?' I ask her. 'Is it really that dangerous here?'

'What, that prostitute stuff?' She laughs. 'Nothing, *nada*, the usual cautionary drivel thrown at women by essentially conservative cultures.'

Julia really speaks that way – *cautionary drivel*. I try to imprint the phrase on my mind, so that I can haul it out one day and impress someone the way it impresses me. Maybe she sees this on my face because she turns to me and says, not cruelly, but quietly, 'You've tried to grow up through books, haven't you? When I was your age I had my own place, my own car.'

'I don't have that kind of money.' I stare out the window. I don't want to look at her. 'I'll never have that kind of money.'

DECEMBER 9, NUEVO LEÓN

Yesterday we saw the sun go down in Mexico for the first

time. It really did look different, russet, its rims sculpted, like a ceramic pot.

We were shocked by the town. I think we were expecting that the second we set foot on Mexican soil we would enter into some exalted landscape vibrating with pain of a folkloric intensity. Instead we crossed into Low Rent USA – a glut of *maquiladores*, McDonald's, liquor stores selling cheap tequila, and four-wheel drives full of Texans on sex-and-bargain-Marlboros daytrips.

The balance of power is shifting between us. Julia might be older but I can speak good Spanish, thanks to two years of university courses. But there are local variations and customs. For example, the first thing we learned this afternoon was the local version of hotel check-in (at least for unaccompanied women): sign your name, pay your pesos, run in the room followed closely by a posse of *gringa*-crazed local men, dump stuff on the bed, whirl round to pile meagre furniture against the door while I yell; *¡Cabrones!* (Assholes!) and *¡Chinga tu madre, Wey!* (Go fuck your mother, punk!).

We lay on our beds and stared at the plum walls while the *cabrones* lurked in the corridor. She propped herself up on her elbow to read the biography of Frida Kahlo she had brought with her. I don't know what it's called: something like *Frida: Life of Sorrow*.

'I want to see Frida Kahlo's house,' Julia said. 'I'm going to add her to my Personal Lesbian Icons.'

'I read that Frida slept with women to annoy her husband. That doesn't seem like the pinnacle of lesbianism to me.'

Julia stubbed out her cigarette. She looked tired. 'Sometimes you take what you can get.'

DECEMBER 12, VERACRUZ

We only came to Veracruz because we wanted to go to the beach. 'No beach here, *mí amor*,' a grinning old man told me. 'It's all polluted. You have to go to the other side.'

'The other side of what?'

His grin widened. 'Of the country, *mí amor*.'

At night gas flares from the refineries rip through the sky like comets. Veracruz is the only place that meets our expectations of Mexico, which I am beginning to realize date from old John Huston or Ava Gardner films. It really is full of jump-ship sailors, people carrying sinister bundles, *cantina*-owners with toxic smiles, the wind-polished faces of sailors.

Our balcony overlooks the pockmarked boardwalk, a hurricane-battered Corniche. This evening we sit on our balcony and look out onto the Caribbean, but it has the same dead, oil-slicked look as the waters of the Gulf of Mexico we saw on our way through Texas.

'This is the kind of place where you wonder if your body really belongs to you,' Julia says. 'Or if it's an independent thing, like one of those ships out there, moored just off your periphery.'

I'm not sure I've ever felt that and I don't know what to say. I look out on to the palm-lined squares and storm-lit vestibules where in summer I imagine women who look like tragic flowers dance stately Mexican twosteps with sloe-eyed men.

DECEMBER 13, MEXICO CITY

We are coming into the capital city. The only thing we know about it is that it is the most populous city in the world and the crime and pollution are terrible. Carjackings are common, so we have our passports nailed to our stomachs and some money stuffed in our bras. Suddenly we see a giant billboard set on high ground, sailing above the valley of Mexico. It shows a grey Christ on the cross, hanging and doleful. Behind him is a wild, cloud-raked sky. Across the bottom of the billboard a neon message flashes off and on, off and on:

No tengas miedo.

Do not be afraid.

In Frida Kahlo's house in Coyoacán we stand looking at the canvases of some of her most famous paintings. They look a little dusty. Someone should give them a wipe. In Frida's bedroom everything is as it was when she lived here. Her spine-reforming corset stands upright on top of the bed-covers, a little ghoulish and lonely in its lack of a body.

'I just love it,' Julia says, looking at the paintings. Frida is see-through, her heart, her womb with her never-to-be-born child displayed. She's ugly, I think, with her mono-brow and her moustache. Maybe they didn't have facial hair removers then, but if I were her I still would have done something about it.

'She was so gutsy,' Julia says, her eyes shining.

I know why Julia admires her. I say nothing. It leaves me cold, Frida's overabandonment to pain. As if she were trying to prove to herself and to the world the depth of her capacity for feeling.

DECEMBER 15, HUATULCO

South of Mexico City the afternoon light pours straight down, a gilded curtain, into amoebic winter fields. The days seem floodlit. Along the roadsides of Puebla are yellow cornfields, the ancient food of the Aztecs. The maize has been raked and arranged in conical shapes that point towards a sloping equinox sun.

I am amazed by this landscape. It looks cruel and empty and shining at once, like a row of beautiful polished tiles.

'I've never seen anything like this,' I say.

'Neither have I,' Julia says.

'But you've been everywhere; the tropics, the Caribbean, Europe.'

'Yeah,' Julia sighs, something she does rarely. 'But none of them have meant much to me. I've been too many places. You get blasé.'

'I want to go everywhere,' I say. 'I always have. When I was fifteen I read the whole of the *Alexandria Quartet*. I remember the way he described colours: brick-dust at evening, lemon-haze mornings. I used to imagine myself there, in Alexandria, surrounded by homosexual druids and ex-spies.'

Julia laughs. 'I knew you were going to say that. The way you romanticize everything. I bet Alexandria is just a big polluted town full of men who think women are on a par with dogs.'

'Why do you say that?'

'It just figures, doesn't it? It's the Arab world.'

Julia is reactionary and conservative, I think. But then she's American. (Canadians are encouraged to have this view of Americans.) Except she's not. But I can see that there is a side to her which accepts the easiest explanation on offer.

We are silent for what seems a long time. It is getting to be night, and there is hardly any traffic. In the twilight the mercury eyes of rabbits glitter as they flee the sides of the road.

I turn to her. 'You wanted company for the drive, that's all.'

'What?'

'I'm saying I think we should go our separate ways in Oaxaca, after Christmas.'

Julia shakes her head but doesn't look at me.

'I thought we wanted the same things. If I can't talk about the books I've read or the places I've been to or the colour of the sun without you laughing at me I'd be better off alone.'

Julia is searching for something to say. I can see she wants to remain nonchalant.

'But we've brought all these books,' she says. She's trying to remind me that this is the one thing we have in common: we are both readers. But I know what she's really thinking, that she wants to live a life full of books, and I want to live my life through them. She will never want this, thinks it's pathetic.

'That's hardly a reason for staying together.'

She reaches for a cigarette. I can tell she doesn't like this kind of emotion, this kind of change. It's too volatile for her. She wants everything to be easy. 'It's as good as any,' she says. 'We get along.'

'Do we?'

'Yes.' Julia nods, exhaling smoke. 'We do.'

The next three hours of flatlands stream by in silence. The only other traffic is busloads of workers going to Villahermosa and the oil fields of Tabasco.

Then we leave the mountains and descend into the Tehuantepec isthmus and its gouged saline bays teeming with crustaceans. We pass through night-sodden towns: Juchitán, Salina Cruz – whole towns of men in white cotton trousers slouching on benches outside blue cafeterias. At midnight these towns have the feel of smothered violence, as if everyone is just too hot and tired to bother knifing each other.

I drive the last stretch to the coast. The moon is full, it punches a hole in the dark fabric of sky and light falls in a haze of angles.

Julia falls asleep. She sleeps with her mouth open, shifting from time to time and uttering sleep-murmurs. She is drooling, so I take a hand off the wheel, lean over and wipe spittle from the corner of her mouth with my hair. It is about two in the morning, winter suddenly doesn't exist, and by morning we will be at the edge of the Pacific, an ocean I have never seen. Above us, I watch the moon ripen from pewter to silver.

DECEMBER 16, PUERTO ESCONDIDO

We slept all day. Finally, at five thirty, I woke and found the bed next to mine empty. I wandered down to the beach. At sunset the sky was the pale flesh of baked salmon and as the sunset progressed it changed, minute by minute, finally blossoming into ribbons of rebellious carmine.

I found Julia sitting in a wooden chair, right in front of the breakers. I touched her shoulder lightly. It was still warm with the heat of the sinking sun. She turned her head and smiled as if she had been expecting me. She was reading a book. 'It's really nice,' she said, without looking up. 'It's called *Monterrey Sun*. It's from the turn of the century.' She wetted the tips of her fingers to turn the pages and began to read.

On the trees the coals
of the oranges burned redhot,
and in the burning light
the orchard turned to gold.

'It's just like that in Mexico at noon, isn't it?' Julia looked up from the book and into the twilit sky. 'Everything looks like oranges on fire.'

The dark gathered around us in a pool. It was a strange darkness, marine and tropical, but with tendrils of cold lapping against its edges. As Julia read on I felt we were being slowly immersed in liquid shadows that had slid down from the lime-dark mountains of the Sierra.

And me the sun stripped bare
the fiercer to cleave to me.

I bear within me so
much sun that so much sun
already wearies me.

No shadow in my childhood
but was red with sun.

At night we lay in bed, heat-drenched. The ceiling fan whirred slowly with a sound like that of winged insects. On the wall opposite the bed was a picture of Christ looking like a moony virgin.

'Have you noticed they look the same?'

'What?' I was half asleep.

'Our feet.'

I looked down to where our feet bobbed above the sea of the bed.

'This is really bad,' Julia said. 'You can't be friends and have the same size feet. I think there's a taboo against it in some culture, but I can't remember which one. They look like fish, don't you think? A little flat. Suspicious.' She rolled over towards me. 'Your feet are covered in sand, you know,' she said. 'Just like Jesus'.'

'How do you know so much about Jesus' feet?'

Julia put her hand on my shoulder and suddenly we were up against each other. We are both so thin only our hip bones and breasts touched. Julia looked at me, her eyes suddenly sharded, diamond-like from the patio light streaming through the curtains. Nothing happened, we just lay there, our skins both very warm from the sun, combining our heat like lizards, before it slipped away.

DECEMBER 22, OAXACA

This morning we woke into a troubled sky. A *norte* had blown in, there was going to be no sun for a few days, so we headed to Oaxaca.

'It's the Night of the Radishes tonight,' I said.

Julia scowled at the guidebook I was holding. 'The night of the *what*?'

'They sculpt historical scenes out of radishes. Religious ones too. It says here the main competition has set themes, but there's a free-interpretation one too. Last year the guy who won it sculpted a piece on The Right of Man to Free Expression.'

'How did he show that in *radishes*?'

I leafed through the guidebook. 'Doesn't say.'

In Oaxaca the streets are hilly and narrow. It was the colours of the houses that most impressed us as we walked around the town: shell pink next to asparagus, banana, then several houses painted the colour of dried cranberries. On some streets whole rows of houses were bleeding into the sidewalk, four or five coats of paint exposed. They looked like they'd been struck by some kind of eczema.

Julia squinted. 'Here comes another patrol of Juan Travoltas.'

A car of the type we had come to know as the Macho Mobile (red, blacked-out windows) pulled up. '*Hsss*,' hissed four squat faces behind a half-opened window. '*Chiquitas*,' they whined. '*Mira, mira que linda*.'

We ran into Santo Domingo, the main cathedral, for cover. Inside it was the temperature of a wine cellar and just as dark. Nuns lurked in the aisles like mummers.

We sat down in a pew and gazed at the giant inscription above the altar – *El Verdad Rey, Nuestro Señor Jesus Christo*.

'*El Verdad*,' Julia repeated. 'What does that mean?'

'The truth.'

'The *truth*.' She paused. 'You know, it's funny how everything seems questionable, now. I kind of miss the bullish certainty I had when I was twenty. I was so determined to get a place of my own, be independent.'

'Is that why you left your parents' house? Wouldn't it just have been easier to live with them?'

She looked at me quickly, then away, towards the gold-leaf altar. 'Because I thought it would be nice to have a lover.'

Something about that phrase really stunned me – *it would be nice to have a lover*.

'Didn't you want to wait for someone to come along who you really loved?'

'They're not exactly inimical.'

'But didn't you have someone in mind?'

'I didn't want to be pathetic.'

'I can't imagine you being pathetic.'

'Well, try to imagine yourself in a world where everyone you're attracted to is poised to ridicule you.'

'Why? Because you're gay? It's not like that any more.'

'It is if you grow up hauled from one town to another in the sticks.'

'So you go about avoiding patheticness by playing it safe? By grabbing the nearest person and making a lover out of them?'

'I'm not playing it safe with you, am I?'

'I'm not your lover.'

We sat in silence then, in the pew, staring straight ahead at Christ dangling on the cross, as if in prayer. I thought how we were surrounded by the desert, and the desert was alive at night – scorpions, snakes, tumbling cactus fruit, the *lobo*, the desert wolf. There was something wolfish about Julia, too. She belonged in this landscape. She was always dry, she never sweated. All of this made me wonder if she knew what it was like to want something and to not get it. I wondered if I should be the person to teach her that.

On our way out, the nuns slid their eyes over our bodies, looking at us from strange lizard angles. We walked out of the cathedral hand in hand. Girls in Mexico go around like this all the time, we noticed – arm in arm, hand in hand, even with their arms around each other's waists. But at sixteen or seventeen this disappears and they're walking with a boy, leaning on him like an invalid.

Julia turned her hand over in mine and rubbed my wrist, kneading the place where my veins came close to my skin.

Out of a silence she said, 'It's nice, isn't it?'

It was one o'clock. Only tourists were on the sidewalks; the Mexicans collected like trout in pools of shade.

We check in at the youth hostel. The manager, Rafael, sports long hair which he ties back into a ponytail, and a goatee beard. He calls his Swiss girlfriend *toucano* – toucan, which makes me distrust him immediately. The hostel is cheap but located in a street full of young men who rev their car engines ceaselessly from morning to night. We agree that we didn't come to Mexico to live opposite a pit stop at the Daytona 500, but neither of us can get up the energy to move.

When we go out to eat we discover the pale green sauce served with tacos is not mushed-up avocados as we thought but in fact some of the hottest chillis known to man. We are such clichés of gringos-south-of-the border with our burning mouths and desperate requests for water. I know what the Mexicans see: two young women who think they can go anywhere, need no one, who have just arrived in your town and started eating the local delicacies and drinking beer as if we've done it all our lives, only to be abruptly caught out by the hot sauce. Where are our husbands, our boyfriends? they think. Where are our children?

In Mexico, so many women our age are already married and have children.

'I want to have a child, one day,' Julia says, when I mention this to her. She sees my face. 'Don't look so shocked.'

'I am shocked.'

'But why?'

'I don't know why,' I say.

But I do know, although I can't tell her. It would somehow spoil her perfection, the hard androgyny she has cultivated. If she had a child, she would be like any other woman.

We go to buy ice cream to soothe our gums. The city is dotted with more ice-cream sellers than I have ever seen in one place before. A plaza outside the Soledad church is devoted entirely to them. We sit by gurgling fountains there, trying flavours one by one.

The next afternoon we went to see the radish sculptures being set up in the Zócalo. Contestants had set out Before photographs in front of their entries, so we could see the raw radishes. They didn't look like any radishes I had ever seen. They were outsize and swollen, enormous hairy tubers, disturbingly like what a flayed penis might look like.

We arrived just as the sculptors were putting the finishing touches to their entries: *The Adoration of Christ*; *The Coming of Columbus* and *The Guelguetza*, a display of Zapotec dancing. We walked past *El Terror de los Toltecas* – The Terror of the Toltecs – which showed the terrible fight between the Toltecs and the Aztecs. The battle scenes were presented in a radish-relief of reversed gore, the skin red, the insides of the lopped-off limbs white.

Suddenly I felt someone clutch my elbow. I turned to find Julia, looking a little flushed.

'What's wrong?'

She hauled me into one of the town's three hundred churches, an old darkened hulk on the periphery of the Zócalo. In the half-gloom I leaned against the cool stone wall, felt the damp seep into my kidneys.

She closed her eyes. 'How many times do you think you can make the same mistake?'

'What mistake?'

She opened her eyes. In the half-light they seemed enormous. 'I can't lie to you.'

'What are you thinking of lying about?'

'Would you love me? I mean, *could* you love me, as a sexual being?'

'I'm not a lesbian,' I said immediately, without even thinking about it.

'I'm not asking you to be a *lesbian*,' Julia said, open-mouthed. 'Even if I were, what's so terrible about that?'

I looked around the church. The Stations of the Cross, serious in the gold and mahogany of Mexican friezes, stared back at me. In one, Jesus was giving Pontius Pilate the moist look of a lover. I dropped my eyes. 'I'm so tired I could cry.'

On the way back to the hostel we were sidelined by the pre-Christmas processions that thronged the streets, crowds holding coloured foil lanterns and singing carols. Snazzy pick-up trucks with illuminated fog lights hauled endless nativity tableaux. A strange woman, tall, pale, with red lips and frizzy hair, staggered into my path. I had seen this woman all night, all over the town, in different places. This time she held a giant sparkler, which she kept waving in my face. A huge star made of lights hung overhead, and strung between the buildings ringing the square was a panel of lights in the shape of a poinsettia.

It's Christmas, we told each other, hardly able to believe it. *Feliz Navidad.*

DECEMBER 24, OAXACA

On Christmas Eve we dine at the Hacienda, a restaurant on the outskirts of the city. Lurking in groves of poinsettias are huge steaming dishes of chicken in *mole*, the Oaxacan sauce made with chocolate, chillies and fruit that both Julia and I find too rich.

We sit surrounded by kaleidoscopic Oaxacan gentry, girls with huge satin bows in their hair and women in cerise dresses.

'I haven't seen *cerise* since the 1978 Sears catalogue,' I say.

'It obviously escaped and is living as a fugitive in Mexico.' Julia is in her habitual monochromes; the whites, blacks and beiges that made me nickname her Julia Armani. She looks retrograde, a silent screen heroine trapped in tasteless technicolour. Her shirt is open to show a brown chest; Julia tans faster than I do. Her lips are parted because she is laughing at something I have just said. She holds a cigarette; she's smoking more now that we're in Mexico and cigarettes are so cheap. She gives me an open look not unlike the expectation of flowers. Her face, her lines, her edges promise some hard skill.

I stare at the slope of Julia's throat and her collarbones; it is delicate, clear. She is baring her throat at me, but it is not at all like the manoeuvre practised by small animals caught by a larger one who know their only way out is through submission. Julia's is a violent throat, the throat of a lover.

I put my fork down, say, 'I don't feel well.' Then I say, 'I've never believed in myself as a lover.'

'Oh.' Julia nods, lips pursed, as if she finally understands something she has been puzzled by for a long time. 'You think that's another kind of luxury I've had.'

Just before sunset we stumble out of the restaurant, stuffed and drunk.

'Shit, it's going to get dark.' Julia scowls lopsidedly into the deserted scrubland surrounding the Hacienda. Above us is a cucumber sky, its skin raked by the coming twilight. 'We should have called a taxi.'

'Why don't we walk?'

'All the way back? That's eight miles.'

'Just to the *cruce*.' I indicate the crossroads with the highway that leads to the Tehuantepec isthmus. 'We can get a cab from there.'

The sky is turning from salmon to the red of pomegranate juice, spilling over the purple lips of the Sierra Madre Occidental. In the crevasses of shadows the evening burns from blue to night, passing through stages of mauve, amethyst, navy, onyx.

Four-wheel drives, the vehicles of wealthy Oaxaca suburbanites. In the twilight they look like giant silver insects.

'I wish we had flashlights,' Julia whispers.

'Why are you whispering?'

Julia grabs my forearm and holds her hand there. 'I don't know. But I think there's something moving across the road.'

We peer into the darkness, where brown forms, like very thin waves, have begun to skim across the road.

Julia is wearing brown leather sandals. I am in my hiking boots. Corded oblongs begin to swish across our toes.

'Jesus Christ. The snakes have just come out for the evening,' Julia says, squinting into the dark. 'They must come out on to the roads at dusk because the asphalt's still hot.'

'I *hate* snakes.'

Suddenly Julia careens into the middle of the road, jumping like a kid on a pogo stick, trying to dodge them. I stay rooted to the spot while Julia yells at the snakes as they slip between her legs.

A silver four-wheel drive passes, tooting its horn at us and managing to crush two of the snakes. We can see their splattered forms, like flat bicycle inner tubes, strewn across the road.

'Why don't they have any guts?'

Julia scowls. 'The four-wheel-drive guys?'

'*Snakes.* They never spill out. They just go flat.'

Suddenly the sky darkens. Besides the cacti, the only visible form against the coming night are the sisal plants spindling into the sky. Against the mountains they look like bodies frozen in the posture of supplicants.

The whispering forms of snakes continue to invade the road, but we have become calm, and don't even try to avoid them any more. Julia is laughing against the red horizon, fast turning to enamelled navy blue. The sky is full of stars now, clumped and curdled. Julia cranes her head backwards so that her eyes slope downwards, and they look clear, infinitely mobile and limbless, like salamanders. We smile at each other and at the sky, and as the snakes converge from all directions, we twirl towards each other with the mistaken grace of intoxicated ballerinas, and kiss.

The Gods of the Savages

We are at Hart House, which is not Hart House any more but an airport. He is leaving – for good, going to Vancouver.

'Everybody always ends up in Vancouver,' someone says.

I watch the plane take off, only it doesn't taxi, but rises into the air vertically, like a helicopter. The next thing I know I have stolen a grey Fuego, that eighties sports car you never see any more. It has a horsetrailer attached to it and I drive across the country, all the way to the end of the Trans-Canada Highway. I leave the horsetrailer and the car with the lights on, climb out of the Fuego's sunroof and run along the road. All around me the earth is parched, a clay-ochre hue. Silvery trees are splattered across the horizon like a line of upright fish. It looks like Mexico.

*

She ducked her head around the door of the tutor's office. A queue of five stretched ahead of her, obscuring the embattled tutor. For a long time the queue seemed to be going nowhere but suddenly the sea of students parted, and she saw him.

He wore a battered blue sweater, from which fell renegade tendrils of yarn. His black jacket was rubbed raw at the edges of the collar and had to be safety-pinned at the cuffs. A white shirt peeked out of the cuff chaos. He looked strangely windswept, as if he had just been blown off a boat. His complexion was an unusual reddish brown.

'Are you ready?'

It was her turn. Where had everyone gone? She realized she had been staring at him for ten minutes. He looked at her through gold-rimmed spectacles. His hair, the colour of rainforest hardwoods – padouk or rosewood – fell around his face, despite his attempts to push it away as he ducked in and out of the textbook, searching for answers to the fumbled questions she had prepared.

As he closed the book she noticed that there was no one else waiting for help. She looked behind his shoulder to where he had scrawled his office hours on the blackboard. He had to be there for another half-hour.

'You're very tanned.' It was all she could think of to say.

'I've just returned from Mexico three weeks ago. I guess the tan has stuck.' He looked down and inspected his arms, turning them over to reveal smooth undersides. She couldn't help staring; his arms were lissome and striated with the kind of sinewy muscles she had only ever seen in pictures of those warrior-like men who cavorted on Greek amphorae.

'What were you doing in Mexico?'

'Fieldwork for my PhD. Actually I should still be there, but I got very ill.'

The suggestion that he could ever be seriously threatened by illness caused a pain of a quite delicate nature to blossom in her stomach. 'What did you have?'

'Oh, the usual. Amoebic dysentery, which comes with the kind of hallucinations where you see giant beetles coming to eat you and God appears in the window. At least it wasn't malaria. I had that when I was a kid.' He paused. His voice had become quiet. 'I almost died,' he added, after a moment.

'But how did you get malaria that young?'

'I grew up in South Africa. My father would take me travelling sometimes, to Zambia or Kenya, and on one of those trips I got bitten by some *evil* mosquito.'

'Wow' – she said it coolly, she was was trying hard not to sound too impressed – 'you certainly got around.'

'Ah,' he said, raising his eyebrow. 'I haven't even mentioned Germany and Sweden.'

She couldn't help herself. 'God,' she said.

When his office hours were over they walked downstairs to the building's concourse.

'I'm Alistair, by the way.' He held out his hand. She looked down and saw long, lanky fingers with square, manly knuckles. They made her think of candlesticks.

She felt the candlesticks fold over her own ridiculous fingers. 'Thank you for your help.'

'Come by any time. I'm not that busy right now. Not until nearer exam time anyway.'

She turned around. She meant to walk back to her residence room, or to get a cup of coffee and a muffin, to go to the library – any one of the daily rituals she employed to give her first year at university structure and to prevent her from descending into the gelatinous realm of the usual first-year temptations of beer-soaked parties and too much cafeteria ice cream.

But, suddenly, as she walked away, she found herself falling into a pit. She realized it had always been there, waiting for her, but camouflaged. The walls were smooth and thick with the kind of canal scum she imagined lined Venetian waterways. She dimly realized she was incarcerated because suddenly, since she had met Alistair – only an hour before – each moment was already filled with the gall of not being with him.

She spent that entire week in the pit, not knowing the exact nature of her entrapment, scrabbling and clawing at the sides to get out.

The next week she went back to Alistair's help session, having concocted some confusion or other with the Treaty of Versailles. As before, she was last in line. Her heart pounded painfully as she asked him her questions. At one point she was sure it was going to leap out of her chest and land on the desk.

At two-thirty Alistair looked at the clock. 'I think I can legitimately knock off now. Would you like to go for a coffee at the GSU?'

In her stupefaction she said, 'Do you think they'll let me in?' She had never been to the Graduate Students' Union. She knew they had a pub where ancient graduate students spent entire days playing chess.

'I think you look convincingly mature.' Alistair smiled, and she caught a glimpse of that extraordinary ability he had to transform his uncertainty effortlessly into humour, then deliver it with kindness instead of an ironic bite.

'So where exactly do you come from?' Alistair enquired, when they were seated in the Union's café.

'You really want to know?'

'Why wouldn't I?'

'I don't know,' she shrugged. 'It's just that people in this city seem so uncurious about your origins. It's as if everyone is a slate that's been erased and now they're writing PROVE YOURSELF on it where their past used to be.'

'I know. It's that New World amnesia. The Past Does Not Exist. Oh, and its close cousin, Only Success Matters.'

She laughed. 'I grew up in Alberta. Now there's an amnesiac place.'

'What, with the cowboys?' Alistair whistled. 'That's lucky.'

'You've been looking at too many Air Canada posters.'

'But what on earth are you doing here? You could have horses.'

She shrugged. 'I did have horses.'

'I have to admit,' Alistair said, 'my sum knowledge of Alberta is mountains and the Calgary stampede—'

'—don't forget those cowboys—'

'Yeah.' He smiled. 'It's hard not to see it as romantic.'

'I could say the same about your' – she searched for the word – 'your background.'

Alistair nodded, a grave, absorbed look on his face, as if he had never considered this before. 'Is your family still there, in Alberta?'

'My father is.'

'What about your mother?'

'I don't have a mother.'

'Were you hatched?'

She thought he might have been making fun of her, but she looked up and found that expression again, the one that was slightly indulgent and kind and which she might have called fatherly in other circumstances.

She was still getting used to the extraordinary effect his eyes had on her. What was it about them? Today they were dark green, the colour of the old leather couches in the Hart House Reading Room. But what made them stomach-churning was the mercury flash that passed slowly, even lazily, through them from time to time; when he laughed, or when he looked at her closely. To her, it looked like desire itself. Whatever it was, this jade bolt transformed his eyes into a cool green fire that ate through her insides.

'I only meant everyone has a mother,' Alistair continued. 'Somewhere.'

'My mother left my dad when I was three. We haven't seen her since. How about you?'

'How about me what?'

'I mean,' she smiled, 'were you hatched too? What about your mother?'

'She's dead.'

She sat up with a jolt. 'I'm sorry. I wasn't expecting that.'

'She killed herself. She jumped off our yacht in the middle of the night, as far as we can tell. She drowned.' He looked down and scowled at his hands.

'How old were you?'

'Twelve.'

'Christ. Twelve, how could she—'

'She was mad.' He said it quietly. She could see it worried him. She could see him thinking: *One day I too might jump off a yacht.*

Suddenly she knew why he had been so familiar, from the first moment she met him: he had the sad clarity of the abandoned. He had lived half his life with the tragedy of his mother's death. She felt herself becoming more and more besotted, if not with Alistair, then with the sadness his story inspired in her.

'What about your father?'

'He's fine. I don't see him much, though. He's always trying to give me things I don't want.'

'What does he do?'

'It's not important.' Alistair looked away.

His sudden reticence had broken the confessional spell between them. He never told her what his father did, and she never asked again. Later, when she had more insight into such things, she would realize it was a sure sign of guilt, that Alistair's father's occupation was probably completely politically incorrect, like aluminium brokering in Bolivia or venture capital raising in South Africa. Anyway, it was obvious Alistair came from a wealthy family. He was far too beautiful to be anything but rich; only successive generations of interbreeding between gorgeous rich people could produce his kind of delicacy.

She found herself staring at the whole effect: his sculpted jaw, his two-day-old blond stubble, his full, well-shaped lips. The boys at home were built like bags of Purina cattle feed. In comparison Alistair was thin, distracted, nervous.

But then there were his limbs, his muscles, which were surprisingly prominent and toned, considering his thinness. Rope-like veins ran down his arms, which ended in the most expressive fingers she had ever seen. Every time she looked at them or caught a glimpse of his leg muscles in outline through his trousers she thought again of those ochre-coloured ancient men on Greek amphorae: men running, throwing things, hunting, driving chariots.

She looked up into his eyes. The expression she found there caused her heart to judder to a halt like a truck with bad brakes. He was looking at her in a way that was appreciative, maybe even desirous, although in an unfocused and desultory manner. She could feel something scrabbling in her abdomen, like a small animal that had been long caged and was suddenly let loose.

'I live with this fellow now.'

He had said it out of nowhere, as if it were an afterthought.

In her head something crackled. What did he mean? *I live with this fellow.*

'I come home and find him dancing in the living room. He's very funny.'

She understood immediately. She knew the dancing-in-living-rooms type: carefree, whimsical, make-your-own-fun. Oh yes, she was sure he was very funny.

*

I'm on a bus and I'm escaping the city, driving through a landscape of estuaries, oil refineries, acid-green light, oil tankers teetering into the horizon. But someone comes after me. I realize it's Alistair's lover. He grabs a scalpel and just stabs me. Then someone is saying, 'You can't get away with a murder like that in August. Too much blood. Too much smell. What are you going to do with the body?'

*

'Ouch.' Alistair winced. 'I didn't think you could pierce there.'

They were studying a book on the body at an 'alternative' bookshop, leafing through a chapter titled 'Apocalypse Culture'.

She peered at the photograph. It showed a man with rings on every available rim of his body, even his chin. 'Christ. What's the use of that? A chin ring?'

'Must be hell going through the metal detectors at airports.'

'Look.' She took another book off the shelf: '*Dreams: the Gods of the Savages*'.

'"Savages"', Alistair sniffed. 'That's a totally unacceptable way to describe indigenous peoples.'

'It's an old book, a classic.' She flipped through the book. 'It says here that the old missionaries used to say that dreams were the gods of the savages.'

Alistair gave her a blank look. 'I'm not sure how interesting it is, anthropologically speaking,' he cleared his throat, 'the views of culturally unreconstructed missionaries vis-à-vis the cosmology of the people they were subjugating.'

She put the book on the shelf. She knew she wasn't politically correct enough for him. It must be something to do with her upbringing, she decided – all that proximity to red meat.

They left the bookstore, passing from the air-conditioned interior into a blare of heat.

'Want to see where we live?'

The *we* made her stomach turn over. 'Sure.'

'Come on, it's just down here.'

They arrived at a busy street corner. Alistair stopped and pointed to the opposite side of the street. She followed his finger to a second-floor window above a restaurant. 'Cockroaches dive-bomb me when I'm writing. Spitfires could have learned a thing or two from my cockroaches. It's just a space.' Alistair shrugged. 'Not even an apartment. More like a big room.'

She thought about that word, *space*. It was so much cooler, freer, itinerant, than *apartment*. *Apartment* would be too domestic to contain Alistair. People like her lived in *apartments*.

'There's no kitchen,' Alistair went on, 'and no bedroom.'

'So where do you sleep?' As she asked the question she felt herself flush red. Suddenly she felt she was breathing not air but hot sand.

'I built a loft, see—' He pointed to a small staircase that she could just make out from the street.

'It's a great *space*,' she said, self-consciously using his word. She stumbled a little.

'Are you okay?' He put out his hand to steady her.

'I've got to go home.' She put her hand to her head.' I'm feeling a little dizzy.'

'Oh.' Alistair frowned. 'It must be the heat.'

'Yes,' she said, turning to walk away. 'The heat.'

*

A very beautiful man is getting married or has just been married, but not to one woman, to several. After the ceremony he roams around a large and old house, like a manor, taking whatever woman is in the way and going with her into one of the house's many rooms, where they make love. The other women (the other wives) wait outside the door until they are finished, then they begin again. I am on the periphery of this. I don't think I am a wife, and when he comes anywhere near me I shrink back. I am afraid but there is something in the whole arrangement I find attractive. I wake up with guilt fluttering in my lungs like a flock of crows.

*

Alistair sat in the library, immersed in a pool of orange sunlight that made him glow like one of the caramel-coloured pieces of furniture that adorned the room. She put her pen down and walked over to him.

'Do you want to get a coffee?'

'Sure.'

When they had got their coffees she took a deep breath. 'So how long have you been—' She stopped.

'What? In the library?'

'No, I mean— How long have you been gay?'

'I'm not gay.'

'You're not?' She frowned.

'No, I mean, I don't define myself as homosexual.'

'What do you define yourself as, then?'

'Nothing.' He frowned. 'Neither one thing nor the other. I think I'm experimenting with my sexuality. Technically I suppose I'm bisexual, but then most of us are—'

'You're *bisexual*?'

'Well, yes. I've had relationships with women.'

Something leapt up inside her.

'But isn't it different, falling in love with a man?'

'Not really.'

They were silent. After a while she said, 'It's so strange, you're so familiar to me; the way you speak, for example. You're' – she struggled for the word – 'you're so light. You're *deft*.' It was as close to a declaration of love as she could get.

Alistair pursed his tensile, quilted lips. 'You feel familiar too.'

Familiar. She let the word sink into her skin. She wasn't

sure if she was pleased or if she was devastated. She said, 'Okay.'

She sees his lover sometimes. She knows him from his visits to the Reading Room, when he walks in swift, low-slung strides to where Alistair is sitting and drops himself on the couch beside him in a graceful, tired *whoosh*, as if his body has never before known solace.

He is one of those thin men who are so light on their feet they seem to walk on their toes. He wears thin-soled volleyball sneakers, dark jeans cut close to the leg, blue cotton shirts. He looks quite like her with his black curly hair, but near his temples she can see his hair is already receding. He has very blue eyes. They are brittle, but have depth, she decides, like the ice on a frozen pond through which you can see leaves and sticks scattered like bones.

She knows Alistair's lover's name but never says it, never even thinks it. If she did, she worries that something might erupt from within her and do terrible damage.

She knows the days when Alistair and his lover play squash together. Of course, she thinks, that is one of the many advantages of being gay: two men can play squash together, equally agile, equally matched in strength and power. She tries to catch sight of them from the overhead walkway. She can hear their shouts ricochet around the court. *Shit! Jesus! Arrgh!* She can't tell who is saying what. When they shout, men seem to have the same voice.

From time to time she sees the toe of his lover's volleyball sneaker or the top of his head. She never sees Alistair; he must like to play back in the court. All she can see are black balls bouncing insanely off the walls. Each time the ball hits it leaves a dark smudge. She stays there on the walkway, her back against the wall, hidden by darkness, watching these scars accumulate on the walls.

Eventually they meet each other on the sidewalk. Alistair

introduces her as 'one of my students', which is not strictly true, she thinks. Alistair is her tutorial assistant; he has finished his Master's and has started his Phhhid, as he calls it, whistling the h's through his lips to make it sound as futile as he thinks it is. She has not yet considered that university might be futile. She is finishing her first year, she goes to Alistair for help. She is explaining this to Alistair's lover when the word *help* gets lodged in her head like a piece of toffee stuck to a tooth. She and Alistair's lover look at each other politely, or rather she gives him a pleading smile. There is something amphibian in the gaze he gives her back and she looks down at her skin to check she hasn't grown scales.

All in all it is one of those excruciating meetings where none of those involved quite understands why it is so unpleasant. After that first meeting, if they run into each other and Alistair is with his lover, she smiles or says hi, but does not stop to speak. If she runs into his lover they do not acknowledge each other. She knows this is strange, even rude, given that they have been introduced. But at the same time it seems part of the unspoken and unwritten command that holds sway over the lives of adults. The truth is she can hardly walk past his lover without wanting to leap upon him and try to smell something of Alistair on his skin.

*

The sky is red, red to a flat horizon. It is like the apocalypse, the end of the world. Alistair and his lover are standing on the street. Alistair puts his arms around him and looks in my direction. I know he wants me to see his face. Tears well up in his eyes. I can see his lover's face, even though he is looking away from me. Alistair's lover is smiling a strange little smile, rather satisfied, as though it weren't the end of the world at all.

All of a sudden I am going to a hotel room which I know I should not enter. I am furious – it has something to do with the scene I have just witnessed. I knock on the door. I know I should not do this. My mother opens it. All of a sudden I am in an incoherent rage, yelling at her; obscenities, terrible things. My mother takes my face forcefully in her own hands. But she is not herself; she is a man, remote, unconcerned with my emotions, sure in his power. With my face cradled in his hands as though I were his lover, this man/my mother says to me: 'Look at how little you are made of. I would be frightened. I would be scared . . . how little you are made of. Flimsy.'

*

She lay on her back on the grass and went to sleep there, her arm thrown over her eyes. She was not sure if it was just one of her many dreams in which he hovered above her like a raincloud about to burst but she woke up suddenly to find him there, blocking out the sun. His face came closer and closer until it swallowed the sky. He kissed her lightly on the lips. He took his face away and she blinked at the sun.

'I've been waiting for you.' Her voice was still thick with sleep. 'I was dreaming of my mother. She was like Medea. You know, one of those women who want lovers more than children. She was in a hotel with her lover and I wanted to speak to her. I was banging and banging on the door. She opened it and told me I couldn't come in. Behind her I could see her lover in bed. He was naked. He had the most wonderful limbs. But then he became my mother and said terrible things to me,' she finished. 'Then I woke up and saw you.'

'Oh dear,' Alistair sighed. 'I'll need some time to analyse all that.'

She stayed propped up on her elbow while Alistair rolled

over to lie on his back next to her with his eyes closed. She watched him soaking up the sun like a lizard, or one of those intently content sun-draining animals.

She could, she knew, reach over and kiss him, even if only to give him the same sort of chaste, friendly kiss he had given her just a few minutes ago as she was waking up. But had it been so neutral? She could have sworn there was something in the way his lips had lingered on hers. But then why kiss her that way? Why not on the cheek? Perhaps he was playing with her, or maybe he had no idea of what she felt for him. Alistair wouldn't know how ardour burned when it has been continuously snuffed out by force, she considered. He probably had never striven, yearned, pined.

Eventually she would simply implode. She saw a television documentary about it once, how spontaneous combustion was dangerously common among young women in their late teens, girls who had fallen precipitously, even chemically, in love. They were burning up from the inside out with love, the reporter said. And then, in one single moment of frustration or euphoria, there was nothing of them left at all. It would be a clean way to go, she thought. There would only be microscopic elements of her left. Only powderdust. Traces.

They sat together on a bench in the courtyard at Hart House.

'I've finally decided to abandon my Phhhid,' Alistair said.

She sat up with a jolt. 'What?'

'I've had enough of academia.'

'But what will you do instead?'

'I'm leaving.'

She turned to look at him. Was it her imagination, or did he look strangely satisfied, even a little smug?

'I'm going to move to Vancouver. It's something I've been wanting to do for a while.'

'Vancouver – Jesus. I mean, why?' Inside her, several screeching children had popped up in her lungs, her fingertips, her brain. *When?* they screeched. *When?*

Alistair shrugged. 'For a change of scene. You know, skiing, fishing. I think I should try the outdoor life.'

The outdoor life. She had lived it for many years, scrabbling over mountains, cleaning the shit out of horses' stalls, freezing her fingers. She had come to the city not just to go to university but to transform herself, to drink cappuccinos at sidewalk cafés, to immerse herself in concrete poetry, to eat arugula, to learn German, Spanish, to dress in black. She had loved Alistair because, in a way, everything about him spoke of these things, everything about him said *in the city*.

But no, she could see him living *the outdoor life* as so many people who were essentially city-dwellers and who had all the privileges of their corporate upbringings called it. She saw him striding across streams on weekend hiking trips, scrambling up screes, skiing down Whistler's slopes, him and his lover in their matching Thinsulate jackets.

'Are you sure you want to go so far away?'

Alistair frowned. 'So far away from where?'

'Here. Europe. Anywhere—'

'It's not that far. I can always travel.'

Yes, she reminded herself. He had money. He could always travel.

At home that night she lay on her futon and watched the cockroaches begin their nightly climb up the walls, like a battalion in basic training. They would get so far, usually about two feet, then they would lose their grip and slip, landing on the floor with a soft papery sound before starting their climb all over again.

In the darkened room she considered the likelihood of it, of their loving each other, her and Alistair, or even of knowing each other. The more she thought about it the more absurd it seemed. Alistair was wealthy, he came from a privileged background. His father still spoke Hungarian, or was it Czech? He was six years older than her. He had been born in South Africa. He had walked through blistering deserts, lived in hills scattered with scrub brushes like so many punctuation marks. He had been to London three times and Paris too. He was gay, or rather bisexual.

What did she want? She tried to see her desires clearly. But any attempt to penetrate her hopes only took her to a wood-panelled room where a chamber orchestra played lush, rhapsodic music. She wanted to walk through darkened palaces with Alistair, listening to the chamber orchestra's fugue, carrying candles from one room to another, like medieval theatre-players or powerful conspirators. She wanted to see Alexandria through his eyes. She wanted to sit with him in cool, darkened rooms during afternoon rainstorms and watch thick marzipan rain drip from the eaves.

Alistair would do these things, she understood, and others. He would see the sun glinting off Vespas in Rome, he would stare at the ceiling of the Sistine Chapel, he would see Rodin's statue of the lovers, their arms entwined in that sensuous way that obliterated the world outside their embrace. She felt the shadow of joy in those hypothetical blurred moments inhabited with Alistair, the delight she would feel, if only she could be there, with him. She tried to catch the feeling of living those moments, but it was cool and wet, like a fish, and it slipped from her grasp.

Suddenly she sat up on the edge of her futon and put her head in her hands. She felt dizzy, she couldn't breathe. She was trapped in a plastic box. It felt like people were chopping at her skin with razor blades. Eventually she passed out.

*

I am swimming through cobalt waters. Every creature who sees me flees, scattering themselves like confetti. I am moving through an intermingling weed packed thick with drama. Alistair is in the water. He has a miniature wound, like a thorn prick, out of which tiny drops of blood fall. I zero in on him for the kill. I am a shark, after all. A beast, an atavistic eating machine, built to consume others, and finally itself, leaving only an impressive set of teeth.

*

'Hey.'

It was Alistair, on the phone. She struggled not to gulp down the sound of his voice.

'I was thinking we should meet up before I go.'

'Yes?'

'I'd like to say goodbye. I mean, normally I just drift away. I think I have a problem with goodbyes, actually,' Alistair said, his tone grim and weighted with uncomfortable self-knowledge.

'Don't worry, Alistair.' That's the way it is, she thought as she put the phone down. We end up reassuring people who don't need it at all. Meanwhile there's no one to pull us out of danger.

They met for the last time in the Hart House cafeteria. They had wanted to have dinner together, but Alistair had called her and said, 'Sorry, this moving stuff is killing me. All the packing and storage, it's such a nightmare.'

She thought how it would be to be part of Alistair's nightmare. She saw herself packing up their spatulas, wrapping the *café au lait* bowls in newspaper, off to start her new life with Alistair amid the exclamation marks of mountains and the floating lozenges of humpback whales.

In that moment, from each extremity of her body, trains

pull out and rush to her tongue. My God, she has to tell him. She has to tell him she loves him. That she would do anything to go with him, to live her life among the detritus of his being, his sinews and flakes of skin, among his discarded hair and tumbling eyelashes. But she finds she can only see the indulgent and pitiful look he would give her if she did. She wouldn't be able to bear that; she couldn't bear to receive his pity. She might kill herself out of rage.

Sitting there with Alistair for what might be the last time, she feels as if she is seeing herself through the wrong end of binoculars. She feels distant, removed from not only herself but from her entire species. All her thoughts have serrated edges; if she touched them she would cut herself. At the same time everything looks blurred and indistinct, as if it has been coated with a layer of gelatin. She feels savage. She could do anything, even harm him, anything to make him realize the violence he is causing her, feel the pitch and roll of her desperation.

All this flashes though her mind in a second. She tries to smile. She says, 'Well, take care.'

'*Everybody always ends up in Vancouver.*'

She has the dream about the grey Fuego and the horsetrailer and her cross-country dash the night before he leaves. She understands that in her dream she is trying to dismiss him as someone average, predictable. Eventually he would buy stocks and have children, just like everyone else.

The day he left there was a ferocious summer storm. Prairie-built clouds in the shape of hammerhead sharks drifted in from the lakes and moored themselves over the city like battleships. By six o'clock it was pitch dark. She sat on her balcony, watching the traffic lumber up and down Spadina, the cars' headlights reflected and blurred in the rain on the streets until each car had four lights instead of two.

She wondered how she would think of it later, when time

had worked the magic everyone said it did. She wondered if she would remember how the minutes she had spent with Alistair had been like flames leaping suddenly from dying wood fires; the sharp crack, the searing illumination. She wondered if she would remember it as love, or rather the dream of it.

The Rainy Season

At first she thinks she is in a kitchen. Light slices at her with knife-like precision from sharp white surfaces. She swims through a brownish liquid she vaguely suspects is her own blood. It is thick and soupy, her arms are as limp as noodles. She keeps on swimming towards the light.

'Welcome back to consciousness.' The voice comes from the end of the tunnel, where the knives of light are waiting to cut her up.

'Check her temperature,' the voice says again. She raises her hand to her head. When she draws it away it is coated with a glycerine-like sheen – her own sweat.

The voice speaks again, and this time it harbours a smile.

'We should call you Mosquito,' it says. 'Look at those legs.'

She had red blotches on her white skin before she had even left the airport. Mosquitoes, it seemed, could smell fresh meat just flown in from the northern latitudes, pale and muscular and ripe as a grape.

In the airport she hadn't recognized him. She was aware that the man in front of her bore a faint resemblance to the friend she had last seen three years ago, but she wondered all the same why this strange man was hovering around her. His face was full, puffed out. His stomach hung over his trousers. In three years, he had completely transformed himself.

'Your beard,' she said, when she had recovered herself.

'Shaved it off two years ago. *As moradoras das cavernas*,' he said, pointing to her arms. Cave-dwellers. Her skin was very white. She laughed. It was the first time she had heard him speak Portuguese.

'I'll give you the dawn tour,' he said. They sped down the highway at sunrise, five thirty a.m. She watched the pink clouds of a tropical sunrise troop along the red of Guanabara Bay. As he drove to the city she lost all sense of direction. They hurtled through tunnels that looked like Space Station Earth – round lights polka-dotting caverns that had been blasted through the mountains. She looked up at the fantastic shapes of the jutting peaks that surrounded the city. She had seen plenty of pictures, but they had not prepared her for the sheer absurdity of the landscape. Meringue mountains sprouted in all directions, sudden and terribly vertical, just like whipped egg whites in a mixing bowl.

They passed bus stops packed with weary pre-dawn workers, who, she noticed after a while, were all black. Jack pulled into a side street and suddenly they were in the middle of a street market.

'Got to get a few things,' Jack said, and hopped out of the car.

At the market they bought fruit she had never heard of – Amazonian fruits from the winterless north with bird-twitter names: *açai*, *cupuacù*. The seasons were reversed, and at the market yellow autumnal pears were being unloaded from boxes marked *Argentina* and *Uruguay*. In the country she had left only the night before, strawberries had begun to appear in the supermarkets. Now she was in the southern hemisphere, which had just slipped over the cusp towards winter.

'Ana's in the States,' Jack told her, in between buying vast bags of oranges and small plump papayas which he told her were called *mamão*. It had been three years since she had seen Ana as well. They had all been at university together and had done the same undergraduate degree. Then Ana and Jack had become journalists and Ana had quickly got her first foreign posting. Jack was still working freelance. 'The rest of the time I'm a house husband,' he told her, and laughed a strange new rough laugh.

She watched as Jack strode around, insanely animated for six o'clock in the morning, arguing about price, shouting in his garrulous American-accented Portuguese. She was still wearing the trousers and shirt she had put on for her plane journey. Everyone in the market crush around her wore shorts and flip-flops. Soon she was sweating, following Jack from stall to stall with bulging bags of fruit hanging off her arms.

When they were back in the car he lit a cigarette.

'I forgot to tell you. We have another guest.' He drew a thick breath of tobacco into his lungs and shoved the car into gear. 'He called me last week without any warning. But don't worry, our rooms are allocated on a first come, first served basis and we knew you were coming a long time ago. At the moment he's staying in your room but I've asked him to move to the one next door.'

Why, she wondered, was he talking like the concierge of a hotel? She knew they had a big apartment, with four spare rooms. But they were friends of seven years' standing.

She looked at him, trying to discern whether Jack's incredible physical change reflected some kind of interior change as well.

'We put up a lot of people,' he continued. 'The BBC are always calling us for a place for their crews to stay. Everybody knows we have a huge place. But at this point we only have Michel.' He stubbed out his cigarette. 'A very good-looking Frenchman,' he volunteered.

*

By the time they arrived at the apartment, she was exhausted. Jack had run several more errands – gas, cigarettes, and a stop at the house of a friend where she had watched another man dressed only in shorts and sandals hand Jack a package while a menacing black dog prowled around the car.

'Michel?' Jack called. For a while no one appeared. Then the kitchen door opened and a very tanned, sleepy-looking man stood in front of them.

'It's eight o'clock in the morning, Jack,' she heard Michel say in Portuguese.

They shook hands. Michel gave her a crumpled smile.

'*Bonjour, ça va?*' she greeted him.

'*Ah, vous parlez français.*'

They sat down for breakfast. Jack was absorbed by the newspaper, so they spoke French, which Jack didn't speak. From time to time Michel turned to Jack and said things in a slushy, purring Portuguese she could not quite understand.

'What do you do?' Michel asked her.

'I'm a student. Well, I've just finished my degree. I'll be an anthropologist.'

He nodded. The obscurity of his expression gave her the idea he might not know what anthropologist meant.

'What do you do?'

'I used to own a hotel, after I got out of gold.'

'Gold?'

'I was a miner. *No interior*,' he said, switching to Portuguese and wagging his head in a north-westerly direction.

She studied his face. He had the look of someone who has spent a long time in the sun. His face was quite symmetrical, attractive, but it was marred by an inelegantly squished nose. This was a rugby injury, he would tell her later, from the days when he had been a professional rugby player.

'Right now,' he continued, 'my ex-partner is trying to buy me out. I'm staying here in Rio while the negotiations go through.'

'And then what will you do?'

He shrugged. 'Go back to France. Perhaps back to Amazônia. I have a girlfriend in Argentina; I could go there. But,' he tried to smile, but it instantly drooped into an expression of disapproval, 'she doesn't love me any more.'

Something ocurred to her, almost independent of the information he had given. He's broke, she thought. And stuck here.

That first night she went running for an hour, sticking to the lit mosaic-patterned sidewalks that hugged the rim of the small peninsula where Ana and Jack lived. On her way back she encountered him on the doorstep to the apartment.

He was on his way out. His hair was damp, and he smelled of cologne. She had forgotten there were men who used cologne.

'*T'as couru?*'

'I tried, but I'm not used to the humidity.' She looked down at her arms, which were covered with sweat.

She noticed he had dispensed with the *vous*. She wondered if this were a comment on the fact that she was younger than him. Maybe he had been away from France long enough to be more casual. But all the same, the *tu* was there between them now, non-negotiable and rushed.

She was surprised how rickety her French was – it had been years since she had spoken the language on a daily basis. She made a note to ask him, politely, if they could speak Portuguese. She was supposed to learn the language better, after all. That was one of the reasons why she had come. But at the same time she knew they would carry on in French, and this seemed to mean something.

*

'And how are you feeling today?' The chrome tone of the doctor's voice has the brightness of refrigerators.

She opens her eyes and says, 'Do you realize that the hunger has to spend his time watching his prey? That he is trapped in his hunger?'

The doctor looks at her.

'I can't think of a duller fate,' she says, closing her eyes again, 'than to want all the time.'

'Toilet paper.' Jack held up a roll before stuffing it in his bag. 'The only thing you really can't go to the Amazon without.' He threw his malaria prophylactics from the case. They landed, rejected, on the bed.

'Aren't you going to take those?' At university she had been told horror stories about anthropologists who had contracted deadly cerebral malaria.

'The best way to avoid malaria is not to get bitten.' Jack lit another cigarette. He really was a chain-smoker now. 'Stay in between five and seven in the morning and evening and wear long trousers and sleeves and you'll be fine. Those pills make you go blind.'

She looked down at her own welt-dotted legs. 'If I don't get malaria I'll probably get dengue fever,' she said.

'I've never heard of any foreigner getting dengue in Rio. Like most things, you only get it if you're poor.'

'So where will you be going?'

'*No final do mundo*,' he joked. The end of the world. 'I'm sorry I can't take you with me, but you know there's only one seat on the plane.'

'That's okay,' she said. She only half believed him. 'Good luck with those officials.'

'Yeah,' he snorted. 'I suspect they're not really interested in talking to anyone about indigenous land rights. All they care about is who can sell them a satellite dish.'

She had a vision of Amazônia from the air, dotted with

satellite dishes like poisonous mushrooms sprouting on the forest floor.

'I love Amazônia,' Jack said, and gave her a big, suffocating hug. She went downstairs to where the taxi was waiting, to see him off. Michel appeared suddenly out of the night to stand next to her. He was still wearing his suit, but the cologne had faded.

'He's going already? I thought it was tomorrow.'

'He had to get a flight out tonight.'

'Oh yes.' Michel fingered his tie. 'It will take him twenty hours to get where he's going.'

Jack struggled to get his bulk and luggage through the cab's back door. 'Hey, Michel,' he yelled. 'Be nice. Show her around.'

'That's okay, Jack,' she said, irritated. She could take care of herself.

'Ana's back on Tuesday,' Jack yelled from the back seat of the cab. 'Make sure to give her my love.' The cab swallowed him and he was gone.

'So,' Michel said, when they were alone in the apartment, 'have you discovered caipirinhas yet? I'll make you one.' He reached to the top shelf and took down a bottle. He turned the label towards her. 'Cachaça,' he said.

'I can read,' she protested.

He took a pestle from the kitchen drawer and proceeded to crush lime slices. They he poured sugar on top of the lime, the alcohol on top of the mixture, and finally soda water and ice.

'I don't drink much.'

'You will.' He turned back to the cutting board. 'You're in Brazil now. Here people drink, eat, go to the beach, have sex. Here people know how to live.' He quartered another lime with the knives kept sharp by Ana and Jack's maid. 'Unlike you Anglo-Saxons, Brazilians actually know how to enjoy the sensuous life. I know, believe me. I've lived here ten years. I'm almost Brazilian myself. But then it was not such a difficult transition for me.'

She looked at him over the rim of her glass. 'Why's that?'

'Because I am a Mediterranean,' he shrugged.

Later, he put on a Tropicalia compilation CD at full volume, and they danced.

'You have no sensuality in your body,' he told her, scanning her limbs. 'Look at the way you move.'

'I like the way I move.' She looked down at her body as if it had betrayed her. She was muscular and fit. She liked tension and containment and the asexual sinuosity she occasionally observed in dancers and tennis players. And in herself. Her dancing usually attracted people, she thought. *She* usually attracted people.

But he shook his head. 'You move like a man,' he said.

The next evening Jack called from the Amazon.

'What's the end of the world called?' she asked.

'Redençao.' Jack's voice hissed down the telephone line. It sounded as if he were calling from overseas. 'As it turns out, it's not too bad. The hotel has satellite and a mini-bar. Although it's full of cattle ranchers and their hitmen. I'm thinking of barricading myself in at night.'

Michel came out of the shower with only a towel around his waist. '*C'est Jacques*,' she mouthed. Michel propped himself up on the table. His fingers kept a delicate hold on the corners of the towel, but it still looked as if it might slip.

'Michel is in front of me,' she said into the phone, in English. 'In various states of undress.'

Jack lowered his voice.' He's not hitting on you, is he?'

'No, no,' she laughed. 'I don't think I'm his kind of woman.'

'That's me in the *drague*.'

The photograph showed a river dotted with amphibious

hulks, all rusted, dredging the silty river bottom for gold. There was another photo of the Cessna he had once owned, and another showed a younger, more muscled version of Michel on Copacabana beach, his unlined face set in a Mr Universe *moue*. The photos were worn at the edges and smudges of fingerprints obscured their corners. Even she could identify the used look of cherished memories.

They were standing together on the apartment's balcony, watching the sun set behind Corcovado. Light spilled from behind the mountain, which filtered the last rays of the sun and sent flutes of alternating blue and orange into the sky like a crisply pleated skirt. It occurred to her that she could watch this all her life, the absurdly lavish quotidian spectacle of a Rio sunset.

'*Le seul chose que je sais est que je sais rien*,' Michel said, looking wistfully into the orange flutes.

She nodded. He was thirty-four, he had a right to say world-weary things. She couldn't help noticing how they sounded even better in a foreign language.

'Look, the *favelas*.' He pointed to the other side of the city. They watched as the sodium lights of the shanty-town houses that clung to the mountains were turned on, seemingly one by one, until they twinkled like a thousand Chinese lanterns.

'Rio is beautiful,' he said.

What was it about the frequency of his voice in this banal statement, she wondered, that made her so immediately go along with it? If anyone said this to her at home it would sound maudlin, so sentimental, but here, watching the Southern Cross appear as the sky turned to black, she found she could only agree: it was so beautiful it hurt.

The next day they went to the beach together. As they laid their towels down on the strip of sand in front of the Hotel Meridien she smelled the stench of sewage drifting off the water. Michel wrinkled his nose as well. There was something very French about his expression just then, she thought, this look of quite violent disapproval. She thought she had seen it on the faces of other Frenchmen when surveying some woman's stomach that stuck out just an inch above her bikini bottom, or a suit whose cut was slightly unimaginative.

As they laid down their towels she was aware of a slight disturbance among the other bodies on the beach, as if people were taking note of their arrival.

In a second she forgot about this, and lay down and smiled. The incongruity of the situation intrigued her. She knew about *garimpeiros* – gold miners. From her university courses with titles like The Anthropology of South America and Ecological Anthropology she knew well enough that gold miners were responsible for, in turn, the hounding of indigenous people, hyperinflated local economies, drunkenness and prostitution, not to mention clearcutting and environmental damage. The previous year they had massacred sixteen Yanomami. At university she had come to equate the word *garimpeiro* with evil. Now she was lying next to one on Copacabana beach.

Then again, he was no longer a gold miner. He had been converted and had turned ecological, he had told her. He had been constructing an 'ecological lodge' on the banks of the Tapajós river, a tributary of the Amazon. He had conceived of the lodge, raised the funds, and built it himself, along with help from his girlfriend, although at times she had been an unwilling partner.

'You can't imagine,' he said to her now on Copacabana beach, 'how much Dominique hated the Amazon.' He whistled at the memory.

'Why did she hate it so much? I've heard it's very beautiful.'

'There's nothing to do, for one thing. Everyone is overly

interested in your business. It is like being under surveillance. No *culture*,' he emphasized. 'And there were always women after me.'

Then, just as the lodge had finished its first successful tourist season, he told her, Dominique had left him and gone to Argentina, where she found the cultural level of the inhabitants much more to her liking. Two months later he had followed her, trailing Ray Bans and Timberland shoes and Sheraton hotel rooms and taxicab rides and other gifts that had cleaned him out of all his money.

'But we made love four times a day,' he said. 'On the floor, in the kitchen. We communicate very well with our bodies. Four times a day,' he said. 'Can you imagine?'

No, she couldn't imagine. It must take up a lot of time, she thought, making love four times a day. When did they find the time to do their grocery shopping? Then again, Michel and Dominique had probably had a maid to do that for them. Ana and Jack had a maid. So did everyone else who could afford it.

She looked up to see one of the drinks sellers who paraded up and down the beach in endless revolutions approaching them. These vendors were always black, or near-black. Their calves were superlatively defined from hours of trudging through the sand.

She couldn't tell whether the face under the white baseball cap belonged to a man or a woman. The skin was dark and pitted, more like a hide than a human's.

'You his girlfriend?'

So it was a she. She shook her head.

'She's had a very hard life,' Michel told her, when the drinks seller had moved on. 'I talk to her when I come here. So nice,' he sighed. 'But so ugly.'

She got up to go back to the apartment so she could walk Ana and Jack's dog, as she had promised to do.

'They'll be so pleased to see you go.' He squinted up at her.

'Who's they?'

'The prostitutes.' She looked again at the bodies on the beach arranged neatly on top of their *kangas*, the Brazilian sarong that doubled as a beach towel. She hadn't noticed before that they were surrounded by lone women. They seemed to have spread themselves at an even distance from each other.

'They leave me alone now, though. I tell them I'm sad because my wife was killed in a car accident and they don't try to hustle me. Some things they respect.'

'And where do I fit in?' she said. 'Am I a friend of your dead wife?'

He propped himself up on one elbow. 'Yes. You are an old friend of hers from France who is living here for a while and I am consoling myself in your company.'

She smiled, shaking out her towel.

'You shouldn't walk through the tunnel alone,' he said, referring to the Tunel Nôvo between Princesa Isabel in Copacabana and the Rio Sul shopping centre. She knew she shouldn't, but now that she was here, nothing about the city that she had expected to frighten her did – not even the ferocious guard dogs who paced round the houses in the fashionable neighbourhood where Ana and Jack lived.

'*A tout à l'heure*,' she said, moving off down the beach, watched, she knew, by nameless eyes. There goes the French friend of his dead wife, grieving with the sad husband. Maybe falling in bed together, locked in grief.

She disapproved of his lies, of course, and felt them unnecessary. But at the same time she liked being a character in his story.

That evening they went running together on the jogging *pista*, the track that ran around the peninsula.

'Do you have a boyfriend?' he asked, as they jogged along together.

'Not right now.'

'You could have any man you want here in Brazil.' He said it enthusiastically, but in his voice she heard the unmistakable tinny note of charity.

'I'm not that interested.'

'What? In sex?'

'I don't think that sex is everything. Besides, I need to be kept whole,' she said. 'Sometimes I don't like sex because it is an invasion. I want to be able to hold myself together.'

He was silent for a moment. She heard only their combined breathing and the thump-thump of their steps. Suddenly he stopped.

She ground to a halt beside him. 'What's the matter?'

'In all my life, that is one thing I have never had any woman say to me. That's just incredible.'

Then his arm was around her neck in a kind of loose vice grip. 'Do you want to be a man in bed?' His voice was low and thick.

She gripped his arm and tried to pull it down. 'No,' she laughed.

'I just want to kick you for being so silly,' he said, releasing her and pretending to kick her off the *pista*, over the edge to where the Atlantic Ocean churned. 'Like you would do with a child,' he said.

And she laughed, because she wanted so badly to be released from herself. She wanted to be a child. Clean, vaguely damp, sexless.

'After you left, she just came up to me.'

He told her how a woman had approached him on the beach at the end of the jogging path. She had gone back to the apartment to have a shower and he had stayed to do press-ups.

'She had the kind of body I like,' he said. 'Big, sensual, tanned. She wants to go to Maxim's,' he said, naming an expensive nightclub in Leblon. 'Can you loan me ten thousand cruzeiros?'

She gave him fifteen thousand. As she handed over the money she felt as though something heavy – pianos, or other large pieces of furniture – were falling through her innards.

'*Qu'est-ce qu'il y a?*'

She couldn't think of anything to say, not in French or Portuguese. She was tired of carrying on conversations in three different languages. She shook her head and put her hand on her stomach. He took her money and left.

'*Très experte*,' he said, over breakfast. The woman had known just what she wanted, and how to ask for it. She was separated from her husband, an airline pilot, and had three children. She was twenty-nine years old. He did not intend to see her again. 'I've got enough problems,' he said.

At night in the giant empty apartment they charted his movements on the wall map of the continent Ana had tacked up behind her desk. SOUTH AMERICA, it said, in *National Geographic* script. The continent looked like a pregnant woman, the stomach of Brazil spilling over Argentina's thin legs.

Rosario. His girlfriend was there, where she had escaped the cultural desert of the Amazon to live on an estancia. *Fortaleza*, a beach-party town in the north-east of Brazil. His Brazilian girlfriend was there. She was twenty-two years old and he had promised her a trip to France. She remembered Jack talking about her, saying that within days of Michel's arrival in Rio she had been on the phone, begging for him, crying over him in the way that only twenty-two-year-old girls can do.

Redençao. Where Jack had called from, the end of the

world. *Tapajós*. There, he said, putting his finger in the middle of nothingness. This was the location of his past.

His finger traced a curved line that began in Venezuela and arced over the Amazon rainforest, then drew it down towards the city where they stood now in a darkened office lit only by the light of a computer screen and the moon. He was drawing Ana's flight; she was on a plane that night, coming in from the States, flying over the night-still jungle. She would be there in the morning.

Within the thick walls of the fever she sees Ana's face coming towards her from a long way away. As soon as it gets close she realizes she wants to kiss her. But then Ana's face retreats in the waves that are also moving the walls, the bed, the ceiling.

Ana had one foot in the elevator and another in the apartment, transferring enormous bags that landed on the floor with a whump.

'How are you?' Ana said.

'I'm fine—'

'Maria!' Ana yelled, calling the maid in an authoritative, commanding voice she had never heard her use before.

'Sorry. Now—'

Michel opened the door. 'Ana.' He smiled. His face had the softened aspect of a supplicant.

'Look at your hair,' Ana said, planting her hand on top of his curls. He beamed like a small boy. 'It's been what? Six months since I've seen you?'

'So what have you been doing?' Ana asked her.

'Oh. Getting to know the city.' She was embarrassed. She hadn't done anything. 'Michel and I went to buy a bikini at Rio Sul.'

'A bikini?' Ana raised her eyebrows. 'How are you getting around?'

'By taxi.'

Ana smiled. She knew what the smile meant: it was a version of the residential snobbery entitled you-really-belong-when-you-know-the-bus-system.

'Oh, I almost forgot.' Ana reached into her pocket. 'I've got something for you.' She handed her a small silver pendant in the shape of a clenched fist.

'It's from Bahia. It's Candomblé.' Ana launched into an explanation of the African religion. She already knew what it was, but she listened politely. Ana had always given her exquisite things.

'Listen,' Ana said, jumping up. 'I've got to make a phone call. Do you mind?'

No, she didn't mind, she said. She got up and went to find Michel. Maybe they could do something together.

All her training had taught her that a new culture must be approached with caution. To remind her of this, she had taken a few books with her. The books told her that an anthropologist had to find a median position, neither hurling himself into the maelstrom of a new reality nor standing back with a crippling aloofness.

When she first arrived she had read these books every night, after she and Michel had drunk their caipirinhas on the balcony and mused upon the sunset city.

'In the view of the ancients, madness was allied to divinity,' she read. 'The mad were already closer to the gods than were the sane. They thus made an appropriate offering, one with which the gods could be expected to be pleased.'

It had always frightened her, the idea of voracious gods who needed to be appeased and who spent the rest of their time lolling in that luscious aphrodisiac realm of those who have their desires fulfilled.

'The only means of compelling fate is to venture into those hazardous marginal areas where social norms cease to have any meaning, and where the protective laws and demands of the group no longer prevail; to go right to the frontiers of average, ordered living, to the breaking point of bodily strength and to the extremes of physical and moral suffering.'

She had wanted to do this, to push herself through that stubborn, opaque boundary that divided her from real life. All she knew about life was through books. Look at Ana, she thought: dangerous, edgy, driven Ana, who went straight to her desk from a nine-hour overnight flight and did her expenses. Look at Michel, who had lived ten lives in one.

'In this unstable border area,' the books went on, 'there is a danger of slipping beyond the pale and never coming back, as well as a possibility of drawing from the vast ocean of unexploited forces surrounding organized society a personal supply of power, thanks to which he who has risked all can hope to modify an otherwise unchangeable social order.'

Could she go there, to that unstable border area? What would take her there?

She put the book down and went to the balcony. Outside the apartment, five floors below, in the streets of a tropical city, men and women clad in shorts, T-shirts and flip-flops eyed one another casually, with a supposedly non-Freudian acceptance of the sexual current passing between them. In Cinelândia and Lapa, the rent boys braced themselves for the arrival of another wave of businessmen poised between the end of the office day and supper with their wives. She saw it when she went running in the evening on the *pista*, where men and women eyed each other openly as they passed. Occasionally deadly coral snakes and long grey vipers would wiggle across the path; out to sea, small islands and supertankers vied for supremacy of the horizon. Everything spoke of beauty. Everything said, It's only sex, it's not that serious. It won't kill you.

The next chapter was about the Navajo myth of transformation. In it an Indian went as far as the earth allowed in search of personal power. He made himself go far from home and enter into a borderland. He did this, her book told her, because he would find himself there. And when he finally arrived, what happened?

'He stood still, weeping bitterly, praying and moaning. And yet no mysterious sound reached his ears, nor was he put to sleep in order to be transported as he slept, to the temple of the magic animals. For there could no longer be the slightest doubt: no power, from anyone, had been granted him . . .'

'An anthropologist, huh?'

The voice comes to her from the bottom of the bed. It takes her some time to realize she is being spoken to. There is a clank of metal against metal. Her chart.

'We see a lot of you guys in here.'

'You have no idea,' Ana told her in a low, alarmed voice. 'Ripping the curtains from the wall. Hurling furniture and crying underneath the bed. How am I supposed to deal with that? He's frustrated in his career, I'm doing better than him. But he's respected here, he does good work and there are people here who love him, who would do anything for him. I just don't understand.'

'I had no idea your marriage was in trouble. Why didn't you tell me?'

'I guess I was travelling. I travel so much in this job it's hard to notice things like my marriage disintegrating.'

Ana took her glasses off and rubbed the lenses with the bottom of her shirt. She was always amazed at the nakedness of Ana's pale face without glasses. Her eyes, shorn of their chic Armani frames, were beautiful: berry brown, candid as almonds.

'To tell you the truth, my work is my refuge. I don't know how to manage my emotional life.'

She remembered how, in another city of autumn leaves and January blizzards, the three of them had done everything together: they had even started smoking on the same day, though she and Ana had given it up after a month only to watch Jack quickly spiral to a pack a day. She remembered the nights they had sat drinking together in the kitchen, the summer barbecues they had hosted. The thought of Ana without Jack and vice versa made little sense to her. It was as if her parents were splitting up.

'I told him he had to move out,' Michel said. They were sitting in the shopping mall coffee shop where they went every morning to share an espresso.

'It's her salary of—' He named a figure, which she could not remember, as Ana's salary. He always seemed to know the numbers of things: the square footage of their apartment, the price of a hotel room at the Hotel Meridien, the dollar exchange rate, which changed every day. 'It's her apartment. Don't you realize what kind of salary she's on?'

She remembered the submissive expression he had greeted Ana with. It was possible he admired her purely for the amount of money she made. She herself didn't know how much money Ana made, and didn't care to. All she knew was it allowed them to live in Third World luxury, with a penthouse apartment, a car, and a maid, although Ana was only a year out of university. Meanwhile she had just finished graduate school, she lived in a basement flat. She had an anthropology degree. She would never make any money.

'How do you know it's her problem?'

He gathered his face into a tired, rather effeminate frown. 'I'm a man.' He replaced his cup with a neat little *clack*. 'It's something I immediately understand.'

*

Next to her bed she has a pad on which she can write things for the doctor. She has not spoken in two weeks, not since she first felt the flashes of fire singe neat paths through her insides.

No one seems distressed by the fact that she can't speak. The truth is, all her reserves are used up. Her muscles have sunk into soft mush, her white blood cell count is very low, and to top it all off, mosquitoes are buzzing in her cranium.

On the pad, the one the doctor solicitously left beside the bed, she performs abstract equations:

1). Experience = transformation (Sennet)

2) Transience = uniqueness (Rilke)

3) Certainty = doubt (anyone who has a brain)

The doctor finds these when she is at last asleep. He writes on her chart: solid food tomorrow.

Ennervé. Désesperé. Déprimé.

A flurry of words exited his mouth, each sounding like the beating wings of a hummingbird. He was waiting. Waiting on lawyers, waiting for money. That way he could buy a ticket to France. He was waiting for news of his girlfriend, to hear whether she would have him back and they could resume their four-times-a-day-on-the-floor lovemaking.

Finally the phone rang. It was his girlfriend, calling from Argentina, demanding money. Argentina was very expensive, she said. He had to help her.

'You can see how mean she is to me.' There were tears in his eyes.

'I can't believe the way his girlfriend treats him,' she told Ana. 'He's trying to do everything for her, and she just chucks it back in his face.'

Ana pursed her lips. 'She's a bitch,' she said, finally. 'But I like her.'

*

'I can't go running with you tonight.'

'Why not?' She had begun to look forward to their twilight runs together. Afterwards they would sit and watch the moon rise over Guanabara Bay and hover above the science fiction shape of the Pão de Açúcar.

He lifted his foot to show where the sole had partially detached itself from his running shoe. 'They've fallen apart.' He frowned. 'Nikes too – I bought them in France. They're a fortune here, especially with the inflation. And I don't see the point of getting inferior running shoes.'

That evening she went running alone and nearly stepped on a snake. It was dusk and the long grey ribbon had appeared out of nowhere and suddenly it was under her feet. She yelped and jumped around, trying to get away from it, looking, no doubt, like a kid on a pogo stick. The other joggers gingerly avoided the snake and merely carried on running. She turned round and ran the two kilometres back in double time.

'*Les serpents ils font la chasse par la nuit*,' he said, when she told him about it, breathless from her narrow escape. He was doing this more and more, telling her things she already knew. She wasn't letting this one pass. '*Je le sais bien*,' she said. She knew very well snakes hunted at night.

In the shops they spoke French, evaluating the running shoes. Nike, or Reebok? No, Nike, he said. They were the only ones he would buy. He wanted the same ones she had. Nike Air, he said. It came out as *Neek Ayre*.

The shop assistants flocked to them. They were rich French tourists visiting Rio, they stayed at the Meridien. They had credit cards that would be billed in dollars, not cruzeiros, which were running at 40 per cent inflation per month. She saw the women shop assistants admiring him. She liked being seen with him. She liked doing things for him. She liked the feeling of knowing herself to be generous.

Now, in her fever bed, she wonders again at how she could have been conned by sex without actually doing it.

'I love women. All the things I've done in my life I've done for women.'

He was crouched, slumped, even, against the wall, just underneath Tierra del Fuego on the *National Geographic* map of South America.

'I am like a woman. That is why women like me. *Je suis très fier de mon corps, comme une femme*,' he said. I am very proud of my body, like a woman.

His face contorted. She saw a cloud of disgust pass across it. '*Je me déteste*. I can't stand myself. I can't understand how I please women.'

He turned to her suddenly. '*Regarde*.' He pulled his shorts up to his hip, showing the outline of his underwear.

She looked. Stretch marks.

'*Comme une femme*.' When she met his gaze his eyes had the look of having come from far away, like those of people just arrived in foreign countries after gruelling flights. They were imploring her, but she could not guess for what.

'*Comme une femme*,' he said, again 'Like a woman.'

Ana did stories on children who lived in the sewers of Bogotá. She descended into that wet, cloacal world at night and teased the male photographer, who was more afraid than he had ever been in his life. She coaxed the children in feral Spanish, promising them things – a warm meal, a pet. The Colombian police considered them vermin and regularly hunted them down. Ana told her all this with her fingers wrapped around a cup of camomile tea.

'When the rain fills the sewers they surface to be shot,' Ana said neatly, as if she had reached the punchline of a joke.

*

Jack was on his fourth gin and tonic.

'I have to talk to Michel.' A note of desperation penetrated his liquor-thick voice. You know, he's been ditched by his girlfriend. He's got no money. You should have seen him in his element, up there,' Jack said, meaning the Amazon. 'Taking care of everything, driving four-wheel drives, cooking a meal on a wood fire, ordering workmen about. He was such a *real man*.' He looked up, a wounded expression in his eyes, shining through a glassy coating of alcohol.

'Is he a friend, really?'

'I don't know,' he said, twirling his glass. 'But I like to watch him.'

'When the crowd roared it was the best moment of my life.'

Michel was talking again of his past as a rugby player, until an injury had put him out of the game. And she saw, in his crumpled incomprehension, a man ten years younger who didn't understand how he had reached thirty-four years of age without hearing that crowd roar again. And although she was young she understood how days became years and the crowd's roar faded forever.

'When we came out of the stadium, it was *hhooooorrh*!' he said, imitating the ear-deafening gush of adulation.

'*J'ai raté ma vie*,' he told her. 'I've wasted my life.'

She suspected that he might be right, and found it impossible not to feel frightened for him, and for herself, that she might one day say the same thing.

'I want him out,' Ana said. 'How dare he hang around in our apartment, feeling sorry for himself.'

'You want me out too.'

'It's just – it's not a good time.'

'Elle va faire le ménage,' he said. She's going to do housecleaning.

'You will have an affair very soon,' Michel told Ana, in Portuguese.

'What, with you, Michel?' Ana said, with a mean bite.

She marvelled at Ana's immunity from his tawdry charms. She so wanted to be like that: tough, discerning. She so wanted to be in control. She was let down by simple things, by the hollowness inside her, by her craving for experience, by her hope, and worst of all, by her body. That childish, smiling, pointing, gesticulating body, her mute self, which was only her betrayer-in-waiting.

In her bed, washed up on the broken shore of her fever, she is circling the truth. But it is well hidden, like marrow in the bone. She must gnaw through something visceral to get to it. Then again, she may not even try. She is less curious about the truth now.

She thinks of the diseased moments when she watched jaguars walk across the sleek sunset shore of her fever, how she felt it then, the truth, circling her like a vulture or a surveillance plane. Then the feeling dissolved and she found she was turning an object in her hand. Like a prism, it separated out the colours of light. She turned it round and round, examining each aspect. Yes, it was very beautiful.

Another line from one of her textbooks:

'Any object which can be examined from all sides gives the illusion of complexity. But it must be remembered that all sides are the same.'

'I don't want to talk about Ana. I'm sick of talking about her. I don't care what she does,' Jack said with a false ferocity that meant: I do care. I care a lot.

But they did talk. Jack took her for lunch and detailed the disintegration of their relationship. With Ana she discussed

Jack's childishness. She was careful never to betray confidences but to frame everything she said in her own opinion.

They also talked to Michel, and she knew he did not apply the same standards. He told Jack Ana's messiest sexual fears. He told Ana that Jack was using her. As for her, Michel spoke to her less and less now, since they had gone shopping for running shoes. He didn't even jog with her any more, only stayed to do press-ups in the beachside gymnasium.

At the time she thought: we are all wrapped up in one another. It was like being in a family: claustrophobic, visceral, and embarrassing. She felt alive again in a way she hadn't in years, in this chaos where everything was breaking down, everyone was talking about their troubles and problems. This is what life is, she told herself. Not the dim cavern of a library, an abstract study, a neat, ordered mind.

She was so wrapped up in the theatrical sinuosity of the situation she forgot to notice that he was winning. Because a fight had sprung up between them. At first accomplices in the empty apartment of their more successful friends, they were now rivals in an intricate struggle.

He was winning because he was making himself more necessary to them, offering each the most useful information, and as journalists they of course could not pass this up. She understood that after all the years she had known Ana and Jack, she was being made to compete with him. Why? she wondered. She would only be able to admit it later: because Ana and Jack made no distinction between her seven years of plodding friendship and his one year of more exciting Amazonian soap-opera life-story *amitié*.

She would leave next week. She invited him for a coffee at the Rio Sul espresso bar, where they had gone together in the first days of their stay in Ana and Jack's flat.

She said, 'I think you've taken advantage of me.'

He turned to her, his face torqued, closed. 'You have a terrible character.'

'Yes, yes,' she agreed, almost absent-mindedly. 'But why did you do it?'

'I perceived that you wanted something from me, so *j'ai coupé*,' he said. 'I cut.'

'Something from you?'

'You knew there was nothing between us,' he said.

Well, that was not quite right. There had been something between them.

'You have a terrible character,' he said again. 'I've never met anyone as awful as you. You don't know who you are. You don't know how to be a woman. You try to be like a man. You are ridiculous.'

Well that's true, she thought, glad to finally have her worst suspicions about herself confirmed.

At the same time she understood that she had colluded with him. She had been a conman too, conning her friends, eating their food and drinking their beer and staying in their apartment for far too long waiting for real life, for adventure to fall upon her head, pondering whether she should go to Argentina or to Ecuador, or to stay in Brazil and live this real life she told herself she was living.

When she first arrived in Brazil she needed the fan to sleep at night. She would come back from her runs drenched in sweat, breathing from within the furnace of her body. Now it is August and she simply cannot get warm. Cool draughts breeze through the bare corridors of the huge apartment, slamming doors and rustling the leaves of shivering plants. The rain falling through the courtyard is a continual deafening gush, wetting the garbage can and the clothes that will never be dry again, their threads marled and buttered. The sound of cascades running down the Morro da Urca, the barren pate of a mountain outside her window, make her feel she is living underneath a waterfall. The violence of the rain wakes her up at three in the morning. She goes to the window. She can see nothing but a malevolent sheet of grey water, falling down bare rock. It's not at all how she expected the tropics to be.

Now that her fever has broken they let her wander listlessly up and down the halls. She takes her coat-rack stand of a portable IV drip with her and it keeps pace with the stiff grace of a tango partner.

She has been hollowed out, wiped clean. She can have no more salt in her body, she imagines. What she did possess she has long deposited into the fetid sheets which she hopes the nurses are at this very moment changing.

How do you measure the value of an experience? She has her fever, of course, and the illness that will always threaten to recur. She has a few limp muscles and extra pounds from all the *choppe* and the *churrascos*. She is down a couple of hundred dollars and two or three friends, depending upon how you look at it.

She shuffles, feeling the liquid piddle into her veins like a puppy pissing on the carpet.

He came to the airport with Ana and Jack to see her off. She wanted to ask him, standing there in the bookshop, what do you want from them? Then she caught sight of him, in the newsstand, reading a magazine. His lips were moving as he read.

He moves his lips when he reads, she said to herself, insanely joyous. And suddenly she was free.

The day she arrived back to a full northern summer in June, hotter than it had been in Brazil, she began to pass out. First in the shower, then sitting down, then wandering around her empty flat. When it had happened the fifth time and she woke up to find herself with her head against a slab of concrete and felt the blood, she went to the doctor.

She is reading one of her anthropology texts. Suddenly she looks up from the book and out the window, where the thick leaves of summer trees are rubbing themselves together.

The truth, she thinks. *Write it.*

She shudders to shake off the thought. She turns to her textbook and reads:

How to identify the constituent units of an institution.

1. Reduce a culture to its structural elements (relationships of opposition, transformation, etc.).
2. Seek to explain homologies between various societies by dialectical terms.
3. Recognize that one simple man, one very charming, seemingly intelligent man, one man who has a great hard-luck story, can be everyone you have ever met. Everyone who has ever been your friend.
4. Societies survive on mutual manipulation. So the host tribe manipulates the visiting anthropologist and vice versa.

A época da chuva. The winter rainy season. He sits sprawled in the armchair. Ayrton Senna is dead, the funeral procession has wound around the black heart of Brazil. The World Cup games have started. *Mais um Brasil!* the television shouts, like a political slogan.

It is a Sunday and the mall is closed. There is nothing to do in Rio when it rains. In the expensive apartment the table is scattered with Brahma beer cans. She sits opposite him, watching television, caught in this pool of wet time.

On the TV the stupendously beautiful newsreader tells how the rains have been the heaviest this century. Rio has been shut down for two days. The sidewalks are underwater and the buses can't run. Pedestrians wade through the floods or clutch the elevated iron fences that front museums and art galleries and haul themselves along above the torrent. In three days, the newsreader says, Rio has received its total expected rainfall for the whole winter.

Nightmap

Helen steps out of the airport at four o'clock in the afternoon. A wet paw of heat swats her in the face. Each breath she takes feels as if she has inhaled soaked cotton which has then been grilled. Broccoli-shaped trees sway in the slanting afternoon sun. The sky seems much closer than it does in London. From the open window of a car she hears a radio announcer say it will be one hundred and two degrees.

'God,' Jocelyn groans. Her forehead is greased with sweat. 'Who would come to DC in August?'

They are sitting on the thin balcony of Jocelyn's apartment near Dupont Circle, eating tortilla chips and drinking beer. The studio apartment – an *efficiency*, Jocelyn tells her it's called in DC – stretches, air-conditioned and uncluttered, behind them. The apartment consists of a bed, a round glass-topped table, a lamp in the shape of a flower stalk, and a kitchenette with a lime-green fridge.

Helen takes another tortilla chip. 'Aren't you glad I came?'

'Sure,' Jocelyn says mildly. 'I just don't know why you had to come now. You could have waited until September. Congress would have been in session then, the museums not so crowded. Every redneck in the country comes to DC in August.'

The telephone rings and Jocelyn goes to answer it. Across the street Helen sees other couples doing exactly the same as she and Jocelyn, sitting on their balconies, sprawled in white plastic deck chairs, drinking beer. It is evening now, a bit cooler, but only slightly. During the day, she notices, everyone huddles in air-conditioned spaces, emerging on to balconies or outdoor cafés only at dusk, like nocturnal animals.

'It's for you.' Jocelyn hands her the cordless telephone.

She hears Ines' voice. 'You don't have to meet me if you don't want to. It doesn't matter.'

'Tomorrow. I'll ring you with a time.'

Jocelyn hangs up the phone and remains standing in the entrance to the kitchenette, her hand on her hip.

'Who was that?'

'Someone I met.'

'Met? You've only been here twenty-four hours. Met where?'

'In London.'

'Does she live here?'

'Sometimes. She's a journalist. She moves around a lot.' Helen puts her beer bottle down, empty. 'Where are we going to have dinner tonight?'

As they walk along Connecticut Avenue that night, Jocelyn tells her another DC horror story.

'Like, there's a guy who came home one night to find a few guys having a good time on the street near his apartment building. You know, nothing threatening, just hanging out.' Jocelyn's heels clack on the pavements. There is no one else on the sidewalk. 'They took his keys,' Jocelyn continues, 'took him up to his own apartment, relieved him of his possessions, and tied him up. It was two days before anyone found him. He was seriously dehydrated. You know government workers on Capitol Hill *never* walk home late at night.'

That's what Jocelyn is: a government worker, walking alone, or rather walking with Helen, another woman, which they both know isn't much better than walking alone. Jocelyn tosses a fugitive look over her shoulder. They lurch like this from one hotel bar to another, taking taxis as the evening progresses, Jocelyn always sighing with relief as she sinks into the vinyl folds of the back seat.

They drive home to Jocelyn's apartment and round the corner of Dupont Circle. On the street outside the Walmart a clump of men are arguing good-naturedly, saying words she has only previously heard in films: *geeze, muthafucka*. She watches them gesticulate in a manner both syncopated and random, as if they were cops directing phantom traffic. In their hands they clutch cans of beer, which they will eventually crush and throw into the gutter. Helen will see them there in the morning, faded and crumpled, silent witnesses to the secrets of the streetcorner night.

'Where's the coffee?'

Helen is rummaging in the kitchen – or kitchenette, as Jocelyn calls it – cabinets. Jocelyn is in the bathroom having one of her interminable showers. Jocelyn's habits haven't changed since they lived together at university: twenty-minute showers, followed by half-hour hair and makeup sessions.

Jocelyn's steam-muffled voice wafts through the door. 'Don't have any.'

'You don't have any *coffee*?'

'I take out.'

They go to the Java House for coffee. It is only nine o'clock but already the morning is thick and glazed with a lemony haze. It smells like afternoon, Helen thinks, although that could be just her jet lag setting in.

Jocelyn picks up her stirring stick delicately and balances it between her painted nails. 'It's not like you to pick someone up,' she says, not looking at her.

'I didn't *pick her up*. We were on a course together.'

Jocelyn scowls into the morning sun, and reaches for her sunglasses. She drinks her coffee carefully, as if it might scald her, or disrupt her lipstick. 'I don't know. I always wait for some guy to choose me like a goddamned plum on a fruit stall.'

Helen laughs. This is one of the things she likes about Jocelyn, she remembers: her honesty, her willingness to see herself with what Helen imagines is clarity.

That afternoon she and Jocelyn go to the Smithsonian. Most of what she sees bores her. But on her way back from the toilet she catches sight of a map on the wall. It's a world map, although black liquid covers most of it. On the left and the right of the canvas are ridges of darkness, uneven and shifting slightly, like the edges of a blanket underneath two sleeping bodies. In the middle is a swathe of light, where the east coast of North and South America shines.

She looks at the sign: NIGHTMAP. The map is calibrated so that it moves to show which parts of the world are in daylight and which are in night. Half of the map is covered by black liquid, like an oil slick. She watches its advance from east to west, its edges wobbling. With every minute it seems to move. She thinks she can feel the edges of that dark blanket sneak over her limbs. England is already dark, as is the rest of Europe. The edge of daylight begins again somewhere east of China. She is in the only part of the western hemisphere free from night.

That evening, Jocelyn takes her to the seafood market down on the banks of the Potomac. Thunderheads brood as she and Jocelyn crack open crabs and suck at the recalcitrant meat. Soon her fingers are coated with crab spice. She wipes them on the paper napkin, leaving orange streaks, and walks to the AT&T payphone.

She excavates a damp quarter from her pocket. As she

dials Ines' number the shrimp spice on her fingers begins to burn.

'I'll meet you tonight.'

'What are you going to do?' She hears the irritation in Ines' voice. 'Sneak out?'

'I'll just tell her the truth.'

'This woman – what's her name?'

'Jocelyn.'

'*Jocelyn*,' Ines says, as if it were a foreign name. 'Well, Jocelyn is just a friend. She has no right to make you feel guilty.'

'She thinks I've come here to see her, and I haven't,' Helen says into the receiver and checks over her shoulder to see if Jocelyn is watching her. She is. 'Sorry, but that makes me feel guilty.'

Before leaving, she and Jocelyn buy two Cokes from the crab-seller. He wears a plaid shirt and baseball cap. His accent has the molasses tones of Louisiana. He works on the boat from seven thirty in the morning until ten thirty at night, he tells them, every day, even Christmas and New Year.

The people who come to the fish market are almost all black or poor whites. Helen watches as enormous women emerge from the kind of cars that are familiar to her only through re-runs of seventies television shows like *The Dukes of Hazzard*. She reads their names – Impala, Reliant. The women make their way in slow-time over to the crab booth.

While Jocelyn is talking to the crab-seller she peers behind the stall. Through a houseboat window she can see a thin blond woman moving, cigarette smoke following her from room to room. Jocelyn is still talking. Jocelyn loves talking to these kinds of people – crab-sellers, ticket collectors. 'I feel I ought to keep in touch with what the man in the street is thinking,' Jocelyn has told her, more than once. Jocelyn works for a government publication that dedicates itself to representing the views of all classes of society, but Helen knows that its staff are all people like Jocelyn, with two parents and inherited money and expensive educations at universities like the one where she and Jocelyn met.

Jocelyn finally prises herself away from Mr Ordinary Joe crab-seller. Helen is thinking about Ines now. She finishes her Coke and crunches her can in her hand just as a gleaming white speedboat skips up the river.

'I like my life as a journalist,' Ines says. 'It suits me.'

They drink beers beneath the canopied café as the skies split open, finally. It has been waiting all day to rain. The rain is so fierce they have to shout. People run by, yelling and whooping, their clothes already welded to their skin. Almost immediately, it is cooler. The rain has broken the heat's back.

'You like dodging landmines in Nicaragua?'

Ines smiles impatiently. 'Yes. But it's not that.' She gesticulates nowhere in particular. 'It's more not knowing, moving, not knowing where I will be, who I will be with.'

'You're with me now.'

Ines swishes her swizzle stick through her drink slowly, not looking at her. 'I'm not on assignment.' She plucks chicken wings from their communal basket. 'I had to write two stories today. There's been some Middle East peace conference proposed.'

'By the Israelis or by Bush?'

'You know,' Ines licks her chicken-coated fingers, 'I'd rather not talk about it. I'd much rather talk about you.'

Ines looks tired, her eyes hollowed by fatigue, her brown-bottle Mexican profile leaning against the brick wall. Helen remembers the first time she saw Ines in the classroom where their course was being held, how her lips were thin and dry, like pieces of kindling.

The staircases of Ines' building are covered in gilt. The lobby is marble, the mirrors in the elevators bronze. Pyramids appear at the end of hallways. In the corners fake palms have sprouted.

'The Cairo's one of the oldest buildings in Washington,' Ines tells her in the elevator. Ines' apartment is on the tenth floor and looks west, to where Washington Cathedral stands white and floodlit, another of the city's many monuments, on the hill above Georgetown.

Helen is not used to being up so high. As she stands in front of the window she feels weightless, like a space traveller or trapeze artist or some other taker of unnecessary risks. She has the impression they are suspended there, in her apartment, breathing thin, oxygen-deprived air.

The next morning they stand in the street together outside the Cairo. Ines seems restless. She puts on her sunglasses. 'Hey, I just heard from my editor. I'm going to cover the Secretary of State's visit to Russia. I've got a seat on the State Department plane.'

Helen feels a flurry of panic erupt in her stomach. 'When?'

'Tuesday. We can meet tonight to talk about it. Damn—' Ines looks at her watch. 'I'm late. Hey, want to see the pictures for my Moscow visa?'

She digs in her purse and takes out two stark photographs.

'Well, they should let you in. You look very post-communist.'

'I look like I've just murdered somebody.'

Ines puts the photos back in their envelope, and kisses her. Over Ines' shoulder Helen sees a man turn around and stare.

*

She buzzed three times. Finally, Jocelyn opened the door. She walked away from it immediately without looking at Helen. On her head was a black sleeping mask and her eyes looked puffy. She got straight back into bed, even though it was eleven thirty in the morning.

Helen sat at the glass table. 'I told you there would be a chance I wouldn't be back last night.'

'I didn't understand why.' Jocelyn had propped herself up against a pillow. Helen saw there were tears in her eyes. 'You're taking advantage of my open-mindedness and tolerance.'

Tolerance. Helen had never heard the word said like that before. The way Jocelyn said it made it sound dangerous. Then, she'd never been on the wrong side of tolerance before.

'I'd feel differently if it had been a guy.' Jocelyn swung her legs over the side of the bed to get up. 'I have to go to the bathroom.' On her way there she stopped and turned around. 'What was she like?'

Helen frowned. 'I really like her. I'm surprised. She's kind.'

'No, I don't mean that,' Jocelyn said. She stood there in her see-through nightdress, her hand on her hip. 'None of this "she's nice, she's kind" stuff,' Jocelyn said. 'I want specifics, like did you have oral sex?'

She thought of Ines: thin and brown, dry as sticks. Her wayward generosity, those sad eyes copied from dusty portraits of seventeenth-century Spanish women. Ines' breath smells of garlic. Helen does not find this at all unpleasant. Her tongue is quick, darting. It seems to be trying to excavate something at the bottom of her. She has become used to men who thrust their tongue in her mouth with the same sausage linearity as a penis.

Helen looked up to find Jocelyn still standing there, her hand on her hip.

'I'm not going to answer your question.'

'I know.' Jocelyn turned around and went into the bathroom, slamming the door behind her.

They lie in bed. The air-conditioner is on full blast.

'How do you know Jocelyn?'

'We met at university.'

'But you never—'

'Oh no.' Helen laughs. 'She wouldn't. Besides, neither would I. Not then.'

Then Jocelyn had been a curiosity: a North American who wore orange jackets and yellow skirts and wasn't afraid to say what she really thought. But now, Helen had to admit, she felt a vague sensation she recognized as repulsion when she saw Jocelyn's perfectly painted mouth, her transparent nightgown, her bulky thighs, her taloned fingers, ready to shred any moment like an eagle with a rabbit in its claws.

Now, at twenty-five, Jocelyn has the heavy sculptedness of matrons. She has tinted her hair since she was sixteen and learned at the same age to wear long, close-fitting skirts of dark material to disguise her hips and thighs. Her nails are always perfectly lacquered. Helen has spent long minutes outside bathrooms waiting for Jocelyn to do her mouth: lipliner, followed by two coats of different-coloured lipstick, then blotter.

What disturbs Helen more, though, is that Jocelyn is beginning to remind her of her mother. She recognizes the tyrannically possessive streak and the clumsy but somehow effective attempts at manipulation. Are all women like this, or only future mothers? And how could Helen have missed these things when they were in university together?

Ines sighs and rolls away from her and on to her stomach. 'So what are you going to do next?'

'Next? You mean, in my life? *Next.*' Helen repeats the

word. 'I can never think that way. I think I want to go to Stanford and study anthropology and end up somewhere in Equatorial Guinea.'

Ines takes a tendril of hair between her fingers, rolls it around them tightly, then lets it go. 'I went to Berkeley for a while.'

'What were you doing there?'

'A course for minority journalists.'

'You're a minority?'

'I couldn't get a newspaper job for love or money, so decided to become an Hispanic. I dropped my father's name, took my mother's and got on this course. Then, bingo, they were falling all over themselves to give this li'l ole minority gal a job.' Ines levers herself off the bed, stretches and yawns. 'It's not good for us to stay in bed this long. Your body collapses, you know. It's two o'clock. We should go out.'

Helen groans. 'It's two hundred degrees out there.'

'Come on.' Ines pulls her off the bed. 'We'll go to an air-conditioned bar somewhere. There's a story I want to tell you.'

Later they sit in the rooftop bar of one of the downtown hotels. The breeze from twenty storeys up keeps it cool. They both order summer drinks – margaritas and daiquiris.

'It was in Chicago, when I was at university.' Ines begins the story she has been saving for her. 'And in walks my first-year roommate, Judy. I knew nothing. But even I could tell she was a dyke. So,' Ines grins, and her smile, molasses-slow, spreads across her face, 'of course, we fell in love. Eventually my mother caught on. She told my sister and they gave me an ultimatum: give up Judy or I would never be allowed to see my nine-year-old niece again.

'I called my sister in Pittsburgh in the middle of the night and asked her for help, but she said she couldn't, and hung up on me. So we split up. But I couldn't stay at college that year. I just cried all the time. I took the year off and moved in with my sister and my niece in Pittsburgh. That was the year I was twenty. I got a job at a bar called Raspberry Rhinoceros, serving cocktails in the evenings. During the day I was a salad prep person working under a very tired black woman. She wasn't very nice to me, but I couldn't blame her. My other part-time job was at a bookstore where it was my responsibility to spray Fantastik on the book covers to make them shine.'

Helen wants to laugh but they move her unutterably, these sad vignettes of early twenties North American failure. She is still there herself to a degree, although American experience always seems so much more outlandish and real. Helen's is an inevitably more genteel English version of career frustration involving low-paid editorial jobs in which her task is to photocopy the manuscripts of famous novelists.

'I could move.'

Ines' eyes narrow. 'Move where?'

'I don't know. I've been in London so long now.'

'You mean move to the States?' Ines' eyes are still watching her very closely, like Helen imagined she would look at a soldier at a difficult border crossing.

'Or I could move to Europe,' Helen stutters. She could see Ines didn't want to talk about her moving to the States. 'I love Europe. Sometimes I just say the names of those cities to myself, but in the proper way, you know, *Athinai*, instead of Athens. *Bucuresti. Beograd. Lisboa. Marseille*. You know my favourite, though? *Odessa*. I think if I had a daughter I would name her that.'

'You could move to Europe.' Ines nods. 'You could go anywhere.'

'Right now I just want to go to your place.'

Ines sighs. 'It's just. I don't – I don't feel very intense

about you. I don't really feel as though I need to see you next month. I think we should just leave it open. I just feel very . . . numb.' Ines stares into her drink. 'I swore I'd never have another long-distance relationship again. I'm looking for someone who lives in the same city, someone to live with. This is what you get from taking up with an old and tired woman.'

For a second Helen thinks Ines is going to take her hand, but Ines' brown fingers scuttle back to the safety of her glass. 'I don't know which comes first – I don't feel intensely for you because you're not here or—'

'—because I'm not here you don't feel intensely for me.' Helen finishes Ines' sentence. 'If you felt "intensely", as you put it, for me then it wouldn't matter where I was.'

'That's why I have my doubts. *God*,' Ines groans. 'I remember myself at twenty-three. I'm still struck by panic sometimes when I go to a restaurant that I'll have to do that again. And when I think of all the jobs I've had since then, the places I've lived, the lovers I've had . . .' Ines folds a napkin over her mouth, wipes her lips on it so that they become, just for a second, transparent behind the thin tissue. 'I'm just a phase for you. You've got so much to go through. I'll just be an interim affair.' *Interim* – the word and its meaning refuses to leave Helen's mind. Interim, meaning, between things.

'I'm just not so comfortable with the idea of a woman lover,' Ines continues. 'I want to have children. I want to be married. I want all that, you know. I can't help it. I've always wanted that. I've just been more wayward than most people.'

Helen tries to say something, but finds there's nothing there, not in her mind, or on her tongue, nor are there any words caught in her teeth like pieces of spinach.

'I've got an idea,' Ines says suddenly. She sounds almost

enthusiastic. 'Why don't we spend the weekend at Rehoboth Beach? Summer's almost over. I haven't been to the beach once this summer.'

'Where's this beach?'

'On the Delaware coast. It's the best beach around here.'

'I don't know.' She had hardly even heard of Delaware. 'What about Virginia, or the Carolinas?'

'Do you know how long it would take to get there?'

Helen shrugs. She really isn't familiar with the distances in North America, except that they are huge.

'We've only got a weekend, remember.'

'Can we rent a car?'

'I have to save my money,' Ines says. 'I'll be all over Russia and Germany. I might even save enough money to come and see you in Europe, when you move there.' She smiles. 'Let's just get the bus. We'll get a room overlooking the beach.'

Helen has a quick vision of them on a wooden balcony. The ocean crashing at their feet. Towels are thrown over the railings. And maybe, who knows? She could change Ines' mind. She sees bed, crumpled sheets, their toothbrushes and hair mousse mixed up in the bathroom.

A gust of wind roars across the terrace bar. 'There's a thunderstorm coming in from Virginia.' The waiter points beyond the Potomac. They both look up from their drinks and see the tor-like clouds advancing.

Ines takes her hand, startling the waiter. 'Come on. Let's go.'

'I'm going back to London.'

Jocelyn stared at her. 'But your flight—'

'I know. But I've got to. I've sorted it out with the airline.' Helen gathered her things in silence so as not to give herself away. Jocelyn sat at her glass-topped table, drinking wine.

'I'll see you then. Thanks for having me—' Helen can barely wait to be out of the apartment.

Jocelyn didn't look up from her wine. She waved her away.

'Oh, well, then—' Helen closed the door behind her.

Then she was on the street, one of those wide-hipped intersections bordered by glassy office buildings and their cavernous interiors of marble and atria. In only a week she felt she had actually absorbed something of the city, its bullying monuments fronted by giant reflective pools, continent-built clouds floating in the water, traffic jams snarling avenues with breezy names, the streetcorner gesticulators, the strange, slow rain.

The bus station is behind the train terminus, in an area of Washington where Helen can quickly tell from the honks of passing taxis that a woman should not be walking alone, bags in hand.

Ines is waiting for her in the foyer. 'I thought you weren't going to come.'

'I thought the same thing.'

They boarded the bus alongside big men with sunburns and drawn-out accents. As they found their seats Helen whispered to Ines, 'Why are we the only people on the bus who don't look like poor itinerants?'

Ines shrugged. 'Most of them are Virginians who work up here. Nobody takes the bus in the States when they can drive. And if you don't have a car you're poor.' Ines said this as if it were a long-practised mathematical theory and Helen just nodded. She understood. It was very simple. In fact, she had decided, things were simpler in the States.

Within minutes they were driving down the interstate. It was late afternoon and soon it would be dusk. Helen watched the city slip by. They glided above rivers, estuaries, and thin houses where women in sleeveless tops, sweat stains between their breasts, lolled in front yards. Whole families sat on the concrete steps of their houses. They watched the bus go by with what Helen imagined were envious eyes.

She turned to Ines. 'It's so different.' What she meant was, *It's so frightening*.

Ines caught her meaning and laughed. Helen thought for a second she might be laughing at her. 'If you think this is bad, you should see Texas.'

'You've lived in Texas?'

'Oh God.' Ines rolled her eyes. 'Have I ever. In Texas they gave me the suburban-axe-murder beat.' She laughed. 'They thought I was good at talking to victims. I can tell you twenty different axe-murder and a dozen drifter stories. You know there's a whole segment of the Texas population dedicated to drifting around those big empty spaces waiting for some woman to come along so they can kill her?'

Helen shook her head. No, she didn't know that.

'Well, I think there should be a public information campaign. They could put up a road sign, you know, like those deer-crossing ones. Drifter Crossing. Beware.' Ines sighed. 'But the thing I hated most about Texas was that it was impossible to get anywhere without driving, and even then it was impossible. One time I was driving to the K-Mart, which was on the edge of the highway. I passed the K-Mart, but it was on the other side. Now all I wanted to do was to get to the goddamn K-Mart, but I couldn't. There was no exit to the other side for about twenty miles. I finally had to pull in at an Arby's and I ate a hamburger out of sheer frustration.'

The bus glided through smokestacks, oil refineries, and occasional patches of coastal sludge. As they neared Baltimore the water of the bay was black. The cars on the highway were white Impalas, red clay-dust skirting the

Virginia licence plates, the same kind of cars that frequented the Potomac crab market.

Helen had never had those kinds of experiences; driving all night, or all day, just to eat a hamburger. In London she had never been more than five minutes from a corner grocer's. Nor had she covered wars, as Ines had done, in Central America. She would be afraid if they suddenly had to get off the bus here, among the oblong warehouses and the smokestacks and the dark, empty streets that snaked between them.

'Ladies and gentlemen . . .' The bus driver, a man with tiny legs and a stomach that hung over his belt, began his announcement. They were coming into Baltimore, where they would have to change to get the bus to the beach.

In Baltimore the station information booth was staffed by a tired-looking white man. In fact, the only white face working in the bus station.

'No bus to Rehoboth Beach here, honey,' he said.

'Are you sure?' Ines said quickly in the voice of a reporter challenging an age-old assumption. 'We were told we should change at Baltimore.'

'Sorry, honey.'

'I don't believe this.' Ines walked away and Helen had to trot to catch up with her. 'Let's go ask a driver. They're the only ones who know what's going on.'

'Sure, I'll get you to Rehoboth Beach,' the driver said as he clipped tickets. 'I'll drop you off at the corner of the I-95, and then you can pick up another bus for Rehoboth.'

'By that time it'll be what?' Ines said. Helen thought Ines' accent had changed, but she wasn't sure. Maybe that was a technique of journalists, to talk more like their subjects and so to gain their trust.

The driver didn't look up from his tickets. 'Eleven-fifteen is the time the Rehoboth bus passes.'

Helen darted a look at Ines. 'What if we miss it?'

'Let's do it. I'm going to get to that beach if it kills me.'

Ines boarded the bus but Helen hung back. She wanted to ask the driver one more time just to be sure. 'This bus is going to Delaware City, honey.' He threw her a tired look. 'No bus for Rehoboth is guaranteed. You might make the connect, you might not.'

Ines was already down the aisle and looking for two seats. Helen tried to get her attention without shouting. Most of the seats were already occupied by women with children eating candy out of large crinkly plastic bags.

'Ines,' Helen called. 'He says we might not make it. We can't stand beside the I–95 in the night.'

'Yes we can.'

A fat man in an aisle seat spoke up. 'No, honey, listen to ya girlfriend. It's not worth it.'

'It's not worth it.' Helen found herself echoing the man. 'Just for a weekend.'

Ines turned around from putting her bag in the overhead rack, frowning. 'What do you want to do, then?'

The locust noise of kids rustling candy wrappers filled the bus. She could feel the fat man's eyes on them. *Whadya wanna do, honey*?

'I don't know.' Helen shrugged. 'It seems useless to go on.'

In that moment Helen sees Ines' face perfectly. Her eyes are deep-set, making her look older than she actually is. Her hair spirals around her face. Her lips are thin, turned down. Here is a woman who has talked her way on to planes, bribed herself through Central America. Helen can see she wishes she were alone. If she were alone, she would have got to Rehoboth Beach.

As Ines comes off the bus, trailing her luggage behind her, Helen says to her (it is all she can think of to say), 'Why do people give you the wrong information?'

*

It's midnight when they get back to DC.

'Do you want to stay at the Cairo?' Ines doesn't say, *with me*.

'I have to,' Helen says. 'I mean, I've told Jocelyn I left town.'

'Okay,' Ines shrugs.

They ride the bronzed elevator to the tenth floor. The other night, when she had kissed Ines in this elevator, the ride seemed to take seconds. Now it goes on for ever.

Ines opens the door. 'I'm bushed.' She immediately falls into bed and turns her body towards the wall. Helen undresses slowly and gets in carefully beside her, saying 'Me too.'

The irregular sound of Ines' breathing seems to fill the room. The digital lights of the television and the CD player blink on and off. But Helen can't get to sleep at all. She lies as motionless as possible on her back.

America seems so far away tonight. She feels she will never know it, but it is out there, somewhere in the distance, she understands, beyond the gleaming monuments of Washington. In the museum the nightmap is swallowing the continent, covering it with a black liquid blanket of night. Jocelyn's body is out there, she thinks, turning over and over in her efficiency apartment. Groups of men on the corner by the Wal-mart are forming and re-forming. Bus drivers are taking people to Delaware. The crab-sellers are asleep in their river-boat trailers, the waveless Potomac a sheet of glass underneath them, their women moving from room to room, trailing smoke behind them. Further away, on the edges of the nightmap's dark crease, the drifters meander through Texas, looking for women to kill.

Finally she gives up on sleep. She slides out of bed and goes to stand in front of the window. The night is black and silky, punctured only by the floodlit bulk of Washington Cathedral standing sentinel over Georgetown.

On the first night she had spent in her apartment Ines had caught her staring at it and came to stand beside her, draping a damp arm around her shoulders. 'Do you know it's the third largest cathedral in the world?' Ines said, her mouth close to her ear. As she settles into the rocking chair for the night she wonders where the other two are. This is the last thing she remembers thinking before she falls asleep.

The Raw and the Cooked

QUAILS' EGGS IN LEMON MAYONNAISE WITH ROMANIAN UPSIDE-DOWN POTATO CAKE

Adrian tapped her on the shoulder. 'You've got a single on table ten. Bad luck, huh?'

Jesse peered through the people strung around the bar and saw a man in a black dinner jacket sitting by himself, studying the menu intently.

'Where did he come from? I didn't see him come in.'

Adrian shrugged. 'Neither did I. He must have been beamed down. Look at him, though – all dressed up and no one to impress.'

She sighed. Single diners ordered half-bottles of wine and no cognac because by that point they were so overwhelmed by their singleness amidst a restaurant of canoodling couples they only wanted to flee. She would make half the tip from a single diner as from a couple, maybe even less. Then again, there was the single diner's mortification tip: when single men were so ashamed of being alone that, should she manage to charm them into thinking she hadn't noticed their singleness, or even that she admired it, they would leave her a ridiculous amount of money.

Jesse went to light his candle, a transparent prismatic disc filled with colourless camp oil. The candles had been carefully chosen by Miranda, the owner. In fact every detail of the restaurant, even the carnivorous-looking flowers that were delivered daily by florists dressed in white doctors' coats, was the result of hours of scrutiny of style magazines on Miranda's part.

She extended the burning match to the wick. As it fizzed into light, Jesse saw his face for the first time – or rather she saw two large, coffee-coloured eyes, and the flame flickering in them.

The fire-eyes turned towards her. 'What do you recommend?'

'Well, for a starter I'd recommend the quails' eggs. For a main course the pork medallions are excellent, very tender. To drink I recommend the Chilean Merlot—'

She stopped to find him staring at her. 'What's your name?' he said.

'Jesse.'

'Is that short for Jessica?'

'I suppose so. No one's called me that since I was four, though. What can I get you to drink?'

'My name's Colin. My wife's just died.'

Jesse blinked. 'I'm sorry.'

'You look like a kind person, Jesse. You look like you could help me.'

'I'm sorry.'

'Can you get me a Scotch and soda?'

'Sure.'

'Will you come for a drink with me tonight?'

'I don't know.'

She turned around and went back to the servery.

Adrian was a bus boy and not yet nineteen, and according to the Ontario Liquor Licensing Act it was illegal for him to deliver drinks to the tables, but Miranda was screaming at the chef in the kitchen so Jesse risked it.

'Go put this on the single guy's table.' She plunked the glass on his tray.

'But, but—' Adrian stuttered.

'Just do it.'

She went around to the back of the kitchen and opened the walk-in freezer. She shut the door behind her and exhaled. Her breath condensed and puffed upwards into the sides of meat that dangled from the hooks on the ceiling. On the dessert racks three of Miranda's chocolate cakes squatted. Beside them were white plastic buckets of pre-prepared raspberry coulis. It was a deep brown-red, like blood.

She wondered what to do. Maybe this was sexual harassment. She thought of all the articles she had read in the student newspaper, the notices posted all around campus like a squad of grandmothers: Have you been harassed? Contact the Officer for Sexual Harassment or your College Ombudsman.

She remembered the look in his eyes as he had said it: *You look like you could help me.* How he had been sad, pleading, yet dignified. When the flush that had spread over her face like a rash had subsided, she took a deep breath and returned to the restaurant floor, short-cutting through the kitchen, where prep chefs were quartering massive tunas, rosé blood trickling from the cutting boards.

She approached his table. This time she saw more of his face. He had a long, straight nose, straw-coloured hair, and a delicate, structured face that looked as though it was suspended on strings. He was quite beautiful, for a man.

'Okay, Colin,' she said, scowling to cover the reaction her new appreciation of his face had provoked. 'But you'll have to wait for me somewhere until I cash out. That may not be till one. How about the Rivoli. I'll meet you there.'

When she walked into the Rivoli she suddenly had the feeling that she might not recognize him. The light in the restaurant was always so low; in the candlelight she could never be sure of the colour of a person's eyes or the exact age of their skin. But then she spotted him, sitting in a narrow booth by himself, stalking a single beer.

'Hi.' He rose. 'Sit down. What can I get you to drink?'

She watched him fight his way through girls in black leather to the bar. In the colder light of the club she could tell he was older. He had very fine lines that crinkled like puff pastry around his eyes, but she had seen the colour of his eyes correctly – they were an unusual light brown, nearly amber.

While he went to get the drinks she scanned the paintings that covered the club's walls: done in lurid, nearly fluorescent colours, they showed people of indeterminate sex in elaborate biker gear wearing tortured expressions.

Colin put two wet bottles of beer on the table. 'Where did these paintings come from? They're dreadful.'

She could hear the faintest trill of a foreign accent, or not so much an accent but a carefully cadenced manner of speaking.

'Where are you from?' she asked.

'I grew up in South Africa. But I haven't lived there for a long time.' He looked furtively over his shoulder as if he were worried about being spotted. 'I don't like being in this city. I look at these people and think of the word "slavish". It's a wonderful word for a horrible thing, don't you think?'

'If you don't like it here, why don't you leave?'

'I am leaving.'

'When?'

'In September. I was only living here because my wife's job was here.' There is a small pause between the *my wife* and the *was*.

'Where are you going?'

'Cape Town. That's where I'm from, originally.'

He began to drill his fingers on the edge of the table. It wasn't the normal sound of drumming fingers: the sound they made was percussive, as if steel were embedded in their tips. Almost immediately he became aware of what he was doing and stopped. He curled his long, fine fingers around his bottle of beer.

'Are you a pianist?'

He looked startled. 'How did you know?'

Jesse nodded towards his fingers. 'You have a piano-player's hands.'

'You're very observant.'

'Hands are one of the first things I notice about people,' she said, her voice betraying how pleased she was to be so observant.

'Yes, of course,' he said in the manner of having long believed this was true without having really considered it.

'Where do you play?'

'Anywhere I'm invited. At the moment I'm doing three weeks with the national symphony.' He gestured in the direction of the downtown concert hall.

'What did your wife do?'

'She was a psychologist.'

'And you think a waitress can help you?'

'You're not a waitress—'

'I am, that's all I am, a waitress—'

Colin shook his head. 'Just because you do something doesn't make you it.'

'It does, in this town. It's easy for you, you do something interesting, something accomplished.'

He shrugged. 'At the moment I find everything interesting.'

Suddenly she was angry. 'So do you go around having dinner by yourself and then picking up your waitresses and getting them to confess things to you they didn't even know themselves?' She wanted to say: *Did you learn this trick from your psychologist wife?*

He frowned. 'You're a waitress. That's not a confession—'

'An admission, then.'

'It's a truth. It's all right to tell the truth.'

'No it's not. People will use it against you.'

'I won't.'

'Listen,' she rose from the booth, 'I've got to go.'

He reached across the table and took her wrist, gently but firmly enlacing it in his long sea-anemone fingers. 'No you don't.'

'You're right.' She extricated her wrist. 'But I'm going anyway.'

'I'm coming in again next Tuesday,' he said. 'I'll ask for your section.'

WARM SALAD OF CORN-FED CHICKEN WITH BALSAMIC VINEGAR AND SESAME SEED DRESSING, TOSSED WITH TUSCAN BOCCONCINI AND ARUGULA

That summer she lived in an attic apartment roughly the size of a closet, strung three floors above the street in a glowering former mansion, now divided into illegally sized apartments. The summer's heat was like the sweat of a fever breaking; no breeze came from the lake and the city had become a great stinking flower, one of those voracious tropical blooms she had seen only on television – orchids or heliconias.

She felt she was moving through a substance thicker than air. She swam through her nights like a fish in an aquarium, surrounded by other gaudy fish doing the same, fluttering their fins, opening their mouths and gulping the rancid air.

The nights she worked at the restaurant she would walk home by the longest route, down Queen Street, passing beautiful people dressed identically in black shorts and sleeveless shirts, Jesus sandals flopping on their feet. At Spadina she turned the corner and headed north into sudden empty blocks of wholesale bridal stores. In their windows satin dresses absorbed the green neon from flickering Vietnamese restaurant signs. She would arrive home at her

Chinatown mansion, heave her body up her apartment steps, unnaturally exhausted, before falling into a black dreamless sleep.

That Thursday he came in again.

'Jesse, you have a visitor,' Miranda hissed menacingly. Miranda hated it when people came in to see the staff; unless she were going to milk them of a hundred dollars, Miranda had little use for humanity.

Jesse saw him standing by the hostess' booth, much taller than she remembered and younger, somehow. Tonight his face had the unlined, unfissured quality of expensive marble.

She walked up to him. 'I can't meet you tonight. I'm going out with some friends.'

'You think I'm pursuing you.'

'Well? Isn't that what you're doing?'

She had never been pursued before. She wasn't even sure that she qualified for it, pursuit. She thought that to be pursued you had to be elegant, mysterious, to project an idea of yourself and lodge it in another person's mind like a hard, unfinished jewel.

'Look,' she said, with more impatience than she actually felt. 'Just tell me, so we can get this over with: why did you think I could help you?'

'I don't know. It was something in your manner. It was just a feeling.' He was silent for a moment and she could tell he had caught something in the music the restaurant was playing. She could almost see him cataloguing its sequences. He turned his attention back to her and looked at her carefully. 'I think you're unusual.'

'What do you mean? Unusual-looking?'

'It's got nothing to do with looks. Haven't you noticed how different you are?'

She frowned. 'Different?'

'The other waitresses, they move as if they're seeking approval. You don't even care.'

'Approval from who?'

'It's even in the way you put a drink on the table,' he said. 'You're straightforward, you're honest.'

'You can tell that just from the way I put a drink on the table?'

'More or less.'

'What else can you tell about me?'

'That you don't know yourself very well. You're sight-reading your own score. Sorry,' he shrugged, and smiled. 'My metaphors are always musical.'

'I don't really go for men. I mean, I'm a lesbian.'

'That doesn't matter. I just need someone to talk to.' His eyes skittered over her face with the delicacy of grace notes. They really were amazing eyes; they had some mercurial quality that made her think they could never belong to a woman. Maybe men had different eyes, perhaps she hadn't looked enough at them. Like the eyes of another creature, like the animals that had inhabited the winter forests of her childhood: a deer, a bear.

'Do you like it? Without your wife?' She didn't know why she said it. She hadn't meant to be cruel.

He seemed unsurprised. 'Sometimes.' He looked away from her. 'Sometimes I feel free. It doesn't last for long.'

He came back the next Tuesday, as he had told her he would; the orchestra didn't play on Tuesdays. They went out for a drink, somewhere on Richmond or Adelaide Street – although she had been in the city a year she still mixed up those wide, eventless streets and their upright, Anglo-Saxon names.

The bar was dark and at first they didn't talk. Each moment Jesse stayed she wondered why she was still there. She had never felt anything like it before, this combination of inertia, fascination, and fear.

She decided to make an attempt at conversation. 'I'm in summer school. I'm taking Canadian History 300. The lectures are really interesting. Did you know that before Newfoundland joined the Confederation—'

'I don't want to hear about it,' Colin said. 'I'm sorry, I don't mean to be rude, but I'm trying to find a way forward. I'm not interested in the past.'

She looked down at her hands. 'Then I don't know what to say.'

'I sit in my room and think of food, even though I've just eaten,' he said, his eyes closed. 'As soon as things happen I forget them. I can't get hold of things. I feel like I'm covered with grease. Slippery.'

'All I want is to know things,' she said. 'Real things.'

'That's strange—' He looked like he was making an effort to keep himself tight and under wraps, as if he really wanted to stand up and start yelling at someone. 'That's just what I don't want any more. I'm sick of knowing things.'

'Then what do you want?'

'I want my wife back. If I can't have that, then I want a lover.' In that light, his eyes were fizzy and opaque, like champagne. 'I want to feel something for someone else again. Something—' He pointed his finger at his own chest. He breathed in deeply, sharply, so that for a second she thought there might be something wrong with him. 'I want to feel *something*.'

'I think you're making a mistake. With me, I mean. You're pursuing me because I'm not available to you. You'd be better off with someone else.'

'And why are you not available to me?'

Jesse sighed. 'I already told you.'

Colin pursed his lips, sat back in his chair. 'Okay, let's just suppose, just for a second, that I am a Martian—'

'Okay, you're a Martian—.'

'—and that I'd never heard of lesbianism. Now, how would you describe it to me?'

Jesse frowned. 'You want me to describe lesbianism?'

He made an impatient gesture. 'I want you to tell me what you think it means.'

'Right. Well.' She pursed her lips. 'There are two types. It's often very difficult to distinguish between them. There's Real and Fake Lesbianism.'

'Tell me about the fake kind first.'

'The fake sort is when you've slept with women but have had relationships with men, or want to. Lesbianism is not defined by the fact that you've had relationships with women.'

'So what's Real Lesbianism?'

'When you are intellectually, emotionally and physically attracted to women.'

'And that's what you are, a Real Lesbian.'

'Yep.' She nodded. 'The real thing.'

'You mean there's no chance of you being attracted to me, just because I'm not a woman?'

'I don't think so.'

She could see a smile trying to break out, but he pulled back the edges of his mouth at the last moment. 'That's not very open-minded of you.'

'It has nothing to do with my mind.'

Colin leaned forward. 'You just said you were intellectually, physically and emotionally attracted to women. Now two of those things at least have quite a lot to do with the mind. Are you sure you aren't looking for an identity in the shape of a sexual orientation? Have you ever had a relationship with a man?'

'Oh come on, I don't need any of this homophobic propaganda.'

He sat back, folded his arms across his chest. 'They're just words you use to attack people because you don't like what they're saying.' He sighed. 'I'm sad you're not more flexible. I'm sad for you.'

She rose from the table. 'I don't need your sadness.'

Then she is on the sidewalk outside the bar on Richmond or Adelaide Street. The CN tower blinks on and off. There is no traffic. As she bends down to unlock her bicycle from the parking meter, she feels a hand around her waist. The next thing she knows, she is hard up against his body. She has just hit a brick wall. But it's not painful, or unpleasant – it's nice, in fact, the way the brick serrates her skin.

They kiss, she doesn't know for how long. A wave of warm liquid spreads slowly through her stomach. She feels as if large pieces of furniture are being slid across a wooden floor that has been greased just for that purpose. She always thought kissing a man would be distasteful, that his tongue would be overly searching or clumsy, or thick and rolled-up, like a sausage. But Colin's is tentative, searching, shy. In the end it is Jesse who grips the skin on the back of his neck and slips her fingers between the renegade tendrils of his hair.

BUFFALO STEAK DONE 'BLUE' IN SINGAPORE SOYA SAUCE

They sat opposite each other, their fingers curled around their beers.

'So if you don't want to be a waitress, why do you do it?' he asked.

'I don't know. I actually enjoy it, you know, sometimes. It's like theatre. I have a role to play for a while, I get to watch people, to be watched. In a way it's a lot more interesting than reading books in the library, but then waitressing isn't going to get me anywhere and studying will. To tell you the truth, I really admire what you do, being a performer.'

He shrugged. 'I just do something I love doing.'

'But did you always know you wanted to do it?'

'My father was a pianist, so was my uncle. In a way I didn't have much of a choice.' He smiled, but there was a twinge in his eyes and she could see there had been some hurt, some struggle involved, before he had arrived at this easy explanation. 'I'm a bit concerned, for you I mean,' he said. 'What do you want to do? What is it you want to be?'

Jesse smiled. 'No one's asked me since the guidance counsellor in high school.'

'I know you don't want to be a waitress. So what is it you want to be?'

'I don't know.' She shook her head. 'It's like . . .' She stopped for a moment. 'It's like you've been using a word – *coercion*, let's say – all your life, and then someone suddenly asks you to define it and you don't know. I always thought I would know what I wanted to do with my life, and now that I'm an adult I can't get close to the idea of a future, of *my* future. It's just, the things I'm supposed to aspire towards – I just can't imagine them. I can't see myself living with a lover and our cat in some upstairs apartment on Bathurst. I can't see myself dressed out of an LL Bean catalogue holding a golden lab puppy and living some lesbian lumberjack fantasy out in the middle of nowhere. Or going to Paris and emulating those women in the thirties, you know, Gertrude Stein and Djuna Barnes. Being a faux-Euro-lesbian and writing deranged novels.'

'But these scenes seem dead to me, lifeless,' he said. 'As if you've picked them up from a book or a film.'

'I know. I'm afraid of that. I never wanted to be one of those people who can only see themselves in poses or frames. I want to get close to something. But I honestly don't know how.'

'The only way I know to get past that is to *do* things,' he said. 'To develop a passion for doing. It doesn't really matter what it is, but I think we can solve fewer things through contemplation than we would like to think.'

'Is that why you're a musician? Because it's based on doing?'

'I suppose.' He pursed his lips. 'At the end of the day I know what I've done, I've got something to show for it.'

He ran a hand through his wheat-coloured hair. Something in this gesture reminded her that he could be ten years older than her. What things would she learn in those coming years, the ones that separated her youth from his gravity?

It didn't come in the form of a flash, a premonition; it was rather like being visited by a future memory. Suddenly she saw that she would try to make sense of the things that Colin was struggling with, and like him she would fail.

'If you don't mind me asking, what happened?'

'To my wife? It was just cancer.' He turned his hands, palms up, on the table, as if they contained explanations. 'It was just cancer. By the time they found out it was too late. Same old story.'

'Same old story as what?'

'I mean. It's not a very original story.'

'But every death is original,' Jesse said. 'Just like every life.'

Before she could do anything about it he leaned over the table and kissed her.

She finds herself drifting off more and more often when she should be concentrating on things like whether the woman on table eight ordered decaf or regular cappuccino, or on her Canadian History course. She finds herself wondering what it would have been like to have lived her life as him – to be a pianist, born in South Africa.

She runs through the little that she knows of him: she knows that he feels most at home in Europe, with the exception of Germany; she knows his grandmother was Jewish and died in Theresienstadt. He is desperate to leave the New World, and in this category he includes Africa. Going back to South Africa to play with the Cape Town symphony, he told her, is just the first step in a series of actions that will get him, eventually, to London, Paris, or Madrid. A concert pianist has to be strategic but at the same time he has to go where he is invited – 'A strange combination of freedom and total dependency,' he had said, and laughed in that way, with a wince in his eye.

She imagines herself there, too, in any one of these cities, although she has been to none of them. She imagines herself with him, walking through hulking grey concert halls, fingering thick tapestries, wandering in and out of bijoux shops on expensive streets that were once the scene of riots and wars.

But what would they do together? Would she sit in the audience night after night and watch him fall in love with the beautiful French principal violinist, or the glamorous percussionist? Colin and the percussionist would go for a drink together after the performance and he would say, 'My girlfriend is a waitress, or a student. *And* a lesbian.' Then they would both laugh, and the violinist or percussionist would take him home to bed.

She tries to imagine what it would be like to lose a wife, a husband. She would feel tricked, like when she used to play hide and seek with girls she thought were her friends. She would have to hide and she hid and hid, and they never came looking for her, just left her there, behind a tree or under a desk, and went off in a group to the drugstore to try on lipgloss. Or maybe it would be more sudden than that: she imagines waking up one day to find her home has been taken by a tornado. It has been lifted up and up, until it is so far above her head that there is no sense in chasing it at all.

On the day his wife dies he goes to work, because it is a Saturday night and he has to play on Saturday nights. There's no one to replace him. It's not as if they can dig up a concert pianist with two hours' notice who knows the entire score and has been practising it with the orchestra for the past month. He enters the grey mirrored hallways of Roy Thompson Hall and smells the astringent fumes of marble and chrome.

The night his wife dies he has to play Khachaturian's Piano Concerto in D flat. It is one of his favourites because its sounds are fractured, minor-keyed, itinerant. Khachaturian was from Armenia, Colin told her. He composed to the sound of earthquakes.

ROAST LEAN DIAMONDS OF TENNESSEE PORK WITH A TART ENGLISH MUSTARD GLACÉ

The next Tuesday they met in an unusual location, a smart bistro uptown. She had become paranoid about anyone from the restaurant or the university or her lesbian friends seeing them together and word getting out that she had abdicated and was now a heterosexual, just like everyone else.

'So tell me,' he began in his awkward way, like a psychiatrist. 'What do you like about women?'

Jesse sighed. This really wasn't something she wanted to talk about. It was too much hard work, all this self-analysis. She wasn't used to it. 'Their hesitancy, I suppose, their capacity for that kind of dreamy yearning for someone. I've never met a man who actually *yearned*, rather than just taking what was in front of him, what was most convenient. And women are so smart, emotionally. You can have an intense relationship with a woman. With a man you're always playing games.'

'I completely disagree. In fact, I think that's utter bullshit. The kind of relationship I had with my wife had nothing – absolutely nothing – to do with sexual games.' Colin's eyes had turned the colour of molasses. He looked at her from somewhere behind these liquorice vats. She could see he was very angry. Then he shook his head slightly, as if to dislodge a fly.

'So where do you go?'

'Go?'

'Where do you go to meet women?'

'Nowhere. I mean, I don't have to go anywhere to meet women.'

'But there must be women's bars.'

'There are.'

'But you don't go there? How do you meet women then? Do you meet women, as a matter of fact?' It came out of his mouth as *fect*. His accent got stronger when he was angry. 'Do you have a girlfriend?'

She flinched. 'No.'

'Why not?'

'Because I don't know what I want.'

'I know what I want,' he said. 'I want a body.'

'Is that what I am? You mean it's true, all that feminist propaganda, that to a man a woman is just a body?'

'Not just a body. A body I can love. You don't think bodies are important?'

'I just don't think they're the most important thing.'

'That's what everyone likes to think.' He shook his head. 'But the *feel* of a body. I mean, the slope of its limbs, the lines around the eyes, the angle of eyebrows—'

'You're talking about it as if it were disconnected from the person.'

'You mean, that's what men do – talk about bodies as if they were things, not people.'

'Have you ever seen a Mapplethorpe photograph?'

He smiled. 'You know, couldn't we just have a soothing conversation?'

'I'd go get yourself a primary school teacher or a nurse or something. That's what you want, isn't it? Female sympathy. You've picked the wrong person.'

'Do you mean you can't understand someone else?'

'I understand. I just can't handle your sadness.'

'*Sadness?*' He said the word slowly, carefully, as if she had pronounced a word in a foreign language. 'Look at me.' He took her hand. She felt him shaking. 'Someone I loved has died. Can you imagine that?' He looked at her. She absorbed his narrowing gaze. He looked like he was deciding something. 'God.' He let go of her hand. 'You're exactly representative of your age group.'

'And what does that mean, *exactly*?'

'Intellectually intelligent but emotionally stupid. A perfect product of this bloody ironic culture that teaches you to be distant from yourself so you won't look silly. You know what that leads to? Inflexibility. As far as you're concerned you've explained yourself to yourself and your responsibility to yourself stops there.'

She ought to have been enraged, but strangely she found she wasn't. She showed him the palms of her hands, so that he could see how transparent she was, that she might be young and stupid but she had nothing to hide. 'There are all these parts of me,' she said. 'They don't always connect.'

For the next two weeks she didn't see him. Each Tuesday she waited for him to appear. When the clock showed eleven or midnight and he hadn't come she didn't know if she was disappointed or relieved.

It rained for the rest of that summer. She watched as drops of rain, thick and yellow like marzipan, collected on the leaves of the tree outside her window. She went swimming every day, then got wet going home. Some quality in these thin, drizzly afternoons made her think: *Nothing of any importance will ever happen here*. Her future looked like the haze that hovered on the horizon at the end of the summer day: thin, transparent, vaporous.

BLOOD ORANGE TART

When it happens it happens *to* her and she has no control over it. It has the finality of any of the scenes in the Canadian history books she was reading that summer – the last buffalo speared by the last wild-living Blackfeet; Louis Riel going to the gallows; men portaging across the glittering prairie. These people had only been doing things, she thought, remembering what Colin had said about *doing*; they were unaware, probably, of the significance of their actions, unaware that they were propelling themselves into an inevitable future.

But it's not a significant episode in Canadian history. It's a Tuesday night in an overpriced Toronto restaurant.

When she saw him come in, Jesse turned to Carrie, who had the section next to hers. 'Can you take my single? I'll finish for you tonight if you will. Please. It would be a favour.'

She watched Carrie walk steadily over to him. She watched his mouth move as he asked her if he was in the right section. Carrie must have told him something. She saw his eyes swivel in her direction. She couldn't bear the look of confusion she saw in them and turned away.

She thought that once he perceived what the situation was, he would leave. But he pored over the menu as usual. At the end of the evening, after she had gingerly avoided his table all night, he scraped out his chair, stood up, and walked straight towards her. He caught up with her just outside the servery, right beside the hand-holding couple on table twenty-two. He put his hands on her shoulders.

She turned around to find his amber eyes there.

'Why are you avoiding me?'

'It has nothing to do with me.' She pulled away from him.

'What?' He frowned. 'What has nothing to do with you?'

'Is everything all right here?' It was Miranda, the owner,

with her falsely concerned face. 'Do you have a complaint about the service?'

'No, it's – it's a personal matter.'

Miranda looked at her. Jesse was going to pay dearly for this. Customers didn't like scenes in restaurants. 'It's okay.' She nodded crisply at Miranda. She turned back to Colin. She knew it would be terrible, but she could not stop herself. It was one of those moments that seemed to grab hold of her and shake her. Instead of her controlling the moment, she was totally under its command.

'Don't you see?' she said. 'It's got nothing to do with me. Its not *me* you want. You just want someone to unbreak your heart. It doesn't matter who it is. If I were to be your lover' – her tongue staggered on the word *lover*, she had always found it preposterous – 'I would just be loving you for your sadness. And before long you wouldn't need whatever it was I had done for you. Then you'd just find someone more interesting.'

She saw the expression in his eyes stagger, then right itself. He walked away from her with a crisp, transparent embarrassment, as if she were someone he had bumped into in a crowded place and wrongly taken for someone he knew.

When she went to give her order, the kitchen looked different. A kind of arcane ritual was taking place, bloody and quotidian. The grill chef and the prep women had become a sacrificial priest and his virgin helpers, white-smocked like mental patients. She watched as one of the maiden helpers sprinkled herbs on steaks to soften their flesh, then anointed them with oil before plopping them on the grill, searing a jail-bar pattern into them.

In a parallel but proximate dimension, in the dining area, couples are gnawing racks of lamb. Men are poring over the wine list, uttering their thick names with the mis-emphasized syllables of the false connoisseur. And beyond the bar, fading into the candle-studded darkness of the restaurant,

Colin is sitting alone, picking at his food, looking around and seeing himself surrounded by darkened people laughing, mouths open, raising glasses of wine, feasting maniacally, their senses made dull by too much satisfaction.

Some time that evening, he left. She was so busy with dessert and dessert wine and cognac that she didn't see him go.

Suddenly it was September and bookings were down.

'Somebody should patent restaurants as early-warning systems. The economy is going down the tubes,' Adrian said one night when there were barely enough customers to fill the section.

The restaurant did not need her that Tuesday, and Jesse took it as a personal rejection. Miranda scowled over the bookings and turned to Jesse with her 'I'm going to be fair' face. 'I tried to get you at home,' Miranda said. 'But you must have already left. I'm sorry.' She whipped off her spectacles – which Jesse knew she did not need – in a gesture of remorse. 'But the bookings are simply awful, and I have to give you the night off.'

She felt panic brewing in her abdomen. She tried to look grateful. 'Just let me drop this shirt upstairs.' She waved the plastic bag containing her dry-cleaning and charged through the kitchen, where the radio was on. It was the summer they were playing Tracy Chapman every three seconds.

She hung up her shirt and noticed for the first time that its cuffs were worn, its colours faded. On her way down the stairs she looked through the back door of the dining room and saw Adrian in the servery. They had shared so many jokes together, they really got along. 'We're a team,' Adrian had said to her, more than once. Now he was laughing at something another waitress was saying, leaning on her shoulder for support. She closed the door behind her.

*

At the end of September she decided to leave the restaurant. On her last night, when the upstairs section had emptied, she sat at one of the tables looking out on to the intersection. The leaves were still on the trees, where they rustled dryly in the breeze. Streetcars rumbled by the intersection at Queen Street, spewing mint-blue flashes of light as they scraped over the rails.

The geography of that particular corner, where she and Colin had merely crossed the street together a number of times, seemed suddenly important – the Café Express, St Patrick's convenience store, the donut shop on the corner, the dry-cleaner's where she picked up her shirts every day, crisp and inanimate, waiting for her body to inhabit them. At the end of the street the CN tower blinked into the night, towering above them all, looking to her more like a dinosaur or some unfinished creature from the past and not the beacon of the future it pretended to be.

Somewhere behind its bulk was the navy metal of Lake Ontario. And beyond that, the wide mouth of a continent, then the ocean. It seemed so far away, she thought, the Atlantic and the rim-named places that hemmed it: Chesapeake Bay, the Algarve, Gibraltar, then down to Accra, Luanda, Cape Town.

She sat like that for a while until she was called down to the bar for last drinks.

Beach Boy

'Ignacio . . .'

'*Ignacio* . . .'

'IGNACIO!'

The third time he hears his name it sounds like a gun going off. He lifts his head above the waves. The waving figure on the beach wears green shorts. His hair stands up, as if he has just got out of bed. It's Tony.

'Come in, Ignacio.'

The boy swims towards the figure.

In his dreams, he talks to sea turtles. They tell him the things he should be afraid of. Fish come to see him too, swimming out of his father's eyes. The fish tell him nothing, they behave in his dreams exactly as they do in water, swimming in shoal-clouds, forming and re-forming.

You're just like a fish, Tony tells him. Always in the water. One day you're going to grow fins and we'll have to build a tank to keep you in.

Ignacio doesn't laugh. A tank is one of the things the sea turtles tell him he should fear.

'There's a letter.'

His father pointed to the white rectangle on the table. Ignacio saw it had been opened already, a ragged slit made by his father's letter opener, the one Ignacio had bent trying to fix one of his toys and which now hacked at the edges of envelopes. Not that they received many letters.

Ignacio gave his father a look that said, *So?*

'It's from your mother.' His father went back to spearing pieces of papaya. He ate papaya three times a day, morning, noon and night. Ignacio had once asked him if he would turn orange.

'Go on, read it. It's for you.'

Ignacio stared at the white rectangle. No one had ever sent him a letter before. He took the envelope in his hands and drew it to his nose. It smelled clean, breezy. Some part of his brain recognized it as the scent of the north.

Dear Ian,
I'm writing because it will be your twelfth birthday soon. I talked to your father on the phone last night, and we both discussed your coming to live with me. You will need to go to a good school from now on. Then you can go to university, if you want. Your father and I feel you should come to live with me. This is what I want, to have you with me, for you to grow up here. Your father wants this too. Of course, you can visit him whenever you want.

He put the letter down. His father darted him a look. Where was Tony? He must have been banished so that they could talk.

'Ignacio? Where are you going?'

He was already out the door. He called over his shoulder, 'For a swim.'

It is ten o'clock in the morning, and already hot. By seven thirty all traces of dawn coolness have been erased. The sun starts its equatorial rise until, by one in the afternoon, it has stunned all creatures into stasis.

Except Ignacio. He is swimming far out, beyond the breakers, dodging the rip tides that move up and down the beach like sidewinding snakes. He knows every rock, every current. He knows how to dodge the wreck of the *Heavenly Body*, the yacht that ran aground on the beach during the hurricane of four years ago, which the villagers still speak of as if it was the end of the world.

The beach has been Ignacio's back yard for the past five years, since his father took him here and built their house right on its sugary sands. One day Ignacio went to school in blue shorts and a clean, pressed white shirt speaking English. By lunchtime he had picked up the playground rudiments – yes, no, don't, piss off. By the next day he seemed to have forgotten he ever spoke English. His father still struggled with how are you, and what's the time? By the time Ignacio was ten he took care of all the shopping, banking, and paid their electricity bill. That was the same year that the first of several Tonys appeared.

This year, his twelfth, was the one Ignacio would remember as the one when his mother found him.

Jorge, the policeman, stopped Ignacio's father in the street one day in May, at the beginning of the rainy season. The air was about to change, everyone could feel it. The farmers watched the skies anxiously for the clouds that brewed themselves out of the mountains.

'Someone's looking for you.'

Ignacio saw his father's face turn pale. 'Who?'

'Better drop by the station,' Jorge said. He ran his hand through Ignacio's hair. Everyone in town did this, just to see if it felt differently and because its silvery blond was the colour of money and considered lucky to touch. Ignacio's scalp shrank under the policeman's hot brown fingers.

In the station they waited on a bench next to one of the town drunks, who mumbled something about turkeys or vultures. The air-conditioner gave off a medicinal smell. When they had waited for nearly an hour the inspector, a citified man in a light brown suit, popped his head around the corner.

'You can come in now.'

As they sat down, the inspector gave Ignacio's father a strange look: even Ignacio recognized it. It had been given to him once before, like an awkward present, by teachers at his school. It said: We know your kind, but we are tolerant, simple-minded people. We welcome good citizens and what they do in their own time is their own business. Half of what the look said was true, half was a lie, although the parts kept changing places and even Ignacio wasn't sure if even his thirty-one-year-old father knew which was correct.

'We received this' – the inspector shoved the fax under Ignacio's father's nose – 'the other day.'

In the local timetable *the other day* could have meant yesterday, or last month.

FBI. Did the FBI really exist? Ignacio was amazed. He thought it was only something dreamed up on television and in the American movies they sometimes watched on video.

Two photographs, both six years old now, looked out from the page. Grainy and streaked with the chatter of satellites, these were recognizably the faces of son and father. Under Ignacio's was written: Ian Parker, and under his father's: Gregory Parker. At the top of the paper was the word MISSING. Ignacio began to read the rest – Do you know the whereabouts of . . . ?

The inspector withdrew the piece of paper. 'Now normally we would arrest you on the spot,' he said mildly. 'Our country has strict laws against child abductors—'

Ignacio shot a look at his father, who looked away.

'—but in this case the local police have requested that you establish contact. We all know each other here, as you know, Señor – Trillo.' The inspector frowned as he said the last name Ignacio's father had given them both, before they even settled in the town. It was really the name of his grandmother, he had told Ignacio. 'So it's almost true.' He could remember his father telling him this, standing in an airport surrounded by stiff palm trees and sweating men.

'The child's mother is willing to talk to you before mounting criminal action,' the inspector continued. 'May I remind you, señor, that in this country proven abductors are always deported, whatever the outcome of these cases. No exceptions.'

Papaya and lime. The carmine belly of the macaw. A smooth stone tumbled in on the rollercoaster Pacific from Australia—

'You don't talk much, do you?' Tony plunked himself down beside Ignacio on the beach, his legs pulled up, his arms resting on his knees.

This was Tony's joke. Ignacio: the silent boy. He had said this since coming to live with Ignacio's father six months before.

Ignacio shrugged. 'Just looking.'

'What's there to see?' Tony smiled. 'A beach. Another beautiful day, as you people who come from up there say. You poor people where every day is not beautiful.' Tony paused. 'You need more friends, Ignacio. You need stimulation.'

Tony was always telling him what he needed. Ignacio's father never did. They had learned their silence from each other. It was their language. When Ignacio found he could no longer speak English and his father's Spanish was still bad they had resorted to silence, to a repertory of smiles and choreographed movements. Fingers on forearms. A shadowy frown. The ripple of a forehead that spelled confusion. Ignacio read his father's face like the waves and was never in any doubt about the direction of his father's currents.

Only Tony kept wanting him to talk. 'Do you remember your mother?' Tony asked.

'No.' Ignacio began to draw a turtle on the sand.

'Do you know why she wants you back?'

'No.' He finished a flipper.

'You know, Ignacio, you used to live with your mother and father. In an apartment. In a city where it was sometimes winter. Do you remember that?'

He drew a curved beak. It was going to be a hawksbill, one of three species who nested on their beach.

'Your father kidnapped you and brought you here. Your mother has been looking for you for five years—'

Finished. Ignacio leapt up, erased the sand-turtle with his foot and ran into the waves.

He heard voices coming from the bedroom.

'You knew it would happen eventually—'

'No I didn't. Who'd ever think of looking here? We're almost at the end of Panama—'

'—where a blond kid sticks out like a satellite dish—'

'—there's a lot of satellite dishes around here. Look at the mayor, he's got one.'

'You know what I mean. Did you really think this would never happen?'

A silence in which Ignacio could hear his father's misery. It throbbed, like a frog trapped in a snake's mouth. 'I didn't think anything.'

Things are changing. His body, for one. All the swimming he does has made his chest wider, his arms heavier. His voice is unreliable; sometimes it comes out as a squeak, other times his father's voice comes from his own throat as if his father's future ghost has taken up residence inside him.

He knows he should no longer hold his father's hand when they walk together to buy rice and fruit at the cooperative. He knows he is no longer welcome on his father's knee.

At the same time he is beginning to hear words differently. *Maricón, maricón*, the boys whisper at school. Not about Ignacio, but anything they don't like. That football team is full of *maricones*. The gas station owner who will only let two of them at a time in to buy sweets is also a *maricón*. Even though it hasn't come his way yet, the word has taken on a spiked appearance for Ignacio, as if one of the smooth iguanas who make their home underneath Ignacio's house were to suddenly grow scales.

It sounds different, too, because now he notices Tony exiting from his father's bedroom wearing nothing, walking through the white curtain separating Ignacio's room from his father's. He notices this happens about the time he gets home from school, three-thirty. He knows what it means but does not know. He wonders with a sense of unease he has never felt before – like when he is sliding down slippery rocks in his dreams, unable to stop himself – what will happen when the boys at school turn their attention on him. Or rather, on his father.

'Ignacio.' His father caught him by the arm.

Ignacio shook him off. 'I'm late for school.'

'It doesn't matter. Not today. Here.' His father drew out one of the two stools that were the only chairs in their kitchen. 'Sit down.'

Ignacio kept his backpack on.

'Ignacio,' his father sighed. 'I mean, Ian, you remember, that's your name.'

'My name is Ignacio.'

'Well, all right. You can keep it. It can be changed. But it's going to give you problems, up there—' His father nodded his head in the direction of the sun, as if the country where he would soon be going was located on top of their heads.

Ignacio shrugged.

'You know.' His father ran his hands through his own hair. His drew his fingers away to see that they were shaking. 'I'd like to ask your opinion on this. I'd like to get your permission. But I can't. You're too young, and they're going to put me in jail if I don't let you go.'

Ignacio shot a look at his father. 'In jail?'

'Yes,' his father nodded. '*Jail*.'

'For what?'

'For taking you here. For keeping you. Your mother says if I let you go she'll drop the charges.'

Ignacio swallowed. 'Will you come with me?'

His father said, in a soft, low voice that was not a voice Ignacio knew, 'I can't.'

'You're going to stay here, with—'

'No.' His father shook his head so hard Ignacio wondered if his brain would come loose. 'I'm going to the city for a while. Then I'm going to think about what to do next. But I'll come to see you every three months. I promise.'

There was a slump, then a crash.

'What's happened?' Tony yelled from where he had been listening next door.

'Ignacio's fainted.'

Something white. Snow. Yes, he remembers wearing heavy boots, and ski pants made of a shiny material. Taking them off in musty winter cloakrooms, changing to school shoes.

He remembers a white hand and a cool smell, like mint. His memory's eye travels up that hand, to the forearm, but gets no further. The memory is faceless and voiceless.

He remembers one night, his father crying. His mother must have been crying too. He had never seen an adult cry and it was like the end of the world had come. He said, What's wrong, what's wrong?

The next day he remembers his father telling him, Your mother doesn't love me because I've done something terrible. Then more tears. Then, I don't know what to dos, all ten of them, said in a row.

Ignacio isn't sure but he thinks his mother went away for a few days. His father's fumbling fingers putting on his raincoat, his father walking him to school through giant springtime puddles.

Then an airport, and aeroplane, his first ride in the skies.

After that he remembers nothing, until the beach.

A week later he has a new backpack and one of those suitcases on wheels that he can pull along behind him. Tony made a trip to the city especially to buy it.

'Remember: ticket, passport, money, ticket passport money,' Tony chants. They are getting ready to leave the house. It will take four hours to reach the airport, but the roads are bad and they are counting on a six-hour journey.

Suddenly Tony turns around to find Ignacio gone. '*Puta madre*—'

Ignacio swims out into the tide. As the current takes him out he finds the energy to lift his head and he looks back at the beach. He sees dogs running, chasing nonchalant egrets who wait for the last minute before lifting themselves off the sand. He sees the rusting engine of the *Heavenly Body*.

The rip tide takes him out and deposits him like a piece of flotsam beyond the breakers. He floats there for a long time. The sun burns his face. He tastes the salt lodged in the corners of his dry lips.

He hears nothing until suddenly arms lock around him. He wants to say, *No. No!* But he is drained of energy. He feels like laughing.

His father's lover says, 'Come with me now, or I'll kill you, I swear.'

Ignacio laughs a strange animal laugh. He is out of breath. Tony hauls him back in against his chest. Ignacio hears his heart beating *thump-thump, thump-thump*.

He feels himself being dragged up on the beach. The sand gets in the back of his shorts.

He looks up into the sky and finds his father's face there. His father is crying. He hasn't seen his father cry since that other terrible day, the one before they left and came to live on the beach.

'Oh my God. We missed you.' His father falls on top of him in a heap.

'Am I dead yet?'

His father says nothing, just sobs against his chest.

Lying there, his eyes full of sky, Ignacio smiles. 'Am I dead yet?'

The Wolves of Paris

It was David who found the apartment for us. I love the name of our street, rue du Dragon, although the only dragons are the women who shop at the Maud Frizon store a few doors down. It's a bijou neighbourhood of expensive boutiques and it wouldn't have been my choice, but David met someone with a place to sublet. He was better than me at meeting people, better at getting things from them – cups of coffee, Parisian sublets, trips to India, love.

It is November now but the days are still warm. It's been one of those elongated summers but you can tell that any day it will be winter. David told me he wanted a winterless year – that he loved the word, *winterless.* I try to picture him in India and I see him in an abstract crush of people, beige hills, wind-sculpted palaces. His skin is raked over elevated cheekbones, like a Peruvian, his eyes the colour of speckled trout, his alert deer posture – he stands there looking as if any second antlers are about to spring from his head. Alain says I have to stop thinking about him. What about you? I say. He's all we ever talk about. Tell me you don't think of him. Alain just shrugs. I think: *So.* He is one of those people who would rather shrug his shoulders than lie.

Alain lives in an immigrant area – Turks, Spanish menial workers. It has a post-1945 look, unmistakable in Paris because all the buildings look the same. I always get lost.

He opened the door.

'What's the matter?'

'I got lost.'

'So. Everybody gets lost. Don't look so sad.'

Alain has a straight nose, brown hair, brown eyes on a small face. He seems delicate and that's his charm – his vulnerability. But there's also something steely about him. Maybe it comes from being brought up in the sticks, then moving here without family or friends. I can see why David wanted him.

Alain flew through the kitchen lifting lids off boiling pans of water, crashing them back like a cymbal player. I'm still amazed by the way the French know their way around a kitchen. Even though he's not French. He grew up in some backwoods place in New Brunswick, but he's lived here so long now he may as well be French.

I said, 'Did I ever tell you I was twenty before I saw a man chop vegetables?'

'I know. Anglo-Saxon taboo. Men chop wood, not courgettes.' Alain threw me that look – quick, darting, like an animal just released from a trap in the woods. He knows how attractive he is. I wonder how many of those looks David received.

I went into the living room and saw a film camera in the corner staring back at me.

'What's that for?'

'What?'

'The camera.'

'Oh, I've started to make films. Just little ones with no plot, characters, no commercial potential, certainly no distribution.'

'Can I see?'

'Not now. It's not time yet.'

I looked at the equipment scattered across the carpet – a few film cans, a filter. What does he mean? *It's not time yet*?

Dinner went as usual. We try to talk about something

other than David. We try not to notice we are attracted to each other. After dinner we sat on the floor, surrounded by bits of film.

'So what's it about, this film?'

'Bad luck to talk about work-in-progress.'

'Just give me a general idea.'

'It's going to be about the city.'

'Paris?'

'What other city would it be?'

'Alain, don't you ever want to go home?'

'*Home*? To a place with women named Rhonda and men who drive K-cars?'

'Don't be such a snob.'

'What are you doing here? You're here because you don't want to go through life talking about life insurance policies and the latest model of four-wheel drive. Look, one day you'll stop thinking about the difficulty of finding a good apartment and the coldness of Parisians and all those expat complaints and you'll wake up and home will seem like the moon. Look—' He gestured out the window. You can see everything from this place – Sacre Coeur, the Bastille. 'You have everything here. What else could you want?'

'I don't know. Wilderness.'

'*Wilderness*?'

'Don't you miss anything?'

'I'm too old to miss things. Missing things is for teenagers.'

'There must be something.'

He lit a cigarette, looked at it suspiciously. 'That's another thing I don't miss – here I can smoke where I please. Okay.' He took a deep breath. 'How about wolves? I miss the wolves who used to live around our house. They used to come and sit in the yard in the moonlight, right under my window. I would look out and see these pools of dark silver in the snow. Their eyes were very beautiful. I was never afraid of them. Oh, and eels. My grandfather had an eel weir on Grand Etang. I used to help him harvest every September. You know, they come downstream in thousands – the river's like a liquid trough of eels. You just put your hand in anywhere and grab one. If we took them out and put them on the bank they'd find their way back to the water. It's their migratory instinct – it's that strong. We used to work all night and at some point I'd look up into the sky and see these flashing eyes and long bodies and tell my grandfather, look, there's eels in the sky. He'd say, those are transatlantic planes. They're going to England, to France.'

'I've got to go.'

He looked at me as if he had forgotten I was there. 'You can stay here if you want.'

'You don't have an extra bed.'

He put his finger on the back of my ear and ran it down to my neck. He saw my face. 'It's not that bad. You'll survive.'

'You think just because you got David you can get me. I'm not going to forget what you did.'

He took his hand away. All these months since David left, even the year since he and David became lovers, I have never accused him of anything, never been angry. I left his apartment and took the elevator down eleven floors, feeling myself decompressing, as if I had been trapped underwater in one of those submersibles I see in the many Jacques Cousteau documentaries they show on TV here. When I reached outside it was winter.

Every day in Paris I feel like a trout squeezed through sargasso weed. I'll never get used to the people – people everywhere, in the Métro, cafés, cinemas, street markets. I wander among them and I think they are in colour and I'm in black and white, a shadowy presence. They can't even see me. I should be used to being on my own now – it's nearly a year since David left me. We don't socialize at my job. On weekdays I stay in and read novels by Algerian dissidents. Weekends I ferret out exhibitions and films. The lonely foreigners who go to these things avoid one another, inching away as soon as they catch the Arctic scent of isolation. I go to clubs but since David left all the men look at me with lizard eyes. Lately I've started going to hear Third World divas like Cesaria Evora and Mercedes Sosa. Alain says this is a sure sign of Male Homosexual Middle Age. I tell him to piss off. I'm not even thirty.

At night I go for walks. You can walk for miles at night in this city and no one bothers you. The Seine looks like an oil slick. Rows of grey buildings act like a giant venetian blind, filtering the light at strange angles. I'm still surprised, even after two years here, to find how a city so old and garlanded by history can be this broken, this animal.

The day David told me we sat in a tiny café on the rue du Bac. It was raining. Outside the café two young Arab-looking men were being interrogated on the sidewalk by the police. David turned to me. 'Have you never seen the wolves of Paris?'

'You mean French men?'

'I'm serious. I met this guy who talks about wolves. He says there are wolves living in the city. You never see them but one lives in the belfry of Saint-Sulpice. He says they insist on living only in places christened by saints and martyrs.'

It had begun to rain and the rain creased the café windows so we couldn't see outside. I felt the same way inside, something was running down me.

'Who is this guy?'

'I've met someone,' he said.

'Oh.'

'Another man.'

I thought, what does he mean: *another* man? Another to him, or another to the many men he has met? I'm a man, the world is full of men—

'Oh,' I said.

Once a week Alain and I go to eat Vietnamese in Belleville. I watch Alain carefully, scour every detail of him to see if I can discover the source of his attractiveness. The way he comes out of the bathroom, for instance, stuffing a tissue in his pocket, and the whole restaurant swirls around him. He seems to attract light and comment and dishes of sizzling noodles.

'What's the matter with you? Why don't you want to go out tonight?'

'You never dance with me.'

He picked up a prawn deftly with his chopsticks. 'We go out so you can meet more people.'

'We go out so you can meet people and do coke.'

'How many friends do you have in Paris?'

'You call all the people you know friends? Thierry or François or Bertrand – they're all the same. All they talk about are this guy and that guy. They're walking proof that youth divests you of character.'

'Fine. You don't like my friends. You don't have to come with us.' He spooned more black bean sauce into his mouth and licked the corner of his lips.

'Blackmail. *Chandage*. At least David was honest.'

'Stop making excuses for him. David isn't that special. He just goes chasing after experience. Like most people, he doesn't *think*.' Alain smiled. 'Gorgeous, though. His shallowness is part of the attraction. It's not fair, is it?'

Then we go dancing – to the Le Tchatch au Tango or the Blue Moon. Around five in the morning Alain drops me at the sublet David had found for us and he goes home with whomever. I go to sleep and dream I am a large whale, wheezing and floundering, beached on some shore that looks like Nova Scotia: low-lying, moraine, waterlogged. I am waiting for the whalers to arrive. They will strip me of my bone so I can be made into corsets to support the waists of women in other centuries, women who were thin and lithe like me.

It is close to Christmas and he takes me to Bofinger. We are surrounded by mirrors, sit on plush red banquettes. Trussed-up waiters flurry towards our table like albatrosses coming in to land. Outside the city is lit for Christmas. Black ice glazes the pavements.

The look he gives me is familiar now, like two streams of water, one hot and one cold, running from his eyes. What does he want with me? He's playing with me. I'm his only link to David.

I scowl at him. He scowls at me.

'What is your problem? Why are you so uptight' Alain says this like a Frenchman – *upthithe*. He draws up his shoulders into a vulture posture.

Suddenly I'm so tired. 'I'm just thinking about how David and I came here to have the kind of conversation you and I are having now. To be in EUROPE. We kept saying to each other that all we needed to make our lives work was to live somewhere more fixed in the world's imagination. We got the idea from a film we saw at the Bloor Street Cinema when we lived in Toronto – *Colonel Redl.* Do you know it? Well, it's set in the dying days of the Austro-Hungarian Empire. Colonel Redl is an Austrian army officer in the war. And the Italians somehow know that he's gay. Or bisexual, at least. And they send a beautiful boy to entrap him. This boy is *incredibly* beautiful. They ride quick bay horses through woods coated with winter. Then they make love and the boy betrays Redl, and the strange thing is, Redl knows all along. And still he goes to bed with him. He knew the boy was a spy, a ruse. Why did he do that?'

Alain is looking at me oddly. The film is still running through my head, but only individual frames, like it has been hacked apart with scissors. Each frame has a separate name, like

Winter.

Couriers of situations.

Horses.

Betrayers—

I walk Alain the ten blocks back to his apartment. The night is cold and still. Alain lights a cigarette. His face is back-lit by the tiny cinder of orange and for a moment his face shows his age – thirty-four; five years older than me. I wonder what I will look like at thirty-four.

'We've really got to fix you up with someone. It's incredible. You've been alone now what, a year? I've never heard anything like it before. It's not as though you are bad-looking.'

'That's the kind of comment the French always think they can get away with.'

'I'm not French.'

'Well, men then.'

'I'm not trying to insult you. I'm trying to help you.'

'*Help* me?'

I ran away. It was stupid – something a child does. After a few blocks I stopped. I could barely breathe. The cold seared my lungs. I was crying. Someone who took my lover. Someone I am attracted to. Someone I want, even. And he wants to *help* me.

I don't know how this happens, how we end up in places that have nothing to do with us. For David it was more clear: David always said that where he came from, being out and gay would have been a death sentence. It wasn't that bad for me, I grew up in a small port city. There were a few places I could go, even if they were full of eighteen-year-old Venezuelan sailors on day leave half the time. David lived with a woman until he was twenty-five and met me. He said he couldn't risk it before then. By that time we were living in a city but David is like Alain, from the country. He can fish, shoot, drive farm vehicles. I wonder if he is fishing in India.

Alain says, 'You're thinking of him.'

'No I'm not.'

'Yes you are.'

Alain leans forward and grabs my wrist.

'Let me tell you a story. It's a short story. Not even a novella. A young man, any young man, well, he is so lonely he sets himself tasks like reading Balzac or Proust or some other hard-work writer in the evenings when he could be going out meeting people. Why does he waste his time like that? Because he is afraid. He is afraid of finding love because he is afraid of losing love. He is so afraid that when he finds love he makes sure he loses it just to confirm the correctness of his theories about the fickleness of people, the transitoriness of experience, the unreliability of love. What he most fears befalls him. All his views are confirmed. And he takes comfort in this because this is how he knows he is real.'

He lets go of my wrist. I roll my eyes. 'Who are we talking about in this little allegory? Okay, let's cut to the dénouement: the young man kills himself.'

'Oh no.' Alain purses his lips, shakes his head. 'He comes to terms with it and has therapy and is subjected to the life-long horror of self-improvement.'

Alain looks tired, suddenly. 'I don't know. I'm not trying to instruct you. I've had so many lovers. How many have you had? Two? What are you afraid of? You're scared to go out into the world, to really live. If you're not careful you'll be thirty-five and celibate and hanging out in the library and obsessing about David.'

'But what does it mean, *really living*? For you it means having a lot of sex. It's different for me.'

'What's going to happen to you? Do you think just because you're in a different country everything's going to change? What's going to happen?'

Alain's phrase takes on this weird echo in my mind and bounces around in there for days afterwards – *What's going to happen? What's going to happen?*

'I need you to do something for me.'

On the telephone two days later Alain's voice doesn't sound like him – he sounds hesitant. 'I need you to come with me to an appointment.'

'What kind of appointment?'

'My appointment with destiny,' he laughs. 'A doctor's appointment.'

'Oh,' I say. 'It's not your first one.'

'No. I go every year or so.'

We sit in the waiting room of the Institut Pasteur. Alain is called in. Behind the half-closed door I can see a doctor who has the bearded look of a psychiatrist but whose actual job is to dispense drugs. All the *Paris Match*es are taken so I pick up a boring history magazine off the table. I look up from the article and into the face of the woman just paged. A chic, well-cared-for face rises from the chair. In her thirties, I reckon. On her hand is a wedding band.

Alain bursts out of the consulting rooms, grinning. He pats his pocket. 'Results tomorrow. Now let's go get drunk.'

In his apartment he sits cross-legged on the carpet, ripping a cigarette rolling paper to shreds between the oval of space created by his legs. Among the scattered pieces of paper is the computer printout he received from the hospital today. He looks up at me as he licks his roll-up.

'You know, the strange thing is, I don't feel that relieved.' He stands up, offers me his hand. 'Come on, let's go to the cemetery.'

When we vault over the gate of Père Lachaise it is three o'clock in the morning. We are surrounded by the tombs of martyrs and a Paris of plaster colours – ermine sky, fish-grey buildings. I think, anyone would be terrified of this city, with its spindly courtyards in which monuments worship past revolutions.

After Alain has had his fill of tombstones we go back to his place. When I wake nothing has changed, it is another grey felt morning – Paris in winter. I go to his window and open the Venetian blinds. Eleven storeys below us the pond behind his building is frozen. I can make out the figures of battered old Algerians, of the facelift ladies obsessively walking their poodles in the park. I realize I will be here for years. Behind me Alain is snoring lightly. Asleep he looks like David.

It is a Tuesday afternoon and the Louvre is eerily empty. Alain drags me through the sculpture section to see Michelangelo's *Slaves*.

'You should see the torture on the faces of the slaves. It's magnificent. Michelangelo made it for the tomb of Pope Julius the Second.'

'How do you know all this?'

'Like a lot of gay men I take refuge in Italian sculpture. When I was first in Paris I would come here all the time. Have you ever seen *David*?' The name hangs in the space between us, just for a second. 'I mean Michelangelo's,' he corrects himself. 'You know, even though it's supposed to be this paean to male beauty I find it strangely unmoving.

David—' Alain says the name in a tone I have never heard before. It is dismissive, as if he has to remind himself which David we are speaking of – the statue or the person who was once our lover.

Suddenly he turns to me. 'You know, I like to think of myself as an intellectual.'

'Well, you are, in a way.'

'But you see, I always fall in love with these shallow people who seem volatile, but they're really strangely unemotional. It's like I'm too lazy to look beneath the surface.'

'It's not your fault. Everyone makes those mistakes.'

'But you know, with David—' He paused again at the sound of his name. 'I don't mean to insult you, but David's a bit dead; it's like he's always waiting for you to do something.'

'I probably responded to that.' In the marbled reflection of statue I could see myself nodding. On my face was a strange expression; I looked like I was going to laugh. 'I really resent people whose attractiveness comes from their passivity. I feel cheated.'

'I know what you mean,' Alain said. 'I always think people should have to *do* something in order to be loved.'

Then we are laughing as we rise on the escalator, through the glass pyramids, to leave the museum. Outside it's sunny and the pyramids create a giant prism and we rise through layers of blue, green, red.

'Do you know where the name of the Louvre came from?'

'Oh no. Another history lesson.'

'It was a wolf house: a *louverie*. That's where the word comes from – Louvre.'

'They kept wolves?'

'The woods of Europe used to be full of them. The kings kept them for sport. To hunt stags. They were like big dogs.

Who knows – they might have fed the wolves to the lions. They did that in Holland. Most of the European kings had private zoos. King Henry the third had a huge zoo, a menagerie, right here next to the wolf house. It was full of the most exotic animals – camels, cheetahs, dik-diks. They must have cost him a fortune. But one night he had a dream that all the animals jumped on him and ate him. So the next morning he shot every one.'

In his apartment Alain is setting up the camera.

'What's it about, this little film?'

'No idea. It's just a series of images. Personally I like to remain as oblivious as possible to meaning.' He switches off the lights. 'I took some of this footage when I was home two years ago.'

'You said you hadn't been back since you moved here.'

'Oh, I just went back once out of curiosity, to see if my family still thought I was the Antichrist.'

'And?'

'The priest was there waiting in the living room. Actually, he was great. He's a friend of the family. I spent most of the time at my grandfather's grave. Classic exile experience: go home, spend your time with dead people.'

Outside it is a winter twilight. A sloping light bleeds the city of its detail. Alain smiles. 'Did you know cinematographers have a name for this time of day? They call it the *chienloup* – the wolfhound.'

The film starts to roll. At first it's just a sheet of grey. Slowly I can see two shadowy figures skirting the edge of the frame. Gradually I realize they are wolves, loping along the sidewalk by the Seine.

'How did you do that?'

Alain turns to me, a mild expression on his face. 'Hmm? Do what?'

The camera goes back to the wolves. Their muzzles

twitch; tiny drops of saliva fall from their gums and catch the streetlight, they shine like mercury. The wolves take the stairs that lead up to one of the Seine bridges in three perfect liquid strides. There's someone walking on the bridge. The figure looks familiar and I realize it's David, walking hunch-shouldered as he always does in winter. I haven't seen him for months, haven't even looked at a photograph. Alain must have shot this at the end of last winter, when they were still lovers. I feel nauseous. That's the strange thing – I don't love him any more, but I look at him and I still feel sick. David's brown eyes are startled. I think again how he looks like a deer. The wolves head straight for him. He stops dead, freezes, but the wolves just slink by him like shadows, their noses to the tundra of the streets.

The Route of Your Evasion

THE PRESENT TENSE

I am thirty. We live on different continents, my mother and I. We trade e-mails about the weather.

I have come to live in the country she left, that she needed to leave. She would only recognize the exoskeleton of it now, the most obvious bones and joints: the beetle-shaped taxi cabs, brown houses streaked by rain, the alarming red postboxes that stand like vigilantes on the street corner.

It is not her country and not mine either. She told me she couldn't bear the weather, the people here, who she thought 'lazy'. That's what drove her to a third country, as they say in refugee applications: you go somewhere first as a waystation, then you go somewhere better.

My grandmother sits on the grass in the white pool of her summer dress, squinting up into the camera. She is only fourteen but her shoulders are already womanly; bronzed and muscled.

'Of course,' my mother says in her *fait accompli* voice, 'my mother was a saint.'

She says the same thing each time we mention her mother. It must be inherited, this mania for extraordinary sacrifice, because my mother is in practice for martyrdom, too. Sometimes I even catch a slight scent of flesh burning. I think of her in words like *petroleum, saint, travel.* They all seem to mean the same thing.

My grandmother's three spectacular brothers stand around her, flanking her like a doltishly pleased Imperial Guard, these prince-named men: Rudolf, István, Tomás. I never met them. All I know of them are these symmetrical polished faces staring out from a black-and-white universe. It's difficult to believed they lived in colour, or that anyone did before 1948 or whenever it was they invented Kodakchrome.

Tomás wears a doctor's coat. It is 1938 and he is studying medicine at József Attila University in Szeged, which my mother describes as 'a vaguely fascist city'.

'How can a city be *vaguely fascist*?' I ask my mother. I am twenty and studying political science at university.

She gives me the hostile look mothers reserve for children who think they know everything. 'It's the place from which thugs set out to murder over five thousand Jews and "Reds" – at least that's what they called them then.'

'When was this?'

'In the White Terror, about 1919,' she says mildly, and she turns the page of the photograph album. 'Szeged was a lovely place.' My mother talks like so many of the children of European exiles, as if these places only existed in the past tense. 'Oh look, here's one of the pool. In the hot summer weekends my mother and her brothers all went to the Partfürdo strand.'

The photos of the river show tall, blond people who have an athletic, sated air.

'Did they know what was going to happen then?' I ask. The date on the back, written in spindly indigo ink, is 1938.

'I don't think they had any idea. They were just living their lives,' my mother says. 'They were all doctors and nurses. No doubt they were put to use during the war.' The phrase, *put to use*, rings tinny and shrill in my ear.

All the photos are taken against a landscape as flat as a cutting board. My mother's family came from the Great

Plain, the area east of Budapest towards the Ukraine and Romania. It is a shimmering, drab fryingpan called the *puszta*. One hundred and fifty years of war, with the Turks and others, had left it home only to mosquitoes, swineherds, wolves and fugitives. Then, in the nineteenth century, to cowboys, lawless men, gypsies. They called it the 'open sea' even though it was landlocked.

'The man on the end, he looks like you.'

'My mother's brother. István. He was homosexual.' My mother's mouth turns into a perfect upside-down arc, like on those yellow sad face buttons.

The last photo in the album looks like a huge family gathering. In the middle is a Roman Catholic priest. He is flanked by two grinning, spectacle-wearing nuns. It might be a wedding because a girl in a plain dress carries a bouquet of what looks like nettles. Two girls to the left strike Louise Brooks poses. They do not look particularly happy, rather knowing. They are all very tanned.

'It must be the end of summer,' I say, using the present tense I always apply to photographs.

'Yes,' my mother says – she is more rigid about her tenses – 'it was summer.'

She turns to look at me with those china-doll features of hers. Even in her fifties, she is still beautiful.

For years I went around with a statement in my head, like a political party slogan: *My mother is much more beautiful than me*. I would whip it out, repeat it to anyone who asked, and even those who didn't.

I'm still not sure if she grew up thinking beauty was an accomplishment or merely a delightful accident. In any case she put it to good use. But was there romance? Beauty should lead to romance. Well, let's see. What is romance? Moments of perfect love illuminated against a black canvas of uncertainty and betrayal? A film shot in Parisian-café colours: olive green and mahogany?

No, that was her mother's story. My mother's story was long hair and Trudeau's corsages, the French bunker architecture of Montréal. She got Joni Mitchell and Janis Joplin. But still she had that face. And somewhere, her face saw my father (who was not the same man as Lucy's father; more of Lucy in a minute), and the accident that is me happened.

The film stops there. That's all I know about it. Fade to black.

SNOW ANGEL

There aren't many photographs of Lucy and me. My mother left most of them behind, in a shoebox in the attic of a flat that now belongs to strangers.

The one I have is taken on Hampstead Heath, at the top of Parliament Hill. We stand smiling under a punitive English sky. I think now how in England the weather makes you look heroic, clouds travelling double-time across the sky, like in vampire films. Just looking at the photograph I catch England's cabbagey smell, can feel Lucy's straight blonde hair blowing into my eyes, how I liked it, picking the thin strands from my sticky eyeball.

The first day Lucy was sick we were in our dark Georgian hallway. My mother was buttoning up my coat, there was a gale outside. Lucy came from the kitchen, a long, dark corridor stretching out behind her like black ribbons. Her face looked like a miniature moon.

'Lucy, darling, what's the matter?'

Lucy said nothing, just gave my mother the long look of someone who has opened a drawer and found horrifying things inside.

A month later my mother explained to me.

'Something has exploded inside Lucy.'

'Exploded?' I pictured bombs, like the ones that kept washing up on the coasts. Sometimes children found them and played with them and lost a hand or an arm.

'Yes. It's blown up and is moving all over her insides.'

'What's moving? Snakes? Worms?'

In the hospital I looked at Lucy to see if I could see them crawling across her eyes, or peeking out from the corners of her lips.

'Go away,' she said, turning her tired, yellow face and giving me a look that I have since seen in eighty-year-old men, a kind of exhausted misanthropy.

In the days after Lucy's death my mother's mind, for punctuated moments, was only wiry scrabblings of desperate music, a Verdi's Requiem sung by schizophrenics. After the funeral my mother paced in the kitchen, her hands grappling around her own neck.

'I've got to get out of here, out of here, out of here,' she started singing in a high, fluting voice that was not her own. *Out of here, out of here.*

I stood, staring blankly, like you would stare at an animal you have never seen before in a cage at the zoo.

'Can't you see I'm being choked?' Her wild eyes swivelled to me. 'Don't you feel it? Don't you feel it?'

'Why do you have to go?'

'*We*,' she hissed. '*We* have to go.' A new look – slow, dull, certain – had taken over one of her eyes. The other one was still its old self, swivelling and shiny.

She pursed her lips and stood in front of me, her hands on her hips. She looked pleased, as if she had just accomplished something.

'Don't you know?' I could see her lips twitching. A smile was trying to break out on her face, like a rash. 'Something terrible is going to happen here.'

The first thing of Canada I remember is the brook by our

house, half frozen, water running through ice channels. Through the meniscus of ice I can see entombed sticks and branches, the frozen leaves, the peat-coloured wedges of rocks.

I remember making snow angels in a full skidoo suit, my eyes full of sky. I used to wonder if God saw them, if he could look down and see a whole country of flattened angels fluttering in the snow.

MEMORIES OF THE FUTURE

Krakow, 1933. My mother's mother leaves this soot city stranded on the plains of Poland. She has a cousin in Budapest and wants to leave Krakow, where she has frozen through the same obliterating winters my mother will come to know in Montréal.

My mother knows nothing of Poland. She is born fourteen years later in a cold Budapest hospital. My grandmother learns Hungarian from her husband, the dark, moustachioed figure in my photos.

When my mother is a girl her mother still speaks Hungarian with a Polish accent. One day they are in an office, queuing for one of the government's endless permits to exist, when the clerk hears her speaking and, through a haze of smoke and dark glances, says, 'You speak our language as if you really had to go to the lavatory. Constipated Hungarian.' Then he laughs. My grandmother laughs too – she is used to apologizing for her foreignness. But my mother, only eight, catches sight of an uncertain hurt invading her mother's eyes, slowly, like weeds.

I am born in London, to where my mother has emigrated from Hungary by marrying an Englishman, Lucy's father, in 1967. For a while, we all live together. When I am very young our family is joined by my great-grandmother, who has come to live her last years with my mother and me.

I quickly discern that my great-grandmother is strange. She wakes up in the middle of the night shouting in a language I don't understand. According to my mother my great-grandmother has visions: they are like a puzzle falling from the sky, the pieces scattered around her feet. A woman slashed down the belly, her foetus visible inside her wrecked stomach. Sawn-off hands. Night in the afternoon, abandoned highways, plane and oak and other northern species turned into spindled silver cacti.

My mother doesn't know where these images come from. My great-grandmother survived the war in relative comfort. My mother doesn't think she ever saw anyone killed. They aren't from the past, my mother tells me, so maybe they are the future. Yes, that's it: memories of the future.

Montréal, 1977. The year we came to live in Canada. It is night, and a snowstorm howls outside. My mother turns over and over in her bed.

There is a ship, or a plane. It is leaving and she is running, running to catch it. She makes it – phew. They close the gangplank or the door behind her and she takes her seat. All at once it evaporates and she is out on the dock or the tarmac, screaming that they are taking her away. She is on the boat, inside the plane, but at the same time she is stranded. The plane leaps into the air in the vertical way only dream-planes can do. She looks down and sees herself, running in circles on the ground.

THE SUBVERSIVE

'Oh, your uncle István—'

'Great-uncle,' I correct her.

'Hmmm? Oh yes. Now he was a real card. "The sensitive brother", my mother called him. She protected him, *you know*.'

She always says it like that: *you know*, in a way that is at once oppressive and dismissive. As if behind the façade of the words is something I could never know and wouldn't want to.

'From what? Himself?'

She looks at me darkly. 'Gabriella. It's a sin.'

'What's a sin?'

'*You know*.'

'You mean being gay?'

'You don't know anything about *the past*,' she says (*the past* is another *you know*).

'I would have liked to know him.'

'I never really knew him. He was just this man who pulled faces and did tricks. Oh well, hard to dwell on the dead.'

Her voice has the quality of snapshots scattered on water after a plane crash at sea; they float to the surface, where their images are slowly erased by salt and sun.

That night I have a dream in which horses are galloping. There's a fire somewhere, the horizon is scorched orange. In barn fires horses have to be forced out, beaten to get them to abandon their stalls. Horses feel safer at home. Home is their refuge, even if home is burning.

From the age of nine to twelve I feel hot bursts of desperate need. I scan my mother's face for clues. *Does she love me? How does she love me?*

She will brush powder on to her face, flicking delicately, the way archaeologists uncovering remains on television documentaries do.

I will leap on her, sniff her neck, trying to get to the bottom of her smell. She will shake me off, shuddering, as if

I were an insect, a monkey. *Back off, Gabriella.* Her voice is warning, dangerous. Once she turns to me, her face is livid, like that of an older sister pursued by the pubescent younger brother. She says, *You are not my lover.* Later I will realize this is a rehearsal for my future love affairs.

I am about to be an adolescent. My mother drifts in like a fog after the one a.m. foghorn. We live in a city prone to fogbanks that file in like pack animals after dark.

She is going out a lot, comes home smelling of beer and cigarettes. The silk dresses she does not allow me to touch are dotted with tiny stains which she will slave over with potions and chemicals before finally taking them to the dry-cleaner's.

I hardly see her, we don't speak for weeks on end. At the age of ten I make my own breakfast, lunch and dinner. Our relationship is like a rehearsal for the countless flatmates I will have in my twenties. We tolerate each other only because we are incarcerated together. You wouldn't call it love.

She is only two or three years older than I am now. She spreads blue eyeshadow in the half-moon crease of her eyelid, her reflection telling me with some ancient female knowledge, both exhausted and voracious, that one has to make the best of one's prettiness while it lasts. She must wonder how she has ended up in wooden houses that smell of wool, and me.

I am twelve and I turn over and over in stranded dreams while she walks under a sodium streetlight, pursued by fictional attackers. The dreams I have are often shadows of the photographs my mother will one day show me: the sleek, elongated thoroughbred horses my grandmother owned, unidentifiable soups, strange telegraph poles that look like crows, trains of laughing dark-faced people, heading to a forbidden quarter.

Also I have dream-photographs that set my mother next to the relatives she never met, the ones who were killed or who died before she went back to her country again. My mother never appears in these photographs, but she is there just outside the frame, a presence, a shadow cast by dusk beside the thick tree, her face stormy, sibylline, dazed with history.

The summer I am sixteen I begin to be interested in the discarded parts of bodies: flakes of skin, fingernails, placentas. In the flat palm of a Canadian summer I brûlée myself, lying like a lizard on the smooth rocks that are the forgotten mementos of glaciers, left behind as they dragged their feet across the continent.

I peel my skin, pulling the muscles in my neck to get at it, my fingers pluck at my back like crows. The skin comes off in large pieces which are jagged at the edges. It leaves my back with a buttered sigh, as if it were relieved to be leaving. I become addicted to that sound, to holding those pieces up to the light. It looks like parchment, its porous, greasy striations.

In the morning my mother finds me surrounded by pieces of skin, like a dissident who has shredded the crucial message in the final moments before detection.

THE ENIGMA

My grandmother's name is Constanz. In one photograph her face even promises it: constancy. She has dark eyes, not at all Slavic, but deep brown and melancholy. Under her eyes she already has lines, or folds of skin, that make her look oddly old.

Lucy looked like her, according to my mother. 'There is a remarkable resemblance,' my mother said, stretching out the syllables: re-mark-a-ble. 'Your grandmother was beautiful,' she added, tactlessly.

Even as a baby, Lucy made the boys cry. My mother's friends would bring their sons over to play. The blank-faced baby boys would take one look at her and burst into tears. Sometimes I think it's a good thing Lucy didn't grow up.

In Canada my mother stays looking young. Men turn to look at her in the street, although they can barely see three feet in front of themselves in that foggy city.

I have taken to calling my mother the Enigma. I am thirteen and we are quite a pair: the Enigma and the Subversive. There she is, the Enigma, with her flair for drama, dressed in a black silk crêpe dress, black stockings, open-toed sandals. And me, slouching around in my then-unfashionable Adidas gym gear, my frizzy permed hair and expensive orthodontal braces, trying to cover my inflating thighs, learning how to vomit discreetly, as teenage girls do.

When I am fourteen she gets married and begins to have more children. For three years she is constantly pregnant: in season, pregnant, drop baby, into heat again, pregnant: expanding and contracting like a child's balloon. A broodmare. (A broodmère.)

None of us, possibly not even her husband, knew where they came from. They just popped up, ramming her from the inside and demanding to be let out. She went to the doctor the way she would slope off to Mass, like a Stasi agent, trenchcoat pulled up around her neck, sunglasses and hat hiding her face. Her husband is a Jewish atheist (she is aware this is a contradiction in terms) and she had to resort to these remarkable tactics in order not to give the game away. It was a small town and he could so easily have come swinging by in his Volvo and caught her at the doors of the Cathedral.

That she wouldn't mention her pregnancies is not that

unusual. She seemed to consider it as she did most of her experiences: as a matter between herself and herself, part of her unusual mania for privacy. My mother did not tell even her own mother she was pregnant, not with me, not with the first of her other children, until she had given birth.

'She came here just a month ago, she must have been five months pregnant,' my grandmother mused sadly. 'And she didn't show. I never guessed. She said nothing. Nothing.' There was a forlornness in her voice. She would have liked to have known.

But my mother hates complicity among women. Her only close relationship with a woman is with the Virgin Mary, whom she prays to constantly.

When I am twenty-nine I have an abortion. I don't tell my mother. To myself I joke that it would be like telling the Pope.

At the end of my twentieth summer I go back to university in Toronto. I live in a neighbourhood of Chinese grandmothers and architecture students. For some reason I feel at home there.

More importantly I have escaped from that gelatinous house and its bowel-milk smell. I don't know how she met that man who is the father of her children. I don't know how they fell in love, when they married. I don't know who my father is. I don't know anything.

Someone, somewhere along the line, has entombed silence in the womb of our family. I dig inside myself, to find this unplumbed well of mute feeling, of never-to-be-described events. I excavate myself for signs of this mania for privacy, but I find only its strange by-product, or its mutation, a shy, reclusive pocket of self which, if you open it, has only a scrap of paper – like a discarded supermarket list – and on it, a single message written in eggs-and-butter code: *You will never have children.*

THE STORY

My mother and I are at the party of our downstairs neighbour. I am twelve, she is thirty-four. She is in perfect Enigma mode and wears a black silk dress, pleated and puffed, and seventies open-toed sandals from which her nylon-stockinged toes poke. I will develop then a lifelong horror of these shoes and the sight of unsightly toes spilling like nail-tipped sausages.

I am at the party early so I witness her arrival. She comes down the stairs, a black-dressed, black-haired creature, and everybody stops talking. You see this from time to time in the movies and of course every girl dreams of making such an entrance, of having the kind of beauty that stops conversations.

In the kitchen, a man, affable and corduroyed – some genial, lonely academic, probably – says my name, smiles to show he means no harm, and says, 'Come on, what's the story there?'

My mother turns a terrifying eye on him.

'Is that what you think? There is always a story?' Her voice is steel, spooky.

'Well, uh—' The man is already wobbling.

'Sometimes,' my mother says, never taking her gaze from him, 'there is no story.' In my mother's voice is the faintest echo of an accent. The man picks it up. She is not some blushing, friendly Canadian, this woman, ready to reveal everything in flat there-that's-said-and-done tones. This is another thing which attracts men to her.

He is looking into his drink nervously, his face forming the angry expression which leaps out so easily from behind so much affability.

'My life is private. I would keep your questions to

yourself, if I were you,' she growls.

Our neighbour, overhearing the exchange, comes up to me and runs her hands through my hair. My mother would never do this and I like it, being treated like an animal from time to time.

'You've got a terrifying mother,' she says, smiling. I roll my eyes and say something like, *Don't I know it*. I am learning to do these things.

'Have you heard from Brenda lately? Do you know she's got a son? He's five years old. Just think, if you'd had a child they'd be able to play together. And Nancy – do you remember, you used to play together – now she's got three boys. Can you imagine! Three. No girls. Poor thing. The Raus are such good kids. Those Indian families are so strong. It's because they respect the mother.'

My mother has decided to take a shortcut to understanding humanity. Now she catalogues people – or women, rather, as men don't figure in her universe any longer (a cunning amnesia) – by their progeny.

I want to say to her, I can't do it. I want to tell her why, about the fear, the nightmares, my certainty that if I have children they will denounce me to the authorities, kill me.

My mother would crack like the rogue pieces of plastering that tumble from my London house every day, if she knew. If she knew what? That I am a throwback, I am her own dark mother, fears masquerading as everyday things and stalking her ankles like sharp-toothed puppies.

NIGHT TRAIN

I take the night train from Toronto. The plane fare is five hundred dollars so I decide I want time to absorb the distance of the country again, to see those hours and hours of glacial fields flashing outside the window for the duration of a journey that would, in another continent, take me from London to Spain.

I stumble dazed off the train. I have spent the whole night awake, sitting in the bubble car, the one with the glass roof, watching a thousand miles' worth of pine trees pass in a haze of angles.

'Of course,' my mother says, when we are settled and home and have the photo album spread across our knees, 'you want to have children to preserve your memory.'

'But memories are so unreliable.'

She scowled. 'What do you mean – *unreliable*?'

'I mean they might not remember you the way you want to be remembered, the way you think you are. They might forget you. You might vanish into vaporous eulogies, or they might feel seething resentment. There's no guarantee your children are going to love you.'

She is silent, her lips pulled tight together in a neat hem.

'You just need to know everything, don't you?' she finally says. There is hatred in her voice – its sheared metal edge is unmistakable. 'You have to know everything and keep it inside where you can control it.'

My mother stares at me, her voice accusing and suddenly small. She has always thought me capable of the most dreadful, atavistic things. Maybe she knows on that in-training-for-sainthood frequency of hers what I have done.

We close the photo album and the relatives vanish once again into its thick leaves. They are all that is left, these tantalizing images. It's for the best, I suppose. They wouldn't have understood, these Szeged doctors, the corn-boiling relatives in my mother's photos, how I have ended up living in apartment buildings surrounded by strangers, my computer humming through the night, keeping in touch by stuttering electronic messages back and forth.

FALSE MEMORY SYNDROME

On Sundays I sometimes go to the café where young people wearing square-framed glasses come to read the *Observer* and sip soyachinos. I think how even relaxation in England looks regimented. Everyone is following some pattern that has been drawn and re-drawn, refined over successive Sundays.

I sit there, in the mosaic-tabled, dark-wood café, among the scattered entrails of *Observer*s. In the news section is a feature on false memory syndrome. I steal glances. The person who owns the paper knows and scurries to cover up the article with the elbowed lozenge of his woolly-jumpered arm. I go back to my soyachino.

My mother is now fifty-five. She lives on the other side of an ocean raucous with the chatter of whales. She has three children whom I do not know, except through hazy snapshots against wide-angle beaches and white billboards that show enormous red lobsters. We keep this space between ourselves because we are exile people and are more comfortable with distance.

I live in the old world now. I have gone back. Eight years of Euro-anxiety in this creaking city of terrorist bombs and proximate wars has taught me something about why she left England.

My theory is, I think she was worried. She knew what happened to people who got caught. She didn't know when history would catch up with her, but she understood that when it did it was like an anxious mother whose child has wandered off in the mall and got lost. She is afraid, but her anger is stronger than her fear. When she finds the child the first thing she does is give it a slap in the face.

THE ROUTE OF YOUR EVASION

'Why do you want to go there?'

This is what she said, when I told her I wanted to come back to England. She said it, *there*, as if I were talking about going to live in Beirut.

'It just makes sense,' I shrugged. 'I don't know why, but I've never felt at home in this country.' It was true: in Canada I was somehow an outsider, in some definitive but undefinable way.

'I can look after Lucy's grave,' I added. But this was a mistake.

'I suppose you feel you are taking something full circle, then.'

'That sounds like an accusation.'

She gave me a long look. Her spinach-coloured eyes had darkened to something nearer stone.

I asked her the one thing I have never before had the courage to ask. 'Why have you always thought me capable of the worst, the darkest things?'

She shrugged. Then she gave me a look of extraordinary clarity and I thought, yes, she really is my mother.

'Because you survived,' she said.

Of course. I felt like slapping my forehead. How could I have been so dumb? But it was effortless, survival. I never really tried.

In London, three years ago, my grandmother is taken into hospital suddenly complaining of a pain in her lungs. My mother looks at the deflated body on the bed, lying like a beached fish in a pool of sticky hospital light.

That night her mother dies, taking with her the memory of her brothers: handsome, ruthless Rudolf; István, the undeclared homosexual; Tomás who died early in the war.

Their ghosts crawl up and down the yellow hospital walls, looking for a joke, anything to comfort their sister. But there's nothing.

My mother and I sit next to each other on plastic chairs in buttery-lit hospital corridors. We say very little, but I can tell it pleases us, to feel the hum of each other, just the mere vibration of our beings. I think in those hospital moments how I have never known who my father is, how he should be the focus of my festival of wondering. But I don't. I don't know why.

Instead it's her I look for, even though I have known her all along. By some trick, she makes me feel that I know less about her merely by having been in her company, that she would have been clearer to me if she had been a character in a novel, or one of those faces in the Szeged photographs.

Now of course we keep in touch: there's the e-mails about the weather, which are strangely enjoyable, and the occasional telephone call. The written form shows her at her best: witty, ironic, self-deprecating. The classic frequency of e-mail communication.

It's hard to believe now that for many years we didn't speak. After she married she seemed to have no further use for me, as if I were a ragged life-jacket that had kept her afloat during hours of shipwreck. Once she was safely in the lifeboat she stripped me off. But I am one of those horrible survivors.

The thing about survival, I am beginning to realize, is that it's not that interesting compared to, say, falling in love, or being loved. And it takes up so much energy, without giving very much back. I feel unable to face the real tasks of life: selflessness, cooking, love, buying garden furniture, having children, but put me in a situation like, say, civil war, and I'd be fine.

Meanwhile my mother has things locked up and hidden inside her, like stacks of forgotten papers piled in drawers of furniture in an abandoned house. If I could find these pieces of paper, what would they say?

My mother's last words. She turns to me, her face ravaged by regret. *Never have children*.

But no, it doesn't end like that. I am sitting here staring out the window at the brown houses of London, my window streaked by rain. She is alive, and not too far from happy. I know from her e-mail message that she is out in her yard now, gloves on, hoe in hand, a forearm thrown across her face against the sun. Her last message to me will probably be *Put your zinnias in early*. For now, though, it is May and she is gardening in the sudden sultriness of an east-coast spring.

Once Seen

Northern Line, 2/4, 5.15. Camden Town to Belsize Park. Me: suit with briefcase. You: girl with Elle bag. You stepped on my toe. We exchanged glances, smiles. Let's meet. Box 439802.
Wigmore Hall Recital, 21/3. Me: brown hair, dark eyes. You: stunning blonde. You sat E19. We chatted briefly at the end. I'd love to see that smile again. Box 999254.
Invention of Love, matinee 28/3. We sat in the front row. Me A14, you A13. Like to invent some love with you. Box 195038.
15/3, Thursday, Long Island Iced Tea Shop. Matthew, do you still want to show me East London? Box 439340.

The column was short in comparison with the Flatshares, the Talking Hearts, the Lonely Hearts. Desdemona closed the magazine. She took out her pen and notepad. What could she write? A restaurant, an art gallery, a public building, or a theatre? In the morning or at night?

April 14th. The South Bank. Evening. Me: girl in green dress. You: writer-type. You startled me. Let's talk more. She folded the piece of paper and put it in the envelope. She turned back to the ads. She re-read their pleas to destiny, how each of them said, in a code of inevitable regret: *We should have talked, exchanged phone numbers. I wish I'd spoken.*

'It could only happen in London.'

Angus went to the fridge and pried open a beer. He perched on a stool opposite Desdemona, beer in hand.

'I mean, picture it yourself. You're in a gallery, and you see someone standing in front of the Francis Bacon or whatever, and you're too shy to say hello, or you can't think what to say: "Hey, don't you just love Francis Bacon? He's so deranged." But you don't say it, and before you know it the person's in the gallery shop buying the catalogue. And then they're through the door. What's the probability of running into someone you've seen once in London? Nil. They're gone, forever.'

Angus' *forever* echoed through his painfully chromium kitchen. She had been living in Angus' flat for nearly a year, but she knew she would never get used to his zen taste in décor. The walls of the flat were studded with Angus' own canvases, the exquisite but vacant objects he habitually painted – empty Mexican match boxes, discarded hair baubles, baby strollers minus babies left in the sunshine, finished cappuccinos. Angus had a fixation with emptiness. Secretly she thought this swept-clean quality was something to do with his promiscuity, his avoidance of messy emotional involvement.

'I don't know,' Angus continued. 'There's something so hopeless about those ads. It's too needy, too desperate. It's like trying to contact a long-lost relative. When you meet them again you remember why it was you never wanted to know them in the first place.'

'These people think they saw someone. I could be that someone. What does it matter if I'm not?' Desdemona shrugged. 'Lots of people meet on false pretences.'

'But what do you want in a man? Do you even know?'

'A *man*?' She said. M-a-n. Suddenly the word sounded childishly simple, and far too short, for what it was supposed to represent. 'I don't want a *man*. I hate the way we're always going around describing ourselves as *men* and *women*. Why can't we just be people?'

'Well, a person then,' Angus conceded.

But she didn't really know. She had never thought that way, making a list like you did to go to the supermarket, ticking things off: job, *tick*. Looks, *tick*. Salary, *tick*. Has read Baudelaire, *tick*.

If she thought about it she realized that what she wanted was someone who would never say, *I know, I know* to everything. Who had not been everywhere, done everything, who had not anticipated every opportunity for absurdity or embarrassment that life had yet to lob their way. She wanted someone who was capable of being surprised, because surprise led so effortlessly to delight. She wanted someone imaginative enough to see beyond their own satisfaction, their own progeny.

'You want to know what I think?' Angus leaned towards her. 'I think you're just trying to create a moment that never existed.'

His face brightened. 'Listen, why don't you just put a normal ad in, like everyone does: "Fair, slim F, twenty-nine, burdened with a Shakespearean heroine name, seeks philosophical, well-travelled M."' Angus beamed. 'Don't you think that just about sums you up?'

She was convinced that if she had been named Jane she would be a different person. She tried to picture herself as a Jane: tall, angular, cool and reserved. *Desdemona*. It had the ponderous scent of an orchid, a ceresius – one of those hothouse flowers that bloomed only at night.

Her parents had named her after a visit to Venice, a trip her mother had come away from pregnant. They had gone to see Verdi's *Othello* and had taken their daughter's name from the programme notes.

Her mother would never know how Desdemona would

squirm through productions of the play, stricken as Othello lurched towards the porcelain neck of his wife. Desdemona sat frozen in her seat, her hands curled around her own neck, terrified that through some kind of fateful synchronicity she too would feel her throat passages narrow.

Othello's Desdemona had been too loved. It was the same with the strangulations, the stabbings of women by their lovers that she read about in the newspapers nearly every day: their assassins were almost always husbands, boyfriends, fathers. Look what love could do, she thought. If you could call that love.

Fernando lights another cigarette, his fifth so far that night. He has not shown in years and he is nervous. He thinks he might see the shadows of his friends – Mark, Paulo, Jaime – struggling with ladders, with power cables and measuring tape, squabbling about who will go out to the off-licence and return with a blue plastic carrier bag full of cans of warm Holsten Pils.

Even though he has to do it alone, there is still a blank excitement to hanging his work in the cold basement space. He loves the empty expectation of galleries, the astringency of their sharpened light.

He peers again at his paintings. Was this really what he had been doing all these months, alone in his studio? The canvases have the familiar-but-unfamiliar look of half-forgotten relatives turning up uninvited at a wedding.

He lights another cigarette, throws the match down on the cement floor and watches it extinguish itself. He wonders if anyone will come.

'Are you Jake?'

A wide, pleasant face framed by severe glasses turned to her. 'Hi. Thanks for coming.' He motioned to the seat opposite. 'So,' Jake said, even before she had settled into her seat. 'You're not English.'

'No.'

'Oh well.' He smiled. 'I saw you in the market, didn't I?'

'The market?'

'That's what your ad said: Ridley Road Market, rainy Saturday. We bought oranges together. Wish we'd spoken.'

She frowned. 'My ad was about a window. And a concert.'

'Concert? You mean a rock concert. A gig? I go to those a lot.'

She thought for a second. 'Are you sure you responded to the right one?'

'Maybe I got the number wrong. I might have taken the one from the ad above, or below.' He shrugged. 'Well, we're here, aren't we? We can just have a chat.'

She found out that chatting, for Jake, meant talking incessantly about himself.

'I love travelling,' he barrelled on, nearly half an hour after she had sat down. 'I went on this overland journey through Africa last year.' He had crossed Kenya and Uganda in a truck with ten other strangers. 'We had such a laugh. We had campfires at night. One night we heard a lion roar; that was really wicked. The Africans were great – there were these two porters and our mechanic. They really helped us a lot. They knew how to carve meat and pitch a tent and all that bush stuff. But mostly we just stuck to ourselves, our group. We really bonded.'

Desdemona stood up and offered Jake her hand. 'Well, good luck.'

Jake looked startled. 'Thanks. Thanks a lot. Good luck to you too. Hope you find who you're looking for.'

'Oh.' Desdemona laughed. 'I'm not looking for anyone.'

The night is blue and ocean-thick; faces stream through it

like fish. Fernando sits on a stool at Bar Italia. Italian cable television roars at the end of the bar. Behind him, the gurgle and hiss of the cappuccino machine.

He is tired and he puts his arms down on the counter and lays his head down on his left arm as bored children do. He sits like this for nearly an hour, watching the procession of faces; in almost every one he sees the abrasive symmetry of beauty. He looks at each face with equal interest, wondering about the passions behind its features, what would happen if he and it were to connect. It's not that he wants to know these random faces, or that he is looking for love, only that this is part of his obsession: he is trying to capture that specific moment, the one before desire becomes memory.

'I haven't been to a private view in ages – two weeks at least.' Robyn said this the way other women complained about not having had sex for a week or so.

Robyn scanned the street for her car, a cowering blue Peugeot. Inside it was littered with pieces of plaster and gold braid. Desdemona got in and they lurched off, Robyn driving recklessly. She had learned to drive in Italy – she had mentioned this once but Desdemona missed the significance.

'Whose is it, one of your friends'?'

Robyn's friends were all painters or artists. In fact Robyn knew most of London's art establishment. That was how she had met Angus, who had introduced her to Desdemona. Robyn was ten years older; at thirty-eight she had dispensed with the furious posing Desdemona saw among the younger art victim crowd. She treated Desdemona as a protégée, but that didn't bother her. It was the way she needed to be treated, at least until she had found her feet in this new world of England, London, the Art World.

'He's a guy I know from my trapeze class,' Robyn said. 'He's from somewhere in South America. He used to be really big when South America was fashionable, you know, around the five hundredth anniversary of whatever it was. Then I don't know what happened. He just dropped out of sight. This is his first exhibition in a couple of years. I told him I'd come. He's very beautiful,' Robyn added in a wistful voice that suggested she had tried for him, and failed.

They threaded their way through a corridor of tall former warehouses swathed in scaffolding and green netting. The gallery appeared in the corner of one of the narrow streets; a tiny door into which a hundred people were cramming themselves.

Robyn handed her a warm beer in a silver can emblazoned with a watery Japanese script.

'Where's the artist?'

'I don't know.' Robyn scanned the crowd. 'He must be here somewhere. God, there's people here I haven't seen in years.'

Desdemona swivelled around to look. When she turned back Robyn had disappeared. She stood for a few minutes, self-consciously sipping from her beer, looking for a familiar face but seeing only the bright, animated faces of people talking in impregnable clumps.

She turned to the paintings – five or six large canvases, abstract in style. The colours were distorted, as if seen through glass, or a smudged window. In their detail she thought she could make out the shadow of a scene: a café, a street, a restaurant. But they were no more than blurs of light and angles. She went closer to read the titles. *One Night Terror. Palacio de la Musica. Momentary Future.*

Robyn appeared out of the crowd. 'Let's go to my place,' she said when she saw Desdemona. 'Everyone else will come later.'

They turned into Robyn's street, an untidy mix of artists'

studios, council flats and renegade grocers run by men of indeterminate nationality.

'How long have you lived here?'

'Ten years or so. I got the lease when you still could. Now I'd have to ask my father to stump up the money for some ridiculous flat called Manhattan or Bowery or one of those New York loft names that have nothing to do with this place and its history.' Robyn opened the door into an oval room and dumped her things on an old sofa, which groaned in protest. She went to the kitchen. Soon Desdemona heard banging and the sounds of chopping. Robyn called something to her from the kitchen.

'What's that?'

Robyn appeared in the doorway, a knife in one hand and a leek in the other. 'I said I want you to meet Fernando, I think you'd have something in common.'

'Who's Fernando?'

'The artist. You've been to some of the same places. Here.' She thrust a glass of wine at Desdemona.

A jagged crash shook the house. Desdemona's glass shuddered. She watched as the wine, now thick and bright, more like the juice of pomegranates than wine, spilled over the lip of the glass with a strange, voluptuous slowness. It landed on the floorboards where it glistened in a fat teardrop.

'*Thunder*. I love thunder.' Robyn lunged across the room. 'Let's turn off the lights.'

They lit two tall candles that stalked either end of the table. Three more crashes tore through the sky. Then, slowly at first, it began to rain. Robyn had kept the door open. Desdemona could see the slanting, almost horizontal rain falling on the old cobblestones of the street. She heard quick, sandalled footsteps going pat, pat, pat up the street.

Two pairs of footsteps crescendoed towards the door. She looked up to see a man, dripping wet, his face pockmarked with rain and dark hair plastered to his head. He was a small man with a chiselled face. His hair was fine and brown, as were his eyes. There was something in their shape and alert expression that made her think of a deer. His expression was uncertain. He looked like he recognized her and was trying to remember where he had seen her before.

Desdemona felt a sensation not unlike that of being on a train about to arrive at a station. She saw a flash of red – red what? – but it was gone.

'Oh no,' she heard Robyn say. 'You really got *caught*. Let me get you towels.'

She watched him walk into the room followed by a blond woman with a smudged Scandinavian face. The woman wore a silver vinyl mini-skirt, white stockings and silver trainers.

She clambered off the stool. 'I'm Desdemona.'

The eyes swivelled towards her. He gave her his hand, which was wet. 'Des-de-mon-a?' He stretched his mouth into an elongated shape.

'I know. It's a funny name.' She tried to smile.

'That's all right. People think I am very *funny*,' he said the word in a way so that she would have no doubt he meant *peculiar*.

They sat down to dinner, Desdemona on the dripping man's left, the smudged woman across from them. As they talked they discovered they had both been in the same city, foreign and remote, at the same time the previous year.

'I can't believe it,' he said. 'You were there in May?'

'Yes, it's amazing, isn't it?'

'For how long?'

'About a month,' Desdemona said. 'But I didn't really know anyone.'

'That is such a shame.' Fernando's voice had a heaviness that suggested he really meant it. 'I wish we had met before, I could have shown you around. I'm sure we passed each other in the street at some point,' he said gravely. 'It's a big city, but everyone goes to the same places.'

'It's possible.' Desdemona nodded.

His voice was like a xylophone, trilling and mellifluous. She was sure she had never heard a voice quite like it before. There were men's voices she was sure came out of the same aural box: gravelly, assured, deep and yet somehow hollowed. But the men's voices she liked were honeyed and light – Angus', for instance. A warning bell went off in her head.

Over the next few hours she studied him furiously. There was something haunted about him – the way his eyes would cloud over between sentences, or his mind would catch on the obstacle of a particular word. When they were speaking about something innocuous – flowers, colours – she watched as his eyes were invaded by this darkness.

'Are you all right?'

'Oh—' He paused. He looked down at the table, frowning. 'What happens is, all my friends they die.'

'All of them?' She pictured plane crashes or bomb explosions.

'Well, a few. AIDS.'

'Oh, I'm sorry.' She really was sorry. In that moment a strange reversal took place inside her. Instantly she retreated to some former conveniently disappointed posture. She let the thought enter her head that what she had in front of her was just another charming gay man with whom she had an immediate rapport.

'Would you like to see a film this weekend?'

She gave him a smile showing just the right amount of disappointment to say she would have liked to, but really, it would be a waste of time. 'I can't. I'm going away.' She stood up. 'It's been wonderful to meet you.' She held out her hand. 'I'm sure we'll see each other again soon.'

A look of disbelief spread itself across Fernando's face,

followed by disappointment. She recognized it and was glad to see it on someone else's face for a change.

On the street the air was thick and humid, the sky streaked orange with London burn. She filled her lungs with air and tasted metal.

Robyn followed her out on to the pavement, mincing on her bare feet, waving her lit cigarette around. 'How did you get along?'

'Very well. He's gay, though, isn't he?' She tried to keep the reproach out of her voice.

Robyn gave her a puzzled look. 'No. Not at all.'

'Oh. Goodnight, then.'

Desdemona was halfway home by the time she remembered something he had said to her. It was when they were talking about both having been in the same countries at the same time. He had turned to her and asked, 'Do you believe in accident?'

'Do you mean chance?'

'No.' He shook his head insistently. 'Not chance. Not fate. *Accident*.'

Before she could answer Robyn had called out that the main course was ready, and the conversation shifted.

Maybe they could have gone for a drink together. Maybe they could have exchanged telephone numbers. Maybe they could have been friends. Had she really done it? Had she looked one of many possible destinies in the eye and let it go, just to see if she could? Because everyone knows there's no such thing as a second chance.

She thinks of herself as living in a place made of glass and edges, like a giant window, streaked by the blurs of faces of people never to be encountered; people streaming up and down escalators, plunging into the bowels of the earth to catch a train, disappearing in and out of doors like water draining from a tub. A team of celestial air-traffic controllers keep them all apart, like planes stacked up in the landing pattern at Heathrow.

She had never felt it anywhere else, but in London she carried the weight of absence, the phantom burden of what it would be to know each of these strangers. Maybe it was the sheer scale of London, or the way that each time she tried to feel something deep and lasting for the city it only bounced her emotion straight back. At other times it struck her that there were simply too many people in the world.

'I saw you over there first.'

Respondee number two pointed across the room and its expanse of polished wood. 'There, by that pillar.'

'Really?' said Desdemona. 'What was I doing?'

'You had your nose stuck in this book. You looked like you were waiting for someone. You must have stayed there for fifteen minutes.'

'I was absorbed. Did you come over and talk to me?'

'I approached you. I asked you what you were reading. You looked at me like you were going to kill me—'

'I hate being interrupted when I'm reading.'

'But you still talked to me.'

He gave Desdemona a furtive, almost shy look. 'I can't believe you read the ads too.'

'Why is that so hard to believe?'

'I don't know,' he said. 'It's just you look—' He gave her an appraising look that travelled up and down her body. She felt like a piece of grass being raked of leaves. 'It's just—' Finally he blurted it out. 'You're attractive.'

'You mean attractive people never have to search for lovers?'

He shrugged. 'That's the whole point of being attractive, isn't it?'

'I don't know.' She didn't feel like debating the sociobiology of beauty. 'I used to be addicted to the Once Seens. They just fascinate me. All those crossed paths, all those destinies denied. It's been a long time since I looked at them, really,' she lied. 'It was just by chance I saw it.'

'I really like it myself.' He reached into his pocket and extracted a rumpled piece of paper. He held it out to her. She took it and read it again:

25/4/98. Royal Festival Hall. Girl in green reading *Great Expectations,* leaning against a pillar. Me, wearing black, glasses, staring at you from the bar. I wish I'd spoken.

'So why did you respond?' he asked.

'Why did you write it?'

'I was curious to see what would happen.'

'Well then.'

So I'm not in love, she thought. At the same time she wondered how one could know so definitively and so quickly. It was like having a little stamp in her hand. One side was embossed *IL*, In Love; on the other *NIL*: Not In Love. She stamped him with the latter. She thought, *Thank God.*

'So what do you do?'

'I'm a project manager.'

'What does that entail?'

'I manage projects.'

She resisted an urge to say, No kidding.

'My job's not that important,' he continued. 'I mean, it's not as though I'm saving the world, know what I mean? But I really enjoy it. I figure it's all in your outlook on the situation. You have to have a positive attitude towards the work. I like working in a big office – meeting different people all the time. It's never boring. I have to talk to all types.'

She studied him. He had a viola face – wide, curved. A honeyed deep sound emanated from it. It was such a shame she wasn't in love. He really wasn't bad-looking.

'I love this space.' He surveyed the Hall with a dreamy expression. 'I don't know about the people, though. Maybe this is what I'll turn into in ten years' time, a guy who drinks organic beer and goes to classical concerts.'

She looked around and saw men wearing overly structured glasses and rust-coloured jumpers, they held pints of bitter in front of their chests like trophies. The women wore opulent fabrics – silk, light cashmere cardigans – textures that anticipate a finger's brush with skin, hair, the soft, folded zones of the body.

'I have a girlfriend.'

'Pardon?'

'I have a girlfriend,' he repeated. He kept his eyes down at the table. 'She's in Romania.'

'*Romania*?'

'She had a fit of altruism.' He shrugged. 'She's there helping out in an orphanage.'

'Grim.'

'Yeah. Apparently Bucharest is full of wild dogs that roam the streets. Sometimes a whole pack will set on a person and kill them.'

'Christ.'

'Well, I don't really know what it's like, but she wrote me that.' He frowned into his drink.

Around them the Hall was emptying slowly, like a film set being dismantled, the extras told to go home. Expensive men and women were already re-interring themselves in Jaguars. Thin-faced commuters seeped from every opened door. Behind them in the darkened concert hall sat exhausted musicians. All of humanity was draining away around them like water, leaving the late-night drinkers, the desperate strangers like residue in a bathtub – hairs, flecks of skin.

'So.' He looked down at the floor.

'So.'

'Until next time.' He stood uncertainly in front of her.

'Yes.' She looked towards the door in anticipation of her escape. She saw him catch the look. 'Next time.'

Desdemona walked through the building, her shoes ringing on the hard floor. Only three hours before, the Hall had been full of people, concert tickets fluttering in their hands. It was like being in an airport; people leaving through doors, disappearing down carpeted corridors to visit distant and unknown cities. Travelling.

His friend the sculptor is the first of three to die. Without him the studio is a hostile place. The room itself seems to be demanding that he leave.

Fernando gathers up his things and puts them into two large boxes. He takes down photographs he has stuck to the wall; one of Henri Cartier-Bresson's from Spain showing a carnival man being shaved by a moustache-wearing woman. These were the kinds of images he had liked as a younger man, five, seven years ago. He wondered if he would keep them. There were pens, pencils, slides, a Stanley knife, also some paint, yellowed letterhead. He puts four years into two medium-sized boxes and closes them up.

He leaves the studio for the last time, stamping as he opens the door to frighten away the dozen or so rats who continually loiter outside like delinquents. He goes out into the streets of Chinatown as he has done so many times, to get a bowl of soup, buy cigarettes or herbal remedies. But today the triangles of silk hanging in the windows, the serpentined pagodas and basins of lychees look disappointed and tinny.

In the restaurant Asian men stay to eat for half an hour at

most, smoking too many strong cigarettes. He wonders what brings them to eat lonely spring-onion soups in these Soho hustler restaurants. He watches as they lift cigarettes to soup-wet lips, their hands fluttering with impatience, or is it fear? Later when he is walking in the rain he will see these men again walking hunch-shouldered, the collars of their cheap leather jackets pulled up, hair dishevelled, the ends of their cigarettes soaked. He thinks of similar solitary men he has seen in the deserted night-plazas of Mexico City, in a Buenos Aires the colour of roses and oysters.

Desdemona put her key in the door and was greeted by the astringent smell of an empty flat. Angus was out again, doing his weekly bout of vigorous clubbing. Tonight he would bring home another of the men she referred to collectively as Dial-a-Redhead. Angus had a thing about Celts, it seemed, possibly because despite his name he himself was olive-skinned and dark.

She saw her post arranged there in a neat pile on the stair. She ripped the most promising-looking envelope open.

This is not really our style, the note read. *Why don't you try a psychic*?

She unfolded the piece of paper inside the note and saw her own handwriting. It looked strangely unfamiliar, less like writing than hieroglyphs.

4 June. The weight of absence. Thai restaurant, Clerkenwell. I have been carrying the idea of you with me like a ghost stone in my pocket. When we meet and I take it out and we examine it, will you recognize yourself? Or will you toss it aside and call it a stone, a dead weight?

She showed it to Robyn. 'I can't believe they wouldn't put it in,' Desdemona fumed. 'I pay the same money every other nutter pays.'

'No one's going to publish ads like that.'

'But you write things like that for your shows. What about that show of yours, "The Banality of Love"?'

'That's art, not advertising for a mate. What about Fernando?'

'I liked him,' Desdemona said quietly. 'I'm sorry I assumed he was gay.'

'Well, if you liked him, why didn't you get his phone number?' Robyn's exasperation crawled into Desdemona's ear and settled there like a beetle. She knew Robyn didn't understand hesitancy where men were concerned. Robyn went through men like water, breast-stroking casually through them as if they were all the same continuous substance.

'Can't you get it for me?'

'I only see him at trapeze class. He doesn't come every week. You know, Desdemona' – Robyn only used her name when she desired the full theatrical effect – 'You have to use more conventional means of meeting people. You have to be more open.'

'Open to what?'

Robyn sighed. 'To experience.'

'I am open. I just want to determine my fate. I want things to be natural.'

'What's unnatural about dinner parties? That's how most people bloody meet. Not through your little appeals to fate. Those nutty replies you get to your fictional Once Seens, they're at least as deluded as you.'

'I hate dinner parties. All those people sitting around a table going blah, blah, blah and coming away from it thinking they've had an actual experience,' Desdemona said. 'If I think I've seen him and he thinks he's seen me, what's the harm?'

'Well, then, *do* something with one of them.'

'Like what?'

'Seduce them.' Robyn exhaled a stream of smoke. 'Get it over with. Get rid of this urge you have.'

'They're not right.'

'What do you mean, not right?'

'They're not the one I'm looking for.'

Robyn narrowed her eyes until she was looking at Desdemona as if she was something untrustworthy, something that had to be watched. 'How are you so sure you'll recognize the right one?'

Desdemona shrugged. 'I just will.'

Robyn sighed. 'Why don't you write a real ad? You know, sit on the tube, go to a concert, whatever. Keep alert for someone you fancy, try to make eye contact, or whatever meaningful interaction these ad-writing people think they've had. Do it properly instead of making up these fictional scenarios. You can't just wait for destiny to pick you up. It may never happen.'

The echo of Robyn's voice accompanied her home. It was what taxi drivers and workmen said to Desdemona when she was walking down the street, deep in thought. *Cheer up, love. It may never happen.*

He steps out on to his narrow balcony twelve floors above the ground. The sky looks porous, like linen. The horizon is soaked with the last stains of blue. He lights a cigarette and looks up into the terse stars of the English summer. He goes back into his flat, where all the lightbulbs have either burnt out or are broken.

That night he cooks on the blue flame of gas, humming a nameless tune. He takes his solitary dinner into the living room, alarming shadows leaping behind his back. In the window a perfect view of the City and the Thames is framed like a photograph. All night he goes from room to room carrying his candle, shuffling like a monk in a manuscript vault, passing through triangles of light, streaks of mint blue, tracked by the sulphur eye of the city.

For the next few weeks Desdemona struggles with her impulse to call him. When she eventually gives in she leaves nothing to chance and writes down what she wants to say, word for word, in order to avoid the nervous stutters of someone who has spent too long thinking of him – the 'I don't know if you'll remember mes', the 'it would be lovely to see yous', and the killing, hesitant laughter.

In the end she leaves a message that sounds like he is being called up to the army.

'My name is Desdemona. We met over dinner at Robyn's. Call me on 241–9482.' Then she thought it sounded too casual so she added, 'It's important.'

She is not surprised when she does not hear from him. Two days pass, then five, then ten. She is in the throes of trying to forget about him when, on the eleventh day, he telephones her.

A concert was letting out as she entered the Royal Festival Hall. She waited at a table by the window, watching as women in opulent fabrics rubbed themselves against important-looking men.

After ten minutes he arrived, threading his way deftly through the foursomes of coffee drinkers. He hovered uncertainly above her for a moment before sitting opposite her, his face tense and agile.

'It looks like a 1950s airport departure lounge, don't you think? I am always waiting for Jackie Kennedy to show up. And the men all look like tango dancers.' He laughed. 'I always think of it as the perfect building for exiles: public, no one owns it, and you always have company.'

'Is that what you are, an exile?'

'Isn't that what we both are?'

'I don't know.' Desdemona frowned. 'I feel less of an external exile than an internal one. *I'm* the foreign land.' She pointed to her own chest. 'It's in here. Most of the time I feel like that quote from Martial, the Roman poet? Do you know it?'

He shook his head.

'You are but a composition of lies, and two thirds of your person are locked up in boxes for the night.'

He looked puzzled.

She tried to explain. 'I have no idea where my desires come from. I just feel at the mercy of my compulsions, as if I'm living in a desert kingdom where some extravagant woman is thrusting pomegranates in my nose and all the men are dressed in white and look like plinths.'

She saw he was frowning, but with an amused expression. He obviously had no idea what she was going on about.

'Oh well.' She sat back in her seat and looked around the foyer. 'I suppose I am an exile after all. Although you can't be an exiled Canadian. What are you going to exile yourself from, an excess of fresh air?'

The amber ring around Fernando's irises widened. Finally he laughed. 'Sometimes it can take me a few minutes to get a joke.' He lit a cigarette. It hovered uncertainly in his fingers before he took his first drag. 'I am dyslexic, actually. Sometimes, with dyslexics, the joke part of their brain does not work very well.'

'Oh dear, there goes the GSOH.'

'Gsawh?'

'It's personal-ad-speak for Good Sense of Humour. It's the one thing everyone seems to agree they want.'

He took another drag on his cigarette. 'Is that something you do, read personal ads?'

She took hold of the stem of her wine glass and twirled it in circles. 'Sometimes.'

'Why?'

'Why not?'

'You are looking for friendship?'

'Not exactly.' She looked down at the table. She was beginning to feel embarrassed. Fernando would never be the kind of person to look for anyone, or anything. People would come to him. She was sure that life divided people at birth, almost arbitrarily, into two camps: The Searchers and The Loved. The Searchers had to go out and look for everything, bang their heads against walls, scrape their fingernails. The Loved just sat back and waited for the magnet that had been planted inside them to take effect.

She said, 'I suppose I'm looking for love.'

'Or sex?'

'I'm not really interested in sex for sex's sake.'

He nodded. 'I agree. Everything does not end up in desire.'

She sat back in her chair as suddenly as if he had smacked her. She had to catch her breath at the sound of the word – *desire*. On his tongue it took the shape of a hothouse. She had a vision of tropical flowers, opening their innards and displaying their petals with the sick audacity of the enchantress.

It was a thrilling idea – that there could be something beyond this opulent, stifling world of desire.

'Don't you ever desire people?'

He shrugged. 'There were many people. But they were just lovers. Really I wanted to forget myself, then to re-remember myself through them. That was not love, that was desire.'

He smiled. His eyes had lightened to toffee. They looked completely different from the dark, mirrored eyes she had met the first night. She realized those eyes would never give her those suffocating desirous looks other men bestowed on women, looks that were like being draped in velvet.

Out of the corner of her eye Desdemona saw gusts of

summer rain sweep down the Thames like sails, blown by winds from the east.

She turned to him. 'We should go.'

They stood in the corridor, jostled by concert-goers. Suddenly he took her elbow. 'I don't feel that way any more,' he said, his voice urgent. His eyes were bright, his hair fell over his forehead, thick and frayed like bunched feathers. 'There's nothing I have to forget in myself.' He dropped her arm. 'I have enjoyed our conversation.'

She wanted to laugh. He sounded so absurdly formal, as if they were delegates to a United Nations conference who had met by chance in a corridor.

'Why don't we take a walk by the river?' The way he said it, it sounded like a promising adventure. He took her hand and they left.

As the train slowed the moment became clearer and she was standing outside a café window, looking into a haze of smoke and faces. For the first time in her life she is south of the Tropic of Capricorn. The city has been scrubbed clean by rain; it is May, the first days of autumn, and the southern light is mandarin and undiluted.

There is nothing to link this moment to anything else in her life; travelling is full of moments like this one, of random cafés, faces, bus stops. But there is something about the alarming red scarves the women wear, the way they coil themselves around necks with the languor of torpid snakes.

She decides not to have a coffee; it is far too expensive. She is not aware how obvious it is, the disappointment with which she turns her face from the window, rotates her body and begins to walk down the street. In that moment her disappointed angle will lodge itself in another mind, one sitting inside the café, cupping his chin in his hand, looking in an unfocused manner out the window and seeing the woman turn down the street, and this will become for both of them less a moment than a forgotten memory.

'Hey, Destinymona, how goes the search for The One?' Angus greeted her with a grin. 'We haven't bumped into each other in, what, twenty-four hours?'

'That's because you've been out with the latest Dial-a-Redhead.'

'Ah-ha.' Angus nodded. 'You don't approve.'

'The truth is, I've given up.'

'Don't believe it. You're resigning yourself to singledom? I so wanted to go on double dates and steal your boyfriend.'

'I wouldn't put it past you.'

She sat on one of the cardboard boxes she still hadn't unpacked and stared at the floor for a while. How could she explain this to Angus? So much of the time she was a stock figure for him: the pathetic yet funny straight flatmate who didn't get it. She was looking for love when she should have simplified her quest to looking for sex. Look at Angus. He managed to bring home a different man almost every night.

She decided to try to explain. 'I started doing this because I couldn't bear the thought that nothing was ever going to happen.'

Angus frowned. 'What nothing?'

'Anything. I hate the passivity of life, that we're just expected to sit around and wait for love to drop on our heads like a piano. Then we say, Oh, it was destiny. It was meant to be. Well, nothing is ever meant. It's all random.'

'Just because you're in thrall to chaos theory doesn't mean some people can't believe in destiny.'

He was right. In responding to Once Seens and writing her own fictional ads she had been pursuing her own theory of human interaction: that everything was perfectly random, from being born versus aborted to who you ended up with as parents, as friends, as lovers, children. She found absolutely no comfort in this theory and that was why she clung to it with such tenacity.

'I just wanted to take matters into my own hands,' she explained. 'I wanted to create the moment, to force something to finally *happen*. But there's no happenings. There's nothing, just this moment lodged in my mind.'

'What moment?'

'Just something I saw when I was abroad last year.' She shrugged. 'It's more colour, you know, a feel, than anyone in particular.'

Angus pursed his lips. 'I think you've lost me there.'

'*Desire*. We focus it on other people like a beam of light, because that's the only way we know how to make sense of it. People have affairs, people fall in love, people have sex just to give themselves the impression that they have a commitment to the moment, to experience. Really all they have is a commitment to themselves.'

Angus was silent. Angus was hardly ever silent. She waited. Finally he rose from the stool. He looked at her long and hard. He seemed to be deciding something. He said, 'You've got some post.'

She tore open the envelope. Another rejection. The ad sat there looking hopeful and blank, the way she imagined newborn babies looked.

Through a glass window. We just missed each other. You were on the inside, I on the outside. Red and flowers. One in the past, the other to come. Please get in touch.

Nights in a Foreign Country

Through a remarkable paradox, my life of adventure, instead of opening up a new world to me, had the effect rather of bringing me back to the old one, and the world I had been looking for disintegrated in my grasp.

Claude Lévi-Strauss, *Tristes Tropiques*

REBELS ADVANCE FROM REMOTE STRONGHOLD

She turns on the tap and hears a sound like an animal choking. There is electricity only between the hours of seven and ten in the evening. She looks at her watch: nine fifty; any minute now the lightbulb will make a tinny *clink* sound, not unlike when moths hurl themselves against its white-hot membrane of glass. Then darkness.

She has been in town only a day and the rebels are taking over. She laughs as she thinks how it sounds like a Hemingway story: *the rebels are taking over.*

By some untraceable accident she has arrived ahead of both the army and the rebels. The town is located in a strategic loop, the rebels stitched it yesterday. But at the time she came through they hadn't yet realized it, like forgetful grandmothers who put down their knitting only to discover they are nearer to finishing the sweater than they thought.

Her paper believed she was still in the neighbouring country. Perhaps she was the only foreign journalist in town. If so, she had work to do. A situation like this could make her career, she told herself. Look at that woman freelance, the only British reporter in town when Kigali blew. Now she was everywhere.

When she arrived that afternoon the hotel desk was empty. She heard the swish-swish of a broom in a corridor and following it found a dark, stout woman sweeping the courtyard. The woman barely gave her a glance as she handed her her key from the full key board.

'There are no other guests?'

The woman only looked around the little plant-filled reception, to the television, a mid-seventies model in the corner, the two skeletal chairs parked in front of it, as if to say, why do you think anyone would stay in *this* place?

She dumped her things in her room then sat at a rickety table in the courtyard; behind her the usual garrulous caged tropical bird chattered. It was pleasant for a moment sitting in the shade, the sun a diaphanous gold curtain dropped a few feet away.

The silent lady was coming towards her from the darkened interior, her face almost completely consumed by a pair of huge square sunglasses like the ones Jackie O wore after she had married Aristotle Onassis. She could see herself reflected in them – a pale face stretched wide in two dark fisheyes, behind her a sepia sky.

The woman put two glasses on the table. 'I thought you might like a drink.'

Her voice was shallow and small, not the guttural flutes she would have expected from a woman of such bulk. Condensation ran off the chilled glasses in rivulets. She sat down heavily and took off her sunglasses to reveal eyes like dried black olives set in corrugated folds of skin.

'Mind you, it's not alcohol. Only lemonade. I don't drink. Do you?'

'Only when I have to.' She neglected to say that this was probably every day.

'Ah yes.' The woman nodded. '*Des coutumes*.' Customs.

'Are you Protestant?'

'Of course not. That's for people with no education.'

They sat in silence for a minute.

'Have you heard any news?' She tried to sound neutral. She had not seen any clues that might alert her to the hotel caretaker's political inclinations.

'Only that they are on their way. They will be here tomorrow. Maybe the next day. Maybe the end of the week.' The woman shrugged. She said, 'Who knows?' But it sounded like, *Who cares*?

When she rose from the table she said, *I am Amélie*.

The city is a low, flat town, surrounded by mangroves. She takes a breath and tastes fried banana. She walks past long-abandoned houses in the old quarter which look like decayed wedding cakes, their once-white stucco peeling off in great curls. Some of them have swimming pools, now empty, their sides cracked and pockmarked by bullet holes. She stops to watch small pink lizards with bulging black eyes dart from the cool cracks.

On the street the women come towards her with a slow-hipped gait. They look quite relaxed, she thinks, considering what's happening. The thin dogs are much more cautious. They trawl the gutters with a low-backed skipping hyena gait. If she reaches out to touch one they shy away, scuttling sideways like crabs.

After only an hour of exploration she has to go back to her room, suddenly overcome by a wave of fatigue. The heat enfolds her body in a wet sheet. She understands now why white men took to drinking in the tropics. She longs for any release from thinking about the next cotton-smothered breath she must take.

She hears the sound of a television in the room at the end of the hall. It must be Amélie's. It is comforting to hear the tinny, wavering voices. It won't make a good story, though: TELEVISION ON IN HUMID HOTEL. These days she is always thinking in headlines – the ones she would yet write.

She falls, suddenly and precipitously, into a dreamless sleep.

*

She heard him shuffling in the kitchen behind her, making noise as he always did to announce his presence and so to reduce the possibility of their having to speak.

She shared only one enthusiasm with her mother's new husband: the national newspaper, delivered to the back doorstep each morning in a tube-shaped plastic bag. The newspaper allowed them to practise their technique of communicating with a certain wordless stealth. They could tell when either was about to get up, or pour more milk, by a complex choreography of anticipation and retreat. She would scrape her chair a second before she actually intended to get up, to give him time to appear not to notice her departure and so save him the ordeal of saying goodbye.

Those mornings they sat spooning cereal into their mouths in silence while their eyes followed the debt crises in Brazil, the war in the south ocean over some misty islands whose names no one could agree on, or the regular deaths of Soviet secretary-generals. Sometimes she would just read the datelines: Lima, Jakarta, Paris.

At twelve years old she dimly understood the imprecise enchantment these names held for her: they were simply anywhere but the town they had moved to when her mother married this man, a place where couples paid teenage boys to mow their lawns regularly and where people drove four-wheel drives through wide, eventless streets. These names, and the words that went with them – *guerrilla, liberation, conflict, détente* – told her there was something hard, even glamorous in a sinister way, at work in the world – some malevolent force. She wanted desperately to know what it was, she wanted to be there.

*

PRESIDENT DEFIANT IN FACE OF ATTACK

Amélie appears in the corner of the courtyard. Her calves, triangular and muscled, stick out from a rigid black skirt. On her feet she wears black Chinese slippers.

'The TV is on. I thought you might want to come and watch with me.'

The olive-stone eyes soften and she can see that Amélie is probably thinking, *la pauvre jeune fille*. Trapped here, and now. That's if she does not think she is a prostitute.

'Thank you, madame,' she says.

'Oh.' She waves her hand in a dismissive gesture. 'You can call me Amélie.'

She sits down, glad to be able to hold a scrap of intimacy delicately between her fingers.

The news shows the President, dressed in khaki and surrounded by soldiers, descending from a jeep. The soldiers' faces are blank and impassive. The President's threatens to erupt into a snarl. He is lighter-skinned than in the pictures she has seen and has lost weight; he looks like a dead lizard paled by the sun. He makes sweeping gestures, speaks in the local dialect, which she does not understand.

'What is he saying?'

'He is appealing for peace. He is asking the rebels to stop their advance on the city.'

The image goes dead and is replaced by black-and-white zebra stripes of fuzz. Suddenly the screen lurches into a different scene. In this one, several women surround a man in a room of what looks like a colonial mansion. A few dusty portraits hang on walls of dark wood. Most of the women are crying; the man's face remains set in a vacant stare.

Slowly she realizes the news has lurched into a soap opera imported from a nearby, more stable country. She can't quite follow the dialogue, which is in slanted local French. The man playing the European administrator looks Italian – a long nose, baleful eyes. He wears a white suit, proof of his European-ness, although in the Kodakchrome colours of Amélie's television it comes out as yellow. He is in the middle of seducing a young unmarried woman.

She mentions this to Amélie, who nods slowly. 'Yes,' she says, very carefully, as if she is about to deliver a great statement. 'That's the way it is.'

'Do you have a – a husband?'

Amélie shakes her head. '*Je suis seule.*'

They go back to watching the programme. It isn't until later, when she is alone in her room, that she remembers Amélie didn't use the usual word for single, *célibataire*. She had said, *I am alone*.

*

Her mother put her to work cleaning his office. She swept the hardwood floor languidly, not taking much care. She looked without interest at the sociology textbooks that lined his shelves. Presents from other academics littered his desk, pictures of their children, copies of their latest book.

The broom scraped on something. She looked down and saw a small white piece of paper caught between the straws.

She bent down and plucked it out. As she unfolded it she

could see writing. It was a list, the kind you make before taking some important decision. It had two columns: Pro and Con. There were more cons than pros. Under 'Pro' were several entries. She only saw 'I want: children' and 'I need: sex'. Under 'Con' she saw her name.

She held the piece of paper in her hand, feeling dizzy, then placed it neatly on his desk.

CIRCUMSTANCES DON'T COUNT

The rebels have taken the airport, twenty-seven kilometres from the the city. Most of the national fleet of aeroplanes have been seized. On the street she hears stories of rebels surprising crews in their cockpits, forcing the terrified pilots to take off again with guns to their heads, even though the plane has only enough fuel to stay in the air for half an hour. Many of the soldiers are poor boys from dusty villages. They have never even seen an airport or plane before. It's like having their own circus ride and they want to have a little fun.

'The President was a scientist,' Amélie said, 'before he became President. He was, what do you call them? Men who study insects?'

'Entomologist.'

'Yes. Entomologist. He had a very big collection. Moths, beetles. All dead and labelled. It was burnt during the last attempted coup. He cried for two days.'

The next day she interviews a government official, a small man with quick, delicate hands. They are in a hot room painted a faded Versailles yellow. In certain places the plaster has been hacked at.

The government official sits in an old, crumbling chair that someone has tried to burn. He places his black hands over two black streaks on the arms.

'The people are wondering who is to blame for their misfortunes,' he says. 'Gods are in line, as are spirits.'

'*Et de circonstances?*' she asks.

He sighs, very lightly. 'Circumstances don't really come into the picture. Here things must happen for a reason.'

She wants to say, the reason is, the people are miserable because they are exploited. The government exploits them. The rebels too. The international aid agencies exploit them for sorrow money. I exploit them for stories.

'So they go looking,' he continues, his voice keeping the same neutral, gelatinous tone as Amélie's, a thick, translucent substance that anyone could see through, if they had the courage, 'for who is to blame. And when they find him they are satisfied' – he clears his throat – 'temporarily.'

*

She leaned against the washer. Her mother was filling baby bottles with apple juice. He came into the kitchen, said something to her mother about the wrong baby formula, then took her mother by the shoulders firmly and began to shake her.

Red blots formed in her head, then spread like ink seeping into cloth. She felt hot. She said, 'Get your hands off her or I'll kill you.'

'You keep out,' sang her mother, in a strangled voice, not her own, not even human. 'You get out from between us.'

She backed away, frightened.

JOURNALIST TRIES TO FILE INCONCLUSIVE STORY

The Novotel is barricaded. No one comes or goes. At the telegraph office a sullen queue of what looks to be a hundred people snakes from its mouth.

She asks a young man in the queue, 'Why are you waiting?'

'Because there is no telegraph.'

'Then why are you waiting?'

He shrugs.

She goes into a bank and pays the fat bank manager with the largest, squarest glasses – even bigger than Amélie's Jackie O glasses; they must be a popular item here – a gigantic sum to use the telephone. But when she dials the international operator she gets a young man's voice, both rough and honeyed. *Âllo, âllo?* she says. The voice on the other end pauses for a moment, then vomits a string of curses. She hangs up. She looks at the bank manager. He is looking at her. She sees a tongue exit from his mouth: small, pink, feline. He looks at her in a way that is unmistakable and licks his lips.

The streets are quieter. People are barricading themselves in. White people are disappearing into cellars. No one looks sick with fear. People generally look well, except for a few beggars and stray AIDS cases, notable for their thinness and an occasional bumpy rash covering their skin, like an attack of boils.

At night the sun sinks behind the blue enamelled mountains and the wind begins to rifle through the sugarcane fields like a many-fingered animal.

'I came to the city because I loved it,' Amélie tells her as they sit in the courtyard. 'I loved the orange nights. I hated the countryside. It was too dark. I was always stumbling into walls, snakes.'

Des serpents. The way Amélie says it, with a curled tongue, hissing on the ssses, makes her wonder if Amélie is talking about snakes, or men.

'I wanted to come here.' Amélie looks at her with eyes that seemed to once have held jokes. Now there are only those glittering olive stones. She sees her mouth twitch into something approaching a shadow of a smile.

*

'We're going for a drive.'

Her mother stood before her, jingling her car keys in a threatening manner. She wore her bloated peach-coloured raincoat, the one that made her look pregnant even on the rare occasions when she wasn't.

'Where are we going?'

'Nowhere,' her mother snapped.

When they were out on the highway her mother turned to her. 'He'll leave me, if you don't change. Is that what you want?' Her mother's voice was narrow. It had edges she had never heard before. 'Is that what you're trying to do? Do you want me to be alone? Is that what you want? For me to be left alone with two kids?'

'Three,' she corrected her mother. Her voice was as flat as the fields that streamed by the windshield. 'You've got three children.'

They returned to the house in silence.

From then on she was the third, forgotten child, the child who was no longer even counted. From then on nothing would ever be more unreal than her days spent in that house, days which refused to pass, got bogged down in their own reality, sat, gelatinous and heavy, on the beating heart of time.

In her last year in the house, when she turned sixteen and got her driver's licence, she found a way to release herself from this unnerving stasis. She would set her alarm for four o'clock, then stumble out to the driveway and get in the car, careful not to shut the door until she had coasted the car in neutral out of the driveway. Lights, engine, action. She drove up and down the provincial highways, the night slipping away like shoals of translucent fish encountered in a black, depthless ocean. At dawn, she turned the car back, sliding it into the driveway as she had left, silently. They never seemed to notice.

AN ACCIDENT

They sat together in darkness, Amélie seated in her rocking chair, moving back and forth like a large pendulum.

'You're not from this city, are you?' She asked the question as gently as she could. Depending on what Amélie said, she might use her in her story.

'I'm from—' Amélie named an area to the north that was mostly desert. 'No one is from this city. The government made it up. It used to be an estuary; only crocodiles are from this city.'

'What about your husband, is he dead?'

'*Oui. C'était un accident.*'

'What kind of accident?'

'It was years ago, during the last rebel siege. He was driving on the road. From here to—' Amélie named a city about forty kilometres from the capital. 'They had taken the road, closed it off. In those days we did not have a radio. It was before I inherited this hotel. We were poor. But he had an old car, a white Fiat.' She smiled. 'And he wanted to see his family. So he went. There was no traffic on the road. He must have wondered. But he kept going anyway. Then, at a certain point, a roadblock, I presume. He must have stopped. He must have got out of the car, gone to talk to them.'

Amélie stopped talking and looked hard out of her window, even though there was nothing there, except a couple of floppy palms she must have seen a million times before.

'*Mais c'était un accident.*' Amélie's voice was flat, toneless. She might have been describing the state of the flowers in the courtyard. 'One of those things that happens. Bad luck. *La chance.*' She looked at her, and shrugged. As if to say, that's all.

'But he died.'

'He died, yes. Although I never got his body.'

'Why not?'

'Because they asked him for a cigarette. He gave them all he had. Then they threw kerosene over him and lit a match. There wasn't anything left.'

The American Plan. The Catholic Church. Everyone has deserted the country. A woman came up to her in the street. She said she was a nun.

'Do you want a place on our helicopter? If you come to the church at two o'clock today we can get you on.'

'I'm here to get the story.'

The nun looked at her. Her eyes were strange. If she had to write about those eyes she really would not have been able to describe the look in them.

'God save you,' the nun said, and moved on.

The nights are yellow; the sky can't quite absorb the sallow glare of the town. In the mornings the sun springs, without warning, over the horizon. Within an hour it is a red cyclops stare.

Sugarcane fields surround the city. They are the colour of light, almost plastic green. The colours are too bright, even out of whack: the sun is green and the rain yellow-orange, the colour of yucca, the vegetable the local women use for their vast stews, cooked slowly in cauldrons that sizzle and squat like giant black reptiles. *Yucca and rain*, she writes again and again, on her notepad. *Yucca and rain*.

*

The snowstorms started in October and ended in April. She remembers snow piling outside the window. Her breath melting a circular hole in the thin layer of frost. Her nose right up against it. Her tongue held out, the taste of window cleaner.

Drifts, blizzards – she watched the snow drift in, accumulate. The same process seemed to be happening in her head, creating sculptures of silence.

She would go to Greece, Brazil, Tunisia. There she would have sweet nights. Coriander and apples. Heat—

THE PRICE OF BANANAS

She decided to try to file again. The same passive queue still dribbled outside the state telecommunications office. Some people had camped out. Others had clearly lost hope and sat in heaps in the dust.

When she arrived back at the hotel Amélie came towards her with an uncommonly brisk movement.

'When are you going to leave?'

'Leave?'

'You must leave. For your own safety.'

'I can't leave. I mean, no one can now.'

There was a pause. 'They don't just kill women, you know.'

Amélie looked at her hard. 'They do things to you first. Then they kill you.'

'I know.' Her mouth went a little dry. 'Aren't you frightened?'

'Me?' Amélie held back her head and laughed – later she would realize it was the first laugh she had heard in three days. 'I'm an old woman.'

In the streets she tries to bargain for bananas. The woman market seller gives her a hostile look. She is not bargaining like a woman should do, clicking her tongue against her front teeth, making expansive gestures that say, too much, not enough.

In the end she takes the bananas and pays the woman some outrageous sum. The woman looks at the money she has handed her, staring at her palm as if she has just spat in it.

Rumours ripple through the city. In the market she hears the testimony of a man who got through. He is thin, shaky. He sits cross-legged surrounded by clumps of bananas, speaking in dialect. She asks him to tell it to her in French.

'It is just before the final assault on my town. The "Freedom Fighters" they come dressed as ... as ...' He struggles with some image in his mind. '*Des femmes. Mais c'est un carnival.* They wore women's cardigans they had stolen from women they had already murdered. They had taken off their ripped stockings and put them on. One even had a red wig. And there was one with a mask.' The man's voice goes cold. He stutters for a minute. His voice drifts back into the present tense. 'At the outskirts they are holding an inspection. One cavorts. He is like a spirit. A small boy. Chattering. "It's been five minutes since I killed someone please let me kill someone. I like the number twenty." The commander, he nods his head. So the boy counts the people from the head of the line, *un, deux, trois*, and drags the twentieth man into the bushes. People are mad,' he says. 'They are mad with blood.'

She goes to her room, turns on the light. Nothing happens. The electricity is gone. She struggles to see beyond the darkness.

*

Every summer she waved goodbye, goodbye to her friends with their families, crammed into cars in which faces turned away from her waving figure just before they rounded the corner. They were driving to the airport. In the winters they went to Florida or to the Caribbean; in the summers they went to Germany, to Italy. *Bye*, she waved. *See you in September*. Keeping her smile for them to see until they turned the corner.

She spent the long summer days crawling through deserted playground equipment, or walking the wide, shaded streets of the city, passing through pools of thick tree-shadows, emerging into sharp shafts of sunshine. In the late afternoon she sat in her room, colouring the models in Sears catalogues with felt markers, giving them extra definition. Blue for eyeshadow, red for lips.

In late August her friends returned just before school started. They had tans, photos, sometimes they spoke different languages for a while, until they got used to what their parents called 'the transition'. They had experiences, which they related in tangled anecdotes about castles or summer language camps. Their parents talked about museums and cruises on rivers. What did you do, what did you do? She opened her mouth to say something but before she could they were talking about trains and cities, parks and gardens. They looked restless. They looked changed.

Now the places change all the time. So do the people, the facts, the details. But essentially all the stories are the same: some betrayal of innocence, reneging on a promise. Hopes dashed when a young son dies, family feuds over lottery money, fish dying because of the asphyxiating properties of the ravenous lily that is eating Lake Victoria. Shiny-faced politicians, men spitting on hot sidewalks, where the saliva dries instantly into a membranous little crust.

That was her escape, writing stories. Being the Eye. Or the I. Even though she never entered her stories, as a character. She was the one with the notepad standing behind the cool, diaphanous curtain of consistently rotating facts, places, trains, oceans, bureaucracies, impeachments, wars. She was the one with all the ponderous detailed analyses buzzing around in her head. She was good at analysing situations, even when they hadn't happened yet. She lived her life that way, in the relentless procession of situations that seemed to make up a day, a week, an existence. It was almost obscene, how often they cropped up, situations, brewing themselves into reality, insisting upon determining things.

There was a distinctive patter her mind took on when she wrote her journalism: aphoristic, deadpan, scanning the horizon for the artifacts of meaning. Strangely, though, the books she liked and habitually travelled with – *Under the Volcano, L'étranger, Tristes Tropiques* – were passionate, even spiritual. Her hands shook a little as she picked up one of these books, now, these damp hotel room talismans. She often wished, at moments like these, that she smoked and could take comfort in the ritual demolishing of dried leaves encased inside a neat white tube.

In her room she put one of those books down. She

couldn't face them and their lacerating pleas for tolerance. She sat on her bed and stared at the wall.

'We're going on sabbatical. We're leaving the house next month. You'll have to pack up.'

'Where am I going to go?'

'I don't know.' Her mother looked tired. 'You're going to university in the fall. It doesn't make much sense to move with us, just for the summer.'

She found a basement room in the house of a widow two blocks away on one of those reassuring tree-named streets common to Canadian cities: Maple, Walnut, Cherry, Elm.

She doesn't know when they left but a week after she moved into the basement she passed the house and found them gone. She felt in her pocket and found she still had her key.

Going from room to empty room she thought she could feel the presence of her mother. But it was the pre-marriage mother, the pre-babies woman, who had tickled her and taken her to a seaside restaurant one Christmas where they had watched the reflections of Christmas lights scatter and re-form in the dark water of the Atlantic.

She sat on the bare floor of what used to be her room. It was that afternoon that she began to really form an idea of her future, tending it like a lush garden. She wanted oleander, bougainvillea. But the garden would also be studded by strange sculptures, by certain incongruities, like swimming pools in wartime, or escape in the middle of torture.

She left the house. Two months later she left the town for good. She never saw her mother again.

She had finally escaped the place she considered fit only for those who accepted the seductive crawl of years. Something would finally happen now, away from the house where her days had been like nights in a foreign country.

WHERE IS YOUR HOME?

Amélie comes into her room, sits down on her bed. Her hand, plump, marked by black liver spots, inches towards hers but does not quite take it.

In the distance she hears a mortar fire. The bed shakes a little. Then another. This one is closer.

'Where is your home? In case something happens. With the – the things. So I can let them know.'

'Oh,' she says. 'I'll give you the details. Who to call. If you can get through.'

'You don't miss it? Home?'

How to explain to this woman, who had struggled to make a living all her life, about the cool, ordered homes? The calculating needs and wants. About people needing, at all costs, to protect themselves against pain. How to tell Amélie that she never wanted to hide. She wanted to go out into the world, to see how much pain and uncertainty she could take. She had thought that would be a useful thing to know.

'Would you like to come and sit with me tonight?'

She nods. 'But first I'll do some writing. I'll stay here and I'll come to you in a few hours.'

She looks at Amélie's face – squat, unattractive, its black stone eyes and wide lips – and suddenly she sees the outline of a young girl's face rise as if submerged, like a long-sunk boat coming to the surface from the bottom of the ocean where it has been kept pristine by cold and pressure.

Amélie is actually very beautiful. In fact, hers might be the most beautiful face she has ever seen.

'I will see you later then.'

She watches the face disappear around the corner.

Five or six hours later she is hovering over sleep, as if she were a fluttering creature – a hummingbird, a butterfly – and sleep were a liquid flower, when a knock, a banging, really, comes at the door. She can't imagine what is on the other side of the knock, to make it sound so urgent, so final. She rises from the bed and lifts her leg to take the three steps it will require to move her from the bed to the door. She is aware of the muscles, the simple architecture of her body. The motion is heavy, like steps taken in a swimming pool. Or the steps the astronauts took on the moon in the year she was born. She has a vision of them in their silver suits and ventilators. How gorgeous it must have looked to them, the distant luminous globe hung on the black canvas of the universe. How they must have loved it, counting their footsteps in their heads in order to keep them from flying off into the blackness; counting one, two, three—